THE GIRL AND HER PROMISE
By Brittany Czarnecki

BRITTANY CZARNECKI

WHITE FIN
MOON WOOD
MOAT BIRGER
TORDENFALL
NORTHERN TERRITORIES
GREY RAVEN
WHISPERING WOODS
GODSTONE
THUNDER TRAIL
ONYX COVE
TONSBURG
BLACKWOOD FOREST
TWISTED TOWER
SPEARHEAD MOUNTAINS
ASHTON
KASPIN'S KEEP
HERCINIAN FOREST
MOORE
SHADOW SEA
HIDEAWAY HARBOR
TEMPLE CITY
HARPER HALL
PORT TSUE
SOUTHERN TERRITORIES
VOLANTAR
CATCHER'S COVE
OLIVE BRANCH
STARRY POINT
PHANTOM BAY
RAHAMA
ISLE OF FIRE
MOAT SUNSET
LAMIRA
TRADER'S ROAD
MARIDIYN
MANDALAIR
SIREN SEA
XANHEIM
SERPENT'S PASS
KAME ISLAND

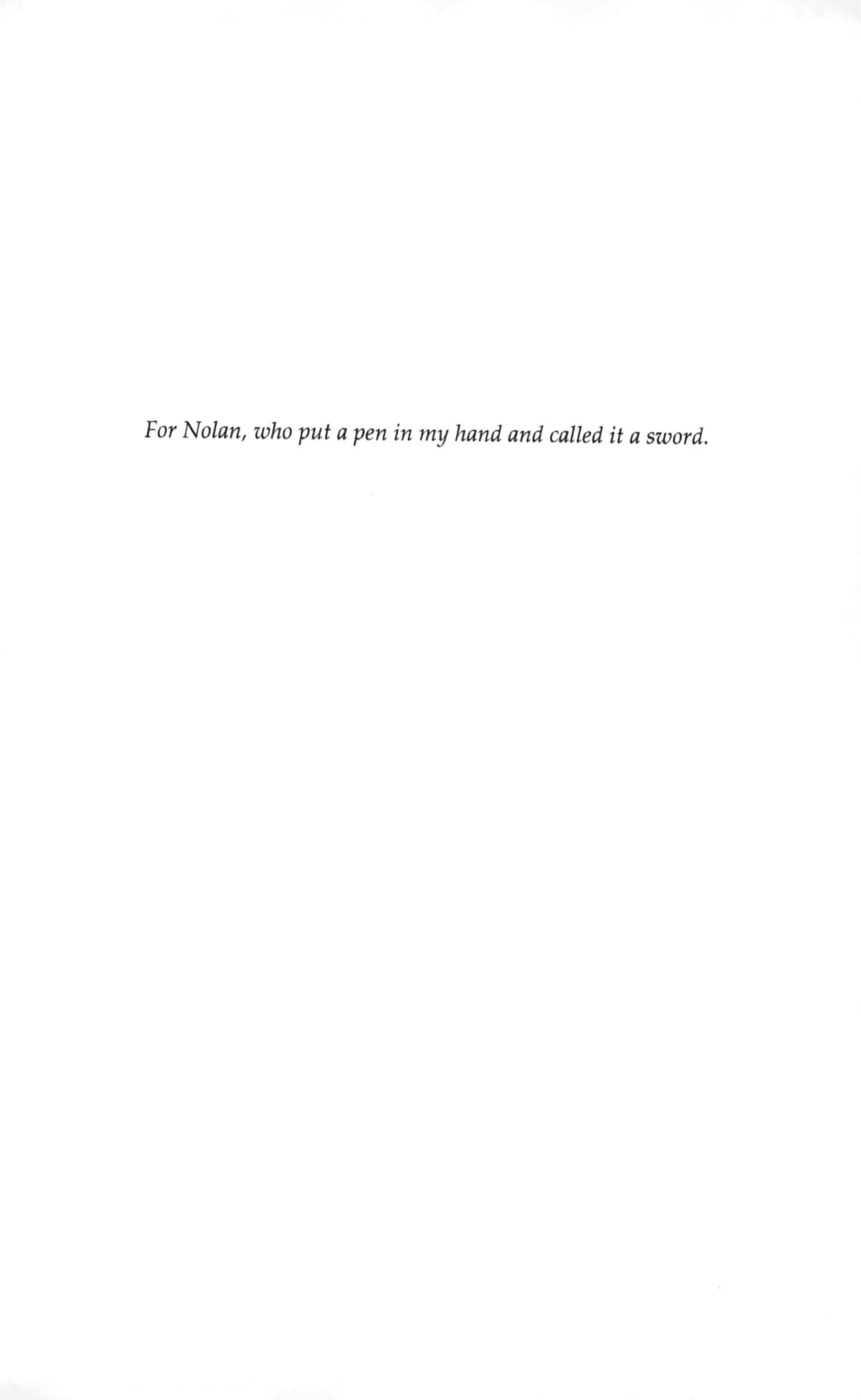

For Nolan, who put a pen in my hand and called it a sword.

BOOK FOUR OF THE BLACKBOURNE SERIES

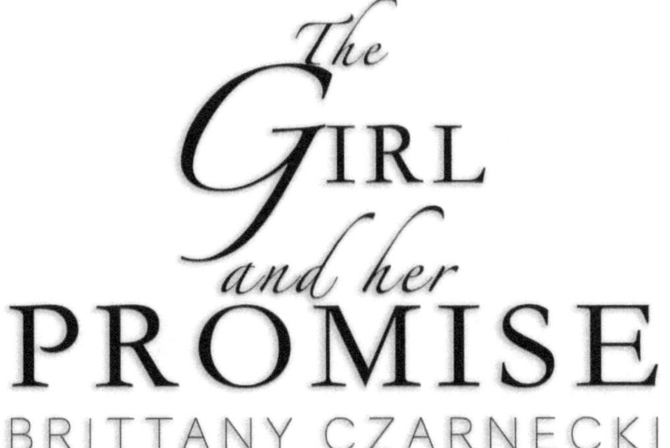

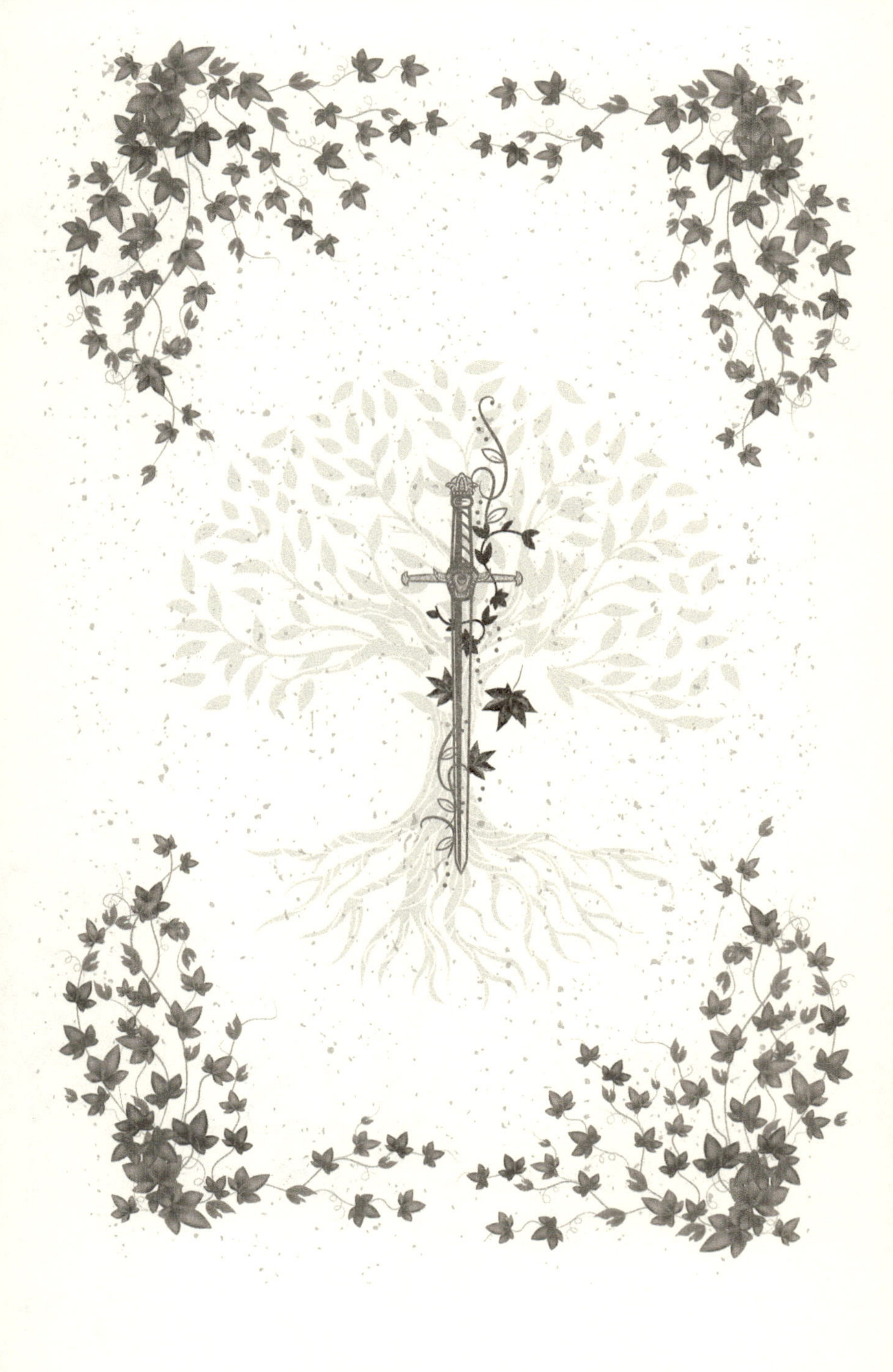

PROLOGUE

A raven soared above, the sun catching the blue hidden in its midnight wings, and Rayner faltered. The sword was just a blur in his peripheral as he ducked, feeling the rush of air whip his hair to the side. Staggering back, Rayner refocused on his opponent, checking his balance, and struck. His blade didn't even come close to its target, and Magnus cracked a prideful yet challenging grin.

They'd been at it for about an hour now, and though Rayner felt the familiar ache in his muscles, he pushed on. Moments like these were becoming rare with his father, so he longed to make the most of them. He knew what it meant to be king, or at least he thought he did. His father was often busy attending meetings, traveling to allied lands to oversee trading himself, or stuck in his chambers writing letter after letter. Now, Magnus was fully focused on Rayner and his training. He'd been teaching him a lot —how to put his weight into his heels when striking to be sure he's grounded, the proper way to hold his sword. A few of his father's knights had gathered around the training pit to watch Rayner practice, among them was Ser Osmund. His armor gleamed in the summer sun, creating an almost ghost-like halo around the old man. He often found time to spar with Ser Osmund when his father was busy, and though Rayner was only ten years of age, he felt confident that he too would be a great knight one day.

One day.

Taking Rayner's averted eyes as an opening, Magnus reached out and grabbed Rayner's hands where they gripped the hilt. Swiftly, his father's forearm slammed into his chest as he hooked his foot behind Rayner's ankle, knocking him to the ground. A grunt of pain escaped as he lay there, and Magnus came to stand above him, blocking out the sun. With his features shadowed, the purple of his eyes almost looked gray, but his hair burned crimson in the light. He wore a cream doublet, unlaced at the top slightly, revealing muscles that had trained and fought for years.

"You were putting too much weight on your left side," Magnus said, his voice deep and patient. "Balance it out, and don't let me knock you over again."

He extended his hand, calloused and rough against Rayner's, and hauled him to his feet. With a pat on his shoulder, his father took a step back, widened his stance, and waited. Rayner was focused now, and with the desire to not disappoint his father burning in his belly, they went at it again. One day, he would be a knight and the king of Godstone, and though he may fall, his father always taught him to get back up. Magnus had never shown anything but determination and pride while training with Rayner, but still, he pushed himself to be better than he was last time.

After a few more minutes, and one lucky blow landed on his father, Rayner caught movement off to the left. Next to Ser Osmund, perched on a stack of crates for a better view, sat his little sister. He smiled at Ivy, who was a constant presence during their training. He knew she took an interest in it, more so than any other young girl in the kingdom. Ser Osmund bent to her ear to whisper something, then made a funny face, earning a giggle from Ivy. They'd always had a special relationship since the day she was born. Ser Osmund was family to them and always would be. Ivy picked up a small practice sword and placed it carefully across her legs, running her fingers over the smooth wood. A twist of guilt coiled in Rayner's belly at the sight. Ivy would never become a knight. His father had banned females within the kingdom from knighthood before Rayner was born, whereas before any female was able to try out, though none ever did. It was as if they needed someone to be the first—to break that mold. Yet before anyone could, it was forbidden. He was unsure of the reasons for his father's decision, but being only ten years of age, he wasn't yet privy to the choices of a king. Perhaps one day, when it's his turn to rule, he could change things.

One day.

Now, he could only focus on bettering his training in the hopes that one day, he might win a match against his father, and then the real work would begin. Magnus raised his practice blade between them, signaling for Rayner to start again. He took a breath to do a mental check of his footing, his grip, and then looked for an opening. Magnus was always calm; he always let Rayner attack first, so he did. Stepping into his strike, Rayner aimed for his gut, but Magnus was faster. Rayner wasn't so naïve— he knew his father slowed his movements some, but not by much. Magnus twisted out of the way before the sword could touch him, and before Rayner knew it, he felt the blade press into the back of his neck.

"Again," Magnus said.

Rayner turned to shove a hand into his father's chest, but only managed to push himself back. He stumbled, cursing himself for even trying. His father was solid muscle, and what little muscle Rayner had was already aching and tired for the day, but the training went on. Magnus didn't react to the move, just kept going. He advanced, smacking Rayner's blade away any time he swung. Sweat beaded at his brow and started to drip down his spine. He tried to focus, carefully stepping back, he threw his head to one side as his father's sword sailed by in his vision. Swiftly, Rayner ducked under Magnus' swinging arm and drove his elbow into his side. Magnus turned and stepped back, a glint of pride in his eyes. They kept going back and forth until Rayner was panting, well and truly out of breath. His father didn't appear to be sweating at all as he lowered his sword and said, "That's enough for today."

Ivy hopped down from the crates and brought with her the practice blade that she'd been holding the whole time. "I want a turn, father!"

Magnus smiled and said, "The queen would have my head if she knew you were dirtying your dress."

Ivy rolled her eyes, fussing with the fabric of her skirts. "I don't like it anyway." Magnus looked closer at the dress—the hemming frayed and tired, blotches of what must have been dirt speckled across the material like blood on armor. He smirked at the state of his little girl. "No, I suppose you don't. Alright, but just a quick round."

Ivy's entire being lit up with glee, and Magnus absorbed a bit of that light, hiding it away for darker days that inevitably lay ahead. He tried not to think of the stress of ruling, not when he was with his family. Moments like these were precious, and so right now, he was a father about to teach his daughter to protect herself. Though a large part of him hoped that she'd never need to use such a skill.

Ivy stood ready with her weapon in hand, grip firm and stance wide, and grounded. A spark of admiration lit in his chest. It was evident that she had been paying close attention to Rayner's lesson. Ivy took a step toward him, eyes alert. She smiled sweetly before attacking. Magnus saw the attack coming, but he slowed his movements, allowing Ivy to get close enough to swing. She aimed for his side, and he easily skirted away, raising his blade to counterattack. Slowly, giving Ivy time to react, he brought his sword down toward her shoulder. She took in a sharp breath at the movement of her dodge. She stood behind Magnus now, and he stayed still, listening. The soft shuffle of her feet told him she was shifting her weight to the right, preparing to swing with her left hand. A small, adorable grunt of effort came from his daughter before her stick made contact with his upper right arm. Magnus feigned pain, releasing his hilt with his left hand to clutch his wound.

He spun to see Ivy's face stern and serious, her stick already swinging through the air again. This time, Magnus truly had to block the attack, stopping her stick with his own. "Well done, sweetling," he said, smiling. A corner of her mouth lifted in a half smile. Widening his stance, Magnus gave her a curt nod, encouraging Ivy to attack again. She gladly obliged him. They went at it until Ivy's breathing was heavy, and her limbs looked stiff and tired, but the determined glint in her eye never faded. Magnus wondered if Ivy may be the one to break the cycle of female knights before he forbade it. He didn't want to think about it too much. After practice, Magnus walked with Ivy along the streets of Godstone. The sun was starting to set, and the last of the light rode on the peaks of the mountains to the North. Magnus made a mental note to extend an invitation to Earl Rorik and his family. It had been too long since he'd seen his friend, and he hoped that one day their children might share the same bond as he did with the leader of Tordenfall.

As Ivy stopped at a vendor booth, admiring the selection of sweets, Magnus' eye drifted south. Over the rolling hills of endless land, somewhere out there, Helvarr waited. It had been ten years since his banishment, but aside from a few rumored sightings, Magnus hadn't heard of Helvarr, and that worried him. Helvarr had never been one to lie down and give up; he's driven and stubborn to a fault, a trait that Magnus thought he even admired at a time, but no longer. The events of that day, of Lady Roe dying in his arms, of the fight with Helvarr still lingered in his mind. To this day, he questioned the decision he made and prayed to the gods that it was right.

"Can I have one, Father?" The nightmarish spell of the past was broken by Ivy's question. Magnus looked up at the vendor—the sweet older woman stood there looking at him, concern crinkling her brow. "Are you well, Your Grace? You look miles away."

Magnus smiled reassuringly. "Fine, thank you." He then turned to Ivy. "Which would you like?"

She gave a little hop of excitement before turning back to the selection. Her eyes drifted over the fresh honey wheat bread, the berry muffins, and the sticky buns until she spotted what she was after. An apple tart. The vendor grinned and cut a big slice, gingerly putting it in a box. "The best apples in the north grow in Godstone," she remarked, folding the lid down and handing it to Ivy. Magnus thanked the woman, paid for the sweet, and continued down the street toward home.

As they approached the main tower, Ivy stopped to pick up a leaf that had fallen from the maple tree. It was the most brilliant red. Ivy carefully tucked it in her jacket, and as they entered the tower, Elana came down the stairs. Her green eyes found Magnus' before sweeping over the state of Ivy. One brow rose as she turned back to the king.

"And what have you two been up to?"

Ivy grinned and said they'd been to the market.

"Mhmm. And before that?"

Magnus strolled up to her, placing a kiss on her cheek. Elana smiled and caressed his face as she said, "Sparring, was it?"

Magnus looked at Ivy, a bemused twinkle in his eye as he shook his head. She mirrored him. "Ivy? Sparring? Never."

"How silly of me. I suppose her dress has been dirtied and frayed while strolling through the market."

Magnus leaned down to whisper in Ivy's ear, but kept his eye fixed on the queen. "I told you."

Elana smirked then and gestured Ivy closer. Her slender fingers worked at the tangles in her hair, careful not to pull too hard. "Supper should be ready," she said, placing her hands on Ivy's shoulders as she stood behind her. "Why don't you go find your brother and Ser Osmund." Ivy leaned her head back against Elana's chest.

"Okay," she said, rather dramatically.

Leaning down, Elana brushed her nose against Ivy's, who smiled in return.

"We'll be right there," Magnus said. She nodded, then threw her arms around Magnus's waist, squeezing tight. "Thank you."

"Of course, sweetling." He kissed the top of her head before she stepped back and headed toward the Great Hall. When she was out of earshot, Magnus turned to his wife to find her already staring at him. "Magnus—"

"I know, darling," he said, stepping up to her and taking her hands. "But she was *so* excited. You should've seen the spark in her eyes. And she has good instincts, she's really not far behind Rayner." Elana was silent for a moment, but she didn't look angry. Instead, fear burned in her lovely green eyes.

"Magnus," she said again, but this time it sounded more tired. "Sparring is not meant to be fun. It's training for those who one day might have to fight. Training for *knights*." The word struck the king's ear like a blade. "Which, if I do recall, was your decision to forbid young girls from this duty. And why was that?" The question was rhetorical, so Magnus only nodded in response. "Because," Elana continued. "*We* have a young girl whom we wish to protect, and keep as far away from this war as possible."

When she was finished, Elana took a strand of golden hair between her fingers and began twirling it. She was right, and Magnus knew it. That day in Ashton, what Helvarr did would always live with Magnus. He had not forgotten, only tried to bury it so that the weight of his decisions wouldn't burden him so much, but it did. With no end in sight to the war, he had to do all he could to keep his family and kingdom safe. But by keeping a sword from Ivy's hands, was he hurting her or helping? Was that truly the best choice? He wasn't sure anymore.

He reached for his wife, taking her hands and cupping them as gently as if he held a baby bird. "I am sorry," he said quietly, gently. "I know you worry, as do I, but..."

Suddenly, he felt all the fear and uncertainty that he tried so hard to keep buried. Elana's shoulders slumped as she stepped up to him, cupping the back of his head and pressing their foreheads together.

"You do not need to carry this alone." Her voice was soft, her breath warm on his lips. "I know whatever decision you make, you do it with good intentions," as she spoke, she placed a hand over his heart. The warmth of her touch radiated through his clothing. "I also know these choices weigh on you, and I'm sorry. But darling, you can't control everything. You can make all the right choices and protect as many as you can, but after all is said and done, our fate lies in the hands of the gods, and we must trust that. What will be, will be."

Magnus repeated the words like a prayer to the gods. Elana kissed his cheek and then headed to the Hall. "I'll be right there," he called after her. A moment later, Luna soared down from the sky and perched on a branch at eye level with her king. Magnus reached out to stroke her snow-white feathers. Luna held his gaze, and in those ancient-looking eyes, Magnus knew that she understood and felt more than any normal animal. Luna cocked her head as if anticipating the question brewing in the king's mind. "You'll look after them, won't you, girl? I know there's more to you," he said, gently tapping her chest. "You've got a power in you just waiting to be released." Luna blinked a few times, observing her king. "Promise me, if it ever comes, you'll protect my family. You'll protect my Ivy." Luna chortled softly. She hopped along the branch to a bunch of leaves, and he observed as Luna carefully selected a fiery orange leaf. She stretched her massive wings, gliding to the ground to lay the leaf at his feet, then lowered her head almost in a bow. Then she gave three great flaps of her wings and took to the sky, off to hunt or simply to enjoy the soar. Magnus smiled as he bent down to pick up the leaf. "Thank you," he whispered, then headed to the Hall.

1

YELLOW ROSES

Somewhere far out at sea and off the coast of the Spearhead Mountains, that's where Rayner thought they were. He guessed it would take another day to get beyond the mountain range, but then what? Where would they go? What would he do when he had to face Helvarr again, or the horned knight for that matter? Just the thought of him sent shivers down Rayner's spine and turned his skin to goose flesh.

"Rayner?" Ivy's voice dragged him from his thoughts. He looked around the table, meeting everyone's gaze. Ivy and Finn sat close with Piotr and Grimm on either side of them. Aska and her family sat down the table next to Kyatta, Earl Rorik, and Lord Cylas. Lord Kevan didn't attend the meeting. He had been quiet for days, and no longer ate supper with them at night. Rayner knew he was grieving and decided not to bother him until they had a solid plan in the works. Elana had fallen ill in the past few days and hadn't left her bedchamber much, though Rayner noted that Cylas went to visit her every chance he got.

The king called the meeting that night to start planning their attack. A large map lay in the middle of the table. It was old and ripping at the corners, but it was all they had. If Rayner was honest with himself, he didn't have an answer or some grand plan to get Correlyn back or their home, so he did what he'd seen his father do many times and asked for the opinions of those at the table.

"Earl Rorik," Rayner beckoned. "What do you suggest?"

"I suggest we stay away from Tordenfall; my home is too close to Godstone, and there may be raiders that have taken up there. We will need to find another place to gather our army before we attack."

Rayner nodded and pointed to the map where a large mountain range lay just north of Godstone. "They may not expect us to come from the north, so that's our best option right now."

"How high are the walls?" Aska addressed Rayner. He explained as best he could the general layout of the kingdom, the walls, and how secure the front gate was, referring to the map and pointing to the places as he described them. Aska nodded with a thoughtful expression, her mind likely turning with ways to kill people.

"We should plan our attack at night so they can use their powers." Ivy gestured to Aska and her family.

"I do have other skills, you know." Aska twisted her mouth into a tight grin.

"Running your mouth is your strongest," Arytin drawled and narrowed his eyes on his cousin.

"Well, if all else fails, we can just send these two in to talk their ears off," Macon suggested. Ivy giggled and turned to her brother, but Rayner wasn't smiling. He was lost in the thought, gears turning with every possible outcome. They were getting closer, and Rayner felt himself retreating further into his head with every passing day. Ivy reached out to touch his hand, snapping him back to reality.

"What are you thinking?" she asked quietly, but the whole table stopped talking to listen. Rayner lifted his gaze to them, scanning the faces and feeling guilty that they might not survive. But the gods must have brought them together for a reason. Why else would Ivy had ended up on Starry Point? Why would Zion involve himself and his people for a war he doesn't agree with if not from some pull of the gods? Sure, Zion claimed it was Luna who convinced him, and Arytin's dead friend swayed him, but those were just sparks that the gods put in place.

"I'm thinking this is a near-impossible mission that you're all risking your lives for," Rayner let out with a sigh.

They all waited, watching the young king but turned their attention to Cylas as he spoke. "This isn't just about getting back Godstone. This is the first step in freeing the whole land, all of our homes."

"Taking back the North will help free the South," Kyatta said softly.

Rayner looked to Grimm, who sat silently with his head bowed, lost in thought or prayer. He turned back to his family, his friends, the people of the stars, all gathered to help win the war and fight for him. He leaned back in his chair, running a hand over his tired face but let a smile spread across his lips as he said, "If any group of people can do this, it's us."

"Together," Finn said, grabbing Ivy's hand and giving her a warm smile.

"Unbroken," the table answered.

Piotr shifted in his seat, leaning his elbows on the table. "What's the plan to get Correlyn?"

The smile dripped from Rayner's face at the mention of his wife.

"I've thought about it a lot, and I think our best option is to have scouts stake out the kingdom first and gather as much information that they can. We need to know the shifts of the guards on the wall, how secure the gates are, and where the weak spots are."

"What if there isn't a weak spot?" Finn asked.

"Then, we'll make one."

"How?" Piotr's brows were scrunched together. Rayner pointed to the eastern gate on the map where Godstone and the black beaches met. It was made of wood, unlike the majority of the wall, and could easily be broken down if need be. They would need to create a distraction on the western side and slip in.

"And who do you plan to send in?" Aska inquired, cocking her head to one side.

Rayner could feel his sister's eyes on him as he answered, "She's my wife, I'm going."

"No, Rayner." Ivy's features twisted with worry.

"It has to be me," Rayner tried to sound reassuring, but Ivy wasn't giving up.

"No, it doesn't. You're our king, and we can't risk it."

"Ivy…"

"If I may," Macon cut in, turning the attention of the table to where he sat. He ran a hand through his wavy brown hair, his dark eyes focusing on Rayner. "Perhaps I could be of assistance." The room went silent as they waited for him to explain. Rayner knew his title, but he didn't know of any qualifications or what he was capable of.

"If anyone can get your wife out safely, it's our Master of Spies," Aska insisted, flashing a smile at Macon.

"You can't go alone," Ivy insisted.

"Why not? I work best alone." Macon reached out and poured a cup of wine before handing it to Aska and pouring one for himself.

"I don't know you very well," Rayner cut in. "How can I trust that you're the man for the job?"

Macon sat back casually in his chair, glancing at Aska and grinning before turning to face Lord Cylas. Rayner followed his gaze, confused. Lord Cylas looked equally confused as Macon gave him a guilty-looking smile. "Lord Cylas," Macon began, throwing one arm over the back of his chair. "You spend much of your time walking through your gardens, don't you?" Everyone but Aska and Arytin turned toward Lord Cylas, waiting for an answer, but the lord didn't speak. Macon went on. "Your favorite part is the yellow rose bush just inside your iron gates. You like to cut your own roses, taking your time, and picking out only the best ones. You then bring them into your house, up to your bedchambers, and set them in a crystal vase with a gold brim. You put them on the bedside table, but not the side you sleep on, the other side. You don't let your maids touch the roses, you don't water them, you just leave them there. After two days, you replace them and start the process all over again, is that correct?"

Cylas sat with his mouth open and eyes fixed on Macon. He looked pale, and the green in his eyes seemed to lose their sparkle. "How—"

"Because I am the Master of Spies," Macon interrupted. "It is my job to keep track of everyone, whether friend or foe. Knowing their plans or how many men they have isn't enough, I need to know how they live, how they think, and what's important to them. No information is irrelevant."

"How did you get past my spies?" Cylas didn't sound angry; he just sounded curious.

"They were easy enough to distinguish; it's my job after all. But don't worry, the untrained eye wouldn't notice them. You've hidden your spies well."

Lord Cylas looked like he had a hundred more questions, but Rayner cut in before he could speak. "Do you have information on King Caato?" Macon gave Lord Cylas a smile that said *I'm sorry* before turning to the king.

"Of course, though there isn't much to tell. He's been a hermit for years, refusing to leave his home... but I haven't been back in months."

"Were you there when I went to Rahama?" Rayner persisted.

"No, I was home. I can't be everywhere at once, but we have our own spies in permanent locations around the land." Macon turned back to Lord Cylas and said, "Don't worry, they know not to interfere with your spies or reveal themselves. They listen, but don't act and only report back to me."

"What will they do now that you aren't checking in on them?" Finn asked curiously.

"They will remain until I tell them otherwise, gathering information for me."

"All right." Rayner held up his hand. "You've made your point, but I still think someone should go with you."

"Who do you suggest then?" he asked with a smug grin, as if no one would be able to keep up with him.

"Akio," Rayner answered simply. "He's King Mashu's lead Shadow. He can be your backup, and don't worry; he won't get in your way."

"And is Akio aware of this?"

"I'll send a hawk over to their ship and tell him. You two can get together once we land and start going over the maps and get a plan working." Macon considered for a moment, looking over to Aska as if to confirm if it was a good idea. She raised a brow and shrugged. He turned back to Rayner, who hadn't taken his eyes off the Master of Spies.

"Fine," Macon finally agreed, leaning forward in his chair as he added, "but if he comes, he has to know that my mission is to get your wife out safe and unharmed. If he gets caught or held up, I won't go back for him."

"Akio can handle himself," Ivy insisted. Macon glanced at her, then turned back to Rayner.

"Fine, send your hawk."

Macon looked as though Rayner had insulted his abilities by suggesting that someone accompany him, but it was the right choice. This might be their only chance to get Correlyn back, and Rayner needed the best people for the job. He wouldn't lose her again.

"All right," Aska spoke up. "So, where are we going now?"

Rayner dragged his eyes from Macon but didn't answer her. He knew they needed to land and reconvene before they hashed out any detailed plans to attack Godstone.

Attack Godstone.

The thought felt strange as it rattled through his mind, that they were about to wage war on their own home. But the people that lived there now were strangers in their home, and it was time for them to leave.

"We need to go to the Moon Wood." Kyatta's voice was soft as she addressed the whole table. All eyes turned to her, and even Grimm lifted his gaze from the thoughts that had kept him trapped for the entire meeting.

"Why?" Ivy asked. Kyatta looked briefly at Grimm, so quick that Rayner almost missed it, but he knew the look in Kyatta's eyes. It was pain.

"There's something there I need," she said, turning her eyes away from Grimm, who went back to staring at his knees.

"What is it?" Rayner tilted his head, trying to search Kyatta's face for some hint, but it was a fortress.

"I just need you to trust me," she said, scanning the faces around her. "If things go wrong, you'll be glad I have it."

"But—" Ivy started.

"Please, just trust me." Kyatta looked so serious that no one else protested.

"All right, so we will regroup when we reach the Moon Wood." Rayner turned to Macon. "You and Akio can get acquainted, and the rest of us will start coming up with a plan to take back Godstone."

Everyone nodded and started shuffling to leave. Kyatta got up first and Grimm's whole body seemed to constrict as she breezed past him. Aska winked at Ivy before getting up and leaving with her family, Finn, and Piotr trailing behind them. Ivy stood and walked to her brother, who brought his eyes up to meet hers. She gave his hand a reassuring squeeze before disappearing through the door with Earl Rorik and Grimm. Only Rayner and Cylas remained seated in the room, and Rayner watched him curiously. He seemed lost in thought, his eyes locked on the table in front of him. Rayner cleared his throat and Cylas slowly lifted his green eyes up to the king at the end of the table. "Why yellow roses?"

Rayner couldn't hide his curiosity though he thought he knew the answer already. Cylas hesitated to answer, but Rayner waited patiently.

"I first saw Elana standing behind my yellow rose bush when her father came to Rahama. Her golden hair put shame to the vibrant color of the roses, but I kept them around to remind myself of her—of what I'd lost."

Rayner lowered his head. He wondered if his mother knew but then decided there's no way she could have known. He twisted his hands in his lap before asking, "Is that why you never married?" There was pain in the lord's eyes as he nodded. "Well, she's here now." Rayner did his best to sound convincing, but failed miserably. It was still strange to wrap his mind around the possibility of his mother being with someone, but he wouldn't stand in the way of her happiness. She deserved to be happy. Rayner pushed his chair back and got to his feet as he told Cylas to get some rest.

Cylas pushed open Elana's door and silently padded his way across the room to where her bed sat. She was asleep on her side, facing away from him, so he crept around the bed and took a seat in the chair next to her. Her golden hair glowed, even in the dimness of the room, and was spread out behind her on a pillow. Elana's soft, sleepy breathing filled his ears like the most beautiful music. Cylas studied her face as he thought of the time they've spent together recently. He held onto every smile, the subtle lift of her brows when she joked, every longing look, the sound of her laugh, and the feel of her fingers brushing up against his hand. He couldn't help but smile at the memories, and he stored them away, neatly filed in his mind. Cylas had been in love with Elana since the moment he laid eyes on her back in Rahama. He didn't know exactly how she felt but held out hope that they could start over once the war was finished.

"You're here." Her eyes were still closed, and her voice was raspy with sleep. She'd been fighting a fever for days now, and her cough had finally started to die down.

"Of course," he answered, not bothering to hide his smile. Elana opened her eyes, and Cylas thought it was like someone\ cracking open a treasure chest filled to the brim with emeralds. Elana sat up, letting the furs fall away from her and propped herself up against the headrest. "What happened at the meeting?"

"Nothing," he answered too quickly. "I mean, we just talked about getting your son's wife back." Elana stayed silent for a moment, studying him, and Cylas knew she didn't believe him. He lowered his eyes and took a steady breath, trying to shake the odd feeling that settled over him as he recalled Macon's words. What else did he know?

Elana leaned forward and touched his arm, whisking away his thoughts. "What is it?"

He leaned forward, resting his elbows on his knees and released a long sigh. "I just... I've waited a long time to see you again, and I don't want to lose you. I can't." His cheeks instantly flared at the confession, but it was too late to take it back, and he didn't want to anyway because Elana was smiling.

Elana shifted to the edge of the bed, and Cylas held his breath, afraid that any movement might change what he thought was about to happen. She leveled her eyes with his.

Elana reached out and put her hand on top of his. It burned and tingled down to his bones. She cast her eyes down to the edge of the bed, then back up to him and said ever so softly, "Sit." Elana scooched back to make room for him and Cylas sat at the edge of her bed, but it felt more like the edge of the world. She settled back into her nest of pillows, fussing with her hair that was messy with sleep. When she looked back at him, he realized he was staring and smiling like a fool. Elana chuckled and stopped fixing her hair to reach out and place her hand on his knee. Cylas felt his heart slam to a stop and fumbled for words.

"I uh… I was just coming to check on you, do you need anything?" Somehow, she seemed disappointed and removed her hand to sit back against her nest.

"Actually, I'm feeling much better," she stated with a grin.

"You look beautiful…better! You look better." Cylas closed his eyes briefly and scolded himself mentally, but Elana laughed and the sound was euphoric. He settled his beating heart, running a hand through his orange hair and shifting his body toward her. They sat in silence for a moment, smiling at each other before Elana asked where they were headed. "To the Moon Wood," Cylas answered. Elana didn't ask why, and Cylas was grateful because he didn't know. If it was mentioned during the meeting, he didn't hear it. The only sound he heard was a dull buzzing in his ear after Macon admitted to sneaking around his house. It sent shivers down Cylas's back to think that the Master of Spies was in his home while Cylas was tending to his roses.

"You should get some rest," he heard himself say though he didn't want that at all.

Elana tilted her head, the movement somehow endearing and calculating at the same time. "I've been resting for days."

He smiled and nodded. "Okay. What do you want to do then?"

She stretched her legs out, wiggling her toes. "I think I'd like a walk."

"It's cold on the upper decks, Elana."

"Then I guess you'll have to keep me warm," she said with a playful smile. Cylas blushed and stood up from her bed, saying he would meet her in the hall so she could change.

He waited a few minutes, tapping his foot on the floor, his hands shoved deep into his pockets before Elana's door finally opened. She drifted into the hall, her hair left unbound, and a long fur cloak hung over her shoulders, fastened at her chest with an iron brooch. He smiled as she approached and offered her his arm, which she gladly took. They made their way up the stairs, Cylas silently commanding his men to leave with a sharp look. The guards scurried off, leaving only Cylas and Elana to wonder the top deck. The night was clear and cold, a constant wind blew down from the north, and as they started toward the bow, it began to snow. Cylas let go of her arm and stood back, watching the way her smile lit up the cold, black world around them.

"Does it ever snow in Rahama?" she asked, tilting her chin toward the sky.

"Not often," he admitted. "Perhaps a few times in the dead of winter, and it only ever lasts until the sun comes up."

"I've missed the snow," she said, and her voice sounded far away. Cylas cupped his hands behind his back to resist reaching out to her. She kept walking toward the bow of the ship, looking up at the sails, the detailed woodcarvings on the gunwale, and the freshly polished deck. It was nothing like Magnus's ship, Cylas knew, and had rarely seen battle.

When they reached the bow, Elana pulled up the hood of her cloak. Cylas stood beside her and took a deep breath. The air seemed fresher out at sea, with no people to corrupt the smell, a place untouched, and constantly moving. He thought about what might happen after this was all over. He turned to Elana, who seemed lost in thought. Her brow was furrowed, eyes far away and her lips twisted into a frown. "What are you thinking?"

Elana let out a long sigh before turning to face him.

"I'm thinking that the gods are playing a cruel trick on us."

"What do you mean?" he cocked his head to one side.

"They have brought us together again, just to rip us apart when the war is over. You will go back to Rahama, and I will..." Tears started to gather in her eyes. "I will be with my family." She rubbed small circles on her swelling belly, taking her eyes from his.

"Perhaps we were wrong about the gods intentions," she said quietly.

"I don't believe that," Cylas answered, taking a step toward her.

"Then why did they bring us together if we will only take separate paths when this is over?"

Cylas stared at her for a long moment, he didn't know what to say. Elana had a point. They lived so far apart, so why had the gods brought them together? Was it some trick as she suggested to break Cylas, dangle what he wanted in front of his face before snatching it away?

Cylas took another step toward her, bringing his arms down to his side. "Elana," he whispered. "Perhaps the gods did have a plan, and our fate has been sealed, but who is to say what that is? We can't know what will happen in the future, but we are here now."

She lifted her chin to look into his eyes. "I can't help it," she said. "I dream about what might happen. Sometimes it's perfect, and other times it's a nightmare. I look at you, and I see a life I never got to live, a fate that was made for me, and I know the gods have a plan. I can feel it the way you feel your heart beating." She reached out and put a hand over Cylas's heart, which sped up on command. "I just need a sign." Her voice was no more than a whisper. Cylas fought every urge, every instinct to reach out, to touch her, hold her. She seemed to be holding her breath as she waited for him to answer, but he didn't have any words left; they had vanished when she laid her hand over his heart. Cylas felt himself break through the wall that had been holding him back.

Cylas placed a hand over hers as he closed the space between them, his other hand gently lifting to her chin. Elana's eyes were a burning green fire as Cylas lowered his head and kissed her. Their lips met, and it was as if he'd always known what it would be like to kiss Elana. She let her hand fall from his heart and brought it to rest against his cheek. Cylas thought his knees would give out, his heart would stop, and his brain would stop making sense of the world around him as he fell deeper into Elana. He wrapped a hand around her waist, gently pulling her closer while his other hand caressed her cheek, drifting back into her golden waves until her hood fell from her head. This had to be a dream. Cylas had dreamt about this moment for years, but those dreams rippled away like a stone in a pond compared to reality. He felt a fire burning in his chest as he parted his lips slightly, deepening their kiss. All the longing and desire he held for this woman, that he'd kept trapped inside finally released and he could breathe.

Cylas broke away, resting his forehead against hers and taking in a shaky breath. Elana's hand still rested against his cheek, and his were still wrapped firmly around her waist. They stayed like that, staring at one another before she finally leaned back. The shy smile that spread across her lips made her look years younger. Her smile faded, and Cylas furrowed his brows, wondering what he'd done wrong and running through all the possibilities of what she might say.

Instead, Elana stepped toward him, placed a slender finger under his chin, and said, "Took you long enough." A wave of relief like no other crashed over him, and then he began cursing himself for not kissing her back on Kame Island.

Cylas smiled and wrapped his arms around Elana, pulling her into his chest. "I've waited years to do that," Cylas spoke softly against her ear. They stood at the bow, tangled in an embrace as the snow fell around them.

Cylas walked Elana back to her cabin, her fingers interlaced with his. He couldn't help but stare at her as they walked down the silent halls of the ship. They reached her door, and Elana gave his hand a squeeze before removing it and placing it on the doorknob. "Well," she said, her voice sounding shy, which gave Cylas some relief, "thank you for walking with me."

"Of course," Cylas answered, feeling like a fool at the way his heart fluttered in his chest. "Get some rest, Elana." She smiled back at him and nodded before pushing open her door.

Cylas remained standing there until the door clicked shut. He let out a breath that deflated his chest, but then her door opened again and his heart skipped a beat.

"Is everything—"

Elana stepped up to him and kissed him. He lifted a hand to rest against her cheek, but then Elana was backing away. He stood there with his arm raised before snapping it back to his side. She tucked a lock of hair behind her ear and whispered, "Good night, Cylas."

He bowed his head toward her. "Good night, Elana," he replied and watched her cheeks blush as she closed the door.

Cylas retreated to his bedchambers at the end of the hall and began unlacing his boots and tossing his cloak onto a chair. He walked over to the other side of the bed, where a crystal vase sat on the table, holding a wilted yellow rose. He had picked the rose just before sailing to Kame Island with Rayner. It was long dead, shriveled up and dry, but Cylas had kept it anyway. Now, he plucked it from the vase and crushed it between his fingers, letting the rose fall in powder to the floor. He didn't need a reminder beside his bed anymore. Cylas had waited many years to be with Elana, and every aching day had been worth it. He took the empty vase from the table and put it in a drawer before crawling into bed and drifting off to meet Elana in his dreams, surrounded by yellow roses.

2

THE MOON WOOD

Ivy walked through a dark forest. All around her, shadows leapt and crawled from her path, and bare branches screeched in the constant wind. A chill wrapped its frigid fingers around Ivy's spine as she beheld the blood moon. Her nerves spiked, but she couldn't pinpoint why she felt this way. Ivy kept on through the woods, her heart picking up speed as her boots crunched in the snow. She came to a clearing, and as she stepped into the red world around her, Ivy's breath hitched.

An army lay ahead. Thousands of men armed to the teeth were charging the hill toward her, and suddenly Ivy realized where she was. Godstone's black walls were painted in the dim red light of the moon, and the snow appeared like a field of blood frozen in time. Ivy surveyed the army, tears forming in her eyes as she took in the sight of her home. She started toward it. Ivy would rather die in the fields of her home than to never see it again. She pulled Promise from its scabbard and took off in a sprint toward the army when someone tackled her from behind. They both tumbled to the ground. Ivy whipped around to see Rayner with his arms still firmly around her waist. "Get off me," Ivy growled, and Rayner blinked at her but quickly made his face stern again.

"It is not our time," he responded, though Ivy sensed a sliver of panic in his voice. What was happening? Why was Rayner running from their home? They had been working toward getting it back for months now. Ivy wasn't just going to lay down and watch it die, not again. She shoved out of her brother's arms and scrambled to her feet. Rayner stood, and Ivy caught sight of her family standing in the shadows of the trees.

Finn and Piotr stood side by side, Grimm next to them with a haunting look on his face. She scanned the group, searching the faces but realized some were missing.

No, she thought. *Not again.*

A dream, this was just a dream, Ivy told herself and prayed to the gods that it was only a dream and nothing more. "You can't save everyone," Rayner said softly. When Ivy tried to speak, tears choked her. Something was wrong.

Ivy turned around to see the army swarming, circling a man as wolves circle their prey. The man stood alone, his back straight and head high as he sliced through raider after raider. Ivy felt her heart leap into her throat. Something about the scene wasn't right, but she couldn't remember what had actually happened.

Because it hasn't happened yet.

Ivy took a step forward, her sword falling heavy to her side as she spotted someone else she hadn't seen before, making their way toward the army stretched out before her. "No!" Grimm's voice cried from behind, and Ivy whirled to see him running, Finn and Piotr trailing behind him. She stood frozen in place as they tackled Grimm to the ground, fresh tears melting the bloodred snow around him. Ivy started to shake all over. She wanted to cry in frustration. These dreams only showed her a glimpse of what was to come, and she never had all the pieces until it was too late. She tried to focus, but already the dream was fading around her. The Blackwoods turned to smoke in front of her eyes and drifted off into the night sky.

"No, no, no," she heard herself muttering. "Wait!" she cried to nobody as the dream began to shift and dissipate before her. She took off running down the hill, frantically scanning the sea of bodies before her as one by one they drifted off, and her vision began to blur. Ivy felt her body becoming light as if it would float off into the sky at any moment, and that's when she saw it. A flash of white and blue smoke swirling around the group of raiders on their knees, crying out in pain.

Ivy woke with a start. She shot up in bed, heart pounding and hands sweating, the sharp stab of the dream fresh in her mind. She was trying to piece together what she saw when Finn's hand reached out and touched her shoulder. Ivy jumped, and Finn quickly let go, propping himself up to look at her. His hair was messy with sleep, but his eyes were fully awake as he studied Ivy. She let out a long sigh and brought her hands up to rub at her face. "I'm sorry," she said quietly. She hated to wake Finn with her nightmares, but he never seemed angry, only concerned. He sat up, pushing himself back against the headrest and rubbing small circles on Ivy's back as she sat hunched over. She took in a shaky breath, and Finn's hand stopped in the middle of her back.

"You're all right," he whispered. "You're here."

Ivy turned to face him, his russet eyes locking with hers. She gave him a small grin and nodded. Finn pushed off the headrest and took her face in his palms, lightly running his thumbs over her cheekbones. "Can I get you something?"

"I'm all right," she responded and watched him crack a grin at her usual response. "I just need a minute."

Finn's smile was soft as he pressed a kiss to her forehead. Ivy watched as he slipped on a shirt, tied on his boots and cloak, and ran his fingers through his messy brown hair. He walked back over to the bed and bent down in front of Ivy, taking her hand in his and pressing it to his lips. "I'll go find out where we are. You come up when you're ready." Ivy lifted her chin and gently kissed him before he turned to leave.

They had been sailing for days and were likely closing in on the Moon Wood. Finn buried his hands in his pockets as he stepped onto the upper deck. The sun had just come up, and the world was cast in a golden haze with hues of soft blue. Lord Cylas's men were busy on the decks, changing shifts, sharpening swords, and dousing the braziers. Finn walked across the deck, his boots lightly crunching on the fresh sheet of snow. He looked to his left and could see Zion's ships trailing alongside theirs, and just ahead, King Mashu's Shadows led them further north. They hadn't had any more run-ins with raiders, and their path seemed clear, but Finn sensed something looming on the horizon. A light fog rose from the sea ahead, and as Finn walked to the bow of the ship, he could see the Shadows disappearing into the mist. He turned his head to the sky at the sound of gulls and let a smile spread across his lips. *Land.*

Finn felt a wave of relief. He hated being on a ship and tried to keep it hidden this whole time, but he had his own nightmares. The last time he'd been on a ship for this long was when he was fleeing his home, headed south with a fisherman from his town. Finn had only been nine years old and already traumatized by the sight of slaughter fresh in his mind. With every wave that carried him further south, Finn had felt a stab of guilt; with every breath he still drew, a choking pain crushed his lungs. He had watched his entire family be murdered at the hands of a raider. Finn wished he had seen the man's face, but at the time, he couldn't peel his eyes from the blood pooling around his father or the look of terror in his mother's eyes or the peaceful sleep that kept Thor from witnessing any of it. If Finn had just seen the man, then maybe he could have found him after all these years. Perhaps he wouldn't have stayed on Kame Island for so long, but instead gone off hunting the man who ruined his life. But then Finn wouldn't have met Ivy.

He closed his eyes at the thought. He knew they had been brought together for a reason and that the gods had aligned their fates. Finn shook the thought from his head when he heard his name being called. He spun around to see Aska stalking toward him, her hood pulled up tight over her face. She gave him a warm smile as she came near, and Finn scanned the deck behind her, expecting to see her cousin in tow. The two bickered more than an old married couple, and their banter filled the supper table every night. Finn missed the usual back and forth between Piotr and Grimm, but Piotr was still mourning, and Grimm seemed quiet the past few days.

"Where's Stormbringer?" she asked as she stopped a few feet in front of Finn.

He grinned at the name. "Why?"

"Arytin is looking for her," Aska said, matter-of-factly.

"Then why isn't he here?"

Aska flashed him a smile. "Because I am his humble messenger bee, carrying his word at his will," she said sarcastically, and Finn chuckled. "He's getting something to eat," she explained. "But he wants Ivy to meet him on the top deck." She pointed over her shoulder to where two sets of steps led up to the highest deck of the ship.

"What for?" Finn asked.

"You are very protective of her, aren't you?" Aska stepped toward him, and Finn met her gaze. "Why don't you come see for yourself, Finn." She turned and left before Finn could answer.

He made his way back across the deck to find Ivy but then ran into Rayner in the hall. The king stopped just before him. "We should be arriving soon," Finn said. "I saw gulls circling the masts. We're close."

Rayner let out a sigh that sounded like relief and nodded in response. "Where's Ivy?" he asked.

"She had a nightmare, I think," Finn admitted. "She wanted a few minutes alone."

"Well, tell her we're close," Rayner stepped forward and put a hand on Finn's shoulder. "It's almost over." Finn watched Rayner walk off down the hall toward Lord Cylas's room. He turned and went back to his bedchambers and found Ivy buckling on her sword belt. She was dressed in black pants, a heavy wool top with her maple tree cloak clipped around her neck. Her braided curled into a knot at the base of her neck. Ivy smiled when she spotted Finn, and he couldn't help the quickened beat of his heart.

"Arytin is looking for you," he said as he went closer. "He wants you to meet him on the upper deck."

"What for?" Ivy scrunched her brows together.

Finn shrugged and wrapped his arms around her waist, pulling her in and resting his chin on top of her head. He waited for a few heartbeats before speaking again.

"Your dream," he started. "Was it…your powers?" He felt Ivy shift in his embrace as she turned her face toward his.

"I think so," she admitted, her voice small. "I still don't get the full picture. It's like taking a painting that's been ripped to shreds and trying to put it back together without all the pieces."

"Should we talk to Rayner about it?" Finn couldn't help the concern in his voice.

"No," Ivy said. "I need to talk to Kyatta about it first."

Finn let out a sigh and hung his head. He hated that Ivy's powers seemed to drain her, especially when they were something that could save them or kill them. Like the gods were only telling her half the story, and it was up to Ivy to guess then ending, but if she guessed wrong…

She lifted a finger to his chin, and Finn's eyes found hers. "It can wait. Let's go find out what Arytin wants."

Finn brushed a lock of hair behind her ear and nodded. "By the way, we'll be arriving soon."

Ivy seemed to shudder at the thought. He wanted to know what her dream was about but knew better than to pry at her. If Ivy didn't want to talk, she would lock herself down and become a fortress of silence.

As they reached the upper deck, they spotted Arytin and Aska leaning against the rail and watching the sea below. Aska turned, and her face lit up when she spotted Ivy. She began to frantically wave them over, pointing down to the waters. Ivy and Finn moved to the rail, and Ivy smiled as she spotted black dolphins, leaping from the dark waters. "Look!" Aska chirped as she pointed to another pod, swimming just under the surface of the waves. Ivy watched as a dolphin shot up through the water and twisted, landing with a splash before another leapt into the air. Ivy had never seen black dolphins before and heard that they only resided in the northernmost waters. That only confirmed what Finn had told her moments ago, they were getting close, so why did Ivy's stomach twist into a knot?

"Are you ready?" Aska turned to Ivy.

"For what exactly?" She looked between the two cousins.

Arytin stepped forward and glanced at Finn before speaking. "You asked me back at Starry Point to teach you about pressure points. Do you still want to learn?" Ivy nodded eagerly and Aska looped her arm through Finn's and escorted him off to the side.

"Take your sword and cloak off," Arytin said as he began to undo his belt of daggers that hung across his chest. Ivy obeyed and handed her belongings to Finn, who gave her a wink before she turned back. Arytin's hair was tied back, his stance relaxed as he stood before her wearing a wool shirt, and light black boots that went halfway up his calf. Ivy shivered in the brisk morning wind and wrapped her hands around herself. Arytin moved over to her until he was mere inches away. He grabbed her arm, but his touch was gentle. He rolled her sleeve up and pointed to the crook of her elbow.

"This is a nerve," he said, his voice deep. He gently gave it a squeeze, and Ivy felt a sharp pain move down her arm, and her hand began to sweat. "Did you feel that?" Ivy nodded. "Imagine hitting that point with all your force—do that, and your enemy's arm becomes useless." Arytin explained that he wouldn't show her all the points at once, just the ones he thought would be most useful for someone new to it.

He moved his fingers up to the inside of her arm, touching the tips to her neck, collarbone, and temple. He brought his fingers down to her center and gave a gentle push, Ivy felt her abdomen contort and stepped away from him, but he caught her by the hand. Arytin lifted her hand to his face and ran his fingers to the center of her palm then to her wrist. He stepped back and ran his eyes down her body, then caught Finn's eye where he stood off to the side. "This one should ring a bell for you." Arytin smiled and pointed to the outside of his thigh. It was the pressure point he'd used on Ivy during their fight. "There is also one here." He pointed to the inside of his thigh. "Think you can remember all those, Stormbringer?"

"I think so," she responded, crossing her arms and looking him up and down.

"Good," he hissed and stepped forward. "Then let's get started."

The two squared up, and Ivy ran over what she'd just learned before remembering something. She glanced down at his feet; she knew Arytin was swift and could move without making a sound. He noticed her lingering glance and flashed her a smile, shifting his feet and making Ivy lunge. She fell right into his trap as Arytin moved aside and jabbed two fingers into her ribcage. Ivy winced and doubled over, bracing herself on the rail.

"That's not fair," she rasped. "You didn't show me that one."

"Then use what I've shown you," he responded.

Ivy narrowed her eyes on him and forced herself upright. She stretched her fingers, preparing to strike as Arytin circled her. Ivy glanced down at his feet again, and when his eyes left hers, she lunged. Throwing her weight toward him, she reached out, jabbing her fingers into his arm as he spun away, but she only barely touched him. She let out a huff and stayed on him, Arytin backing up further and further as Ivy tried again, failing to hit her target. The mockery in his smile lit a fire in her belly as his arm shot out at lightning speed, hitting her in the upper arm. A tingling sensation spider-webbed down her right arm and then it went limp. Arytin tsked her as she rubbed at the spot, trying to course life back into her dead limb.

"Not fast enough, Stormbringer."

"It's not over yet, *Ary*," she mocked. Behind her, Aska cackled madly and Arytin lost his smile, whipping his head back to scold his cousin. Ivy lunged at him and slammed into his chest, Arytin tripped and went crashing down on the snow-covered deck. Ivy grabbed hold of his arm with her hand, but her other arm was still numb and shook as she tried to lift it. Arytin chuckled at her attempt as he stabbed his fingers into the outside of her thigh. Ivy winced and felt her leg go numb, but she didn't stop. She grabbed hold of his collar and rolled his weight on top of her before letting go and aiming her fingers into the base of his neck. Arytin growled and winced from the blow, which made Ivy grin. He quickly recovered and put both hands beside her ears before flipping his body over her and landing above her head. Ivy tried to stand, but her leg was still numb. Instead, she reached her good arm out and jabbed at a random spot on his lower calf. Arytin's leg buckled, and Ivy grinned, pulling herself up to a sitting position and swinging her arm out, catching him in the leg and watched as he crashed down to one knee.

His features twisted with curiosity, and the ghost of a smile lifted a corner of his mouth. "How did you know about that one?"

"I guessed." Ivy tried to strike again, but Arytin caught her wrist.

"All right, all right," he breathed, pushing her hand away. "Let's call it a draw, shall we?"

Ivy let a smile spread across her lips as she leaned into him. "I got you." Arytin gave her a playful growl in return as he staggered up to his feet and offered her a hand.

The sound of applause came from behind, and Ivy turned to see that they had an audience. Grimm stood with his arms crossed and a broad smile on his face. Rayner and Piotr stood alongside Finn and Aska, who was still clapping as if she had just watched a show rather than a fighting lesson. "Bested by your own student on the first lesson," Aska tsked as she stalked toward them. "Does that mean you're a good teacher or a lousy fighter?" she teased.

Arytin gave Aska a shove to which she stuck out her tongue in retort. Ivy rubbed at the spots Arytin had struck, feeling the numbness fading and her limbs returning to her.

"You think you can beat me without a sword now, Iron Heart?" Grimm's usual playful tone lifted her heart. Grimm had been quiet the past few days, and Ivy didn't know why but decided not to pry at him anymore. She swore she wouldn't interfere with whatever was going on between him and Kyatta and so stayed silent, letting Grimm work it out the way he wanted.

"Why don't you come and find out," Ivy bit back. Grimm chuckled and flashed his teeth before stepping forward.

"Your Grace!" a knight ran up the steps of the deck, drawing everyone's attention to him.

"What is it?" he asked.

"We've spotted land." Everyone looked at Rayner before taking off down the stairs and running the length of the ship. They blew past knights and Lord Cylas's guards as they scrambled to the bow. And there, rising through the fog ahead, trees reached up into the sky, and Ivy spotted the first bit of land since leaving Starry Point. The North. Home.

As if Kyatta could sense it, her eyes opened, and in her heart, she knew she was back in the Moon Wood. She rose from her bed and rubbed her tired eyes. Kyatta hadn't slept soundly after that night with Grimm on the bow of the ship. Kyatta had almost kissed him. She'd wanted to, and at the time, she thought that Grimm wanted it to, but when he pulled away, he took a piece of her with him. Kyatta knew about Grimm's past and understood that it was hard for him to get close to someone, but she thought he would have realized by now that she was different. Kyatta had always wanted a close-knit family like Grimm wanted, and she thought she made that clear, yet he still shut her out. Kyatta never knew her mother, and after her father died, she had no one except the elderly women who taught her how to control her powers. But that wasn't enough. They weren't family, they were teachers. She'd been selected at a young age to be the leader of the Moon Wood when the old leader died. Kyatta thought that her people would become her family, but she was wrong: she struggled to have any sort of relationship with any of them. They only saw her as a leader and a weapon, not family.

Now, Kyatta slipped on some black pants and a wool, blue tunic before clasping on her white cloak with the blue feathers. She hoped she didn't look as tired as she felt and that Grimm wouldn't notice. She didn't want his pity or the sad looks he gave her, she wanted all of him or none of him and Kyatta was adamant on sticking to that.

She strolled down the hallway, shoulders back and head high as she passed by Grimm's door. The deck was filled with people moving about, bringing up chests and barrels from below and men rolling up the sails. She spotted Lord Cylas walking hand in hand with Lady Elana, and Kyatta felt a wave of jealousy. She averted her eyes and made her way toward the bow where she saw a group of people standing. Kyatta paused briefly when she spotted Grimm's towering figure amongst the group, but she drew in a breath and pushed on. She wouldn't let him rattle her. She wouldn't even look at him. There were bigger things to worry about now.

As she drew near, Ivy spotted her and then immediately looked to Grimm, but Kyatta held on to Ivy's face, fighting the urge to look. "We're here," Kyatta said to Ivy.

"How did you know?"

Kyatta didn't answer but instead moved to the bow and looked out to see the Moon Wood just ahead. The land was covered in frost that shone in the sun and lay crusted over a foot of snow. The white trees of the Moon Wood stretched out for miles and miles, their bare branches adorned with icicles. They were already anchored, and Kyatta spotted some of her people making their way toward land in rowboats. She felt a strange pull and noticed that Ivy was staring at her. She turned to her, feeling another set of eyes on her but ignoring it.

"What is it?" Kyatta could sense something was wrong.

Ivy hugged her arms around herself and lowered her head. "I had a dream."

Ivy turned to look at the group around her before grabbing Kyatta by the arm and ushering her a few steps away. She looked worried, and Kyatta felt her heart start to leap in her chest. "Ivy?" she persisted.

"I had a dream," she repeated and then began to explain quickly. "We were outside Godstone with the whole army of raiders coming after us, and there was a blood moon, Rayner tried to stop me from fighting, he said I couldn't save everyone, and then there was something in the middle of the raiders, it was—"

"Wait." Kyatta held a hand up to stop her rambling. "Did you say a blood moon?" Ivy nodded and opened her mouth to speak again, but Kyatta was already moving away. Her heart drummed in her ears, and she felt Grimm and others staring at her as she briskly walked back down the deck of the ship. She thought about her first encounter with a blood moon, and a frigid chill crawled down her spine. They came a few times every year, but she managed to keep track so that she was safely indoors, hidden from its dreaded face. Had she lost track? Was it already time for another blood moon? Kyatta shook her head and made her way to the other side of the ship, where rowboats were setting off. She stopped one of her people and ordered them to gather her things and bring them to the Moon Hall, Kyatta's home.

I vy, Rayner, Elana, and Finn followed Kyatta in another rowboat. Elana sat huddled in her fur cloak, gently rubbing her belly and humming to herself. Ivy couldn't help but smile; she hadn't seen her mother happy in a long time and was grateful that the gods brought Lord Cylas to them. Though it still felt strange, Ivy had to admit that she would give anything to see her mother happy and healthy when the baby arrived. Elana may not have been a warrior, but she was always the glue that held Magnus together. Without her, their father might have fallen apart. Her mother was stronger than she looked—a beautiful, cunning fox clad in an armor of wisdom.

Ivy almost cried when her boots touched down on the white pebble beaches of the Moon Wood. Finn took her hand as they made their way through the thin white trees, following silently as Kyatta led them to her home. The woods were oddly silent as they passed through, and Ivy craned her neck up to see light dancing off the icicles that hung like teeth from the branches. Small woven strands lined with beads and bells jingled softly in the wind as they passed through to a clearing. The path was covered in snow freshly broken from Kyatta's boots. The town opened up before them, and it was nothing like Ivy had expected.

White stone buildings lined the streets, and blue doors sealed almost every home. Ivy could see fires flickering to life in the windows as people made their way back to their homes after many months spent away. The white trees dotted the side of the street as they made their way through the town. A large stable sat off to the left where some men were leading their white horses, and next to it was a large wooden structure with an overhanging roof. Bells and beaded rope hung from the roof low enough for people to have to pass through. Tall iron rods lined the streets with blue glass lanterns swinging off their hooks. It looked like a place from a storybook that Ivy had read when she was a child. Everything was white and clean, snow-covered rooftops, accents of blue everywhere, and people milling about. Though, when Ivy looked to Kyatta, her face was grim and stern.

They moved to the edge of the town where a large building shot up from the snow. The wood still held its white bark, and on the doors, a full moon was carved, split in two as Kyatta pushed them apart and entered the building. Ivy noticed the chipped red paint on the moon door as she passed and reached a finger out to brush over it. As they entered, Ivy's gaze immediately went to the rafters and the large windows that stretched across the ceiling. The roof was at such a steep angle that the snow couldn't cling to the glass, leaving the windows open to the sky above.

"This is your home?" Rayner's voice echoed in the large hall. Kyatta half-turned and nodded to him as she made her way down the center. To the left was a large bookcase with a hearth set in the center of it, and couches placed atop white fur pelts. Large wooden beams broke the room into sections and to the right was a round table with plush chairs enough for ten people. Kyatta made her way to a door at the back before slipping inside, leaving the group to wander about her home.

Grimm took a seat on one of the couches with a loud sigh, and Piotr joined him. Rayner stood leaning against one of the beams while Ivy and Finn walked down the long bookcase. Lord Cylas popped his head in for a moment to let Rayner know he was going to get his mother settled in a nearby inn. Earl Rorik, Lord

Kevan, and Ronin came in after a few minutes, stomping snow from their boots.

"Where's Zion?" Rayner asked Ronin.

"Getting his men settled and taking inventory of our supplies."

Ivy nestled herself on one of the couches, Finn coming to sit beside her and wrapping an arm around her shoulders. Kyatta emerged from the back room, dressed in a long blue gown that covered her feet and a dark blue cloak with her hood drawn up around her white hair. Grimm stood suddenly, and Kyatta stopped. The tension between them crackled through the air like lightning and it seemed to grow with every word left unsaid. Grimm lowered his eyes from Kyatta and moved to the hearth to start a fire. As it roared to life, Ivy was thankful for the crackling wood to kill the silence in the room. Kyatta moved to a nearby tray and filled a blue glass with red wine and handed it to Ivy without saying a word. Rayner stood up to help her, and once everyone had their drink and settled around the fire, only then was the silence broken when Aska burst through the door, shivering and rubbing at her arms. "By the gods, I swear it's colder here than it was on that ship."

"You get used to it," Kyatta insisted, staring into her blood-red wine. A moment later, Macon and Arytin came in and immediately moved in front of the fire, holding their hands out. Kyatta smiled faintly and got up to retrieve some fur blankets from a shelf. She handed one to Aska, one to Ivy and Finn, and the other to where Grimm and Piotr sat. She didn't even look at Grimm as he took the blanket from her hands, and she quickly moved away to take her seat by the bookcase.

Rayner turned to Macon. "Come with me, I'll introduce you to Akio, and you two can start hashing out a plan." Without any protest, Macon followed Rayner back out into the cold. Ronin looked to Earl Rorik, who stood behind his son. "We should go as well; there is plenty to do before nightfall."

"There is a small cottage down the way," Kyatta said. "You

may take it for you and your men." Rorik thanked her and disappeared through the chipped moon door with Ronin.

"Father," Piotr said, and Lord Kevan seemed to snap out of thought. "What do you need me to do? You should rest." The look in Piotr's eyes was nothing but worry as he stared at his father.

Lord Kevan shifted and beckoned for his son to follow. "Come, we can help unload the rowboats."

Aska huddled under the fur on the couch next to Grimm after Piotr left, and Arytin stood by the crackling fire. Ivy prayed for once that they would bicker at one another, anything to fill the silence of the room and the growing tension between Kyatta and Grimm.

"So," Aska drawled. *Thank the gods,* Ivy thought. "How long are we planning on staying here?"

"Once Macon and Akio have a solid plan, I imagine we will move on," Finn answered.

"Will all of your people be joining us?" Aska looked to Kyatta.

She sipped her wine and shrugged her shoulders. "I'm not sure. Returning home might have swayed their hearts. We may lose some numbers, and I cannot force them to fight if they don't want to."

"But you're their leader," Aska insisted.

"Leader. Not commander." Kyatta caught sight of Grimm cracking a grin though he didn't look at her. She averted her eyes and focused on the dancing flames.

"Where should we stay?" Arytin asked. Kyatta knew her town wasn't big enough to house all of the people and knew she would have to keep some within her home. She drew in a breath before answering, "You all can stay here, in my home."

"We don't want to impose," Ivy urged.

Kyatta grinned at her, "I'm afraid I don't have room for everyone, so you'll have to stay here unless you prefer to pitch a tent outside."

"Oh no." Aska perked up. "I'll freeze out there."

"Are you sure you can't order her to stay outside?" Arytin joked, and Aska gave him a vulgar gesture.

Kyatta smile at the comment. "You can tell Piotr and his father that they are welcome as well, I have plenty of room. We can set up cots and furs, and some can sleep on the couches if they don't mind."

The sun began to set, and the town began to settle. Ivy looked out the door of Kyatta's home and could see smoke rising from all the buildings and some tents lining the edge of the woods. Ivy couldn't believe they were finally here in the North, with thousands of people willing to fight with them. It felt like a dream, too good to be real, yet Ivy knew their work was just beginning. Tomorrow they would start to plan their attack, Macon and Akio would have a plan to save Correlyn, and then, they would get their home back.

Luna came sweeping down from the sky and blew past Ivy, perching herself in the rafters of Kyatta's home. Ivy closed the door and crept back to her spot on the floor beside Finn, just in front of the fire. Everyone had turned in early after several days of sailing; it felt good to sleep on firm ground. Kyatta had long since retreated to the back room, and Grimm decided to stay with his father at the local inn rather than sleep under the same roof as Kyatta. Piotr slept a few feet over, his father turning restlessly in sleep atop the couch. Rayner made up a bed of furs for himself beside the bookcase and seemed fast asleep as Ivy lowered herself into her nest of blankets. Finn was half-asleep as he tucked his arm around her and pulled Ivy into his chest. She nuzzled her face into the crook of his neck, breathing in his scent and drifting off to sleep, where she hoped nothing waited for her.

3

FEVER DREAMS

orrelyn dreamed she was back in the cell under the central tower of Godstone. The room was pitch black, the only light coming from under the wooden door that led to the spiral staircase. She tried to sit up, but her head spun, and her pulse pounded in her ears. Correlyn clawed at the stone wall to get into a sitting position. A shooting pain ripped through her, making Correlyn double over. She felt under her shirt and gently pushed against her ribs, choking back a sob. They were definitely broken, but Correlyn tried to focus on the other pain in her body. She brought a shaky hand up to her face and felt the swelling around her eyes, the split in her lip, and a burning sensation in her shoulder. Correlyn snapped her eyes shut before lifting a hand to her shoulder—it was hot to the touch, and her hand came away wet, but it wasn't blood. A fever was setting in, and her shoulder was infected, but from what? What happened? Correlyn started to drift in and out of consciousness before finally curling up on the stone floor and letting sleep carry her away.

Correlyn snuck around to the back of the local inn, trying to keep the crunching of her boots on the snow silent. The town was asleep, and she'd left Cass tied up to a tree about a mile outside town. After the sun had set, Correlyn started to make her way toward the town with the small pouch from Ser Oby, and her sword strapped on her side. As she got closer, Correlyn could discern the local inn from atop the hill and decided that was her best chance at finding food. She would leave behind some money and slip out before anyone noticed and hopefully be miles away by the time the sun came up.

Now, Correlyn pushed open the back door and peered into the kitchen. It seemed empty, but she stayed there in the doorway for a moment, listening for any movement. When she was satisfied that she was alone, she crept into the dark room and began searching for food. Correlyn quietly began to open cabinets, taking out a large heel of bread and a jar of preserved fruit before moving over to the countertop. She gathered some dried meat and a handful of apples, gently tucking them away in her bag before pulling out the leather filled with coins. She left behind two golden coins and said a silent prayer to the gods before slipping back out into the night.

Quickening her pace to a brisk walk, she glanced over her shoulder to see the town still peacefully asleep and unaware that a stranger that been lurking in their kitchens. She felt odd sneaking around like she was a fugitive or criminal. The plan was to head east along the coastline until she got closer to Harper Hall. There she could rest for a few days and perhaps find some maps and start planning her trip further south. Correlyn had to get far enough south to be able to find a boat willing to take her to Kame Island. A strange fluttering sensation began to fill her stomach as she thought about Kame Island, where her husband and family awaited her. Correlyn didn't know what she'd do when she saw Rayner again, but she had dreamed of the moment for months, and she was ready for whatever came next.

Correlyn rounded the wooded area where she had left Cass

tied up, taking her bag from over her head as she moved toward the horse. Cass stomped his feet in the snow and let out a whinny, backing away from Correlyn. She stopped in front of the horse and felt a shiver run down her spine as she spotted a dark figure just inside the tree line. Time seemed to slow as Correlyn reached for her sword, but it was too late. An arrow sliced through the air and embedded in her shoulder. A scream tore up her throat as she dropped to one knee, clutching the wound. The arrow was deeply lodged into her flesh, and Correlyn's heart sank as she noticed the raven feathers at the end of the arrow.

She looked up with tears in her eyes as a dark figure drifted toward her out of the wood line. Cass was thrashing against the reins as Lady Oharra stepped past him to stand over her daughter. "Hello, Correlyn, dear."

Correlyn's eyes flew open. The cold stone floor pressed against her cheek and her infected shoulder throbbed with pain. *This wasn't a dream.*

Gritting her teeth, she forced herself to sit up. This wasn't a dream, the pain was too real, her broken ribs too real. The throbbing and cold sweat that coated her body was all too real. Her entire body was shaking, yet she her skin burned beneath her clothing. She held back her tears and curled herself into a ball on the floor as she drifted in and out of her fever dreams. She dreamt of her mother and what she had done to Correlyn outside of Ashton.

Correlyn dropped to both knees, as her blood began to melt the snow around her. Her heart was racing, pushing more blood out through the wound. Oharra walked up to her daughter, bow still in hand, smiling her wicked grin. Her hand shook as Correlyn reached for the hilt of her sword. Oharra tsked her as she did. "I wouldn't do that if I were you."

"I'd rather die than go back there as your prisoner," Correlyn hissed.

"Well, I'm not going to kill you," Oharra said, and Correlyn felt her heart leap into her chest because whatever was coming next…death would be the easy way out. "Once I'm through with you, though, you'll wish you were dead."

Oharra lunged, quicker than a viper, but Correlyn rolled away, painting the snow red as she continued to lose blood. She drew the dagger from her boot and got into a crouched fighting position. Oharra threw down her bow and flashed her teeth before charging forward again. Correlyn shot to her feet, slashing her knife through the air, but only just missed her as Oharra stepped aside and reared back, throwing a punch and catching Correlyn in the eye. Correlyn staggered back a few paces, breathing hard. She shifted on her feet, waiting for Oharra to lunge again, and when she did, Correlyn slid from her path and landed a punch to her mother's ribcage only to be met with chainmail. She drew her hand to her chest, shaking it out and taking in her cut knuckles. Oharra sneered. "Correlyn dear, I thought I taught you better than that. You know I always have my armor on."

Correlyn growled in anger and tried to focus on the image that was the monster before her. Her shoulder screamed at her to stop, to give up and lie down in the cold snow and let death take her, but Correlyn wouldn't quit. Darkness crept in from the corner of her vision, and before she knew what was happening, Oharra had moved directly in front of her and slammed her open hand into Correlyn's throat, grabbing her and throwing her to the ground. She lost grip on her dagger as Oharra's weight pinned her to the snow-covered grass. Madness danced in her mother's eyes.

Oharra reared back and sent a punch into Correlyn's ribs. She coughed at the blow and tried to hunch over, but Oharra sent another fist into the same spot. Over and over, her mother punched Correlyn with all her strength and then there was a snap. Screaming was near impossible with the wind knocked out of her. Only a pathetic yelp managed to escape. Oharra let her go and Correlyn rolled over and curled into a tight ball. She couldn't crawl away, she couldn't even stand, and she knew Oharra had won. Correlyn was going to die in the snow by the hands of her mother, still hundreds of leagues from her family.

Oharra grabbed Correlyn by the hair and yanked her to her knees before sending a powerful blow to her face. Blood trickled down her cheeks and chin, the throbbing behind her eyes intensifying as Oharra leaned in and whispered, "Don't die on me yet, dear. I'm not done with you." Correlyn watched the fading image of her mother as Oharra sent one final blow to Correlyn's temple, and darkness pooled in from the edges of her vision. It felt warm and smelled of death.

The muffled sounds of footsteps echoed down the staircase. Correlyn propped herself up as her vision focused in and out. She shivered violently and looked down to see her clothes soaked through with sweat. Her heart jumped to her throat as a set of keys jingled in the lock. Her world flooded with light as a figure stepped into the room, holding a torch. She clutched her ribs and held up a hand to try to block out the flame. The figure put the torch into the metal ring on the wall before taking a few steps to where Correlyn sat in the corner. For once in her life, she prayed to the gods that it was Helvarr…her father. He'd grown to care for Correlyn, and although the thought sickened her, he might be her only chance. He once told Correlyn that he might be the only one here who wants her alive, and Correlyn was starting to believe him.

Instead, Oharra came into view as she bent over to catch Correlyn's eye. She felt a sick twisting in her stomach at the sight of her mother, her gray dress and black hair braided up, the cold calmness in her eyes. Oharra gave her an innocent smile. "How did you escape?"

Correlyn hesitated. Is it possible she didn't know about Ser Oby? No, her mother was too clever; this was a trap, so Correlyn opted to stay quiet. Oharra huffed out a sigh and put her hands behind her back, straightening to her full height. "I'll tell you," Oharra answered for her, pacing around the cell casually. "You jumped into the sea and scaled the cliffside, I know, because I saw you on top of the hill looking back before you took off." Correlyn was going to be sick.

"Then, Ser Oby, the loyal knight that he was, went after you. You snuck up on him, punched him in the face, and stole his horse. Does that sound right?" Oharra stopped her pacing to stand in front of her daughter.

Correlyn kept her eyes trained on the stone ground. Her entire body was shaking as Oharra went on. "No, that's not right." She tapped a finger to her chin. "Let's try that again. Ser Oby expected your escape and gathered supplies and went after you. He told you to injure him to add to the story, and then he handed over his horse, his saddlebags filled with supplies, and told you to run. Isn't that right?" Bile burned in her throat, but she kept it down. Ser Oby wouldn't have told Oharra anything. Was her mother just guessing? And where was Ser Oby?

She shifted on the floor and forced herself to look up at Oharra, mustering as much command into her voice as she could. "What did you do to him?"

"Oh, don't worry about him. His body is cold by now," she said with a smile. Correlyn snapped her eyes shut. Ser Oby had known the consequences of crossing Oharra, and yet he did it anyway. So why did she feel so guilty?

"He was a tough one. He didn't tell me anything," Oharra went on, picking at a string on her shoulder. "I put it together pretty quickly, but still, his betrayal couldn't go unpunished. Would you like to know how I tortured him?"

Correlyn sat frozen in place. She could only imagine what her mother had done to Ser Oby. Oharra stepped forward and went to a crouching position in front of Correlyn, forcing her to look into those mad eyes.

"Well, first, I had his fingers broken one by one. Of course, I had to come after you myself, and so a few knights took my place while I was away, but when I got back, I saw to his punishment myself."

Tears started to fall down her cheeks. She closed her eyes, but Oharra grabbed her chin and jerked her head back to her.

"I whipped him until his back was nothing more than shredded ribbons of skin. When he passed out, I branded his chest until he woke up screaming. I was patient and tried to talk to him, but he told me to go to hell and so I continued. I forced a few guards to help me hold his head in a bucket of water. He thrashed like a wild beast, and yet still, he did not give you up."

Correlyn was sobbing uncontrollably by now. "Stop, please…" she said through tears. She didn't want to imagine Ser Oby's pain and suffering. It was her fault; if she hadn't escaped, then he wouldn't have taken the opportunity to help free her.

"Don't waste your tears on him. He's a traitor." Correlyn remembered Oharra's letter and forced herself to look back up at her.

"You're the traitor," she spat. "You killed your own brother and had an entire town slaughtered! My friends, our neighbors! You're a monster," she growled. "And you can blame me for whatever you want, but I didn't aid your madness."

Oharra smiled and leaned in closer, "Correlyn dear, we are of the same blood. My madness runs through your veins. You just need a push."

"I'm nothing like you."

"We'll see about that. If you survive your injuries, perhaps I can start to rebuild you again now that you've been properly broken." Correlyn felt a sudden panic. Magister Ivann was dead, and no one was going to come to help her.

"I need a healer." Correlyn's voice sounded timid.

Oharra stood up and looked over her injuries, tsking as she said, "Pity, I imagine you don't have much time then." Oharra moved to the door and opened it to leave.

"Wait!" she called. "Where's Helvarr?"

Oharra stopped with her hand on the handle and turned back to her daughter. "You won't be seeing him for a long time," she answered. "Perhaps not ever if you don't survive your fever." Oharra slipped through the door and came back in with a tray of food, sliding it over to Correlyn. A bowl of porridge sloshed over the brim of a bowl, and a small cup of water sat on the tray. Oharra slammed the door shut again and left Correlyn in the dark. She would have thrown up at the smell of the food, but her stomach contorted and heaved, nothing coming out. She forced herself to drink the water and then curled into a ball, hoping it would stay down.

She had no idea how long she'd been there. Had it been days? Hours? Correlyn couldn't remember much of the ride back to Godstone—only flashes of snowy fields, a blue sky above, and the smell of her own blood.

Correlyn suddenly thought about the people back in Ashton. Did Oharra know she went there? Were they all right, or did her mother send men back to kill them? Another wave of nausea overtook her, but Correlyn forced herself to sit up. She had to tell Oharra that those people were innocent, that no one saw her, or helped her in any way. She couldn't have more blood on her hands, there was already too much.

She scratched at the stone floor, pulling herself across the room toward the door. Her head was spinning, and a loud buzzing sounded in her ears as she strained to crawl across the floor. When she reached the door, she put all the strength she had left and pounded on the wood, the movement sending a shockwave of pain to her shoulder. She bit back tears and pounded again when she heard footsteps, angrily stomping down the stairs.

Correlyn backed up until the stone wall pushed back. The door swung open, and Correlyn was blinded again by the light coming from the hall outside. She willed her eyes to focus and lost her breath as she looked at the man before her. "Ser Oby?" she said, her voice raspy from crying.

The man stepped closer and crouched in front of her, a nasty smile plastered on his face. His blond hair was pulled back, and his hazel eyes shone with hate. *Not Ser Oby.*

"Not quite, darling." He snickered, and Correlyn pushed so hard into the wall she thought it might crack. "But you're going to wish he was still here." A shiver skittered down her spine, something in her mind telling her to run, but she couldn't move. The knight grabbed her by the collar and balled his hand into a fist.

"Wait!" she cried just as his fist contacted her jaw, and she slammed back into the wall, the lights in her eyes going out before her head hit the stone.

And then she was dreaming.

Dreaming of Rayner, standing under the archway on the beaches of Godstone. It was their wedding day, and the sun was shining as Rayner leaned in and kissed Correlyn, loud applause roaring up around them. Correlyn turned to see her family and friends, all on their feet and clapping to their happiness. She let herself smile, but it quickly fell when she spotted her mother moving down the aisle. Oharra wore a dress, blacker than the beaches, and her hair hung limp around her face. Correlyn's eyes were drawn to the bow in her hand, and before she could say anything, Oharra lifted the bow and sent the arrow plunging into

Rayner's heart. Someone screamed, and it took Correlyn a moment to realize it was her. All around her, people seemed lost in a fog as they continued clapping, smiles painted on their faces and tears in their eyes as Rayner fell to the ground. Correlyn caught him, his weight dragging her down with him as he bled out, his blood hot and sticky on her fingers. He tried to speak, but more blood came from his lips, and then he was gone.

Correlyn couldn't form any words. Her throat was dry, and her mind was blank as she stared at her dead husband. She looked over her shoulder to see Oharra, nocking another arrow and aiming for Ivy next. Correlyn screamed again as Ivy dropped to the sand, blood covering her dress and the purple dimming in her eyes. One by one, Oharra killed the members of her family while Correlyn was frozen in place, only a viewer in Oharra's play. She wanted to yell at them to run, to do something, but she realized that they were as frozen as she was. They all kept clapping until Oharra's arrows sliced through their throats or pierced their hearts.

Oharra wore a wicked smile the entire time, and when everyone was dead, Oharra finally dropped her bow and held her arms out to her side. Correlyn watched as a murder of ravens seemed to appear from nowhere. They blew past her mother in a wave and came barreling toward Correlyn, swarming her until all she saw was black.

4

ALL OR NONE

It had been a week since Rayner's army arrived in the Moon Wood and came up with a solid plan for Correlyn's rescue. They would set out tomorrow, where they planned to hide out at the base of the mountain range just north of Godstone. Akio and Macon had sat up most of the first night, looking over maps and listening to Rayner lay out every inch of the kingdom. After hours of planning, debating, and memorizing all they could, Rayner was convinced that Helvarr would be keeping Correlyn under the central tower where a small cell was.

When they were wrapping up their discussion for the night, Lord Kevan had come in and insisted that he accompany them.

Surprised, Rayner told the lord, "That's not necessary. Akio and Macon have it covered, there's no need to risk you." He said this as gently as he could, pointing out the fact that Piotr had just lost his mother.

Lord Kevan looked tired. His usually shiny, blonde hair was unkempt, and his eyes looked haunted. He worried Rayner. "I insist," Lord Kevan said, meeting the eye of the king.

"Why?"

His gaze wavered for a brief moment. "Because," he said in a soft voice. "I need to do something. I've been...I haven't been myself lately, haven't been useful—"

"That's not true—"

"But I can be useful now," he went on, staring at Rayner with pleading eyes. "If I can be a part of reuniting my king with his queen, then that's what I want to do."

Rayner stared at the lord, then looked over at Akio and Macon. They were both capable men and very skilled in what they did, but was it a good idea to send a grieving man to the place his enemy resided? Rayner had known Lord Kevan his whole life, and he was a good, honest man. Akio and Macon both stared at the king, allowing him to make the final call. It felt like the weight of the world. Rayner turned back to Lord Kevan and nodded slowly. "Very well. You can go."

"Thank you," Lord Kevan said, bowing his head.

In truth, Rayner didn't have it in him to deny Lord Kevan. Not after seeing the pleading look in his eyes or the way he stood timidly in the door. The lord had taken his wife's death hard, and Rayner knew how it felt to want to throw yourself into something to distract you from the grief. For Rayner, it had been taking over as king after his father died. He'd spent so many hours planning and regrouping that he didn't allow himself much time to grieve for his father or the capture of his wife.

Kyatta had taken count of her people the past few days and which ones would be coming with them. Only about half of them decided to go along, and the others would be staying home in the Moon Wood. Kyatta couldn't blame them; after so many months away, they were all tired, and seeing their home again sealed their decision. Many of them feared that if they left again that they wouldn't return, and Kyatta didn't have the heart to try and persuade them.

After Ivy had told Kyatta about her dream, she couldn't think of much else. Her mind ran over it again and again, but there was only one part that Ivy mentioned that made Kyatta's blood run cold.

The blood moon.

She poured over the calendar she made years before and had been studying the moon for the past two nights, and Ivy was right, a blood moon was coming. Kyatta had been so distracted the past few months after the battle, fleeing, planning their attack, and then there was Grimm…

There had been so many things rattling around in her mind that Kyatta neglected to keep track of the moon the whole time. It wasn't like her to forget something so important, and yet, if Ivy hadn't had that dream, Kyatta might not have caught it before it was too late. She thought about what happened during the last blood moon, and a shiver of fear snaked down her spine. She pushed the memory from her mind and made her way back to her home.

The day was bright with a crisp snap to the wind as she crunched through the snow and up the path to her home. The town around her was bustling with movement as people carried supplies to the stables, loaded up wagons, or sat on the steps of their home, sharpening their weapons. If Rayner didn't need them so much, Kyatta would have told her people to stay behind with their families, that they didn't need to sacrifice themselves now that they were home. Kyatta knew what she had to do once the blood moon arrived, and she couldn't put it off for much longer. She would need to talk with Rayner about it and warn him.

She paused in front of the wooden moon door of her home, running a hand over the chipped red paint as she pushed through the entrance. The paint had been chipped for years, after Kyatta had clawed at it in a frenzied state. It was after the first blood moon where she'd harnessed her powers… after what she did.

Inside, Grimm was standing off to the left just in front of the bookcase, staring into the fire. He spun around as Kyatta pushed through the doors, and his whole face went white. She looked around and realized no one else was there, likely helping the others pack for their trip south. She tried to settle her pounding heart, lifting her chin and strolling across the room to the round table. This was her home, and she wouldn't allow him to make her feel uncomfortable under her own roof. Kyatta stood over the table that was covered in maps and books, feeling Grimm's eyes bore a hole in the back of her head. She began to roll up the maps when she heard Grimm take a few steps closer.

She snapped upright, arms full, and walked across the room toward the bookcase, blowing past him without so much as glancing in his direction. She started to place the books back in their spots, opening a wooden box to set the maps in, waiting for him to leave, but instead, he crept closer.

"Kyatta…" Her hand froze as she was straightening a book. His voice sounded raspy and sad, but she refused to give in. *All of him or none of him*, she reminded herself.

The floor creaked as Grimm took another step forward until he was standing just behind her. His presence was overwhelming, almost as if he were touching her. Grimm took in a breath and shifted on his feet, but Kyatta spoke before the words could leave his mouth. "Shouldn't you be helping with packing?" Her voice was cold, her words clipped.

Kyatta counted the seconds it took for him to answer.

"I wanted to talk to you." He stepped even closer, and Kyatta hunched her shoulders, wanting to disappear.

"We don't always get what we want, do we?"

"I *needed* to talk to you, Kyatta. Please."

"I think that time has passed," she answered, forcing herself to turn around and finally look at him. His eyes were sad, and his long hair was messily braided down his head. "Don't you?" She finished and crossed her arms against her chest, hoping to mute the pounding of her heart.

"Kyatta—"

"I thought I made myself clear that night on the ship about what I wanted, yet you still shut me out, you pushed me away, and I'm tired of resisting. You won. Now get out."

Grimm's face crumpled and he looked utterly destroyed. His mouth hung open, and his crystal blue eyes held onto Kyatta for a long moment. She bit back her tears, pushing her shoulders back and standing straight. Grimm didn't bother to try to compose himself. He hung his head and slowly turned around, heading for the door.

Kyatta watched his back until the door closed before collapsing into a pool of her blue skirts and silently crying beside the fire.

All or none.

She repeated it like a mantra until it was branded into her mind because if she didn't, it would destroy her.

Rayner walked through the streets of the Moon Wood with Ronin, Luna soaring high above the white trees, a spark of orange against the blue sky. Rayner hadn't slept much in the past few days since coming up with a plan to get Correlyn back. He was filled to the brim with anxious energy, a tightly wound ball of nerves. He buried his hands in his pockets and inclined his head to Ronin, who walked with his hands behind his back and eyes forward. "Do you think Macon can handle it?" Ronin asked before Rayner could speak.

He turned his gaze back to the men around him, packing up and preparing to leave. He gave the only answer that he had, "He has to." He was putting his trust in Macon and his skills. "He's been spying on Lord Cylas for years without his knowledge. What about Akio?"

Ronin didn't miss a beat. "Akio is the best Shadow King Mashu has, I know he will do everything he can to get her out."

Rayner knew he must be bothering everyone with his constant worries, but he couldn't help it. They were so close now, and they couldn't afford to lose, not again. Rayner wouldn't survive if anything were to happen to Correlyn. His people had named him Rayner the Unbroken, but his breaking point ended with her. His worry must have shown on his face because Ronin reached out and placed a hand on the king's shoulder. "You should get some rest," he said. "We can handle the rest of the packing. You'll need your strength."

Rayner turned to his trainer. Ronin's face was unreadable as usual, but concern hung in his voice. Rayner knew he wouldn't rest—*couldn't*— not until his wife was safe and back in his arms. He nodded anyway and thanked Ronin before moving away, watching Ronin walk off toward Zion and his men. He spotted his sister standing with Finn and Piotr as they oversaw some men from Godstone loading a wagon with supplies. Aska and her family were walking toward the stables, and Rayner didn't need to hear their conversation to know Aska was bickering with her cousin. Arytin's face was twisted into a sneer as he rolled his eyes at something his cousin said. He let himself smile as he made his way toward Kyatta's home.

Rayner had tried to convince his mother to stay behind since not all the people of the Moon Wood would be joining them, but her stubbornness wore him down. Elana wouldn't leave her family, not when they were so close to getting their home back. Besides, she wouldn't leave Lord Cylas when they had just been brought back together. It added to Rayner's worry thinking about his pregnant mother being so close to an inevitable battle. But their mother was hard-headed, which was why she was here now and not safely back on Kame Island.

He pushed open the moon door, stomping snow from his boots as he entered. Perhaps he should take Ronin's advice and lie down for a little while. His body begged for sleep, but when he stepped into the home, he stopped in the doorway. Kyatta sat on the floor by the fire, quietly sobbing to herself. He was about to turn around when she snapped her eyes up to him, freezing him in place. She seemed embarrassed and quickly wiped away her tears with the back of her hand, grabbing hold of the bookcase and pulling herself to standing. They stared at each other for a moment before Rayner spoke up.

"I'm sorry." He averted his eyes. "I can go." He started to turn around, but Kyatta sniffed away the last of her tears and beckoned for him to come in.

Rayner obeyed and closed the door behind him, making his way over to one of the couches. Kyatta wrapped her arms around her waist, staring into the flames as Rayner settled himself on the sofa. He felt uncomfortable the longer she stayed silent, but he'd interrupted a private moment and didn't expect her to confide in him. When she finally turned to look at him, her face was set, with no signs of fallen tears.

"I have to talk to you," she said, making her way to the opposite couch. She glanced at the door as if expecting someone to walk through before turning back to the king. "There's a blood moon coming," she started and cast her eyes down to the white fur pelt. "Your sister had a dream of it. She saw Helvarr's entire army coming after us during the blood moon, and you need to know that when the time comes, you can use me."

"Use you?" He scrunched his brows together. "You're not a weapon, Kyatta."

"You have to trust me. When the blood moon comes, and I harness my powers, I'll be unstoppable. If Ivy's dream is accurate, then you'll need me at my most powerful." Rayner leaned his head back against the couch, rubbing a hand over his eyes. He knew Kyatta couldn't control her powers, and he had to admit, she scared him. Rayner looked back to Kyatta, who was studying him intently.

"I won't ask you to do that, whatever is coming, we can handle it."

"No, you can't. If you want any chance of getting your home back, you need me." He sat forward, narrowing his eyes on her, and remembering how adamant she'd been about coming here. But if Kyatta hadn't known about Ivy's dream when she suggested they come, then what was her reason? Kyatta shifted nervously, fussing with the skirts of her dress as Rayner studied her.

"Why are we really here?"

Kyatta snapped her eyes back to him before getting to her feet and walking off to the back room. Rayner watched her go and waited a moment before she reappeared, fist clenched around something. She sat down on the couch next to him and slowly opened her hand.

Rayner reached out to take the stone, but Kyatta jerked her hand away. "What is that?" he asked.

"It's a bloodstone," she answered, gently cradling it in her palm. The stone seemed to glow from its core, radiating pure power.

"What is it for?"

Kyatta rolled it around in her palm before digging in her pocket and pulling out a silver chain circlet and placing the stone in the center. "It was given to me by the elderly women who taught me to harness my powers. When I use my powers, it's like something takes over, and I don't know friend from foe." She lowered her head, and Rayner wanted to reach out and comfort her, but he stayed still. "They told me that this stone, when worn, will delay that initial fog and allow me to aim my powers rather than just destroying everyone in front of me...but it only lasts for so long. Once it wears off, nothing can stop me until I either kill everyone in my path or until the sun pushes the moon from the sky."

Rayner felt a shiver run down his back. He could only imagine how that must feel, to have so much power yet not being able to control it. Kyatta was more powerful than Aska and her family, but her lack of control also made her more dangerous. "I can't let you do that," he said and watched as Kyatta peeled her eyes from the stone.

"I'm not asking, and this isn't up for debate. I was giving you the courtesy of warning you because when the time comes, I'll need you to point me in the direction of Helvarr's army and then get the hell out of my way."

Rayner blinked at her tone. It was as if she'd decided long ago to walk into the belly of the beast and tear him apart from the inside. He shuddered to think what she could do, especially under a blood moon when her powers would be at their peak.

Rayner reached out and touched her shoulder. "Kyatta, we'll figure out something else. I won't send you to your death."

She squared her shoulders, closing her palm around the chain circlet with the bloodstone before standing. "You won't be," she insisted. "It's the death of an army you'll be sending me to, not my own." She turned to leave before Rayner could say anything, leaving him with more to worry about than when he came here. He let out a sigh and leaned back into the couch, listening to the crackle of the fire until his eyelids became too heavy to keep open, and then the king was asleep.

Kyatta sat in the local inn until nightfall, mulling over her conversation with Rayner. He wasn't happy with her choice, but it was what needed to be done. She ran her thumb over the stone in her pocket as she sipped her wine. Kyatta had only used the stone one time and only because the elders forced her. She snapped her eyes shut at the thought and scanned the room. A few locals sat about, eating their supper or drinking horns of ale, a glimpse of a normal life.

She looked out the window to see the blue lanterns flickering to life along the street as snow began to fall from the sky. Kyatta finished her wine and left a few coins for the innkeeper. She pulled up the hood of her cloak and stepped out into the snow. Kyatta looked up the street to where her home stood and hesitated. She didn't want to talk with Rayner anymore about her decision or see Ivy's worried glances. Instead, she turned and headed down the silent streets toward the woods. Candles danced in the windows of every building, and Kyatta could hear laughter coming from somewhere up the road. It felt strange to be back in her home with so many strangers filling it.

Though this was her home, Kyatta always felt obligated to stay and lead rather than out of her own desire. She had no family left, and Kyatta admitted she had been glad when Earl Rorik summoned them last spring. After the dream she had of Ivy, Kyatta knew in her heart that her world was about to change, but she couldn't predict what was to come. The gods had failed to show her anything else in the form of a dream. Ever since Kyatta had transcended Ivy, it was as if the gods didn't bother with her anymore because Ivy held power to see the future. As if no one needed her anymore. But Kyatta could still do something to help the people who had become the closest thing she had to a family.

Whether she died on that battlefield wasn't even a concern of hers. She would be leaving no one behind, and her people would elect a new leader after her death. The thought saddened her, but Kyatta couldn't deny the lack of love from her own people. The only ones who ever seemed to care about her were the elders who trained her, but Kyatta had ruined that. They were gone now, and Kyatta had been alone ever since.

She walked into the white trees and through the strings hanging from their limbs with bells tied off at the ends. They jingled lightly as she pushed them aside and strolled deeper into the woods. Kyatta always liked it out there—no people to bother her and no sounds other than the whisper of the wind through the branches. She paused and held her breath, trying to hear the sound of the snow falling, but the world was silent. Kyatta followed a small path lined with the same blue lanterns that hung from hooks along the streets of the town. The dim blue light danced off the white world, creating small circles of light along the path. Her hood fell from her head, and snowflakes clung to her eyelashes.

She came to a clearing at the end of the path. A circle of trees surrounded her, all of them decorated with hanging bells and beaded string with smaller lanterns dangling from the lowest branches. She pushed the fresh snow to one side with her boot, revealing the stone beneath it. The circle was large, and Kyatta took the time to walk around it, brushing the snow away to reveal a new face of the moon. At the center of the stone circle, a full moon was carved, encircled by every other face of the moon. Kyatta touched at her arm, where the moon faces stained her skin. The elders told Kyatta that she was born during a blood moon and then brought her to the stone circle, where they thanked the gods for sending her to them. They didn't know at the time that the baby they prayed for would be the end of them.

Kyatta shook her head as if to erase the thought. She couldn't change the past. She needed to focus. Closing her eyes, Kyatta stood silently in the snow when she felt a pair of eyes on her. Her skin pricked up as she opened her eyes and twirled around, reaching for a hidden dagger to see a figure walking toward her. Kyatta dropped her hand as Grimm came into the blue light of the circle. He stopped just outside of it, lowering his eyes and looking at the moon carvings under Kyatta's feet. Her cheeks burned with anger at the sight of him. She thought he would finally leave her alone after what she said earlier, but apparently, he was adamant about torturing her.

Kyatta crossed her arms over her chest as Grimm stepped into the circle, his hands buried in his pockets. The snow caught in his beard and clung to his green cloak as it continued to fall around them. Did she have to be cruel to Grimm to get him to leave? Being around him was too painful, and Kyatta was done holding out hope that he would change. Instead, she lifted her chin and glared at him before asking, "Why are you following me?"

He took a step toward her. "I talked with Rayner…" Her pulse spiked and the anger spread from her cheeks to warm her entire body. She didn't need a lecture from Grimm about what she planned to do and couldn't believe Rayner told him. "Kyatta…"

"He had no right to tell you," she snapped. "And it's none of your concern."

"Yes, it is."

Kyatta snorted and shook her head, trying to reel in her anger and focus. Grimm took his hands from his pockets and stepped closer, Kyatta backed away. "Kyatta, please," he started.

"I don't want to hear your excuses, and stop looking at me like that."

"Like what?" Grimm narrowed his eyes.

"Like I'm some broken, naïve little girl." She stepped up to him. "I know what I'm doing, and I know Rayner only told you to talk some sense into me, but I wouldn't waste your breath."

Grimm stared at her for a long time, his anger giving way to fear. It splintered across his features like a crack in a frozen lake. Kyatta shook her head and went to storm past him, but Grimm grabbed her wrist.

"Don't touch me," she bit out, and Grimm bristled at her tone but let go of her arm.

"Just wait a minute," Grimm pleaded. "Rayner did not send me to talk to you."

Kyatta rolled her eyes and turned her back on him, but he ran in front, cutting off her path. "Grimm, please. I can't do this anymore. Just let me go."

"No." His answer was so final that it gave her pause. She stared into his eyes, searching for the truth.

Grimm ran a hand over his face and let out a deep sigh.

"I have thought a lot about what you said." He looked into her eyes, and Kyatta found herself holding her breath as he went on. "You told me that you never had anyone close after your father died, that you have been alone ever since." Kyatta turned away, looking at her boots.

"That's not exactly true," she responded.

Grimm knitted his brows together and waited for her to explain. She drew in a deep breath, feeling the weight on her chest shift as she began to explain. "The women who taught me about my powers, they became the only thing I had after my father died. They raised me, and I thought of them like family at the time, but I was wrong. They were my teachers, nothing more. Years back during a blood moon…" She closed her eyes, trying to block out their screams. Grimm stepped closer, and Kyatta didn't back away that time.

"It was the first time I used this." She reached into her pocket and pulled out the circlet with the bloodstone in it. The stone seemed to glow in the palm of her hand as she explained what it was for, Grimm never taking his eyes from her. "They forced me to use my power while wearing it, and they assured me that everything would be all right. That it wouldn't be like the other times. They brought me here." She spread her arms out and looked around as if expecting to see the three old ladies. "I didn't want to do it. I was scared, but they forced me into that state by… by trying to kill me. They knew my instincts would take over, and they were right.

"I summoned my power, but it felt different, stronger, and I could feel it fighting against the shield that the stone held in place. I was still me—I could think and feel, whereas usually, I can't tell who the enemy is. They thought the power of the stone would hold out for the entire night, but they were wrong. They studied me, but it wasn't long before I could feel the stone losing its grasp and my power starting to take over. I tried to warn them, but they brushed it off, insisting it would hold. When the last of the stone's power left, I felt it like a jolt through my body. My mind went blank, and the women who had raised me suddenly became the enemy in my eyes. I reached my power out to all three of them at once, pushing their blood through their veins, twisting their muscles until they were all on their knees before me, crying out in pain, and begging me to stop. I could hear all of it, the cracking of their bones, their screams, but I couldn't stop. I didn't know what I was doing until the blood moon was pushed from the sky and my powers left me. I threw up when I saw their bodies, what I had done. They were twisted at odd angles, eyes bulging from their sockets and blood already cold, draining into the middle where I sat in the full moon carving. This stone won't stop me—it will only delay that state until I can get away from you all and get to Helvarr's army." She wiped a few tears from her cheeks and blinked the rest away.

Grimm stood complete still, staring at her with a sorrowful look on his face. "You're not the only one who hurt someone close to you," she said, meeting his gaze. "I'm a monster in disguise, and I suppose I was naïve to think I could ever be close to someone. Most of my people are afraid of me, and I don't blame them. So, whatever you came here to say, save it because you were right to push me away." Kyatta stepped around him and heard Grimm shift on his feet.

"I am always right," Grimm called after her, and Kyatta rolled her eyes. "But there is a first time for everything." Kyatta paused and Grimm came to catch up to her. "I am sorry," he started, standing only a foot away. "I am sorry they did that to you and that you think you do not deserve to be close to anyone because of it. But you are not a monster, Kyatta."

Grimm took in a deep breath before continuing. "I have thought a lot about what you said, and you were right. I did push you away; I kept you out because I could not handle losing someone like that again...not after Fey."

"Grimm, you don't need—"

"Please, I have to get this out of my head." Kyatta felt her stomach flutter with nervous energy at the way he was looking at her. There was so much tenderness in his cold eyes.

"My family is the most important thing to me," Grimm said, "and all I have ever wanted was to share that with someone. Ivy has become my family, her brother, Finn, Piotr; they have all become my family. But you have become something more to me."

Kyatta couldn't breathe. She told herself this wasn't real and to turn around and run before he could say anything else, but she stayed frozen in place.

Grimm shifted on his feet, looking nervous yet somehow confident, and every word passing his lips was nothing but the raw truth. "I told myself to stay away," he went on, "that I would only hurt you, but I could not do it. No matter how I try, I gravitate to you. I am just sorry I wasted so much time."

"Grimm...I—"

"I think you are beautiful," he blurted out, and Kyatta saw his cheeks redden. "You *are* beautiful," he said with more confidence. "You are strong and stubborn, terrifying yet gentle. You care so much about the people around you when no one else has ever shown you that level of care. You came to help Ivy and her family just because of a dream you had; you have risked your life for all of us without a second thought. I cannot tell you not to use your powers; I have no right. I just needed to tell you how I feel before we get to Godstone because no matter what Ivy's dream told her, we cannot know what will happen. I could not live with myself if I lost you before I could tell you that I am in love with you."

Chills spread down her back and Kyatta's heart hammered so hard it felt like someone had punched her in the chest. Her mouth hung open as she stared at Grimm. *Now what?* He studied her intently, waiting for her to say something, anything. Kyatta stepped toward him, and Grimm's body went rigid as she did. She balled her fists to stop the shaking in her hands as she squared up on him. "You can tell me whatever you like, but I told myself that I would have you, all of you, whole and unguarded or I wouldn't have you at all, so if you think—"

Grimm threaded his fingers through her hair, and pulled her in, pressing their lips together. All the fear and nerves melted away as Grimm kissed her. Kyatta's eyes were still open in shock, but as Grimm held her in his hands, she slowly closed her eyes and gave in. Kyatta wrapped her arms around his neck and lifted on her toes. Grimm smiled against her mouth and pressed his chest into hers, tilting her head back farther. He held her so gently in his large hands. Grimm slid his hand from her hair and rested it against her cheek while the other slipped around her waist. The touch had Kyatta burning from her core and spreading like wildfire to every nerve, muscle, and bone in her body. She parted her lips and Grimm's whole body seemed to relax as a deep sigh melted his body to hers. His lips captured her mouth again and he slowed the kiss until both of them were still. Leaning away slowly, Grimm opened his eyes and smiled at her, the sight so welcomed and needed that Kyatta could've cried.

"Now what?" she whispered. Grimm ran his thumb over her bottom lip, then to her chin, his eyes tracking where his skin touched hers.

"Now, we go win this war."

Kyatta leaned back in, surprising Grimm with another kiss. The two stood in the center of the stone circle, wrapped in each other's arms, under the moon whose face would soon run red with blood.

5

THE SPY AND THE SHADOW

The army had been traveling for just over a week now and, finally, they had made it. The snow-capped mountains just north of Godstone came into view. Just the sight of them gave Rayner more hope than he'd felt in a long time. Alongside him, Ivy reached out across their horses and grabbed hold of her brother's hand. Rayner peeled his eyes from the mountain to look at Ivy, then turned back to where Macon and Akio rode side by side. The spy and the Shadow had been going over the plan for the whole journey, and Lord Kevan had been there for every discussion since deciding to help with the mission.

"It's almost over." Ivy's voice drew his attention back. "I can feel her. We'll see her soon." Rayner managed a smile and gripped his sister's hand in his before releasing it.

They set up camp at the base of the mountain on the north side to keep the smoke from their fires out of view. Rayner and Akio had sent a handful of knights and Shadows scattered in all directions. They were instructed to go miles out and keep an eye out for raiders. Rayner had no way of knowing what Helvarr was up to or how many men he had left, but he wasn't taking any chances. They had been working for months to get back home, and he wouldn't tuck tail and run just miles from its walls.

The sun would set in only a few hours, and with every inch that the shadows grew, so did Rayner's worry. He knew the plan and trusted the trio, but there was still that part of him that felt strange like something was going to go horribly wrong. Yet anytime the king expressed his concern, Macon wouldn't hear of it. The Master of Spies had been given that title for a reason, and Rayner had to believe in it. The decision had been made, and it was too late to change it now.

Everyone had been quiet throughout the journey, but Rayner could feel the unease surrounding them like a shroud of mist. It lingered thick and heavy in the air.

"Where's Aska?" he asked once they'd settled around a fire.

"She wanted some time with her family before Macon leaves tonight," Ivy responded. Rayner plopped down on a log with a sigh, running his hands over his face and up through his knotted hair. "I know you won't sleep," Ivy said quietly. "So how about some wine?"

Rayner nodded and watched as Ivy moved away to find a barrel to tap. Finn wrung his hands in his lap, and Piotr sat quietly, staring into the flames. "Are you all right?" Rayner inquired of Piotr. He lifted his eyes, and Rayner thought the blue in them seemed duller.

"I'm fine," he said unconvincingly.

"If you're worried about your father..." Rayner started but stopped himself. He was the one allowing Lord Kevan to go along.

"I'm not worried," Piotr responded. "My father can take care of himself." Rayner just stared at him, unable to come up with words of comfort. Finn seemed to notice and caught the king's eye before motioning behind him with an amused smile. Rayner turned around and saw Grimm and Kyatta making their way toward them. Grimm was entranced in her as Kyatta spoke, his eyes never wavering. As he turned back he caught the ghost of a grin touching Piotr's lips before it vanished.

"Well," Piotr drawled, his tone was playful, but the smile

didn't quite reach his eyes. "What are you two talking about? It sure looks interesting."

Grimm grumbled something too low to hear.

Kyatta moved forward without a word and took a seat across from Piotr, motioning for Grimm to join. He hesitated but nestled himself close to Kyatta on the log. When Ivy came back balancing cups of wine, her eyes immediately went to Grimm and Kyatta and their closeness. She opened her mouth to speak, but Grimm interrupted. "I would suggest drowning your words in that wine if I were you, Iron Heart."

Ivy flashed him a challenging smile but moved about, handing out the cups and taking his advice, sipping her wine in silence. Elana had come to sit next to her son while Lord Cylas left to help set up a tent for her.

They all sat around the fire, talking and laughing, almost like things were normal. After a while, Elana wrapped her arm around Rayner and kissed his cheek before getting up to go find Lord Cylas. Aska and her family eventually joined them just as it was getting dark outside. Rayner looked to the trio assigned to rescue Correlyn and felt a knot in his stomach. Macon's mop of brown hair shadowed his eyes, and he was dressed head to toe in black. Akio dressed similarly and had his black hair tied back, while Lord Kevan had settled for a black cloak, gloves, and his sword secured at his hip. They were ready to set off as soon as the last of the sun died.

Ivy tilted her head up to the sky. "Do you think you'll be able to see the stars tonight?"

Aska, Arytin, and Macon all turned their heads up, taking in the few clouds that floated across the crimson sky. "I hope so," Aska whispered. When Aska looked back at Macon, he was standing, checking his belt that held a sword and long dagger. Macon looked to Lord Kevan and Akio, then back to the sky. "It's time."

Aska had tears in her eyes as she said goodbye to Macon, and Arytin gave him a quick hug, wishing him luck. Ronin had come to see Akio off, and Rayner stood like a statue in the crowd as he watched the three men about to set off to bring back his wife. Fear coiled tightly around his heart, making it difficult to breathe.

Piotr walked up to his father, who grabbed his son and pulled him into an embrace. "I have to do this," Lord Kevan said against Piotr's hair. "Your mother sacrificed herself, and I know she would want me to help in any way I could."

"I know," was all Piotr could manage as he pulled away from his father, looking him eye to eye before Lord Kevan stepped away and pulled up the hood of his cloak. Everyone stood in silence as the trio walked off toward Godstone under cover of darkness. Rayner prayed that come morning, he would see four figures walking back.

Macon and Akio followed Lord Kevan east along the base of the mountain and toward the coast. They would make their way down a narrow path in the cliffside and end up right on the beaches outside Godstone. From there, Lord Kevan would be their map inside the kingdom and lead them to the central tower where they hoped to find the king's wife. Macon knew the eastern wall was made of wood and that the gate there would be easier to break through. They had decided not to create a distraction on the western side of the kingdom. Rayner feared it would give away something, and he wasn't willing to risk it. The king wanted them to become shadows, to slip in and out undetected, but Macon was doubtful. He had always worked better alone. He shook his head and tried not to let it worry him. He couldn't be responsible for Akio and Lord Kevan should they get caught.

Once they were down the cliff and on the beaches, that's when it really hit Macon. Usually, he spent months in one place, learning the streets and studying the buildings until he knew them like the back of his hand. It was why he was able to spy on Lord Cylas for so long and never be caught—because he knew the city so well that it became second nature to blend in. But Macon had never set foot in Godstone before, and he was beginning to feel slightly nervous when something grabbed his attention.

Floating in the harbor, under the pale light of the moon, was an armada. He swept his eyes up the masts and found one that had been blown loose in the wind, and when he saw the sigil, his breath caught. The solar eclipse surrounded by a ring of fire silently flapped in the dying breeze. King Caato and his men where there, in Godstone. He motioned for Akio and Lord Kevan to look, and the same look of panic contorted their features.

Lord Kevan whirled on Macon. "I thought you said he was a hermit."

"He is… he was."

"Perhaps the king isn't here, and it's just his men," Akio offered, looking back to the ships. Macon shook his head and pointed to the ship right up front. It was larger and obviously better cared for.

"That's the king's personal ship. He's here." Macon racked his brain for all the information he'd gathered on King Caato over the past few years. The man had been a hermit, though now it seemed he was starting to come out of his shell.

"Well," Lord Kevan said, "what do we do?"

Macon balled his fists, trying to calm the rage in his head. He hated the king and everything he'd done to the people in the South, everything he'd put his family through. Macon swore that he would end it one day, and he supposed now was a good a time as any.

"Where would the king be staying?"

Lord Kevan looked confused. "Why do you need to know that?"

"Just tell me." His whisper was harsh.

"Likely in the central tower where we are headed, but I'm not sure which floor. Why do—"

"All right, change of plans," Macon started.

"Absolutely not," Lord Kevan protested. "If King Rayner knew—"

"Don't worry," Macon interrupted. "We'll get his wife, but I have a stop to make first."

"You want to split up?" Akio asked.

"Only once we get to the tower. You two will head to the dungeon and get his wife. I'm going to pay the king a visit," he said with a dangerous grin. Lord Kevan looked like he was going to argue further, but Macon persisted. "We can stand here and argue about it, or we can kill two birds with one stone. Either way, you can't stop me." Lord Kevan twisted his mouth and looked to Akio, who offered nothing. Eventually, he nodded, and they started toward the gate.

Macon was surprised to find it unguarded, and he quickly picked the lock and slipped inside before closing it behind them. The town was mostly quiet: a few lanterns lined the street and some candles burned in windows, but no voices sounded. They moved to the right, staying in the shadows and alleyways as they crept closer to the tower. Lord Kevan led them through the streets, navigating them as Macon did Rahama. A few raiders could be seen just ahead, walking toward them. Macon glanced up to the sky, where a few stars could be seen behind the slow-moving clouds.

"Don't even think about it," Lord Kevan hissed. "King Rayner doesn't want anyone to know we are here."

"Then let me do my job."

"They're going to see us. We have to move."

"It's too late."

The guards were getting closer, and Lord Kevan glanced around, looking for a place to hide. The alley was too open, and a lantern was positioned just at the entrance, creating a dim glow that would reveal them. Macon could hear the crunching of their boots in the snow as the two raiders drew closer. He pushed Lord

Kevan back into the wall, and Akio slipped into what shadows there were just as the raiders came into view.

Macon summoned his powers, feeling it course through his veins like lightning. He stood in the middle of the alley, just under the lamp as the guards walked by, but one of them stopped as Lord Kevan shifted behind Macon. He said a silent prayer, hoping Lord Kevan would stay hidden as the raiders stopped just in front of Macon. They wore black leather uniforms with swords hung at their waists. One of them put a gloved hand to the hilt and scanned the alley. "What is it?" the other asked. The raider stepped forward, just a few feet in front of Macon, his eyes passing right over him. "I thought I heard something," the raider said warily.

"Just the wind," the other offered and started to move along. Macon eyed the raider until he lifted his hand from the hilt and turned to walk away.

Macon released his power, sending it back up into the sky and watched as a few stars flickered back to life. Lord Kevan stepped away from the building, and Akio emerged from the shadows, both gaping at him. "They didn't see you. Why couldn't they see you?" Lord Kevan shook his head as if expecting Macon to disappear before his eyes.

"That's why you've never been caught," Akio said with a knowing smile. "That's why Lord Cylas never saw you."

"Most of the time, I was right in the room with him." Macon grinned in return. "It's like a different breed of the same species— my powers differ from the others. While others can convince people that they see something else, none can hide in plain sight without shifting the world around them. I can stand right in front of you and convince your eyes that I'm not there. It takes a lot, and I usually reserve that power for my missions, but this is a special occasion." He smiled at Lord Kevan who still stood shocked.

"But we could see you," Akio said.

"That's because I didn't touch your minds."

Akio grinned, "You would make a good Shadow."

"This spy doesn't need shadows," he responded with a playful grin.

They moved along silently through the alleyways, keeping to the shadows whenever raiders passed by, and hugging the walls of buildings. The central tower rose before them, and Macon noted the dim light coming from the top room and one just below it, deciding that's where the king would be. He turned to Lord Kevan. "How do we get in?"

Lord Kevan described the covered bridge that led to the maids' quarters.

The Great Hall sat next to the tower, and as they passed along the backside, voices and music could be heard inside. Lord Kevan led them around the back to a small door used by the maids and quietly pushed it open. He poked his head in to find the room dark and empty, so signaled to Akio and Macon to follow. Lord Kevan drew his sword as they walked through the empty building, devoid of any signs of life. They stopped outside a small room, and Lord Kevan gently pushed the door open. Moonlight came in through a window. There was a shelf with a few empty bottles, and remnants of torn tapestries on the walls. Nothing remained in the room save for a bed in the corner with a layer of dust on the covers. Macon presumed that this used to be a Magister's room, and Lord Kevan looked troubled and dazed.

"We have to keep moving," Macon urged, trying to snap him out of it. "Where are the stairs?" He ushered them up the steps that led to the covered walkway before stopping in front of the door. He turned to face Akio and Macon.

"You don't have to do this; Correlyn is our mission, not King Caato."

Macon only stared back at him before saying, "I'll meet you two in the apple orchard as planned. If I'm not out in ten minutes, take her and go." No one argued any further, and they pushed the door open to find the bridge empty. When they stepped inside the tower, Macon took one last look at them before heading to the stairs.

Macon's footsteps were silent as he padded his way across the hall and up the stairs. He watched the ground, making sure he didn't step on any loose pebbles or patches of dirt. As he rounded the top of the stairs, he heard voices coming from the end of the hall. Macon would be exposed as he passed by the threshold of the stairs that kept leading up. He waited for a few heartbeats before poking his head up over the top stair. The men were clearly the king's, as they wore beautiful metal armor and swords adorned with jewels in the pommels. There were three of them. Macon slid the dagger from his belt, knowing he couldn't rely on his powers if he couldn't see the stars and from his angle he couldn't see the sky from any window. The men were walking closer, and Macon slowed his breathing, waiting to pounce. Two of the guards stopped and entered a room halfway down the hall, and the last one came walking toward the stairs.

Macon crept back and hugged the rounded wall of the stairwell, listening as the guard stepped on the top stair and began to make his way down. Quickly and silently, Macon slid from the wall, putting one hand over the man's mouth and the dagger to his throat. The guard squirmed and writhed, but Macon dug the knife in deeper, hushing him until he relaxed. "I was hoping you could point me toward your king," Macon drawled. He turned the man around, looking into his panicked brown eyes. He pushed him up against the wall, slamming his head into the stone and leaning in. "What room is King Caato in?" he hissed.

The man's knees began to shake, and Macon rolled his eyes, sliding his knife along the man's neck until a thin trickle of blood disappeared beneath his armor. The guard spoke into Macon's hand, and he leaned in closer. "If you scream, I will cut your tongue out and let you choke on your own blood. Understand?" When the guard nodded, Macon slowly removed his hand, keeping his knife pressed against his neck.

"King Caato is on the fourth floor, last room to the left," he blurted out in a raspy whisper.

"Thank you," he said and cupped his hand back over the man's mouth and slit his throat.

Macon picked up the guard and dropped him into the first empty room before making his way to the fourth floor. King Rayner might be angry that Macon went against his orders, but he would be forgiven when he brought news of King Caato's death. If not for King Caato, his people wouldn't have had to stay hidden on Starry Point, wiping the minds of anyone who discovered them. Arytin would have never lost his friend Nova, and Macon wouldn't have had to spend so many months away from home.

Every time he left for a scouting mission, it broke his heart. Aska, Arytin, and Laeke were always like his family. He never knew his parents and had grown up alongside Aska and Arytin. He considered them like siblings, and they were all he thought about when he was alone in a city, spying on kings and lords. He shook the thought from his head; he would see them again, and soon, they would return home, and maybe they wouldn't need to hide anymore.

As Macon turned the corner of the stairwell, he cursed to himself as he saw two guards posted outside the king's room at the end of the hall. He sat down on the steps and thought for a moment before springing to his feet and going back down the stairs. He found the dead guard right where he'd left him and made quick work of removing his armor and slipping it on. Macon felt silly—he'd never worn armor in his life, and it felt stiff and rattled when he walked. It set his nerves on edge to hear his own movement echoing off the stone walls. He was so used to being silent. He drew in a deep breath, adjusting the guard's sword on his hip before stepping into the hall.

Macon strolled down the hall toward the king's room with his head high and shoulders back. The other two guards barely acknowledged him until he stopped in front of the door. "What do you want? The king is asleep," the taller one said, looking over Macon from head to toe.

"I have a message from Helvarr," Macon lied, the words feeling foreign on his tongue.

The stout guard narrowed his eyes on Macon. "What message?"

"Seeing as how you're not the king, I would imagine it's none of your concern," he bit back. The tall guard took a step toward him, his accusing eyes searching Macon's face, and he knew he'd been discovered the moment the man reached for his sword.

Macon drew the dagger from his back and quickly sliced it through the air before the guard could pull his sword. Blood spurted from the guard's throat as he choked, but Macon was already eyeing the stout guard. He had time to draw his sword, but Macon was on him. He thrust his blade forward and clamped a hand over the guard's mouth as the knife dug into his flesh, just above the collarbone. The other guard was already dead and lying in a pool of his own blood. Macon quietly lowered the other one to the ground, catching the falling sword with his boot and dropping it to the stone. Macon drew his knife from the man's flesh and watched him sway until his head fell back against the wall. The blood poured from the wound, but the man was still alive. Macon leaned in, trying to hear what the guard was saying.

"Who…who are you?" he rasped.

Macon leaned back and smiled, wiping his dagger on the man's sleeve before answering, "No one."

Macon slipped into the king's room, his eyes fighting to adjust to the dimness. He noticed one candle still burning in the window and a loud breathing mound atop the bed. He had taken off the guard's armor and dragged the two bodies across the hall and left them in an empty room. There was nothing Macon could do about the pool of blood, so he'd have to be quick, before the guards changed shifts. He moved silently through the room until he stood at the end of the bed, watching the king's chest rise and fall. Macon had watched this man for years. He knew what he liked to eat, his mood based on how his shoulders hung that day, even the song he liked to hum at his son's grave. Macon knew the man enough to know that he wasn't sleeping.

The king shot up in bed, but Macon didn't move. He stood still at the foot of the bed, a tight grin spread across his lips. King Caato searched the room for anyone else but found no one but Macon.

"Who are you?" he demanded.

Macon let out a sigh and walked around the side of the bed, running his fingertips along the wooden beam. "I suppose the fact that you don't know means I've done my job well, and so have you."

"What are you talking about? *Who are you?*" Macon could sense the panic in his voice.

"As I told your guard outside, I am no one, and my people are no one, thanks to you."

King Caato seemed utterly confused as he stared at Macon, circling his bed like a predator.

"Have you heard of Starry Point?"

"Of course. The land is barren, no one lives there..." Macon smiled as he watched the king start to put it together. "Those people are only legends," the king muttered.

Macon put a hand over his heart. "I'm honored you consider me a legend. But we are real, I assure you." He glanced out the window behind the bed to the night sky. "Would you like to see?" Before King Caato could say anything, Macon harnessed his powers, and pure, raw energy flowed through his veins. He navigated the king's mind like a bookshelf until he saw what he was looking for. Macon forced the memory to the front of the king's mind and watched as his face twisted in horror.

King Caato scrambled out of bed, falling to the stone floor as he tried to escape what he was seeing, but the image of his wife's charred body seared into his brain. Macon felt nothing as the king began to sob, heavy tears streaming down his cheeks before he let go, and the king collapsed to the floor. The king was shaking uncontrollably as Macon bent down in front of him, snatching his chin and jerking it up.

"You're a monster!" the king exclaimed.

"No, I'm a Cosmian," Macon answered simply before thrusting his dagger into the king's heart. Caato's body shuddered as Macon pulled the knife out and pulled the king into his chest. He stroked Caato's hair as the blood pooled around them. "You took freedom from my people," he whispered. "But now, we will win it back. I've thought about how I would kill you for years, and the more I watched you, the more I realized that there was nothing left. You're an empty shell of a man with no one in his life. I'm doing you a kindness by taking that pain from you."

Macon leaned back to see Caato's eyes spilling over with tears, but somehow they looked relieved. He let the king sink to the floor and felt a weight lift from his chest.

L ord Kevan and Akio entered the common room of the central tower. No guards or raiders were inside, and Lord Kevan thanked the gods. He moved over to the wall where an iron key hung from a hook. Snatching it, he and Akio quickly made their way down the winding staircase, his heart pounding louder with every step. He fumbled with the key in the lock while Akio grabbed the torch from the hall, and they entered the room.

The dark shadows skittered away as Akio swung the torch to the corner of the room where a small figure lay curled up. Lord Kevan dropped to his knees as Akio stood over him, casting light on a bundle of blankets with black hair draped over the back. He couldn't believe what he was seeing. Correlyn lay unconscious in a pile of wet blankets. "Correlyn," he whispered, reaching out and gently brushing the hair from her face. Her skin was clammy and burned under his skin.

Panic ripped through him as he uncovered Correlyn and took in her bruised face, the seeping wound to her shoulder and the way her hand clutched her ribs even in sleep. "Correlyn." He gently shook her, but she only mumbled in return. He scooped her up in his arms without wasting any more time, and he turned to Akio, but someone else was in the room. Akio caught Lord Kevan's glance and quickly drew the sword from his back and spun around to see a massive man blocking the doorway. The knight stood a head taller than Akio and held an ax in either hand. His blond hair was tied back, and his eyes beamed with rage.

Akio eyed the man as he stepped into the room, his gaze going to Correlyn, who hung limp in Lord Kevan's arms. "She doesn't belong to you," the knight said, his voice deep and raspy.

"She's not your prisoner anymore," Akio said, moving aside but the man mimicked his movement. Lord Kevan glanced eagerly at the door as the knight stepped away. He caught Akio's eye one last time and then made a break for it the second Akio attacked the knight.

Lord Kevan barreled up the stairs, taking them two at a time as the echoing of metal on metal chased him up the stairs. He couldn't think about Akio right now; he knew what he was doing. His job was to focus on Correlyn. He glanced down at her face; she was still unconscious, and worry coursed through him. She had a fever and an infected wound based on the smell. If Correlyn didn't get treatment, and soon, it would be too late.

"Hold on, Correlyn," he begged her as he rounded the corner

and ran across the bridge. He knocked a few boxes from the counter as he ran through the maids' quarters and out the back door.

He stole a look back over his shoulder to see a few men running to the central tower, where a figure emerged, but it wasn't Akio. Lord Kevan ran faster, crashing through the snow and trying to focus on the apple trees ahead. He couldn't see anyone standing among them. He heard a few shouts behind him and swords being drawn from scabbards. He shot through the trees, their branches nothing but a flash of brown in his vision. His heart was thundering madly, and his arms shook as he tried to gently cradle Correlyn. He spotted someone ahead and stopped dead in his tracks, blinking to try to adjust his vision.

Macon ran toward him, his eyes immediately lowering to the limp figure in his arms. "Is she…"

"She's alive," Lord Kevan answered quickly. "But we need to move. Now." Macon took a look around.

"Where's Akio?"

Lord Kevan only shook his head and glanced back to see guards and raiders swarming around the tower. A few pointed in their direction, and he snapped his attention back to Macon.

"We have to go!"

Macon ran alongside Lord Kevan, heading toward the northern gate. A few guards ran atop the wall, and Macon stopped in his tracks and tilted his head toward the sky. Lord Kevan watched his eyes glowing in his head as he reached out a hand to the guards on the wall. The men dove from the wall and landed with a sickening crunch. Macon didn't even look at Lord Kevan as he ran ahead and climbed the stairs. They reached the top of the wall, and Macon quickly pulled a tightly wound cord of rope from under his cloak and with swift and sure fingers, looped it around the breaks in the wall, and threw the end over.

Some of the guards had reached the apple orchard while more gathered on the wall. Macon stretched his hand out, and the guards dropped to their knees, clawing at their throats, some screaming and curling into a ball. Lord Kevan gently set Correlyn down and drew his sword as a few raiders came up the steps. He skewered the first man and kicked him back, sending him and the rest of the raiders tumbling down. An arrow whizzed by his head, and Lord Kevan spotted the archer, running along the edge of the wall toward them. He turned to Macon, and spun him around, looking into his burning white eyes, they surged with power.

"Take her and go," Lord Kevan urged.

Macon drew his brows together and released his power, his dark eyes pushing away the light. "I can hold them off," Macon started, but Lord Kevan picked up Correlyn and forced her into Macon's arms.

"I'll do it, just get her out of here."

"There's too many—"

"Go, Macon! We don't have time to argue about this." He gave him a gentle push toward the rope as a raider came back up the stairs. Lord Kevan turned and slit the man's throat before turning back to Macon. They locked eyes for a brief moment before Macon climbed over the wall, holding Correlyn over his shoulder and starting to lower himself. An arrow whizzed by again, and Lord Kevan broke his eyes away from Macon and charged the archer.

Macon quickly lowered himself down the stone wall and shifted Correlyn until she was cradled in his arms again. He took one last look up, hoping to see Lord Kevan before turning to run. The snow crunched under his boots as he ran north, following the dark mountain that stood before him. Macon heard screams and glanced back to see men with torches running along the wall and a figure cutting through them. He slowed down when he spotted Lord Kevan jump up onto the wall and grab the rope in his hands. Macon stopped, his heart racing as he watched Lord Kevan cut the rope and his only chance for escape.

"Oh, you fucking idiot."

Men closed in around Lord Kevan, who still held the rope in his hands. He tossed it over the wall, and then his body went rigid. A sword could be seen protruding from his chest before it was ripped out. Macon's feet drew him a step closer, preparing to run back and then Lord Kevan toppled over the wall.

"No." The word fell softly from his lips. His instinct was to go back, to not leave Lord Kevan behind, but he knew the man was dead. Besides, that had been his plan all along. Instead, he looked down at Correlyn who was pale, and her breathing labored. She wouldn't make it without medicine. Macon took one last look at Godstone, to the men filling the wall, calling out orders, and running off to search the kingdom. Macon had to complete the mission, but he'd lost two men in the process. He wasn't used to the guilt that pressed down on his shoulders. He always worked alone so that he wouldn't have to be responsible for others, but they made their choice and knew the risk.

Macon drew in a deep breath, trying to calm himself. The mission wasn't over yet. He took off running toward the mountain, listening to Correlyn's breathing and the crunching of snow underfoot. King Rayner would have his wife back, and King Caato was dead. He wondered if King Rayner would be angry or pleased. The king had lost a knight and a Shadow tonight in exchange for his wife back, safe in his arms, delivered by the Master of Spies.

6

THE QUEEN

Rayner felt suspended in time as he stood just outside the camp. The voices behind him barely registered in his mind as his eyes stayed focused on the stars. And there it was. A group of stars flickered back to life in the night sky. Aska tilted her head up as she came to stand alongside the king.

"Come back, Macon." She whispered. If Macon had used his powers, did that mean that something had gone wrong? Was the group in trouble? They were supposed to be in and out without anyone noticing, and yet, Rayner knew in his gut that something wasn't right. The stars above had been flickering in and out for almost an hour now.

He whirled around, blowing past Aska.

"What are you doing?" Ivy called to him as Rayner hurried toward the horses.

Aska came running up to Ivy, her face twisted with concern. "He used his powers again," she explained. Ivy turned back to Rayner, who was saddling a horse.

"Rayner, stop," Ivy reached for the reins before he could.

"They should've been back by now. Something is wrong, I have to go." His voice was shaky, but Ivy wouldn't let go of the reins.

"You can't. It's too risky," Ivy responded.

"I have to!" Rayner bellowed as fear coiled tightly in his heart. "I can't lose her. Not again." Ivy stepped forward and put a hand on Rayner's shoulder, but he brushed her off. Finn and Piotr came running over at the sound of the commotion.

"What's happening?" Finn asked, looking from Ivy to Rayner.

"We don't know—"

"Help!" A cry came tearing through the night. Everyone snapped their heads up and started scanning the field ahead. Rayner took off running before Ivy could grab him, and Piotr followed.

When a dark figure came into view, Rayner sprinted toward it, tears blurring his vision.

"We need a healer," Macon said in raspy voice, his breathing heavy as he came to a stop in front of the king. Cradled in Macon's arms was a limp figure, black hair cascading over his arm and a pale face, bruised and beaten. Rayner stepped forward, a low sob escaping as he looked at his wife. His queen.

"She's alive," Macon said. "But she needs medicine. Now."

Rayner moved forward and took Correlyn from his arms, taking half a second to look at her before turning around. The group had caught up to them, but they all stopped dead as they saw Correlyn. Ivy's eyes shimmered with tears as Rayner walked with her toward the camp.

"She has an infected wound," Macon called out, and a ripple of fear began to course through the king's veins. Ivy immediately reach for her sword belt and pulled out the bag of medicine from Miko.

"We need to get her inside," Ivy urged and took off running with Rayner.

Aska crashed into Macon, wrapping her arms around him and crying in relief. "Are you all right?" Arytin asked. Macon only nodded as he hugged Aska. Piotr stepped forward, his eyes frantically scanning the empty field ahead. Macon felt his heart sink into his boots, but before he could explain, Piotr stepped closer, tears burning in his eyes.

"Where is my father?"

Macon released Aska, who began to search the fields as well.

"He's...they didn't make it," Macon said quietly, hanging his head. Piotr's face twisted with disbelief as his eyes still scanned the fields. "No..."

"Piotr," Macon stepped forward. "I'm—"

Piotr took off running, slipping through Macon's fingers as he barreled out into the night. His father couldn't be gone. He *had* to be alive. He'd just lost his mother, he couldn't bear to lose both parents. Why did he volunteer for the mission? Why had Piotr let him go? Panic and fear pushed away reason as he ran toward Godstone.

Piotr crashed into the snow as someone tackled him from behind. He didn't even turn to see who it was before scrambling to get on his feet again. The pair of arms grabbed him around the waist as Piotr tried to crawl away, tears streaming like a river down his cheeks. Finn spun him around, holding him at arm's length. "Let me go!" Piotr roared. "I have to save him, I have to —" He choked on a sob, and Finn let him go. Piotr sunk back into the snow, his body violently shaking, and his stomach twisting into knots.

Finn put a hand on his back. "Piotr—"

"Tell me this isn't happening, Finn." Piotr cried, his eyes glued on the empty field ahead. "Tell me I'm wrong, tell me I'm crazy, but don't tell me he's gone." He looked up at Finn, whose face held such sorrow. Finn seemed lost for words as he crouched down in front of Piotr, placing a hand on his shoulder.

"I'm sorry," was all Finn could manage.

Tears blinded him as Piotr lowered his head and sobbed. Finn wrapped his arms around him, pulling Piotr into his chest as he cried, as his world continued to crumble at his feet.

Rayner tore through the camp with Ivy at his side. Men moved from his path as the king ran toward his tent, the queen wrapped in his arms. He pushed through the tent flap, Ivy moving ahead and swiping everything from the table, metal bowls, and glass crashing to the fur pelts that lined the ground. Ivy dumped the contents of the bag onto the table beside Correlyn, looking for the healing balm that Miko had given her. Rayner pulled his dagger from Ivy's belt and began to cut Correlyn's sleeve off, revealing the wound. He stopped when he saw the wound—it was angry and swollen, pus coming from the cut and dead skin surrounding it.

"Shit," he breathed to himself. Ivy put a hand of Rayner's shoulder, but he couldn't peel his eyes from Correlyn.

"We need Finn," Ivy urged. "His mother was a healer; he'll know what to do." Without another word, Ivy ran from the tent, leaving Rayner alone.

Rayner moved over to a bowl and dipped a towel into the water, touching it to Correlyn's brow. She was sweating, but her body shook as if she were freezing. She shuddered at his touch but didn't wake.

"Correlyn," he whispered, fighting back the tears. "It's me, you're all right now. You're going to be all right." He said the words more so for his sake, convincing himself that it was true, it had to be. Ivy returned a moment later with Finn, Grimm, and Kyatta. He could hear a commotion outside the tent, but Grimm ordered one of the knights to not let anyone in. They moved over to the table, Ivy grabbing Rayner's hand and gently leading him aside. Grimm started a fire in the brazier while Kyatta piled furs over Correlyn's legs. Finn rolled up his sleeves, sweat covering his brow as he rummaged through Miko's kit. He looked at Correlyn's wound, twisting his mouth as he thought. Finn turned to Grimm and motioned for him to come over.

"What are you going to do?" Rayner asked.

Finn didn't look at the king as he spoke. "The skin around the wound is dead. We need to cut it away, clean the wound and seal it."

Kyatta stepped back to make room for Grimm at the table. "What do you need?" he asked Finn.

"Hold her down while I cut away the skin. If she wakes up and starts moving, I could cut the artery." Grimm gently placed his hands on Correlyn's lower arms, and Finn motioned for Kyatta to do the same with her legs. Finn grabbed Rayner's dagger, but paused and locked eyes with him. "This is going to hurt her," he said gently.

Rayner looked at his wife, then to the dagger. "I know," he whispered, then set his face and looked at Finn. "I trust you. Do it."

Finn nodded and turned back to Correlyn. The first few cuts were easy, but as Finn moved into the open wound, Correlyn's eyes shot open. They looked the way a corned animal's do, wild with panic. Finn moved faster, trying to keep his hands from shaking as Correlyn began to wriggle. She let out a loud cry as Finn dug deeper into the wound. Rayner was by her side in an instant, grabbing her clammy hand in his and trying to catch her eye. She screamed again, and Finn hesitated before cutting away the last piece of dead flesh. He moved over to the fire, sticking the dagger in the coals and waiting until it was glowing red.

"Correlyn," Rayner said, but as she looked at him, her eyes seemed far away. Grimm leaned over her, trying to keep her from wiggling free, but she seemed to recognize Rayner at that moment and stopped moving.

"Rayner?" she breathed, her voice harsh and raspy.

Tears pooled in his eyes. "It's me, Correlyn. You're here, we got you."

Correlyn rested her head back down, staring up at nothing. "This is a dream," she said to herself.

"No, Correlyn." Rayner squeezed her fingers gently, "You're really here. I promise." Correlyn's eyes widened, and she squeezed his hand back, running her finger over his skin. She looked back up at Rayner before sliding her eyes to Ivy and Grimm, who stood over her. Finn came back over with the dagger, and Correlyn began to wiggle again when she spotted it. Rayner moved closer. "We need to seal the wound, Correlyn." But her eyes were locked on the knife.

"No, no, please. I can't take it anymore. Just kill me..." She began to sob, and Rayner's heart shattered at her fear. What had they done to her? Grimm gripped her arms tighter, and Kyatta struggled not to get kicked in the face.

"Rayner..." Finn said quietly.

Rayner looked from him back to Correlyn before leaning in and whispering in her ear. "I love you." He kept his eyes on his wife as he nodded for Finn to do it.

The scream that came from Correlyn was blood-curdling. She thrashed and screamed like mad as Finn struggled to keep the blade pressed against her skin. The smell made Rayner sick to his stomach, but he tried to ignore it. Correlyn's eyes glazed over as she slumped back onto the table.

"It's all right," Finn said. "She just passed out." Once the wound was sealed, Finn gently cleaned it then took some healing balm from Miko's kit and began to dab it onto her skin. Grimm and Kyatta stepped away as Finn wrapped her wound and began searching for more. He pried one of her eyes open. It was bloodshot, and the skin around them was black with fresh bruises. She had a small cut to her lip, which Finn gently dabbed with more healing balm. "Someone go get Macon," Finn ordered, and

Grimm immediately moved through the tent and disappeared through the flap.

Rayner sat next to the table, wringing his hands and staring at Correlyn. Ivy stood behind him, watching Finn as he lifted the blankets and rolled up her pants, checking for any more cuts. Macon came back into the tent, and Grimm motioned for Kyatta to follow, leaving the spy alone with Rayner and his family.

"Did she say anything when you got her from the cell?" Finn asked. Macon lowered his head and hesitated before speaking.

"I didn't go get her," he admitted. Rayner peeled his eyes away from Correlyn to look at Macon.

"What do you mean?" Rayner demanded.

"I sent Lord Kevan and Akio without me. I had something I needed to do first."

Rayner stood up suddenly, and everyone in the tent tensed up. "What the hell do you mean? She was your mission." Rayner pointed back to Correlyn, letting the anger fill his voice. "Lord Kevan and Akio are dead." Rayner stepped toward him, and Ivy shifted, ready to interfere. "So, you better start talking." Macon didn't back away but locked eyes with Rayner.

"King Caato was there."

Rayner blinked at him in disbelief, but before he could talk, Macon began to explain. He told Rayner about the ships in the harbor that he knew the king was there, and he couldn't let the opportunity pass.

"You killed him?" Ivy stepped up behind her brother. Macon didn't look away from Rayner, only nodded in response.

Rayner slammed into Macon, wrapping a hand around his throat and pinning him up against a post. Ivy and Finn started to move, but Macon held up a hand.

"Do you know what you just did?" Rayner hissed. "King Caato's entire army is in Godstone! Do you think they will flee now that their king is dead, or will they stand with Helvarr?"

Macon hesitated for a moment. "I don't know."

"No, you don't know. Because you didn't fucking think before you murdered their king!" Rayner's hands were shaking with anger. Macon could have gotten them all caught tonight, and Correlyn would have never made it out of Godstone alive. King Caato was dead, but Correlyn was still fighting for her life. Rayner squeezed harder, and Macon coughed, but made no move to push the king away. "You could have ruined everything," Rayner went on, leaning in closer. "You could have been caught, and she never would have made it out. If she dies"—his eyes burned with anger as he leaned in closer—"I will fucking kill you."

"Rayner," Ivy begged. "That's enough." He let go of Macon and stalked back to Correlyn, tucking the fur tighter around her. "Get out," Rayner ordered over his shoulder, and Macon obeyed.

The next night, as Rayner sat in the chair beside his wife, he thought of all the time they had spent together. Correlyn had come to Godstone last winter with her mother to help Magnus defend the North against raiders. He had always liked Correlyn and thought she was beautiful and smart and brave, but it surprised even him how quickly he'd fallen in love with her. Rayner couldn't explain the feeling he'd had for these past months when he was away from her. She had held him together, kept him going as he fought for his life, but now she lay on the table, broken.

Correlyn was tough, but when she begged for death last night, a part of Rayner died with her. He couldn't imagine what she'd gone through, the beatings she took, and the pain she suffered in his place. It was a weight like no other on the king's shoulders. It was him that Helvarr wanted, and if Rayner could have switched places with Correlyn, he'd do it without a second thought.

He lifted the blanket to check the wrapping around her

shoulder and lifted her shirt to look at the bruising around her ribs. Finn thought that one might be broken, but there was nothing they could do about it, she just needed to rest and heal. Rayner had sent out more men last night to keep an eye on Godstone and make sure none of Helvarr's raiders or King Caato's men were coming after them. So far, everything had been silent, but that worried Rayner even more. He couldn't believe that King Caato was dead. A part of him had to admit he was relieved, but the fact that Macon put that priority over Correlyn angered him. He didn't know exactly what happened to Akio or Lord Kevan since he sent Macon away last night without letting him brief Rayner on the mission. Did it really matter though? They were dead, and though he had Correlyn back, he still felt guilty. No one was supposed to get hurt, but they had all offered to help, knowing the risks.

Rayner should be planning their next move, but he couldn't leave until he knew Correlyn was all right. He had thought a lot on the trip to Godstone about Correlyn, the battle last spring, and the knight who had taken her. Rayner felt a chill creep down his spine at the thought. The horned knight had tried to kill him twice and then used Correlyn against him in the end. Rayner didn't need to see their face to know it was anger that fueled them, and after turning it over and over in his head, Rayner had pieced it together.

Correlyn began to stir from sleep, and Rayner shot up from his chair, taking her hand in his. Her eyelids fluttered before finally cracking open and searching the room around her. Rayner reached out and brushed the hair from her cheek as Correlyn turned to face him. Her brows drew together as she searched his face.

"Rayner?" She lifted a shaky hand to his cheek, and Rayner couldn't help the tears that began to form in his eyes.

"It's me," he whispered. Correlyn snapped her eyes shut as tears escaped and rolled down her cheek. Rayner reached out and gently wiped them away as she quietly sobbed.

"This isn't a dream?" she asked.

"No, Correlyn. We got you. You're all right now." She opened her eyes again as Rayner cradled her head in his hands, catching her tears with his thumbs.

"You came for me." She smiled as more tears spilled over.

Rayner pressed a kiss to her wet cheek. "Of course," he said, lightening his tone. "I'm no king without my queen."

Correlyn smiled but it seemed to take a lot of effort. "You'd still be Rayner."

Rayner shook his head, his voice becoming serious again. "I'd be nothing without you."

Correlyn frowned at that then a sudden pain seemed to take over as she clutched her ribs.

"Finn said you have a broken rib. Try not to move."

"Finn..." Correlyn said his name like she was trying to remember. She turned to look at Rayner. "Is Ivy here? Where are we? And Elana, is the baby—?"

Rayner gripped both her hands in his. "We're all here, everyone is all right. We're just north of Godstone." Correlyn released a sigh and settled back down. "I have a lot to tell you," Rayner said, smoothing her hair back.

He helped Correlyn drink some water and made her comfortable. She insisted on sitting up, so Rayner walked her over to their bed and piled all the pillows and furs for her to lean up against. Once she was settled, she began asking questions, and Rayner told her everything. About the assassin that went after Ivy, her engagement. He described Zion and his people, the history between Lord Cylas and Elana. The attack in the Siren Sea, who they had lost, and who they gained. Aska and her family, their trip to the Moon Wood, and what Kyatta was capable of. Correlyn listened to all of it intently. Rayner went silent when he got to the part about her rescue. Correlyn reached out and grabbed his hand, urging him to continue, and so he told her that Akio and Lord Kevan had died trying to get her out.

Correlyn released his hand and sat back in the furs. She looked back up at Rayner, worrying the blankets between her hands as she said, "Magister Ivann is dead." Rayner felt his stomach sink as the words settled on his shoulders, adding to the weight of guilt. He didn't ask what happened, and Correlyn seemed reluctant to go into details. Rayner wasn't going to push her to talk about what happened to her. He could see the pain in her eyes, and it made his blood boil over to think about it.

Correlyn reached out, bringing Rayner from his thoughts. She smiled, and suddenly his anger melted away. "I've missed you," she said softly.

Rayner moved closer to her, careful not to shake the bed too much. "I thought about you every day," he told her. "I've been fighting to get to you since the day you were taken. I'm so sorry, Correlyn—"

"Don't." She grabbed his face in her hands. "Don't do that. This isn't your fault." Rayner shook his head in protest as Correlyn leaned in and kissed him. Rayner grabbed hold of her wrists, bringing her hands away from his cheeks as he returned her kiss. They came apart, and he rested his forehead against hers, closing his eyes. "I love you," she whispered. Rayner kissed both her cheeks before gently wrapping his arms around her neck, stroking her midnight hair.

"King Rayner," a voice called from outside the tent. He peeled himself away from Correlyn, kissed her hand and then moved over to the tent flap. He drew it back to see one of his knights, urging him to step out of the tent. Rayner looked back to Correlyn before reluctantly stepping outside. Fires roared all throughout the camp, and Rayner was surprised to see how many people were still awake. He knew it was late, but as he followed the knight a few paces, many people lifted their attention to him and began to walk closer.

"What is it?" Rayner asked the knight while scanning the crowd around him. He handed Rayner a note, and he quickly read it, aware of the eyes on him. Rayner read the note twice before looking back to the knight. "A parley?"

The knight shrugged his shoulders, just as confused as Rayner. Ivy walked over, and Rayner willingly handed her the note. She snorted and handed it along to Grimm, who stood behind her.

"This does not sound like Helvarr," Grimm said.

"It says he wants to talk," Rayner explained even though Grimm had just read the note.

"It has to be a trap." Ivy crossed her arms over her chest. "Since when does Helvarr follow any rules? He's trying to lure you out." Rayner pinched his brows together, trying to think.

Lord Cylas and Elana came walking up followed by Ronin and Earl Rorik. Piotr was nowhere in sight, but Rayner wasn't surprised. A few others gathered around, knights waiting for orders, all eyes on the king.

"If Helvarr wants to talk, then that's what we'll do," he said.

Ivy shook her head, "The time for talking is over, Rayner. We can't trust him."

"That's why this is going to be on my terms." Rayner turned to the knight who had given him the note. "How did you get this?"

"It came on a raven," the knight explained. Rayner felt his heart start to race but kept his face neutral.

"Send a note back, tell him to meet us in the western field outside of Godstone in two days at sunset. Let him know I'll be bringing my men with me because I'll expect him to have an escort. Tell him I'll hear him out, but if he tries anything, I won't hesitate to kill him myself." The knight nodded and took off to write the note.

Elana stepped forward. "You can't meet with him." Her voice was quiet.

Rayner stepped up to his mother. "I have to. It will allow me to get close enough to see the size of his army and the damage. Any advantage we can get, I have to take it." Elana reached up to brush his hair from his forehead and gave him a half-smile.

"I'm coming with you." Lord Cylas stepped forward. Rayner looked around to everyone gathered outside his tent.

"You're all coming with me." He looked over at Ivy, Grimm,

Aska and her family, Ronin and Zion, all of them. Rayner would need all of them if things went wrong because if King Caato's men stayed behind, then he knew they were vastly outnumbered. Suddenly, everyone's eyes drifted behind Rayner, and he turned to see the queen.

"I'm coming too." Correlyn leaned into a stick for support as she stood at the entrance of the tent. All eyes were on her, and Correlyn tried to stand up straighter, but her ribs begged her to stop. Rayner was at her side in an instant, cupping her elbow and placing a hand on her lower back. She waved him away and stepped out into the snow. She looked around to the familiar faces of her family and those that were foreign to her eyes. They all watched her silently, waiting for her to speak. "I'm coming," she repeated.

Ivy stepped from the crowd and came into view. She smiled at Correlyn, but her brow was wrinkled with worry. "It's me Helvarr wants." She tried to keep her voice stern. "And if I'm there with you, he will not attack. He wouldn't risk it."

"What do you mean he wouldn't risk it?" Ivy came closer, searching Correlyn's eyes.

Correlyn glanced at Ronin, who stood like a statue, his face the same as it ever was, unreadable. She turned back to the crowd, took in a deep breath before speaking the words that had haunted her for months. "Helvarr is my father."

A collective gasp sounded throughout the crowd, whisperers began to float into the sky, but Correlyn looked only at Ronin. His face morphed into confusion and then realization in an instant. It was strange to think of her trainer as her grandfather. Correlyn knew by the look on Ronin's face that he had no idea. He looked like he was about to say something but then stopped himself.

Rayner stepped in front of Correlyn, horror and confusion plastered on his face like a mask.

"He told me. It's true," was all she said. She would have to explain everything eventually, but not tonight. All they needed to know was who she was and what they were walking into. Correlyn took a step around Rayner, and the crowd settled.

"I know what some of you may be thinking." She paused, taking in the different looks on people's faces. "Helvarr has done horrible things to get what he wanted. To get to me. But he will not harm me." A few harsh whispers traveled through the crowd. "He did not do this." Correlyn pointed to her bruised face and the wound to her shoulder. She snapped her eyes shut at the memory. Correlyn pushed on.

"He is a monster, and I will not defend him. But when one goes searching for evil, you're bound to find something darker lurking in the shadows. He knows I'm gone, and this parley is going to be a bargain to get me back, so if I'm there, he will not risk me getting hurt by attacking. I know what you must think," she repeated. "But I am not my father, and his actions are his alone…"

"Correlyn." Ivy stepped up to her. "No one here would ever blame you for the evil of your father." She took Correlyn's hand in hers.

"She's right," a knight called out and stepped through the crowd. Correlyn recognized him as a man from Godstone, one of Magnus's knights before his death. "You are not your father. You are our queen." The knight placed a hand over his heart and got down on one knee. "Correlyn Blackbourne!" the knight yelled. "Queen of Godstone!"

Ivy released her hand and backed up a few steps before dropping down to a knee. Correlyn felt tears burn in her eyes as everyone bowed before her, calling her name.

Rayner stepped up beside Correlyn, taking her hand in his as he stood infront of her. He smiled warmly before lowering himself to the ground before her. Rayner lifted the back of her hand, pressing a gentle kiss to her skin. "All hail the queen!" Rayner shouted, keeping his eyes locked with Correlyn. She lifted her head as the crowd roared around her.

"All hail the queen! All hail the queen!" they shouted.

Rayner stood up and leaned into his wife, pressing a soft kiss to her lips. Another roar went up, and Correlyn smiled against his lips. He stepped aside, and the crowd rose to their feet, clapping and shouting their names.

Correlyn turned to Rayner, who was watching her with a prideful look and full smile. She leaned in to be heard over the crowd of people. "Let's go get our home back," she said with determination. Rayner brought his lips to graze against her ear as his hand snaked around her back.

"Let's get our kingdom back," he whispered and pulled away, giving Correlyn a playful bow. "My queen," he said with a smile, and Correlyn knew that they would get it back. They would get it all back, and then she promised herself that she would kill her mother.

7

THE EXCHANGE

Correlyn couldn't believe she was riding toward Godstone, the place that had been her prison for the past few months. Alongside her, Rayner kept a watchful eye. Correlyn's rib was still broken, and every time her horse stepped on to an uneven patch of snow, she felt it. The bruises around her eyes had started to turn a yellowish-green, so she knew they were healing. Finn had come to change her bandage twice a day and said he felt confident that it was improving, but she would have a bad scar. "Just add it to the ones you can't see," she had responded.

Correlyn still couldn't bring herself to talk about everything that happened in Godstone, but Rayner didn't pry. She would tell him everything in time.

She glanced at Rayner to find him already staring at her. They smiled at one another then Correlyn looked over her shoulder where Ivy rode just behind them. Her face was twisted with worry, but when she caught Correlyn's eye, she tried to muster up a smile to which she failed. Ivy was wary of the situation, and so was Rayner, but he did well to hide it. They had no way of knowing what Helvarr intended or what was waiting for them. The news of her relation to Helvarr was a shock to everyone, she knew that, but she worried about how Rayner was taking the news. He seemed lost in thought as they rode toward Godstone, and Correlyn wondered what he was planning.

The previous night, Rayner had hosted supper within his tent. Piotr hadn't shown up, but Rayner could hardly blame him after what happened. Rayner hadn't talked to Macon again since that first night, but he would need to get answers from him eventually. He decided not to waste energy on something that he couldn't change. Correlyn was there, and that's all that mattered, Rayner would figure out the rest later.

They all sat at a round table as they methodically ate their supper. Rayner noticed the mood of the table and for once, hoped that Aska and Arytin would start their usual banter. Instead, Aska told Correlyn the story of how she saved Ivy from a Siren, the history of her people, and painting a picture of Starry Point. Correlyn listened intently but turned to Rayner in disbelief when Aska started talking about their powers. He motioned to Macon, who sat on the other side of the table.

When Correlyn looked to him, Macon offered a sad smile before explaining that he'd used his specific powers to keep them hidden until they got to the tower where she was being held. Correlyn had gone silent after that.

Rayner watched Correlyn throughout the entire supper. She ate everything on her plate and even went back for seconds. Rayner smiled as he watched his wife, thankful that she was feeling well enough to start eating again. They would all need their strength tomorrow when they went to meet Helvarr. When Aska began to poke at Arytin, Rayner let out a sigh of relief. He watched the looks that passed between Grimm and Kyatta, the way she smiled at him, and how he tried to hide his nervousness. Aska was teasing her cousin about some fight they had years ago, Correlyn giggling as she listened, but when Rayner turned to Ivy, she seemed lost.

Ivy locked eyes with her brother and gave him a small grin before turning to Finn. "I'm going to find Piotr," she said, starting to get up from her seat. Finn grabbed her hand, pulling her back down and gently kissing her.

"Do you want me to come?" he offered. Ivy shook her head, running her fingers through his brown hair and kissing his brow before getting up to leave.

Aska's laughter followed Ivy out into the cold night, but faded as she rounded a corner and started to walk through the camp. Ivy couldn't comprehend what Piotr must have been going through and didn't pretend to. After her father was killed, Ivy had let the guilt and grief consume her even when she had so many people around that loved her and only wanted to help. Ivy needed to let Piotr know that he still had a family with them and that he wasn't alone. Though, as she crept through the camp, she became doubtful that she'd be able to convey that message. Ivy came to the edge of the camp and spotted a small fire with a figure hunched over it. She moved toward it, recognizing Piotr immediately and taking a seat next to him on the log.

He didn't even look up as Ivy took a seat, the only noise was the crackling of a fire and the distant howling of wolves. Behind them, the camp was quiet, many men finding their beds early in preparation for tomorrow night. Ivy glanced over to Piotr, whose eyes were locked in the direction of Godstone, where his father had been killed. She racked her mind to try and find the right words, but what could she say that would mean anything?

Instead, Ivy reached out and took hold of his hand and immediately realized how cold he was. How long had he been out there? Ivy didn't hesitate to remove her cloak and drape it over his shoulders. Piotr seemed not to realize the gesture and stayed silent, his eyes focused south. Ivy wondered what he saw in those empty dark fields. Did Piotr see his father walking toward him, unharmed and smiling? Or did he see the ghosts of his parents, walking away from Piotr and leaving him behind?

Ivy shivered at the thought and began to rub her hands together, reaching out to the fire in front of them. Piotr seemed to snap out of his fog and noticed her cloak draped over his shoulders. He stared at Ivy before starting to untie it to hand back. Ivy grabbed hold of both his hands to stop him. "Thank you," he said quietly. Ivy nodded and wrapped her arms around herself for warmth.

After a moment, she turned to face Piotr, but his eyes were lost again. "Piotr...."

"Don't," he started, looking up and meeting her eyes. "Don't tell me you're sorry. Please." Ivy snapped her mouth shut and stared at him. "I know my father was broken," he went on. "I just didn't see the cracks in time to realize he didn't want to be put back together. He wanted peace, and now he'll never see this world in that state. He died during the chaos."

Ivy thought for a moment. They had all seen that Lord Kevan was devastated by his wife's death, but still, they let him go. Maybe Piotr was right, and what Ivy thought was defeat was actually a plea for peace in the afterlife. She grabbed Piotr by the chin, gently lifting him to face her. The blue in his eyes looked dim like all the light had been sucked out with his father's last breath.

"*You* will see this world restored to peace." Piotr's eyes flickered as she held him. "You are a part of the change we are making. You're..." Ivy chose her next words very carefully. "You're the Lord of the Twisted Tower, and it's up to you to decide what you'll do with that title. You can still help us change the world, or you can stand by and watch it crumble at your feet."

Piotr grabbed her hand and pushed it away from him, a flicker of anger sparking in his eyes. "Both of my parents are dead because of all this," he gestured in the direction of Godstone. "My father was reluctant to get involved in the first place, but he felt obligated, like he somehow owed your father his life."

"Piotr…"

"And now they're dead!" He snapped, whirling to face Ivy. There was anger on his face, but there was also sadness. "And I'm here, alone, expected to rule the Twisted Tower and swear to House Blackbourne—your brother. Am I to die too?"

Piotr had tears in his eyes, making the brightness of the blue come back out again. Ivy stared at him in shock, feeling the guilt and sorrow crash into her. It broke a part of her to see him like this. Piotr shook his head and turned away, angrily wiping his tears. Ivy didn't leave his side as Piotr cried, but instead wrapped an arm around his shoulders and he allowed the touch. He was grieving and Ivy knew not to take his words to heart.

After a while, Piotr drew his knees into his chest. His face was red, eyes swollen from tears. "I'm sorry," he said, so quietly that Ivy almost didn't hear him.

"There's nothing to be sorry for."

"It's just…how can you be so optimistic after everything that's happened to you?" he asked. Ivy considered but gave him the only answer that made sense.

"Because I have no other choice. It's that or lie down and die, and I'm not ready to go yet."

Piotr turned to her, then threw his arms around her neck. He gripped Ivy, pulling her to his chest like she'd float away and leave him too. Ivy hugged Piotr tight. He brought his lips to her ear and whispered, "The gods couldn't handle your wrath, Ivy Blackbourne."

She chuckled and leaned back. Piotr cupped her cheek then let his fingers fall away.

"I'll always be here for you," she assured him. "We're your family, and nothing will ever change that." Piotr nodded and opened up the cloak she gave him, wrapping Ivy in it with him. He tucked his arm around Ivy's shoulder as she leaned her head against his chest. They sat together for a long time, listening to the fire and watching the stars.

Now, Ivy scanned the people around her, all had similar looks of worry or pure, unwavering rage. She felt her emotions twisting into a tight ball that would burst the moment she saw Helvarr. She snapped her eyes shut and focused on the rocking motion of the horse. Ivy couldn't let Helvarr rattle her. She had to keep her emotions in check and her face passive, but it would be the hardest battle she'd ever fought. Finn caught her eye but didn't smile; instead, he stared at her, his russet eyes searching.

"I'm fine," she offered. Finn didn't crack a smile at her usual response, so Ivy reached across their horses and grabbed his hand. "It will be all right, Finn."

He squeezed her hand before releasing it. "I hope you're right."

Ivy was about to respond when she spotted the walls of Godstone. Tears immediately threatened to fall, but she choked them back. Her home looked just as she remembered—even the walls that had been damaged in the battle were repaired. She scanned the distant wall, seeing small figures moving about and smoke rising from the buildings within. It seemed like any other kingdom with people going about their day, guarding their walls, and living their lives. Except they weren't their walls, they were Rayner's walls, *her* walls, and she was eager to remind Helvarr of that.

Rayner turned around as they drew closer, motioning for everything to tighten the ranks, and for archers to have their bows ready. Just ahead of them, outside the western wall of Godstone, an open tent had been set up. Ivy's heart was drumming at an irregular pace when she spotted a familiar head of black hair. Her skin pricked up, and anger rose to warm her cheeks as she laid eyes on Helvarr. He sat in the middle of the tent across from a row of empty chairs and raiders at his back. Ivy was so focused on Helvarr that she nearly fell from her horse when she spotted the horned knight. He stood unmoving, just behind Helvarr's left shoulder with his hands clasped in front of him. Ivy looked at her brother, but his back was straight, head held high and eyes forward. Beside him, Correlyn did the same, revealing nothing as they closed the space between them and the tent.

Ivy jumped down from her horse and quickly made her way to Rayner's side. Finn followed her, but everyone else hung back, archers watching the Blackwoods and knights standing guard, forming a half circle around their king. Grimm, Kyatta, and Piotr stood behind the empty chairs as Rayner made his way around to stand in front of Helvarr, who did not get up. Ivy looked back to see Aska and her family standing with Lord Cylas. Ronin lingered in the back of the knights, not wanting to cause any problems during the parley. When she turned back, Rayner and Correlyn were standing side by side, and Ivy and Finn moved to their spots opposite them.

Helvarr ran his copper eyes over all of them, a smug grin twisting at the corner of his lips. Rayner stood tall, his back rigid but face blank. Ivy didn't know how he managed to keep his rage under control, but she praised him for it as she started to feel hers creep up the back of her neck. Helvarr stood suddenly, and Ivy put a hand to the hilt of Promise, her earlier plan failing her as a sneer crossed over her face. Helvarr didn't even look at her; his eyes bore a hole into Rayner. The tension was so thick that Ivy thought even her sword wouldn't be able to cut through it. Helvarr gave a bowed to her brother. "I'm so pleased that King Rayner the Unbroken has graced me with his presence."

Rayner didn't miss a beat. "Drop the act. What do you want?" Helvarr gave him a surprised look before lowering back into his chair. Rayner hesitated a moment but then motioned for his family to sit. Ivy noticed that Correlyn didn't take her eyes off the horned knight, and Helvarr barely acknowledged his daughter.

Helvarr leaned back as if this were nothing but a friendly meeting between friends. "I want to offer you a deal," he said, shooting a look at Ivy. She fought back the words bubbling in her throat and stared him down until he looked back at Rayner.

"Here's a deal," Rayner said, leaning forward. "Get out of my home before I have to force you."

"Oh, a feisty king," Helvarr grinned. "You know, your father—"

"Do not talk about my father," Rayner growled. Helvarr playfully threw his hands up in submission, and when he lowered them, he glanced over at Finn, doing a double-take. Ivy scrunched her brows together as he studied Finn, running his cold eyes over his face. Ivy balled her fists together and was about to say something, but Helvarr dropped his eyes before looking back at the king.

"I'm not here to fight with you, King Rayner." He said the title as if it were a joke. "I have a real offer." Ivy snorted, and Helvarr shot her a menacing look. She glared back, challenging him to do something. Instead, he flashed his teeth and raised a brow to her, silent submission.

"What kind of deal?" Rayner's voice was turning hostile.

"One where we both win," Helvarr went on.

"I doubt that."

"You haven't even heard it yet." When Rayner didn't answer, Helvarr started to explain. "If my memory serves right, Kaspin's Keep is unoccupied at the moment." Ivy suddenly got a flash of Meisha and Queen Narra, what the enchantress had done to her, and how Helvarr used them. The wave of anger was rising, and Ivy couldn't stop it.

"If your memory serves right?" Ivy snapped back at him, and Helvarr seemed intrigued. "You're the reason they're gone. You're the reason they betrayed us, and we almost lost our home!"

Helvarr wagged his fingers in the direction of Godstone and smiled. "But you did lose your home."

Ivy shoved back her chair and reached for Promise. The raiders behind Helvarr began to draw their swords.

"Ivy!" Rayner's voice cut through her. The rage was blurring her vision. She could do it right now. She could kill Helvarr and hold off the raiders until her family got away, but then what? She thought of Ronin, likely back there watching her. She removed her hand from Promise and released her anger in a long sigh. Helvarr watched her with a knowing smile until she sat back down.

"Now," Helvarr went on. "As I was saying. Kaspin's Keep is without a leader, I have some raiders there, but they are just keeping it safe for me."

"For you?" Rayner questioned.

Helvarr smiled, "That's right. I will give you back Godstone." He waved a dismissive hand toward the kingdom as if it were nothing. "If you make me King of Kaspin's Keep." Everyone turned to look at Rayner, whose eyes were narrowed on Helvarr.

"Why would you want Kaspin's Keep now? Why take Godstone if you could have conquered that kingdom instead?"

"Because I could." He said, turning to face Ivy, but she remained in her chair this time. "Because your father took everything from me, and it was time to repay the gesture, and now I have."

Rayner balled his fists, and Helvarr held up a hand, sitting back in his chair.

"What makes you think I'll give you such a title? After everything you've done."

"Like I said, I didn't come here to fight. I'm tired." It was the most honesty Ivy had ever heard in his voice. "But if you refuse, I'll keep what I've got and destroy your army."

"With your raiders?" Rayner gestured to the men standing behind him, his eyes passing right over the horned knight.

Helvarr let out a low chuckle. "I'm sure you know by now that King Caato is dead, thanks to one of you." He scanned their faces and those of the people behind Rayner. "But the king was smart enough to bring all of his men here, which I now have control of." Ivy looked at Rayner, who tensed up slightly. This was the worst-case scenario. If Helvarr did have all King Caato's men, then they had no chance of winning the battle. She looked at Helvarr, the same wicked grin plastered on his face. Could he be bluffing? They couldn't see the harbor from here, so they would have to take his word for it and send out scouts later tonight to confirm. Ivy turned and looked out to the western fields. The sun was setting, and soon the world would be dark, and the stars would come out. Ivy felt some comfort knowing Aska and her family would have an advantage if things should go wrong, but she knew Rayner didn't want to risk it. Not until he had all the information he needed.

Helvarr observed the king, waiting for an answer.

"What's the catch?" Rayner finally asked.

Helvarr chuckled in response, almost as if he were delighted at Rayner's assumption. "I wouldn't call it that, but there is something else I want." He finally rested his eyes on Correlyn, who stiffened under his gaze.

"Forget it," Rayner snapped.

"You haven't even heard my condition yet."

"I don't care. She's not part of this deal." Correlyn reached out and grabbed hold of Rayner's hand. He turned to her, his face softening as he looked into her eyes.

Correlyn turned to face Helvarr. "What is the condition?"

"Correlyn—" Rayner pleaded, but she squeezed his hand a little harder, and he went silent. Helvarr suddenly looked a little nervous as he faced his daughter, but he pushed on.

"When I am king, I will vow never to set foot in Godstone or your allied kingdoms in exchange for you allowing my daughter to visit me for the entire summer, every year." Correlyn released his hand and sat back. Helvarr watched her carefully, and Ivy wondered if he really thought Correlyn would agree to that. Rayner immediately shook his head, but Correlyn leaned forward in her chair to address him.

"How long would you make me keep coming back?" she asked.

"For the rest of my life," he answered. "But I would hope after some time, perhaps you would want to keep coming back."

Ivy snorted a laugh, but Helvarr and Correlyn stayed staring at one another. Correlyn looked up to the horned knight before glancing down at her boots and releasing a sigh.

Rayner shook his head. "That's not happening. She's my wife and the queen, and you don't get to command her."

"She's my daughter," Helvarr said back with some heat.

"And you screwed that up. She shouldn't have to pay for your mistakes." Helvarr growled in response, but Correlyn shifted until his eyes left Rayner and looked at her instead.

"I'll consider it," she said.

"No!" Rayner and Ivy said in unison.

"It's my decision." She closed her eyes. "If this exchange will bring peace and get our home back, then I have to consider it."

Ivy glared at Helvarr. "There will never be peace as long as he's still breathing." Helvarr flashed her a grin, another challenge.

Rayner turned to his wife, "Correlyn, I can't let you do this."

She cupped his cheek in her hand, "I'm not doing anything yet. But I need to consider it. I am queen, and I will not see more of my people die, knowing I could have prevented it."

Rayner stared at her unblinkingly and Ivy was just as shocked. Correlyn had been imprisoned for months, beaten and tortured, yet here she was, still healing from fresh wounds and willing to open up another one. She would do anything for her family and their people, even if it meant her own misery.

Correlyn released Rayner and turned back to Helvarr. "When do you want your answer?" Helvarr thought for a moment, stroking his short black beard and looking out to the west. The sun was no more than a sliver on the horizon, and they only had a few moments before it would set. "Tomorrow evening," he said.

"Two days," Ivy countered and shot a warning glare to Rayner.

He seemed to understand and repeated the counteroffer. "Back here, same time, two days from now." Helvarr tried to read the look that passed between brother and sister, but Rayner's face gave nothing away.

He sighed but agreed. "Fine, I'll see you then." Helvarr got to his feet.

"Not so fast." Rayner stood as well, but his family remained seated, confused. "I need assurances that you won't attack before our meeting." Rayner looked behind Helvarr. "I want to exchange hostages." Ivy got to her feet, but Rayner wouldn't look at her. Beside him, Correlyn tugged on his sleeve, but still, the king only had eyes for one person.

Helvarr placed his hands behind his back, twisting his mouth in thought. "Very well." He turned around. "Ser—"

"Oh no," Rayner interrupted. Helvarr turned back and looked at Rayner curiously, but Rayner wasn't looking at him. "I know who I want." Rayner's voice was sharp. He lifted a finger, and everyone followed his gaze to the horned knight, who didn't move. "I want Lady Oharra."

Ivy felt her heart slam to a stop and a knot twist in her gut as she looked at the horned knight. What had her brother just said? It couldn't be true. Correlyn would have said something. Ivy looked over to Correlyn, whose face was white, and her eyes averted. It didn't make sense. Why wouldn't Correlyn have said anything and why wasn't she looking at her?

Helvarr even furrowed his brows together but quickly

recovered. He motioned for the horned knight to step forward and remove the helm. Ivy thought she was going to be sick as he beheld Lady Oharra, her black hair sweeping across her cold face as she removed the helm and tossed it to the ground. Ivy's hands were shaking, and Rayner sensed her putting one hand on the hilt of Promise. Lady Oharra snapped her attention to Ivy, who froze under her gaze. Rayner put a hand on Correlyn's shoulder without looking at her.

"Did she tell you?" Lady Oharra's voice was like a sinister whisper.

"No," Rayner responded. "I figured it out."

Oharra raised her brows and nodded.

"Very well, King Rayner. I will come with you." Oharra turned back to Helvarr and cupped his cheek in her hand before walking toward where Rayner's knights were waiting to disarm her. They bound her hands behind her back and ushered Oharra to a horse.

"Is that really necessary?" Helvarr asked.

"Yes," Rayner hissed. Correlyn rose to her feet, worry dancing in her eyes as she looked at Rayner. He grabbed her hand and pressed a soft kiss to her cheek before she turned to face Helvarr.

He held up a hand to stop her. "You got to pick your hostage. Now I get to pick mine."

Everyone looked confused. Why wouldn't he want time alone with his daughter? Ivy was sure Helvarr was going to choose Correlyn, but instead, she followed his gaze.

"Him." Helvarr pointed his finger at Finn, who went rigid.

Ivy stepped forward, hand on her sword. "Absolutely not."

Helvarr only raised a brow to the king, who looked at Ivy with an apologetic look. Why would he want Finn?

Finn stood up, facing Helvarr with a curious look.

"Why him?" Rayner asked.

Helvarr peeled his eyes from Finn. "That's none of your business. I didn't question your choice. Now," he smiled with teeth like a hungry wolf. "Give him to me."

Finn didn't know what to feel. Confusion, anger and fear all coiled in his stomach, making him feel sick.

"Finn…" Ivy's voice cracked. He turned to Ivy, whose eyes were growing shiny with tears. He balled his hands to try to stop the shaking, but to no avail.

"I'll go," he said.

"Finn, no," Ivy walked over to him. Finn wrapped her in a hug before she could say anything.

"It will be all right," he whispered against her ear.

Ivy's whole body was shaking as she hugged Finn. It didn't make sense. He had nothing to do with this. Was this Helvarr's way of punishing Ivy for speaking out? It had to be. Everything was a game to him, and he was winning. Ivy released Finn, and he unbuckled his belt, pressing his sword and ax into Ivy's hands.

"Keep them safe for me," he said.

Ivy let a tear escape, but Finn wiped it away and pulled her in, kissing her forehead and allowing his lips to linger for a moment longer. He looked at Rayner, who seemed just as confused as Finn felt. "It's all right," he tried to assure them, but Rayner's face was still twisted, and Correlyn looked shocked.

She gave Finn a hug, bringing her lips to his ear as she whispered, "Don't play his games."

Finn withdrew and looked back to the rest of their people. Grimm stood with his arms crossed over his chest, his face stern as he stared daggers at Helvarr. Piotr looked at Finn with a sorrowful gaze. Finn tried to muster a smile, to tell them that it was okay but he failed. Instead, he nodded once and turned back to face Ivy.

The look on her face broke his heart, but he would not be another casualty of Helvarr. "I'll come back to you, my Ivy."

She couldn't speak, only smiled and kissed Finn.

He walked over to Helvarr's raiders, who produced metal cuffs chained together. Helvarr waved them off. "There's no need to bind him."

Ivy stepped forward. "If you hurt him, I'll fucking kill you," she said through her teeth.

Helvarr placed a hand over his heart. "I would expect nothing less." He flashed a grin, but Ivy sneered at him until he turned his back on her.

Helvarr stood before Finn, gesturing him toward the awaiting horses. "Shall we?"

Finn followed him, looking back over his shoulder to see Ivy still standing there. Everyone else left the tent, but he knew Ivy wouldn't leave until he was out of sight, behind the walls of Godstone. Finn felt a strange knot forming in his stomach and something pulling at his mind, like a warning. He shook off the feeling as he mounted a horse and couldn't help but gasp when he recognized Cassius, Ivy's horse. Cass seemed to recognize Finn and greeted him with a small whinny as he scratched him behind the ear. It had to be a sign from the gods.

Finn looked back to see Rayner's men still lingering in the field. He couldn't believe that Lady Oharra was the horned knight and wondered how long Rayner had known. Why didn't he tell any of them? Why hadn't Correlyn? He felt an intense stab of sorrow for Correlyn and wondered how she had survived all these months being held in her own home by her parents, two monsters formed from the same evil.

8

THE MONSTER WITHIN

As soon as they returned to the camp, Rayner motioned for a group of knights to escort Lady Oharra to an empty tent. He didn't know exactly what to do with her now that she was there. Correlyn stepped in front of him. "Why didn't you tell me you knew?" She glanced over to the tent that held her mother.

"Why didn't *you* tell *me?*" Rayner asked, then gestured out to the camp. "Or them? Did you feel like you couldn't tell me?" He stepped closer to Correlyn and took her hands in his.

"Of course not," Correlyn said, then lowered her eyes to the ground. "I just... I guess I didn't know how to tell you. Or what they would think of me."

Rayner furrowed his brow and tilted her chin up to look in her eyes. "I'm sorry you felt like that, and I'm sorry I didn't tell you. I should have."

She shook her head and wrapped her arms around his neck. Rayner buried his face in the crook of her neck, hugging her around the waist.

"What a mess," he whispered against her hair. Correlyn chuckled lightly and leaned back.

"We're a team, you and I. We need to inform each other of our decisions."

He smiled and cupped her cheek. "You're right."

Correlyn grinned. "I know."

He laughed then leaned in and kissed her softly. When he pulled away, he caught movement out of the corner of his eye. Ivy was storming across the camp toward them.

Her face was a swirl of anger and fear. She stepped up to Rayner, jabbing a finger at his chest. "How long have you known?" she demanded.

Rayner glanced back to see Grimm and Kyatta standing with Piotr, all eyes on him and Ivy.

"Long enough." He looked back at his sister and saw she wasn't satisfied by his answer.

"Why the hell didn't you say something?" She was angry, but Rayner knew that part of the heat in her voice was worry for Finn. He didn't have an answer for her, not one he was willing to admit in front of everyone. He tried to calm his shaky hands. He'd been terrified to bring Lady Oharra here and face her again. When he pieced it together, he doubted it for a long time and told himself that he'd lost his mind. But he was right, and Rayner had to come to terms with the fact that he couldn't run from her forever.

"I'm sorry," he answered. Ivy's eyes were shiny with tears as she glared at Rayner. "I messed up. I didn't mean to keep this from you, but I thought it was my burden–my monster to deal with."

Ivy crossed her arms and sniffed back her tears, but to little avail. "You need to tell us what you're planning. It doesn't only affect you." The look in her eyes pulled on his heart.

"I know." He hung his head. "I'm sorry, Ivy," Rayner reached out to her, but Ivy brushed past him, bumping his shoulder with hers. Rayner whirled around and took a few steps forward, "Ivy, wait—"

Correlyn grabbed hold of his arm, and Rayner watched his knights leap from Ivy's path as she stormed across the camp. "Let her go," Correlyn whispered, dropping her hand from him.

Rayner hung his head, rubbing a hand over his eyes. He was tired, but they still had work to do.

Rayner scanned the crowd that was gathering around the tent and motioned for Macon to come over. He hadn't spoken with the spy since he brought back Correlyn, and Rayner owed him an apology and a thank you, but that could wait. Macon came strolling up to the king with his hands clasped behind his back. "Go to the harbor to see if King Caato's ships are still there. Stay hidden," Rayner urged, and Macon nodded. "If Helvarr is bluffing, he'll likely have raiders waiting to intercept you if you get too close. Do *not* engage them." He looked up to the stars. "Use your power if you must just get to that harbor and get back here as soon as you can."

Macon nodded that he understood and turned away. Macon wouldn't get caught if he sent him alone. It was what he did best, and Rayner had a feeling that Helvarr was bluffing, which meant he would need to start planning their next move after they came to a decision about the deal.

Rayner looked away from Macon when he heard voices moving toward the tent. He spotted his mother as knights parted way to let her through. Rayner knew the moment he looked at Elana's face that someone had already told her. He stepped in front of his mother, who had tears in her eyes.

"Is it true?" she demanded.

Rayner felt his heart sink to his boots. He nodded, and Elana snapped her eyes shut as Lord Cylas came to her side. Correlyn stepped up beside him.

"What do we do with her?" She gestured toward the tent. Rayner knew that he needed to talk with Lady Oharra, but he wasn't sure if he had it in him tonight.

Before he could answer Correlyn, Elana pushed past her son and stormed into the tent. Rayner ran after her, Correlyn and Cylas following. His mother stood in the middle of the space, staring at Oharra as she rose to her feet. The tension and anger rippled between them as the two women glared at one another.

Lady Oharra made the mistake of cracking a grin as Elana walked up to her.

"Elana—"

Oharra's words were cut off as Elana slapped her across the face with such a force that Oharra stumbled to one knee. Everyone froze.

Oharra at least had the decency to look shocked as she rose back to her feet, her cheek beet red. Elana turned on her heels and stalked out of the tent without a word. Rayner stood there shocked as Cylas ran out after her. He'd never seen his mother hit someone before, and never had he seen her anger get the better of her. But then again, Oharra was a special type of monster. One that could get under your skin and burrow so deep that you'd rather lop your arm off than to feel the itch.

Correlyn eyed her mother from across the tent, and Rayner tensed, ready to step in this time. Correlyn lifted her chin and turned around, leaving Rayner alone in the tent with Oharra, who glared at him like he was the one who had just struck her. A few knights came running in. Rayner would bet they heard the slap throughout the camp. He held Oharra's gaze as he addressed his knights. "Keep a guard on the tent. I'll deal with her tomorrow." Oharra narrowed her eyes and grinned at him until he turned his back and left.

The next day, Rayner went off in search of his mother. Macon still hadn't come back, but Rayner didn't have time to worry about that right now. He had to trust the spy to do his job; he just hoped Macon didn't get any more ideas about doing things himself.

As he strolled through the camp toward his mother's tent, he passed by Ivy's. Rayner poked his head in to find her tent empty, the bed made up neat and no signs of his sister. He sighed and hoped that someone was with her. He knew exactly how Ivy felt, with her free and Finn trapped with Helvarr. Rayner had felt it every day for months, and the guilt was unlike any other, but they would get Finn back tomorrow night. He still couldn't figure out why Helvarr wanted to take Finn rather than Correlyn, but he supposed it didn't matter and thought Helvarr was just getting back at Ivy.

Rayner stopped just outside his mother's tent and took in a breath before pushing through the flap. Elana and Lord Cylas sat side by side on her bed, his arm wrapped around her waist. They looked up when Rayner entered the tent, and he lowered his eyes. "May I have a moment alone with my mother?" He glanced up to Elana, whose face was stern.

Cylas nodded and leaned over, placing a gentle kiss against her cheek. "I'll be right outside." He gave Rayner a sorrowful look as he passed and disappeared through the tent flap.

Elana didn't move as Rayner came to sit next to her, releasing a sigh as he settled onto the bed. "I won't apologize," Elana said sharply. Rayner cocked his head to look at her, but her eyes were on the fur pelts below her feet.

"To her or to me?" He tried to make his voice sound playful, but Elana wasn't smiling. Rayner knew how difficult it must be for his mother to accept what Lady Oharra was. They had been friends once, but Oharra destroyed everything, all while hiding in plain sight. Rayner would never expect his mother to forgive or forget what Oharra did. He just needed her to understand why he didn't tell anyone that he knew. Rayner turned slightly to face his mother.

"I'm sorry I didn't warn you."

Elana stayed silent, rubbing small circles on her growing belly. Rayner felt a nervous wave run over him as he considered what to say. He wrung his hands together and began tapping his foot on the floor. Rayner drew in a deep breath.

"I didn't tell anyone because I...I was afraid I might back down on my own choice, and I couldn't have people looking at me like that again. Like I'm broken."

The weight of the confession made it a little easier to breathe. Elana turned to look at her son, and he leaned his elbows on his knees, bouncing his foot nervously. "I still have nightmares," he went on, staring at his boots. "About that day... The horse stomping over me, the fire, feeling myself dying...but I'm king now, and I can't afford to show my weaknesses. By keeping the identity of the horned knight to myself, I could still change my mind about facing her again, and I would have never asked for a hostage." Rayner felt lost as he spoke. He hung his head so that his hair curtained his eyes.

Elana reached out and grabbed both his hands, and he peeled his eyes away from the ground to look at his mother. "You are not only king. You are my son, you're a husband, a brother, a friend, and a knight. You are allowed to have fears, and you shouldn't feel ashamed." Rayner turned away, but Elana quickly grabbed his chin, lifting it back up to meet her eyes. "Do you think no kings before you have ever been afraid of something?" Her eyes were searching, but he didn't answer. "Do you think your men out there have never been afraid? Do you think you would lose their respect because you showed them that you're human?" Elana leaned in closer and softened her voice. "We all have something that scares us, and you shouldn't be ashamed of your decision."

Rayner furrowed his brows but still didn't respond. "She may have broken your body." Elana moved her hand from his chin to cup his cheek, "But she could never break *you*." She pointed her finger at his chest, and Rayner felt a few tears roll away from his closed eyes. "You remind me so much of your father, but there are things I see in you that are all your own. Look at me."

Rayner pried his tear filled eyes open, and Elana took his hands into her own. "You are Rayner the Unbroken, and you will remain that always. So do not apologize for keeping your fears to yourself, but never be ashamed of them. Let your fear lead you, not use you."

Elana grabbed his face in her hands, wiping his cheeks. "You have had a hard time as king, I know. It came too early, and no one was prepared, but you handled it better than any of us. You carried the weight of everyone's pain, suffering, anger, and guilt and took it upon yourself, never giving yourself a chance to heal from your own demons. I could not be more proud of the man you've become, but I see in your eyes that you're tired, Rayner. You have so many people around who love you, people who are here because they want to help, so let us help. Don't carry your fears and worries about with you. Talk to us. You don't need to carry all the weight on your shoulders. We can take some of it for you."

Rayner let his tears silently roll down his cheeks, finally releasing his fears that he kept bottled up for months. Elana pulled him in, and he rested his head on his mother's shoulder as she gently stroked his hair. Perhaps she was right, and Rayner had been trying to carry too much weight alone, not knowing it was breaking him from the inside out. Rayner never did get a chance to deal with his fear of what happened that day with the horned knight, but he would fix that. The scars from that day would remain, but Rayner wasn't going to allow any more.

He composed himself after a few moments, and already he felt better. Elana smiled at him, pushing his hair back from his brow. "If it's any consolation," Elana said with a grin, "she scares me too."

Rayner furrowed his brows. "But you said to let my fear lead me, not use me."

"Yes, that's right."

Rayner narrowed his eyes and smiled slightly. "But you let it use you. You slapped her, Mother..."

Elana twisted her lips but couldn't hide her smile. "I let my fear *lead* me to slap her. If I let it use me, I would have killed her."

Rayner blinked at her and didn't think she was completely joking, but they both chuckled. Rayner let out a sigh and got to his feet. He knew he couldn't waste any more time running from the monster that waited for him in the tent. He picked up Elana's hand and pressed his lips to it. "Thank you, Mother." She winked at him before he turned and left the tent.

Rayner headed back through the camp, turning his head up to

the sky as he felt something wet on his cheek. Grey clouds loomed overhead, and snow began to drift down from them. He paused and closed his eyes, feeling the cool flakes melt against his skin. Someone ahead of him scoffed, and he looked down to see Aska, bundled in a heavy cloak, walking toward him with Arytin at her side.

"Does it ever stop snowing?" she asked, pulling her hood tighter.

Rayner grinned. "Not until spring, I'm afraid."

"Well, hopefully, we'll be gone by then," she responded and then realized how it sounded. "Oh, that's not what I meant, I mean—"

"It's all right." Rayner held up a hand. "I know what you meant."

"Where's Ivy?" Arytin looked around.

Rayner studied him a moment before shrugging. Arytin seemed disappointed and told Aska he would find her later before walking off. Rayner turned back to Aska then spotted Macon walking toward them. Aska saw the look on his face and twirled around before breaking off into a run. She leapt into Macon's arms, and he spun her around before gently setting her back on her feet. Macon's smile faded as Rayner came up to them.

"What took you so long?" he demanded.

Aska whirled on the king. "Spying is an art, it takes time," she defended, but Rayner only looked at Macon.

He smiled at Aska and ran a hand through his messy brown hair. "You have good instincts," Macon started, grinning at the king. "It's like you suspected. King Caato's men have left. The only ships in the harbor of those of raiders."

Rayner felt his heart start to race, his mind working on new plans. "You're sure?"

"Positive, I even heard some guards discussing it. After they found the king dead, his men fled back to Lamira. But Helvarr still has a sizeable force with his raiders." Rayner nodded, biting his lip and considering. Macon wrapped an arm around Aska and gestured to a nearby tent that smelled of fresh bread.

"Macon," Rayner grabbed his shoulder. "Thank you." They stared at each other for a moment before Macon bowed his head and moved along.

Rayner stopped outside the tent that held Oharra, steeling himself and taking a few deep breaths. The knights held open the flap for him before closing him off, alone with her. Lady Oharra sat in a pile of furs on the floor, her hands now bound in from of her so she could drink and eat. Her black hair hung like a sheet around her face, and her eyes seemed colder than ever. Rayner willed his pulse to slow as he took a few steps forward and sat in a chair before her.

"King Rayner," she addressed him with a mocking tone. "Where is my daughter? She hasn't been to see me."

"You're dealing with me now."

"Oh, I believe I've *dealt* with you before. As I recall I didn't turn out so well for you."

Rayner kept his face stern; he refused to give her what she wanted. "I'm not the one tied up right now. So, I would watch how you talk to me."

"Oh, dear Rayner. We both know you can't touch me. Not when my Helvarr has your friend."

The image of Finn being taken into Helvarr's custody materialzed before his eyes. He pushed the thought away. Finn had to be all right. Rayner leaned over his knees, clasping his hands together. "That day on the Thunder Trail, when we were attacked by raiders and were forced to retreat. When I got hit from behind and had to be carried back to Godstone, that was you. Wasn't it?"

Oharra flashed him a smile and leaned back into her fur nest. "You have pieced it together, haven't you? Too bad it took so long." Rayner felt his cheeks begin to flush with rage but tried to keep it from reaching his eyes. "Too bad you're missing pieces too." She was baiting him, but Rayner took it anyway.

"Such as?"

Oharra leaned forward. "How much did Correlyn tell you about what happened these past months?"

"It doesn't matter, I know all I need to about you." All he felt was utter disgust as he looked at her.

"Ah, but do you know all you need to about your wife?"

Rayner sat back. He wouldn't let her rattle him. She was just trying to get a reaction out of him. Oharra waited patiently, but Rayner wouldn't answer, so she persisted. "Do you know she tried to kill me twice?" Rayner blinked, and Oharra grinned triumphantly. So what if that was true? He knew Correlyn was a skilled warrior and would do anything to protect herself or her people.

Rayner shrugged and sat back. "I would have tried to kill you three times."

Oharra tilted her head back and laughed, but Rayner knew it wasn't genuine. "She nearly got me the second time too. The clever girl used a chicken bone from supper, stuck me right here." She pointed to a small scar above her collarbone. Rayner smiled and raised a brow, waiting for Oharra to explain why he should care.

"When was that?" Oharra said to herself, tapping a finger to her chin. "Ah, yes! I remember. That was right after I had that Magister dragged into the hall and slit his throat like a pig in front of her."

Rayner felt his chest cave in and rage rushed through his veins. Oharra smiled at the reaction. "There's the face," she snickered. "The Magister and Correlyn had become close. He would tend to her wounds after she was beaten and bruised. And yet, she still never gave you up. All those scars are because of you."

Rayner looked away for a moment. His mother was wrong, he wasn't ready to face her.

"Breaking her physically wasn't working, so I had to break her mentally, starting with the only friend she had left." Oharra watched as Rayner struggled to keep his shaking hands in his lap.

"It took some doing, but I learned something about my daughter. I learned that, when pushed, she is capable of as much hate as I am."

"Correlyn is nothing like you," Rayner said through his teeth.

"Ah, but she is. There is a monster that lies within her, same as me, and sooner or later it will show itself, I just had to give her a push."

"Correlyn would never kill innocent people," Rayner retorted, trying to maintain his anger.

Oharra picked at some dirt under her nails, "Oh no?" She scooched closer, locking eyes with Rayner. "Do you remember what happened in Temple City?"

He remembered all too well, Correlyn had saved him from being killed while Oharra likely delayed her progress on getting the door open so they could escape. "The girl," Oharra said softly, and Rayner suddenly remembered. "She killed a young girl who ran from us. Was she not innocent?"

Rayner shook his head, "She would have gotten us killed." It wasn't a justifiable answer, but it was the one Correlyn had given to him. He never asked exactly what she did to that young girl, but he didn't want to know.

"Is that what she told you?" Oharra asked as innocent as ever.

"Enough." Rayner stood up. "You aren't going to paint my wife a monster just because the image is so familiar to you. She's not like you, and no matter what you think you did to her, Correlyn is good. She deserves a better mother than you." Oharra seemed disappointed and sat back in her furs. Rayner moved over to the table and poured a cup of water for himself, downing it in one gulp and snapping his eyes shut. He could feel Oharra staring at him from behind, but he needed a moment to compose himself if he was going to face her.

"Tell me why Helvarr really wants Kaspin's Keep." Oharra

sighed as if she were bored, fussing with the furs and nestling herself in.

"He wants to be king," she said simply.

"There has to be another reason."

Oharra looked down at her hands and drew her brows together. Rayner watched her and swore she looked sad but didn't think her capable of such an emotion. When she looked back up, her face was cold again. "He wants to be king," she repeated. "But mostly, he wants a relationship with his daughter."

Rayner was taken aback. Helvarr, the man who had ruined their lives, now wanted another shot at his? "Why?" Rayner couldn't help the curiosity.

Oharra looked right at him, her eyes narrowing. "Helvarr has come to care for her. She's the whole reason he did this; well that and revenge for what your father did."

"My father was right to banish Helvarr."

"Was he?"

Rayner thought for a moment. Magnus never did anything without thinking it through, but was that a habit formed before or after Helvarr's banishment? If Magnus had never banished Helvarr, Rayner wouldn't be here right now. But who's to say how things would have turned out? Perhaps things would have been worse than they are, but maybe Magnus would still be alive. He rubbed his eyes, trying to get his thoughts straight.

"Helvarr made his choices," he answered. "It's not my fault he chose wrong."

"Yes, but your father made one for him. A very important choice. When he banished Helvarr, I was pregnant with Correlyn at the time. So, really, he was banishing Helvarr from me as well since I was allied to your father. From the North and his home, he banished Helvarr from meeting his daughter, watching her grow up and teaching her things. He took that from Helvarr. He didn't choose to lose everything; your father made that decision."

Rayner sat unblinking at her, surely if his father had known, he would've reconsidered. Rayner knew how close the two were when they were young, they were like brothers, Magnus wouldn't have taken away the chance at a family for Helvarr, especially since he thought he was alone. He wondered how different Helvarr might have turned out if Ronin had just confessed to being his father. He couldn't think about that. Oharra was distracting him, and he was allowing her to do it. He took a gamble. "You and I both know that my father was unaware of that when he banished Helvarr."

Oharra grinned. "Fine. Just because he didn't know, doesn't mean his choice didn't help shape Helvarr into what he became. Magnus is just as responsible for his own death as Helvarr."

Rayner leaned back, letting out a sigh. "So Helvarr wants to make up for lost time? That doesn't sound like him."

"Well, you don't know him very well." Oharra hung her head, worrying a string from her tunic.

Rayner narrowed his eyes. "You mean to tell me that he truly wants to build a relationship with Correlyn and get to know her?"

"Sounds simple, doesn't it?" Oharra still didn't meet his gaze. "I don't like simple."

"And what do you get out of this deal?" Oharra was acting strange at the mention of Helvarr and Correlyn. What had happened between the two?

Rayner waited for her to answer, shifting in his seat and crossing his arms over his chest. She finally looked up at him, but something had changed in her eyes. "This deal is not for me. He made it for himself alone. It's what he wants."

"And what do you want?"

She smiled, but it seemed…sad. "Helvarr wants to rebuild his relationship with Correlyn and have control of a castle… to live out his days behind walls."

"But not you?" He couldn't keep the curiosity out of his voice.

"I have done all I can to try to get Correlyn to see my way, and I've done all I can with him. He's changed, I can see it in his eyes. He may put on a mask for you"—she waved her bound hands toward him—"but he is tired of fighting. All he wants is to live in peace."

Rayner found that hard to believe. Helvarr had fought tooth and nail to get what he had, and now he was going to give it all up? For a daughter he doesn't even know and who he helped to have captured?

"So, what will you do?" Rayner asked.

"You think I'm going to tell you my plans?" She cocked her head and smiled.

"But you don't plan to go with him if I give Helvarr Kaspin's Keep?"

Oharra shook her head.

"Does he know that?"

"Why would I tell him if you have not made your decision yet? He will find out soon enough."

Rayner couldn't pick out what he was feeling. Helvarr had made a choice, one that would benefit him, and Oharra was planning to leave him because of it. What should he care? Both of them had ruined his life, and yet, a part of him felt bad for Helvarr. He shuddered at the thought. What would Rayner have done in his position to get back to his family? What *had* he done already? Perhaps Oharra was right, and Correlyn did have a monster within her, waiting to be let out when pushed. But Rayner had one as well, and he was going to unleash it when the time came. Rayner stood up, and Oharra watched him. "Where are you going?"

"To find Correlyn," he answered, turning his back. "I've made my decision."

9

THE SCAR

Finn watched as a few raiders led Cassius back to the stables. If felt odd, being back in Godstone but not getting to roam around free, with Ivy at his side. He told himself it would be soon enough, but even that felt too long.

Helvarr gestured for Finn to follow, a few raiders lingering behind just in case Finn tried anything. He glared back at them, but they only snickered in return, not threatened at all by him. Helvarr strolled casually through the streets with his head high. It made Finn angry to see him so comfortable in a place that wasn't his. They headed toward the central tower, and Finn caught a glimpse of Ivy's maple tree. His heart began to flutter as he craned his neck up, looking to the highest branches where he once sat with Ivy. The limbs were covered in snow and the ends bare save for a few stubborn leaves at the very top, unwilling to let go. Finn recalled the day he sat with Ivy, high in the arms of the tree. Finn was about to propose to her, but then she spotted riders, which turned out to be Queen Narra and Meisha. It all seemed like a lifetime ago, but he remembered every detail.

He followed Helvarr up the stairs of the central tower and down a hall. Finn knew where they were going before they even stopped in front of the room. It was the last one at the end of the hall–Rayner and Correlyn's old room. He felt a stab of pain and wondered what had become of the room he shared with Ivy. Did someone else now sleep in their bed? Or had Helvarr boarded it up, trying to seal off his past?

Helvarr stopped to unlock the door before stepping aside and allowing Finn to enter. He smiled at Finn as he slipped into the room and then followed him in. It was empty save for a mattress in the corner by the window. The room felt cold, and he wondered how much those stone walls had witnessed. He reached out to touch it and swore he felt the sadness etched into them. When he turned to face Helvarr, he found his gaze fixed on the window. What game was Helvarr playing?

"I allowed Correlyn to stay here," Helvarr said quietly as if to assure the room he meant no harm. Not this time. "But she continued to disobey us, and her mother…." He trailed off, his eyes sliding from the window to the floor as he hung his head. Finn took a step toward him, and Helvarr snapped his attention back to Finn.

"Why am I here? Why wouldn't you want more time with Correlyn if you care about her so much?" His tone was sharp as he recalled Correlyn's words: Don't play his games.

Helvarr cocked his head, observing Finn. The smallest grin lifted one side of his mouth. "I'll have one of my men bring some water," Helvarr said as if he didn't hear the question. He turned to leave.

"Wait," Finn called after him, but Helvarr was already out the door, locking it behind him.

"Fuck." Finn paced around the room, searching for anything that could be used for a weapon, just in case. Finn doubted Helvarr would try anything, not when Rayner had Lady Oharra, but still, he couldn't be trusted to play by the rules. When Finn found nothing useful, he huffed a sigh and went to stand by the window. The night was clear, with an almost full moon. He stared out in the direction of the beach, hoping to make out the ships that sat in the harbor, but he was too far. Finn noted that he hadn't seen any of King Caato's men wandering around Godstone, but that didn't mean that they weren't there.

Something caught his eye, and as Finn searched the sky, a handful of stars burned out. He couldn't help but smile. Rayner must have sent Macon back to find out if King Caato's men really were in Godstone, or if it had been a lie. He said a silent prayer to the gods for Macon, and then the door opened.

Finn turned to see a large man standing in the threshold, holding a tray with a cup of water and slice of bread. The man had long blond hair that was pulled back, and a blank stare. He moved closer, and Finn couldn't help but tense up, ready to fight.

"You know," he drawled, "that girl sure could take a beating."

Finn's cheeks began to burn with rage. Correlyn had become his family, and it pained everyone when she was captured.

"She broke eventually, when her mother caught her after she escaped."

That caught Finn off guard. "Correlyn escaped?" Why hadn't she mentioned anything to them?

"You didn't know?" The man seemed genuinely curious, but his smile said otherwise. "This was her third attempt. She made it pretty far too, all the way to Ashton before her mother hunted her down and brought her back."

Finn wondered how Correlyn had planned to get to them on Kame Island. Surely, she had some sort of plan, though if she had been successful, she would have found out that her family was no longer there. Had the gods intercepted her escape because they knew Rayner was about to risk everything to get her back? He snapped out of his thoughts as the man crept closer.

"The knight that was assigned to watch over her allowed her to escape. He helped her, and Lady Oharra tortured him for it." Finn didn't look away, but glared at the man, balling his fists. He couldn't imagine the guilt that Correlyn must feel. She'd been through much more than she let on, more than any of them realized. Without saying another word, the man set down the tray and left. Finn drank the water and sat down on the mattress, leaning his head back against the stone wall until he eventually fell asleep.

The next morning, the man from last night came to escort Finn to the Great Hall, where Helvarr was waiting. The first thing he spotted upon entering, was Magnus's throne. He assumed that Helvarr would have destroyed it, but there it sat, dark and sinister at the back of the Hall. No lanterns hung from its branches, and Luna's nest had been taken down. Finn was surprised to see that Helvarr wasn't sitting in it. He had kept it for a reason, so why wouldn't he use it?

Instead, Helvarr sat at the end of the table on the dais. No one else was in the Hall, and when Finn stopped to look around, the man shoved him and ordered him to sit next to Helvarr. Finn ground his teeth together as he sat down, taking in the spread of food before him. He looked back to see the man lingering in the shadows, like a wolf ready to pounce.

"Are you hungry?" Helvarr's voice drew his attention back. Helvarr poured a cup of dark ale then held the flagon out to Finn. When he didn't take it, Helvarr poured another cup and placed it in front of Finn's empty plate. Finn's stomach growled, betraying his stern face, but he still refused to take anything. Helvarr sat back, eyeing him curiously as he sipped his ale.

"Why am I here?' Finn asked again. Helvarr smiled over the brim of his cup before setting it down and leaning his elbows on the table. His eyes traveled over Finn's face and settled on his scar.

"I remember you." Helvarr still avoided the question. Finn's heart thumped a little faster in his chest as he recalled the day Helvarr killed Ser Osmund. He didn't think Helvarr had even noticed him that day, too focused on Ronin who showed up too late.

"I remember you too. You killed Ivy's knight." Finn leaned forward. "And don't think she's forgotten." Helvarr seemed utterly delighted.

"Ah, Ivy. She is a fierce fighter." Finn balled his fists under the table to keep from clawing at it. "Ser Osmund never liked me, you know." His tone was casual.

Finn snorted, "I wonder why."

Helvarr flashed his teeth in warning but sat back and began to fuss with a chip in the armrest of his chair. "Ever since I was a young boy," he went on. "Ser Osmund always had one eye on Magnus and one on me, but for different reasons. I guess he was the first to realize what I would become, but he was too late to stop me."

Finn didn't know why Helvarr was telling him this. Was he fishing for sympathy?

"In a way, it is people like him who made me the way I am."

Finn snorted again and grabbed the cup of ale. At least he could numb his senses if he had to sit through this.

"If you've already made up your mind about someone, it's hard to see them in a different light," Helvarr said then lowered his head. Was he talking about himself or someone else?

"Is there a point to this story," Finn asked.

"I've been painted as a monster, so that's all you see when you look at me."

Finn narrowed his eyes, searching his face. "Looks pretty accurate to me."

Helvarr's mouth twitched like he was about to yell, but he took a deep breath instead. "You don't know me," Helvarr went on. "Not really. You know what you've been told to focus on, what other people see. Relying on others' ideas of someone is dangerous—it's why none of them saw what Lady Oharra really was. They saw a loyal ally of Magnus because that's what they'd been told to see when really, if you looked hard enough, you could pick out the cracks in her mask."

Finn sat back in his chair and ran a hand through his hair, focusing his gaze on the table in front of him. Was he right? Did no one suspect Lady Oharra because they had all been told she could be trusted because that's what Magnus believed? He shook his head, Helvarr was just trying to eat up time. *Don't play his games,* Correlyn's voice came to him. He looked back at Helvarr. "I didn't need someone to make up my mind for me. I see you as you are. Now, tell me, why am I here?"

Helvarr sighed. "You don't know me," he repeated, looking Finn up and down and flashing that familiar wicked grin. "But I know you."

Finn felt a shiver of fear run down his back, but he didn't know why. "Yes, we've established that—"

"No," Helvarr interrupted, leaning forward. "I remember you...*Finnick.*"

Finn's skull felt like it was caving in on itself. His mouth hung open as chills danced along his spine, making him shiver. A wave of panic shot through him as he looked at Helvarr, *really* looked at him. The black hair, the strong shoulders but lean build, the way his eyes lit up with the promise of violence. Finn thought he was going to be sick. He hunched over, trying to catch the breath that suddenly escaped him.

Finnick.

No one had ever called him that other than....

"What's the matter, Finnick?" He could hear the smile in Helvarr's voice. Finn fell from his chair to his knees. His heart was beating so fast he was going to pass out. This wasn't real. It couldn't be. "That's some scar you've got." He gestured toward Finn. "I believe I gave it to you some years ago."

Tears blinded Finn as the image of his family came to the front of his mind. His father had tried to save Finn, his mother screamed at him to run, and Thorman had lain asleep in bed, unaware of the death looming in the room. His heart shattered all over again, and the pain he'd buried for so long dug its way back to the surface. Helvarr got up from his seat and crouched down in front of Finn, taking him by the chin until they were eye to eye. "Like I said, you don't know me, but I know you. And I have many masks you are unaware of. Don't make me use them."

Finn couldn't form any words.

"I assume that was your family. Too bad about the boy, I guess it's a good thing he was asleep—"

Finn launched himself at Helvarr, knocking him off his feet. They crashed to the floor, and Helvarr grunted in pain, but that smile remained on his face. Finn reared back and sent his fist into Helvarr's nose before he could catch him. His head snapped back, smacking the stone floor beneath him. Helvarr kneed him in the ribs, but Finn hardly felt it. The adrenaline rush was like no other, and blind rage guided his hands. Finn grabbed hold of his throat and squeezed with everything he had, completely losing himself in his anger. Helvarr's eyes began to water and Finn squeezed harder, snarling as tears poured down his cheeks. He heard something behind him, but realized it too late. The blow to the back of his head knocked Finn away from Helvarr, and he crumpled to the ground as his world went black.

The room spun around him as Finn cracked his eyes open. It was dark, no light coming in from the window. Finn sat up and immediately plopped back down on the mattress. His head screamed, and a dull ringing sounded in his ears. He brought a hand up and felt a lump on the back of his head where he'd been hit. Taking a few steady breaths, Finn pushed up and rested his back against the stone wall. He took a moment to allow the room to stop spinning before he stood up, bracing the wall for balance as he made his way to the window. The moon was almost full but not quite. Finn hadn't missed the exchange which meant he had only been out since that morning.

He sat back down on the mattress, finally feeling where Helvarr had kneed him. He pulled up his shirt to reveal a small bruise around his lower ribs. Finn couldn't believe what he had heard, the real reason he was here in Correlyn's place. Helvarr had been the man that night who killed his entire family. Finn was only nine years old at the time, and he was so consumed with fear that he never paid attention to the hooded man who had cut him. Now he knew why Helvarr kept looking at him like that: he'd recognized the scar. Finn's hands started shaking at the thought. He wrapped his arms around his legs, burying his face in his knees, and silently cried to himself. Finn promised himself he wouldn't let his family's deaths haunt him anymore, but how could he not? Now that he knew who it was that had taken everything from him. The man who had taken everything from Ivy and her family. Was this some cruel game the gods were playing? Was this the reason Finn and Ivy were brought together?

He snapped his head up when he heard keys jingling in the lock. Finn wiped his tears away and stood up as Helvarr stepped into the room. His eyes immediately went to Helvarr's nose. It was red with large purple bruises creeping out on their side just under his eyes. Finn allowed himself to smile—at least he got a punch in before he was knocked out. Helvarr dragged in a chair and set it in the middle of the room before closing the door behind him. He sat down with a sigh, running his fingers through his black hair and staring out the window. When he looked back at Finn, he cracked a grin, and Finn felt his anger bubbling back to the surface. He could kill him right now before any guards could stop him. Helvarr had taken his family away, and for what? His village had never taken part in the war; they were just more casualties in its path.

"How is your head?" Helvarr asked, which made Finn even more enraged.

"Why the hell do you care?" he said through his teeth.

Helvarr leaned forward. "Because there are rules in a parley, and I need to keep you safe until I get Oharra back."

He didn't care, not really. He only wanted to make sure Oharra got back to him safe and sound, and then he'd do whatever he wanted. Finn balled his fists and held his stare.

"Come now, Finnick—"

"Do not call me that!" Finn roared.

Helvarr held up his hands in submission. Finn's head began to throb again, and he fought not to sway on his feet. Helvarr took notice and stood up, offering the chair to Finn. When he didn't move, Helvarr crossed the room, and Finn tensed up, stepping back into the wall. "You can either sit down willingly, or I'll knock you down," Helvarr hissed. Finn swayed and bumped into the wall behind him. Helvarr stepped aside and waited until Finn reluctantly crossed the room and sat down in the chair.

He brought his hands up to rub at his temples, trying to soothe his aching head. Helvarr stared out the window, his back turned, and hands clasped behind his back. Finn wondered what he saw out there. His home or just another stop on his path of destruction. Finn couldn't believe that Helvarr only wanted Kaspin's Keep just so he could be king and have a safe place for his daughter to visit. Correlyn would never agree to his terms, and neither would Rayner, so what were they going to do? He started sweating at the thought. What if things went bad tomorrow night when they returned hostages, and Helvarr used Finn to get the deal he pitched? Finn couldn't allow that. If Correlyn had survived months alone with him, Finn could handle another night; he just had to start coming up with a plan in case the exchange went wrong.

Helvarr kept his back turned as he spoke. "What do you think King Rayner will say about the offer I proposed?"

That you're insane; that it will never happen; that he's going to kill you.

Finn couldn't say any of those things, so he kept his mouth shut. Helvarr sighed at his silence and turned around, taking a few steps toward Finn. His copper eyes were bloodshot, and he looked tired. Finn made a mental note.

"You still have another day with me. Are you going to remain silent the whole time?" Finn glared at him, clenching his hands to keep from punching him again.

"What was the name of your village?"

Finn's eye twitched at the mention of it. He knew Helvarr was just trying to get him to talk. *Don't play his games.*

"How about the name of your brother?"

"Shut up," Finn hissed. "You don't get to talk about him." He closed his eyes, trying to fight back his tears and keep his face stern, but he was failing. He sniffed them away and glared back up at Helvarr, but something in his face had shifted.

Another mask.

Helvarr twisted his mouth and looked down at his boots. "I'm sorry about your family," he said so quietly, Finn almost missed it. He scrunched his brows together, waiting for Helvarr to say something cruel, but he kept his eyes down.

"You're not sorry," Finn responded. "And I don't want to listen to your bullshit reasons about why you did it either." Finn stood up, and Helvarr met his gaze.

"They did not deserve to die. My people were innocent farmers and fishermen, and you slaughtered them like livestock." Tears began to roll down his cheeks. "So don't stand there and tell me you're sorry. You made your choice, and whatever comes next, you deserve worse." Helvarr stared at him. Finn was shaking with anger, his face stained with fresh tears.

"Like I said before, you don't know me. I have many sides—"

"I don't give a shit!" Finn yelled.

Helvarr took another step closer. "Your brother—"

Finn shoved his hands into Helvarr's chest, making him stumble back, but Finn persued him. "You killed him! He was a little boy, and you fucking *killed* him!" Finn shoved his hands into Helvarr's chest again. "He was sick! I just saved him and promised nothing would happen to him!" Finn gave him one final shove, and Helvarr's back slammed into the stone wall. He grabbed a handful of his shirt and balled his fist, ready to fight a monster. "I should kill you right—"

"They were going to sell him!" Helvarr roared, and Finn froze.

He blinked at Helvarr. "What did you say?"

He straightened up, prying Finn's fingers from him and rubbing his chest where he'd been struck. "They were going to sell him. He would have been a slave...or worse." Finn's head began to spin, and he stepped aside, bracing himself on the wall.

"What are you talking about?"

Helvarr stepped away, giving Finn some room. "That band of raiders was filled with outlaws. They all had deals on the side that King Caato didn't know about. Some of them were former traders. I wasn't in charge of them. We were led by a man named Hal, and he used to sell children as slaves or into pleasure houses in the larger cities." Finn slid down to the floor, clutching the back of his head.

Helvarr stayed standing and continued. "King Caato ordered us to go north and search for men to fight for him. We came to your village, but Hal had other plans. He ordered us to burn the village and only take the children and leave no one else behind. He must have known the men wouldn't come willingly to fight for a southern king, so he didn't even give them the option. I warned him against it, but we attacked the village anyway. I made my way around to as many homes as I could, trying to grab up the children. I didn't know what I'd do with them, but I had to try and get them out." He looked down at Finn, then turned and sat back in the chair.

"I was going to take you, but your father stepped in, and your mother was making too much noise." Finn snapped his eyes shut. He could still hear his mother's scream. "I didn't mean to cut you, I tried to grab you before your father could stop me. I didn't even notice the other boy until after and then I forgot about you. I could hear raiders making their way to the home, and see the fires outside the window. I knew it would be too late. Hal would've taken your brother and sold him to a southern city to either a pleasure house, or he would have been forced into King Caato's army once he was old enough. He was already asleep, and I thought... I thought death would be easier than a life of misery..."

Finn couldn't believe his ears. Helvarr had to be lying. He was cruel and twisted. Why would he show mercy to a child?

"I heard you run from the home, but when I turned around, you were already gone, and some men came in right after. I told them the child was already dead and covered his body to hide the blood. Hal got his hands on a few children, and I couldn't stop him, but when he got back to Lamira, King Caato wasn't pleased that Hal went against orders and had him killed. I never did find out where he sold those children to, but they're out there somewhere." Finn felt like he was going to throw up. All these years, he thought he had been the only survivor, but could it be true that some of his friends from childhood were out there? He looked up at Helvarr, trying to discern the look on his face.

Helvarr sat back and sighed as if a weight had been lifted off his chest. "I know you don't believe me, but I don't care. That's what happened, and I thought you'd like to know."

Finn leaned forward. "Why did you tell me at all? Why did you tell me it was you that killed my family?"

Helvarr lifted the corner of his mouth into a grin. "I recognized you at the exchange, I thought I was seeing a ghost, but it's you. I was curious to see what kind of man you've grown into. How did you get away that night?"

"A fishing boat, one of the men was fleeing. I climbed into his boat, and he brought me south."

Helvarr nodded. "I always wondered what happened to you."

"Why did you tell me?" Finn demanded.

Helvarr leaned over his knees. "Because I saved your life once. You see it differently, but if I hadn't been there, who knows where you would be right now? And I wanted to remind you that I have many different sides, ones that you won't like, so you shouldn't push me." His familiar wicked grin returned to his face.

"You think that because you saved my life once that I'll spare yours?" Finn asked.

"I expect nothing of the sort, and should we meet on the battlefield one day, I will not hesitate to kill you this time."

Finn snorted. "Good luck."

Helvarr chuckled. "I'll add you to the list of people who want me dead. But for now, you can't touch me, and I can't touch you." Finn looked at his bruised nose and cracked a grin.

"You're fast I'll give you that." Helvarr admitted, sounding genuinely impressed. "But you'd do well to remember who I am."

"You may think that you spared my brother from something worse." Finn stood up, resting a hand against the wall. "But he's dead, and that's your fault. No matter what you think his fate would have been, I will never forget what you did to him–to me. But you've done worse to others, and it's their revenge that will kill you, not mine."

Helvarr raised a brow and looked at him curiously. "So, you are sparing me." He put a hand over his heart. "How generous," he mocked.

Finn growled. "I'm sparing you from nothing; it's the wrath of my family that will come for you."

Helvarr grinned. "What do you think Ivy will do if I use you?" That forced Finn's heart to race and his stomach churned.

"They will kill Oharra if you touch me."

"Oh no, Ivy wouldn't allow anything of the sort, not when I have her fiancé in my grasp."

Finn narrowed his eyes. He must have noticed Ivy's ring.

"You are very important to her. I can see it in her eyes when she looks at you," Helvarr went on casually. "You think I took you just to torture you with your past? I never make a choice if it doesn't have multiple benefits, so remember that. I will use you if I need to." He stood up. "I just hope your king makes the right decision." Helvarr slammed the door shut behind him.

Finn sank back down to the floor, bringing his hands up to his face. His head was throbbing madly now, and he felt faint. There was too much rattling around in his head. If Helvarr had been telling the truth, then that meant some of his people might still be out there, and he had to find them. He said a silent prayer for Thorman. If it were true, then how could Finn say that death was crueler, when Thorman may have been sold off to a pleasure house? The thought made him sick, and he shook his head to banish it. All he knew was that his family was dead, that Helvarr had killed them, then tried to justify it. Finn couldn't change what happened to his family, but he could still help those who were taken that night if he survived tomorrow.

He knew Helvarr meant what he said and that he would use Ivy's feelings for Finn if he had to. Finn knew in his heart that Rayner would never give Kaspin's Keep to Helvarr; he just hoped Rayner had a plan. Finn wouldn't let himself be used to hurt his family. He had to think of a way to get a weapon, just in case, but the pain in his head was blinding him. He touched the scar on his chin, feeling the line of smooth skin, the mark from Helvarr. Finn had many scars, both visible and not, but the one from Helvarr had haunted him for years because of the memory attached to it.

If Finn wasn't going to survive the exchange, the least he could do was take down Helvarr with him. He thought of all the people who had personal reasons to want Helvarr dead and the promise Ivy made to Magnus. He didn't want to take that from her, but he would if he had to. If Finn could get a weapon, he would kill Helvarr if things went wrong, but if he couldn't get a weapon, he would have to somehow convince Ivy to leave him and run. Finn smiled to himself. Ivy was the most stubborn person he knew and convincing her of something she didn't want was like trying to convince a drowning man that he could breathe underwater.

Finn had to come up with a solution, but the more he thought about it, the more his head screamed at him to stop. He lay down on the mattress, curled into a ball while his head settled its constant throbbing. Finn drifted off to sleep, and the next morning when he woke, a tray had been set by his mattress with a cup of water and some fruit, cheese, and bread. His head felt better, and Finn ate as much as he could. When he looked out the window, he saw that it was snowing and the moon was still lingering in the sky despite the sun's arrival. Tonight they would exchange hostages again, and the blood moon would rise in the sky. He hoped Kyatta had a plan for tonight because Finn finally decided there was no way he'd be able to kill Helvarr before someone killed him. He put his faith in his family and prayed to the gods he would live to see tomorrow.

MISSING PIECES

The pressure of what tonight would bring was wearing down on Rayner. He knew there would be a blood moon, and they were set to exchange hostages, but he couldn't know what else might wait for them. He had an answer for Helvarr, but Helvarr was unpredictable, and Rayner had no way of knowing how he might react. He was eager to get Finn back—they had become like brothers, and Rayner felt as if a piece of his family was missing with his absence. Besides, Ivy had been worried sick the past two days, and it killed Rayner every second to see his sister in pain.

Rayner walked through the camp in search of Ivy. He left Correlyn back in their tent where she'd fallen asleep. She would need her rest to heal, so Rayner thought it would be a good time to talk to his sister. He found her sparring with Ronin while Zion stood off to the side, watching her with a grin on his face. Ivy moved around her trainer with flawless ease, though it seemed her swings were powered by anger and that Ronin was letting her hit him to work through it rather than suppress it. He stepped up to the circle they had dug in the snow and Ivy spotted him, but quickly turned back to her fight.

Ronin stopped fighting and looked to Rayner, putting his hands behind his back. Ivy huffed out an angry sigh.

"Can I talk to you?" Rayner stepped into the circle.

Ivy turned to face him. "I don't want to talk. I want to fight." Ronin nodded to Rayner, who stepped up to take the sword from his trainer. He turned to face Ivy and didn't even have a chance to open his mouth before she swung.

Rayner blocked the blow and stepped around her as Ivy lifted her sword again. "Ivy—"

She smacked her dull blade into Rayner's shoulder before slipping from his path.

"I'm sorry," he tried again, but Ivy was focused on the fight. She aimed for his chest, but he smacked her sword away, dodging her blows but not attacking. "I should have told you about Lady Oharra."

Ivy cringed at the name and swung her sword into Rayner's back hard. He paused and stared at her, but Ivy didn't stop. Rayner moved just as her sword crashed down into the snow. He gave her a light shove, but Ivy launched herself at him, forcing him further back. She swung again and struck Rayner in the shoulder. He winced and Ivy widened her stance, ready to swing again.

"I was afraid!" Rayner yelled, and Ivy halted. She kept her sword up but didn't move. Rayner sighed. "I *am* afraid." He lowered his eyes and dropped his sword in the snow. He saw Ronin and Zion shuffle off, giving them some privacy.

"I'm afraid of her," Rayner continued. "And I didn't tell you about her because if I backed down, I'd look weak."

"He has Finn," she said in a low growl.

"I know. I'm sorry. I never would have thought Helvarr would take Finn, but we're going to get him back tonight." Rayner stepped forward as Ivy lowered her sword and hung her shoulders.

"You should have told me." She released the words with a sigh.

"I know."

"I'm your sister, Rayner. You can talk to me about anything. I would never judge you for something like that because I know you wouldn't do that to me." Rayner could only stare at her as she stepped closer. "I'm sorry for taking my worries out on you, that wasn't fair. I know every decision you make is difficult, but you have people around to help you." She smiled soflty and wrapped her arms around his neck. Rayner pulled her to his chest, squeezing her gently. "I love you, Rayner. And you're right. We'll get him back."

"I love you, too."

They came apart, and Ivy looked to the snow as she asked, "What are you going to do tonight?"

Rayner sighed, he knew about the dream Ivy had. "Try to prevent your dream from happening," he answered. "But prepare for it anyway." Ivy only nodded; she knew there was no way they could fully prepare, not when she still had pieces missing.

Grimm walked through the camp, his mind overloaded with thoughts and worries about tonight. Kyatta had told Grimm everything about the blood moon and what it would do to her powers. He also knew about Ivy's dream and would do anything to prevent Kyatta from having to use her powers tonight. Rayner was taking precautions, and Grimm trusted him, but Kyatta was as stubborn as Ivy and would willingly throw herself to the wolves if she had to. He snapped out of his thoughts when a burst of fire shot up into the sky. He looked to his right to see Zion and his people practicing their fire skills. They stood beside a brazier, drawing the flames to themselves and shooting them up into the sky or creating walls around themselves. Grimm tilted his head up to watch the fire and spotted Luna, turning her head curiously as she watched.

Grimm continued on and eventually found Kyatta at the edge of the camp. She was a swirl of blue in a field of white, her winter hair neatly braided and cascading down her back. Her head was tilted toward the sky, and though the sun was still out, he knew they didn't have much time before they needed to leave. He strolled up alongside her and watched as she closed her eyes, drawing in a few deep breaths. Grimm gently wrapped his fingers around her hand, "Kyatta…" he said softly.

She opened her eyes. "I know what you're going to say, but I have to prepare for the worst." Grimm lowered his eyes and squeezed her hand.

"I know, I just do not want you to think you are alone in this. We fight together." Kyatta turned to look up at him.

"You know what Rayner's decision is. I have to consider the fact that Helvarr will react poorly, and I'll have to use my powers. That's why they chose tonight, when I'll be at my most powerful."

Grimm sighed and reached out and ran a finger along her hairline and behind her ear, gently caressing her cheek. "You speak as though you are a sacrifice or a weapon." He looked her in the eye and leaned in. "You are not, Kyatta."

She smiled at him, but it was weak. "Then what am I?"

Grimm dropped his hand. "You know that you are like family to them." Grimm gestured to the camp behind them.

"Rayner would never do anything without thinking about it."

Kyatta placed a hand on Grimm's chest, and his heart sped up on command. "He can't think of everything," she said quietly.

"He can try." Grimm offered a small grin, and Kyatta couldn't help but return it. He took her face in his hands and Kyatta closed her eyes, leaning in to his touch.

"Grimm," she whispered and opened her eyes. He was leaning in, his blue gaze fixed on her lips. Kyatta straightened a little before speaking. "If things go wrong, I need you to promise me that you'll stay away. I couldn't live with myself if I hurt you."

"You will not—"

"I'm serious, Grimm." Her voice was stern, no longer quiet and soft. "I won't be the girl I am now, and if you get in my way, I will kill you. So, I need you to stay away."

Grimm dropped his hands and sighed, closing his eyes. He didn't want to think about it and knew he would never just stand by while Kyatta fought alone. Grimm had grown to care too much about her to watch her die after just having come together.

Kyatta grabbed his face in her slender hands, forcing him to look back down at her. Her pale eyes were lined with worry, but they bore into him the longer he stared. "Promise me," Kyatta pleaded.

Grimm stayed silent for a few moments, looking back and forth between her eyes, but finally gave in. "I promise."

Kyatta slid her hands away from his face and rested them against his chest. Grimm smiled at her and leaned down, Kyatta rose on her toes to meet him. He kissed her deeply, snaking his fingers around her slender waist. Kyatta threw her arms around his neck, parting her lips for him and his tongue brushed against her teeth. Grimm fought the urge to scoop her up, bring her to a tent and keep her there until the exchange was over, but he knew Kyatta would find a way out. His cheeks flushed as she kissed him, and Grimm felt another urge that he didn't wish to fight.

Someone behind them cleared their throat, and Grimm reluctantly pulled his lips away to see Ivy standing there with Aska and Arytin. Ivy had a smug grin as she stood there, arms crossed, staring at him. Grimm took Kyatta's hand in his and returned Ivy's smile, but he knew his cheeks were red with desire.

"I think the two of you are adorable," Aska chirped, and Arytin rolled his eyes. Kyatta looked at Grimm and couldn't help but giggle.

"Can I talk to you?" Ivy looked at Kyatta. She nodded and lifted on her toes, pressing a soft kiss to Grimm's cheek and leaving him to be mocked by Aska.

K yatta and Ivy walked out of camp toward the base of the mountain range. Ivy kept her hands buried in the pockets of her jacket, and every few seconds she'd bite her lower lip then catch herself and stop. "You're worried about tonight," Kyatta stated.

Ivy nodded, keeping her eyes on the snow in front of them. She told Kyatta that she recalled seeing her in her dream at the last second, but there was someone else in the middle of the army fighting the raiders. "I don't know what's going to happen tonight," Kyatta said. "I'm just going based on what you told me."

Ivy stopped walking. "I never get the full picture, so how is this even a useful power?"

Kyatta stopped alongside her, searching her face and noting the bags that hung under her purple eyes. Ivy looked drained, but she would need to be fully awake tonight during the exchange. "Ivy, you have the ability to see your future. Perhaps the gods aren't giving you all the pieces because it's still up to you to change it."

Ivy sighed annoyingly. "But I don't know what I'm changing if I can't see the ending!" She began to pace nervously, wringing her hands, but Kyatta reached out and grabbed her shoulder, grounding her. Kyatta now saw the fear that danced around in her eyes, it was bright, skittering around like a cornered animal.

"I know it's frustrating," Kyatta said, her voice calm and soothing. "Sometimes your powers feel more like a burden rather than a gift, but I wouldn't have transcended you if I thought you couldn't handle it."

Ivy released a sigh and said, "I just need to make sure we have Finn back before you unleash your powers."

"We will get him back," Kyatta assured her, though some voice in the back of her mind told her nothing was certain. They stood in silence for a moment before Kyatta lifted her head toward the darkening sky, taking in a shaky breath. "It's time to go."

Rayner ordered some knights to gather Lady Oharra, putting her on a horse and surrounding her as they made their way south. Oharra didn't protest or utter a word as Rayner's knights lifted her onto a horse and encircled her. Rayner rode ahead of his men, alongside his queen. To his right, Zion, Ronin and their people walked alongside the mounted knights. He knew Zion and his people were carrying flints in order to make their own fire. Rayner had witnessed Zion's power during the battle on the Siren Sea. He would be a valuable asset should the meeting go wrong. To the right of the king, Aska and her family rode close by, along with Kyatta's people. Rayner thought he might have an advantage, having so many people with different powers, but it didn't give him any comfort.

Luna circled above their convoy, her orange feathers burning in the dying sun. Rayner had tried to leave her behind with Elana. He was afraid that Luna might lose her temper and burn everyone before they had Finn back, but Luna seemed reluctant to leave her king's side, and so Rayner gave in.

He looked over to Ivy to see her eyes focused on Godstone as they drew closer. There was a tent in the distance, set in the middle of the western field outside the kingdom. Rayner turned around, finding Grimm's eyes and gave him a tight nod. Grimm motioned to Kyatta and Piotr, who then gave the signal to Ronin and Lord Cylas. They all broke off from the group and moved over to the Blackwoods along with a handful of knights. Rayner needed to have people hidden who could come and back up their small army if needed. Rayner didn't dare take all of his men to the meeting, fearing that Helvarr would try something in their absence.

Ivy turned to watch the group break off, catching Piotr's eye and offering him a small smile. Piotr didn't smile back but held her gaze until they were behind the dark trees of the Blackwood. They were getting closer, and Ivy's heart was pounding wildly. She could see some figures under the tent ahead and a handful of raiders standing behind them. Ivy let her eyes drift over to Godstone; the gates were closed, and Helvarr's army was still inside. The sun was starting to set and the sky grew darker by the minute. She racked her brain for any detail she might have missed in her dream. Who was the person with Kyatta? And why had Rayner stopped Ivy from running back to fight? They had worked so hard to get where they were now, and Ivy wouldn't give up.

She felt eyes on her back and turned to see Lady Oharra, staring at her with a blank expression. A ripple of anger hummed through her body. She hadn't spoken with Lady Oharra the whole time she'd been captive in their camp. Ivy didn't trust herself not to kill her if they were left alone, so she decided to stay away. Injuring Lady Oharra when Helvarr still had Finn was not a risk she was willing to take. Her heart fluttered rapidly as they came closer, knowing she would see Finn again and hoping that this would all be over soon.

Ivy looked ahead to Correlyn, riding alongside Rayner. She didn't even acknowledge her mother's presence, and Ivy thought that Correlyn might kill her too if she had the chance to be alone with her. She noticed the bow strapped across Correlyn's back and the sword hanging at her side. Correlyn was ready to fight if needed, even with a broken rib and wounded heart. Ivy wondered how long it would take for it to be over. The pain, anger, fighting, and loss. Ivy wished she could step through time and into the future. But what would it look like? Who would be left after everything was over? Would Ivy ever be there? She shook the thought away, running a hand over her tired eyes and trying to focus on the figures coming into view under the tent. Ivy was here now, and she still had a say in her future, no matter what fate the gods had in mind.

BLOOD MOON

The sun had just about set as Rayner and his party trotted up to the tent. He slid from his horse and helped Correlyn down from hers before approaching. Ivy put a hand on the hilt of Promise, eyeing Helvarr as she followed her brother into the open tent. Helvarr had a few more raiders with him this time, but Rayner had more men still. Ivy turned to see three knights escorting Lady Oharra toward the tent, a smug grin painted on her cold face. Ivy felt a shiver and turned her head toward the sky. The blood moon wasn't out yet, and she began to panic. What if something went wrong, and Kyatta couldn't use her full powers? She couldn't think of that right now—all that mattered was getting Finn back safely.

A few of Helvarr's raiders held torches and created a half circle behind him, filling the tent with dim light. Helvarr sat in his chair, leaned back, and tapped his fingers anxiously on the armrest. Ivy spotted Finn, and her heart began to race as she scanned his face. Something was wrong. Finn wouldn't look up. He kept his eyes trained on the ground and seemed to be lost in thought.

Rayner and Correlyn took their seats opposite of Helvarr as Lady Oharra was pushed to stand beside the king. "Ivy," Rayner said quietly and gestured to her seat. She looked at her brother and then back to Finn. He didn't have any marks that Ivy could see, and when she looked at Helvarr, she noticed the bruises around his nose and under his eyes. Rage coursed through her veins, and she took a step toward him. "Finn…"

He lifted his eyes, resting them on Ivy. He looked broken and hurt, and it made Ivy angry. Finn lowered his head again, and Rayner noticed too. "What did you do to him?" Ivy snapped and stepped in front of Helvarr.

He smiled and waved her off like she was a child. Ivy growled at him, and Helvarr stood up suddenly, forcing her to step back. Rayner shot up from his seat, grabbing Ivy by the arm and pulling her back. "I suggest you take your seat," Helvarr hissed. "The sooner this is over, the better."

"Ivy," Rayner warned, but she kept her hateful gaze on Helvarr.

She shook Rayner off and lifted her head. "I told you if anything happened to him, I'd kill you."

"And I believe you," Helvarr said with a smile. "He is perfectly healthy; I assure you."

Finn lifted his eyes to Ivy and seemed to be pleading with her to sit. She felt a wave of sorrow crash into her. Finn looked dim and defeated. She hung her head and turned to take her seat.

Helvarr sat back down and looked over to Lady Oharra, giving her a warm smile, which she didn't return. He furrowed his brows and turned back to Rayner. "So then, King Rayner. Have you come to a decision?"

Rayner's palms began to sweat—he'd told his people what he decided and some weren't happy, but he didn't see another choice. Correlyn reached across to grab his hand, rubbing her thumb along his for reassurance. He drew in a deep breath and lifted his head to Helvarr. "First, give me Finn, and then I'll tell you."

"That's not how this works. You tell me your decision, and then I give you back your friend."

"I'm telling you this is how we're doing it, so we can sit here and argue, or we can trade and move on." Rayner's voice held all the authority of a king.

Helvarr twisted his mouth, tapping his fingers on the chair. "Very well." He motioned for a raider to bring Finn forward, and Rayner did the same with his knights. He tried to catch Finn's eye, but he wouldn't look at any of them. Lady Oharra's ropes were cut by a raider, and she took her place beside Helvarr. Finn stayed behind their chairs, and Ivy kept turning around to look at him.

Rayner couldn't worry about Finn. He seemed uninjured, and that was good enough for now. He turned back to Helvarr.

"Happy?" Helvarr snickered.

Rayner narrowed his eyes. "Not quite. Now I want you out of my home."

Helvarr chuckled softly. "So, you have made up your mind then?"

"I made up my mind the moment you pitched that ridiculous request." Helvarr lost his smile to be replaced by a grimace. Rayner leaned forward. "You'll never be king of anything, and I'd rather die than allow you to keep my wife and queen for any amount of time." Helvarr growled, but Rayner went on before he could interrupt. "Kaspin's Keep will never be yours, and I will appoint a high lord to run it. There will be no other kings. I am the only king in the North now, and you've just been keeping my seat warm for me."

Helvarr balled his fists, "You think I'll just give you your home back?"

"Oh, I don't expect you to leave without a fight, but now I know we have a fair chance of winning." Helvarr stared at him, his anger palpable. "My friend informed me that King Caato's men did, in fact, leave after that same friend killed him in his own bedchambers."

Helvarr was fuming, his cheeks turning red with anger.

"So, you can either lay down your weapons and get the hell out of my kingdom, or we will take it back, kill all your men, and save you for last." He looked to Lady Oharra; her face was blank, and she sat utterly still. Helvarr stood suddenly, but Rayner remained seated. "There is a third option," Rayner went on, and Correlyn and Ivy snapped their heads to look at him. He hadn't told them about it because he knew they would talk him out of it. Perhaps Rayner didn't want to be seen as weak, but who is to say what weakness is? Magnus never thought that showing mercy was a weakness, and he showed it the day he banished Helvarr from Godstone.

R ayner stood up slowly, placing his hands behind his back. "You can save yourself and your men." He gestured to the raiders behind him. "I will allow your banishment from my father to continue, but you must leave the North for good, give up Godstone, and never come back." Ivy shot to her feet, her eyes wide in disbelief.

"You can't be serious?" She whirled on Rayner, but he kept his eyes on Helvarr and addressed him only.

"My father believed in sparing a life when he could. He banished you that day, not knowing of your relationship and that he was denying you of a future with a family, but not telling him was your negligence. Magnus would have reconsidered if he knew. So, I will give you that chance again, to spare both of us from losing people in an unnecessary battle. Magnus could have killed you for your treason, but he showed mercy and let you go. You can die here for the place you fought to claim, or you can live out your days in exile with what family you have left."

Helvarr looked somewhat shocked but also angry. Oharra's face was unreadable. She kept her eyes downcast and seemed disappointed rather than angry. Helvarr balled his fists. "You expect me to give up and run? After all that I've done to get here?" He no longer looked shocked, only angry.

Rayner put some more depth behind his voice. "After all you've done, I *expect* you to be grateful that I'm giving you the option to keep your life. Don't be foolish. Take the deal and leave." Rayner glanced over to Correlyn. Her eyes were on Helvarr, and she looked to be pleading with him to consider it.

Correlyn had told Rayner all that Helvarr did while she was being held in Godstone, the good and the bad. Though Correlyn didn't try to justify his actions, she said that if it weren't for him, she would likely have been dead long ago. That was something that Rayner could try to repay by giving Helvarr his life. He hated Helvarr and wanted him dead like so many others, but he gave Helvarr this option for Correlyn. She had remained strong, and though Helvarr had done evil things, he also kept his wife alive.

Correlyn stepped forward. "Take it," she said softly to Helvarr.

He looked at her with a confused expression on his face. "I fought to get back to you, Correlyn." Rayner didn't know how to discern the sorrow in his voice, it was like he was another person when he spoke to Correlyn.

"If you don't go, you will die here," she urged.

"You would kill me?" There was genuine curiosity in his voice, and Rayner knew he was counting the seconds it took for Correlyn to answer.

She hesitated, looking to Oharra then back to Helvarr. "You helped me, I know that. I know you tried to do the right thing, but she held you back." Correlyn shot a hateful glare at Oharra. She hung her head, wringing her hands. "I don't know if I would kill you should we meet on the battlefield." She looked back up to him. "But I know there are others here who wouldn't hesitate. This is your last chance to live." She drew in a shaky breath, clenching her fingers until her knuckles turned white. "Father..." she pleaded. "Take the deal."

. . .

Helvarr's mouth hung open in surprise, but his face was twisted in an unreadable mixture of emotion. Beside him, Oharra let out a sharp laugh. "After everything he's done, you're just going to let him go?" Oharra took a step forward. "You are weak," she hissed, locking her gray eyes on Correlyn. "You've always been weak, Correlyn dear, and one day it will get you killed."

"What is your decision?" Rayner spoke up, drawing Helvarr's attention away from Correlyn.

Helvarr stayed silent. Rayner wasn't sure what to hope for. None of the options led Helvarr to a life with his daughter, the one thing he had been working toward for all these years. He probably never expected to be banished again, to live out his life in exile with Oharra. Rayner glanced over at her; Oharra's attention was pinned on Correlyn. Helvarr turned his gaze west. The sun had set, and the world was growing darker.

Oharra stood and stepped toward Correlyn, and Rayner tensed up. Ivy put her hand to Promise. She looked back quickly to see Finn watching the discussion, his eyes trained on Helvarr. "You think this deal makes you a good person?" Oharra questioned. "Because you are sparing a life?" She looked around the tent to meet Rayner's eyes, then Ivy's before turning back to her daughter. "Did you tell them how you got Magister Ivann killed?"

Ivy furrowed her brows and looked over at Correlyn, but she wouldn't meet her gaze. She balled her fists and sat back down, lowering her head and taking some deep breaths. "No? How about what happened to Ser Oby because of you?"

"That's enough," Rayner growled, but Oharra ignored him and stepped closer, bending down to get eye to eye with Correlyn. "How about what happened at Grey Raven?" Everyone went still. "It was your fault they died."

"Stop it," Correlyn pleaded and closed her eyes.

"Oharra..." Helvarr warned, his tone changing to hostile. Rayner stepped up to Correlyn, gently placing a hand on her shoulder, and he could feel her shaking.

Oharra leaned down to whisper to Correlyn, but Rayner stepped in front of her. Some of his knights shifted behind them, putting their hands to their swords. Correlyn shot to her feet and stepped around Rayner, standing face to face with Oharra. She seemed delighted by the challenge and grinned at her daughter. "You'll never escape me, Correlyn, dear." She narrowed her eyes and held out a finger to point at Correlyn's heart. "My blood runs through your veins, and if you think that we are nothing alike, then you have much to learn."

"That's enough," Rayner warned again and looked to Helvarr. "Make your decision, or it's off the table, and we leave here having resolved nothing."

Helvarr ran his hands through his black hair, looking back and forth between Rayner and Correlyn. Oharra turned to face him, her expression soft as she walked up to him and caressed his cheek. "Helvarr, my love, will you lie down and give up so easily?" He drew his brows together and took her hand away.

"Oharra, will you not consider it? Aren't you tired of fighting?" Oharra glared at him and stepped back, removing her hand. She turned around to look at Rayner, who kept his face blank and stern. Rayner knew that Oharra wasn't planning on going with Helvarr, no matter what the offer, but he didn't dare say anything. That was Helvarr's problem; Rayner just hoped Helvarr would take the deal out of his love for Oharra.

Rayner looked outside of the tent. The sky was dark, and though the tent blocked the view above, he could make out a reddish shimmer in the snow. His heart began to pound. He cast a look at Ivy, and she followed his eyes out into the field. Her face went pale, and she stepped back to where Finn stood, whispering something in his ear before stepped back to their horses. Rayner turned back to Helvarr. "You've had enough time to consider, what will it be?"

Correlyn looked at the snow outside and craned her neck out to look at the sky, trying to get a glimpse of the blood moon.

"Correlyn..." Helvarr's voice sounded weak. She turned back to him, avoiding the look her mother was giving her. "Did you ever even consider my offer?" She looked to Rayner, who averted his eyes, crossing his arms over his chest.

"Of course, she didn't!" Oharra answered with a sinister laugh. Helvarr searched his daughter's face but took her silence as an answer. Correlyn watched as his face morphed, and he slipped on the all too familiar mask of the man who killed Magnus, the man who ruined their lives and didn't do enough to protect her when she was taken captive. She felt her pulse quicken and went to speak, but Helvarr stepped forward suddenly, locking eyes with Rayner.

He bared his teeth. "If you want your home, little king, then come and take it."

Rayner growled in retort, Helvarr shot a warning look to Correlyn before turning around and storming off. Correlyn was frozen in place. She *had* considered his offer, but it was too late to tell him now. If Correlyn could do anything to keep her people safe, she would have, but Rayner talked her out if it. He assured Correlyn that they had a chance of winning with King Caato's men gone and that he wouldn't allow her to go through anything like that again. Helvarr was the reason they were all here, and Correlyn needed to remember that.

Helvarr's raiders parted for him as he stomped his way to his horse. Rayner grabbed Correlyn's hand and began to lead her away when Oharra snatched her daughter from his grasp. The king's knights stepped forward, ready to draw their swords, but Correlyn held a hand up to stop them. Rayner looked back and forth between mother and daughter, trying to distinguish the look in Oharra's eyes. She leaned in to Correlyn, and Rayner strained to hear her words. "You will never have peace," she said in a hiss. "I will haunt you until your last days and make you regret turning me away. You are no daughter of mine, and you were never fit to rule Grey Raven."

Correlyn's eyes began to water, and Oharra tightened her grip on her arm. "You are weak and foolish." She drew back to look her daughter in the eye. "First, I will kill your new family on the battlefield. Then I will make you watch as I slaughter your king, taking my time to break every bone in his body until he begs me for death, and then, when no one is left, I will kill you Correlyn, dear, and bury your body where no one will ever find it. You will have no peace, neither in this world or the next." She shoved Correlyn away, Rayner catching her by the elbow. Correlyn let out a sob as she watched Oharra turn her back on them.

C orrelyn wanted to sink down to the ground and cry until she was numb. Her hands shook as she wiped away the tears, only to make room for more. "Correlyn…" She pushed out of Rayner's grip, sniffing her tears away and blowing past Ivy and Finn. She couldn't do it. She couldn't live in a world where a monster like her mother existed. Correlyn ignored everyone in her path as she stalked over to her horse. Rayner mounted his horse, and Ivy and Finn followed. Correlyn climbed up on her horse, avoiding Rayner's gaze and kicked her horse to start walking forward. She watched Helvarr and Oharra saddle up, the raiders already making their way back to the gates of Godstone. That was their home, and she'd be damned if she let Oharra spend one more night in it.

"Correlyn?" Worry hung in Rayner's voice, but she ignored him. Rage burned in her cheeks as she stopped her horse and watched through her tears as Helvarr turned back to look at her. Rayner's men began to turn around to rally up with the group who waited in the

Blackwoods. Rayner brought his horse alongside Correlyn's. "We will get it back," he said softly. "We just need a plan." Correlyn didn't respond, and Rayner huffed out a sigh and turned back, leaving Correlyn still mounted next to the tent. She tilted her head up, and her eyes went wide. The blood moon hung in the sky, casting a blood-red glow across the field of snow. She snapped her eyes shut, but when she opened them again, Oharra was staring back at her with a wicked smile. Correlyn lost it. She looked back to the Blackwoods where her friends were. "I'm sorry," she whispered to herself.

Correlyn let the rage fuel her hands as she reached back and unslung her bow. Her shaky hands went steady as she wrapped her fingers around the wood and drew an arrow. Before she could think about stopping, Correlyn drew back the arrow, aimed, and fired just as Rayner called out to her.

"Correlyn, no!" Rayner yelled, but it was too late. Her arrow tore through the night air with a faint whistle and hit its target. Correlyn didn't even blink as she watched the arrow embed itself in Oharra's back. Time seemed to slow, and Correlyn felt like she could breathe again as she watched her mother fall from her horse. She wasn't too far away that Correlyn couldn't make out the expression on her face. She was smiling, and it sent shivers down Correlyn's spine. Oharra was speaking, and Correlyn walked her horse forward, looking at her lips as she mouthed something over and over. The shaking returned to her hands, and Correlyn felt sick to her stomach. *My little monster.* Oharra's dying words.

Helvarr jumped down from his horse and ran to Oharra, as a pool of blood began to form around her, creating a dark circle that enveloped her. Rayner brought his horse up to Correlyn's trying to catch her eye, but she was locked on Helvarr. He fell to his knees, cradling Oharra's head in his lap as her eyes closed for the last time. Tears streamed down his face, and when he looked up, he looked right at Correlyn. She felt her body go numb and her heart stop from the look he gave her.

"What have you done?" Rayner's voice sounded so far away.

She tried to move, but Helvarr held her captive in his copper gaze. He dropped Oharra's head and rose to his feet, his raiders forming around him, weapons drawn. Helvarr kept his eyes on Correlyn as he ordered his raiders, "Kill them all."

F ear danced in her mind as Correlyn suddenly realized the full reality of what she'd done, but it was too late. "We have to go," Rayner urged. "Now!" Correlyn turned her horse and kicked, following Rayner toward the Blackwoods. She wondered if the group had seen what she'd done, but they needed to get to them. She turned back to see figures making their way back to Godstone. No one was coming after them. She ground to a halt and leapt off her horse, burying her shaky hands in the snow. Rayner fell beside her, taking her face into his hands. Correlyn's heart was beating too fast, and her stomach was flipping inside her.

"Correlyn," he pleaded. "Stay with me, we have to move." He pulled her to standing, and they ran the rest of the way through the trees, calling out to Grimm and the others.

Piotr came around a tree, and from the look on his face, he had no idea what happened. Rayner blew past him, "Where are the others?"

"Grimm and Kyatta are further west," Piotr called back. He caught Ivy by the arm, "What happened?"

Ivy was breathing heavily as she answered. "Oharra is dead."

Piotr let go of her arm and took a step back, "What? How?"

"Correlyn killed her."

"Why the hell did she do that? Helvarr didn't take the deal?"

"I don't know, Piotr!" she roared. "We need to get out of here before—" But she stopped when Kyatta came in to view just ahead. As she approached them, Ivy walked up to meet her.

Kyatta's face was not in its usually calm demeanor, but rather it was streaked with fear. Grimm grabbed her by the wrist and turned her around before Ivy could speak. His eyes were intense, darting back and forth between hers. Lord Cylas ran to where Rayner and Correlyn stood. "We can fight them."

"No!" Rayner bellowed. "We weren't prepared for this. Half of our men are back at camp."

"And you want to lead them back there?" Cylas's voice piqued with worry.

"We don't have a choice," Rayner snapped back. "We need more men." Everything was happening too fast. They had only brought half their men, not wanting to show their exact numbers to Helvarr in case they ended up battling. Correlyn could see her husband working over something in his mind. His brows were drawn together, his bottom lip pulled between his teeth. What was he going to do? Lord Cylas was right: if they led Helvarr and his raiders back to camp, he'd be putting his mother in danger.

"Rayner…" Correlyn said softly, drawing him back to her. He looked at her, then turned to the empty field now turning red under the moon. He squinted into the night and Correlyn followed his gaze, her eyes going wide. Helvarr's entire army of raiders was pouring out the gates of Godstone, headed their way. It was too late; they were coming, and Rayner wasn't prepared for what would happen next.

THE WEAPON & THE LEGEND

Kyatta didn't need to look. She knew what was coming, and it was too late. Rayner whirled around and began shouting orders at his men to form up. He wouldn't lead the army back to their camp. It was too much of a risk, and they were out of time. Correlyn stood like a ghost, pale and still, at the edge of the wood line. Ivy turned around to face Kyatta. "You don't have to do this," she pleaded, but Kyatta closed her eyes, preparing. "Grimm, tell her!" Ivy shouted at him, but he stayed silent, his face hard.

"We need to go." Ivy was panicking. This had been Ivy's dream, and they all knew it… so why was no one running?

Kyatta stopped Rayner as he was running by. "Tell your men to stay back."

"Kyatta, no. You're not—"

"A weapon?" she finished. "Yes, I am. Now stay back, or I won't be able to tell your men from his." Rayner stared into her eyes for a moment, still not wanting to budge. Rayner's men froze around him, looking back and forth between their king and Kyatta. She turned around before he could argue; there was no time for that.

Grimm came up to her, taking her hands in his. His eyes were creased with too many emotions and it broke her to see that look on his face. Yet even as he stood there, gripping her hands as if asking her not to do this, Kyatta knew there was no other way. The gods had given her a part to play in Ivy's life, and Kyatta had been trying to fill the role ever since. Perhaps this was what she was really meant for, to save Ivy and her family, even if it meant her own destruction.

"Kyatta, please…" Grimm's voice broke as he fought for words. Kyatta lifted her hand to his face and smiled.

"You promised me you wouldn't stop me."

"I know," he replied, leaning into her hand. "But I cannot let you go." Tears began to build in his eyes, making them appear more vibrant blue. Grimm closed his eyes before they could fall.

Kyatta took a breath. "I'm not asking you to let me go. I'm asking you to let me help."

"Kyatta, I…" Grimm's voice trailed off as Kyatta harnessed her powers, and his eyes shot open. "What are you…" Grimm stumbled, but Kyatta caught him with her other arm, forcing him to sleep. His eyes went wide as he struggled to fight it. "Do not… do this," he said through his teeth, trying to pull away from her, but Kyatta's hand remained firmly against his brow, her moonflower tattoo glowing bright with power.

"I'm sorry," she whispered as Grimm crashed to his knees. She lowered herself into a crouch next to him, forcing her powers into his mind, but he was fighting. "The more you struggle, the worse it will feel." Grimm's breathing was rapid and uneven. He fought to keep his eyes open, to keep Kyatta with him, but she could feel him slipping.

"Please," he begged her.

Kyatta closed her eyes, a single tear rolling away as she gave one last push. She pressed her lips against his ear as Grimm began to fade into sleep and whispered, "I love you." Grimm's eyes shot open at the words, but Kyatta forced the last of her powers into his mind, and Grimm slumped over. She pressed a kiss to his brow and stood up.

All eyes were on her, but no one spoke a word of what she'd done. Grimm would have done anything to stop her, and Kyatta couldn't have him getting in her way. She pulled her hood down and stepped out of the wood line, Rayner and Ivy following her. Kyatta dug out the circlet with the bloodstone and put it around her head. She looked over to Rayner, ignoring Ivy's worried glance. "Tell your men to stay back," she repeated and tilted her head up to the moon. She felt her powers spike and shoot through her with the force of a falling star. It warmed her blood and powered her heart, and when Kyatta opened her eyes again, she set her sight on what she had to do.

She removed her cloak, letting her tattoos show. They were glowing bright red from beneath her skin, and the crescent moon on her face looked like it was dripping blood down the bridge of her nose. Her eyes were solid black with bright streaks of red shooting through them like veins. Ivy stepped back at the sight of her but tried not to show her fear.

"You'll freeze," Ivy said, looking at her bare arms.

Kyatta turned her eyes back to the army. "I want them to see me coming."

Why?" Rayner asked.

Kyatta turned her blood-streaked eyes on him, her tone grave. "To give them a chance to run."

He just shook his head. "But they don't know what you are."

Kyatta took in a breath, closing her eyes for a moment and focusing her powers. She turned to look at Rayner and Ivy one last time before stepping forward and responding, "They will."

She could feel the bloodstone working its powers as she stepped out onto the field and made her way toward the army, but it would fade. Kyatta quickened her pace, knowing she had to be well out of range before the bloodstone failed, and she was transformed into someone else. Her heart was racing, but her hands calm as she glided over the shimmering red snow. She felt bad about using her powers on Grimm, but it was only just enough to knock him out for a few minutes so she could get away.

Grimm fought her the entire time. He was too big, and it took a lot out of her to control him like that, but the blood moon filled her veins with a different power. It pulsed, twisting, and turning, like a snake writhing against a predator. The army before her screamed and shouted as they closed in, unphased that they faced only one woman. Some were on horseback while others tore through the field on foot. Kyatta paused in the middle of the field and took in a breath, thinking about the last words she said to Grimm. Kyatta glanced back. She was a good distance away from the wood line, and as long as no one came after her, they would be safe. She lifted the circlet off her head and dropped it into the snow beside her boot, crunching the stone beneath her heel.

The wave of power that hit her was unlike any other, and already Kyatta could feel herself slipping. It was as if she was tucked away into the back of her own mind, who she was ceased to exist, and only darkness surrounded her. What emerged was not Kyatta. She closed her eyes, welcoming the darkness and letting it wrap around her in an embrace. She could hear the pounding of hooves, the rattle of armor, and the shouting of men; it surrounded her, swallowing her whole, and now it was time to show them what real fear felt like.

Kyatta opened eyes and held out a hand, fingers splayed out before slowly curling them into a fist. A handful of raiders dropped to their knees, their swords sinking into the soft snow and their screams rising to greet the moon. They writhed in pain, clutching their chests as blood began to stream from their eyes. Kyatta snapped her head to the left. Three horsemen galloped toward her, spears in hand. She reached out the other hand, pulling the blood of the horses until they ground to a halt, throwing the men from their backs. Kyatta released the horses and focused on the men, scrambling to get to their feet, but she already had them in her grasp. She squeezed, feeling their hearts constrict as if they lay in her palm, releasing them when they stopped beating. An archer shot an arrow, just missing Kyatta's face. She whirled around, stretching out both arms and controlling the men surrounding the archer. They advanced on him, and the archer had a look of utter horror as his men cut him in two. The fear on their faces made her blood run faster as she watched them kill their fellow raider. Her mind was as clear as the sky above; no trace of Kyatta remained, and the space left behind was filled with rage.

The raiders circled her; some looked confused, some fearful, and others still filled with enough adrenaline to try to attack her. She stepped up to them, reaching her hands out and grabbing hold of an entire group. They dropped to their knees, screaming in agony and sobbing as Kyatta forced their hearts to stop, constricted their muscles, or simply stopped their blood from flowing. "Archers!" one of them yelled. Kyatta looked up to see a line of archers already releasing arrows into the sky. She grabbed the first man she could, forcing him to run to her side and hold his shield above her head. The raider was pierced with arrows, but Kyatta kept her grasp on him until they stopped falling, and only then did she let him die.

Ivy bounced from one foot to the other, her nervous energy building up as she watched the distant figures dropping to the ground around Kyatta. She had to do something. She couldn't just stand there and allow Kyatta to die for them. Aska, Arytin, and Macon stood over to the left, harnessing their powers and trying to focus on the raiders down below. Ivy couldn't tell if they were being controlled by Aska and her family or Kyatta. The distant screams rushed across the empty field to where she stood and it gave Ivy chills down to her bones. Beside her, Arytin sighed deeply and when Ivy turned to him, his eyes had gone back to normal. Aska and Macon did the same, returning to Ivy's side. "What's wrong?" she asked.

"It's not working," Arytin answered, rubbing the back of his neck.

"What do you mean? What's not working?"

Arytin gave her a sorrowful look. "I think it's her." He gestured toward Kyatta. "It's like she's blocking us out, or her powers are. I don't know how to explain it, but when I tried to control their minds, I couldn't get in. It's like there's a wall I can't break through. Either that, or we're too far away to pick out specific people."

"We need to get closer." Macon stepped forward.

"No." Ivy's answer was final.

"But we can help." Aska came up beside Ivy. "It's why we came." Ivy snapped her eyes shut. She couldn't let more people risk their lives for them.

"I didn't ask you to come," she growled, and Aska stepped back, furrowing her brows. Ivy didn't want to hurt them, but it might be the only way to save them.

Arytin took her hand in his. "Stormbringer," he said, his eyes soft, "we want to help if we could just get—"

Ivy snatched her hand from his. "You can't help," she snapped, then lowered her head, sparing herself the hurt on Arytin's face. "No one can."

Aska turned on her heels and stomped off toward the woodline, Macon running after her. Ivy lifted her eyes back to Arytin, and they stared at each other for a moment before he left her side. She let out a long sigh, rubbing her hands over her face. What was she going to do? Kyatta wouldn't be able to kill every one of the raiders, and then what? They waited for Kyatta to get overwhelmed before they stepped in? Ivy wouldn't accept that, she couldn't. Kyatta had become her family, too, and she wouldn't just stand by and watch her die. She reached down to the gold scarf from her father, rubbing it between her fingers and remembering his words: *I'll always come home.* Magnus hadn't lied about that, he did always come home. No matter where he'd been or what else was going on in his world, he always came back to his family. But in the end, he had died in his home, trying to protect it. Ivy thought that if she were going to die, at least she'd fall in the field where her father had been felled—at least she'd be home.

She took a step forward, but a strong hand gripped her shoulder. Ivy turned, ready to yell at Rayner or Finn, but it was Ronin who stood beside her. His eyes were trained on the army as he asked, "What do you think you're doing?" Ivy moved out of his grasp, and he let her, folding his hands behind his back. Ronin's hair was tied in a tight knot, and he wore his usual dark, loose robes. When she didn't answer, he turned to face her. His dark eyes found hers, and Ivy thought something seemed different. Ronin had always guarded his true feelings behind his calm demeanor, but Ivy saw something in his eyes now.

"I can't just let her die," she finally said and thought, if anyone, her trainer would understand. Ronin turned back as if he hadn't heard her. Kyatta was still dropping men as they swarmed her, but they were starting to get closer.

Ronin pulled out a small object from an inside pocket next to his heart and began running his thumb over it. It was a small copper bracelet. Ivy watched his eyes, which seemed lost in another world. "I gave this to my wife, Yacira, the day Helvarr was born." Ivy had never heard that tone of voice, far away and longing. "I had no idea I would be taking it off her dead body just hours later." He wrapped his fingers around the bracelet before tucking it back into his pocket.

Ivy knew all about Ronin's past. He had told her and Finn right after Helvarr had killed Ser Osmund. Ivy had been too enraged at the time to really hear what he was saying. Ronin had always tried to teach Ivy to control her anger whenever they trained, but she thought that impossible. How could someone fight with no emotion? If Ronin used anger or hatred to fuel his sword hand, then he did well to hide it. He was a legend throughout the land–it was what brought him to Godstone in the first place. She wondered what he saw now as he looked at the place that had once been his home.

Ivy put her hand to Promise and stepped in front of Ronin. "I have to do something, Ronin. This was my dream, and I can't stand by and watch it play out."

He smiled, really smiled, and Ivy was taken off guard by it. "I know," he said, reaching out and putting a hand on her shoulder. "You have been the most stubborn, hard-headed student I've ever trained." Ivy cocked her head but Ronin only smiled bigger. "But, you have also been my best student." She dropped her hand from Promise as he went on. "I didn't want to train you at first, I admit that. But I was wrong about you, Ivy. You are quick to learn, strategic in your fighting. You use your body as a weapon, not only relying on the sword in your hand. I think that one day, you could even be better than me." Ivy felt a knot in her stomach; no one was as good as Ronin. He leaned in closer. "Your enemies are rocks, so be like water and flow around them."

Ivy held his gaze as he dropped his hand back to his side. "I'll never be as good as you," she admitted because, in her heart, she knew it was true.

"No," he said, then winked. "You'll be better. You will be a legend." Ivy furrowed her brows, she didn't understand why he was telling her this, why now? Ronin lifted his gaze back to the raiders, and the haunting calmness settled over his face again. "You know," he began, and something in his voice gave Ivy chills. "After I lost her, I had nothing." His eyes drifted over Godstone. "That idea of a peaceful life died with Yacira. For years I fought, I trained, and I killed and for what? I thought perhaps the gods were leading me toward something, that I would find the life I had before here, with your people." He turned to look at Ivy, and she found herself holding her breath. "I thought this place might bring me a bit of peace like I once had, but I was wrong. This place will give me a different kind of peace, one that men run from. I once believed this place was a beacon of hope in a world of chaos…but it was just a mirage."

Ronin drew the sword from his back, and dread pooled in Ivy's stomach. "What are you doing?" she asked, hating how little and scared her voice came out. Ronin kept his eyes ahead and took a step forward. "What you were about to. It's been a pleasure, Ivy Iron Heart."

Ivy grabbed for him, but he slipped from her hands without even looking. He walked with a purpose down the hill, and Ivy started after him, but being Ronin, he heard her coming. He called over his shoulder, "Stay. Your family needs you." Ivy halted, knowing he would hear her if she ran after him.

"Ronin!" she called, but he ignored her, his pace steady. Tears rolled from her eyes as she watched her trainer walk into the belly of the beast.

Ronin steered clear of Kyatta, keeping a safe distance as she killed more raiders. A few turned their attention to Ronin and ran toward him, swords raised. He glanced at their feet before dropping under the first blade that swung at him. He sliced at the back of the raider's ankles before springing to his feet and thrusting his sword through the man in front of him. He dropped with a *crunch* to the snow. The other lay bleeding and screaming, gripping his ankles. Two more came barreling toward Ronin, and he slid around them as if they stood still, slicing the sides of their necks before they had a chance to raise their swords. He glanced over to Kyatta. Her tattoos seemed to be pulsing with red light, her fingers nimbly working their way into raiders' bodies. He moved away, focusing on a group of raiders who clearly avoided her, but they would find no more comfort fighting him.

They advanced on him, screaming with the thrill of battle. Ronin cut through the first two like they were made of smoke, twirling around their falling bodies and sending his sword through one's neck. He stepped aside as a blade came down, forcing Ronin to take his hands off the hilt. The raider swung again, but Ronin caught his arm and kicked the front of his knee, bending it at a sickening angle. The raider shrieked in pain, dropping to the snow as Ronin retrieved his sword.

Just then a spear landed in front of him, and when he looked up, archers were nocking back arrows. Ronin ran to the nearest man, grabbing him by the collar as the arrows flew straight toward him. He used the raider's body as a shield, feeling the jerking motion as the arrows sunk into his flesh. Ronin released the raider, leaping over his body and charging straight at the archers.

His confidence gave them pause, and many hesitated as he ran to them. Some dropped their bows and turned to run, preferring to feel Kyatta's wrath rather than die on his sword. One archer leveled his aim on Ronin at the last second. Ronin smacked the arrow away midflight and drove his sword deep into the archer's gut. Then he reached back and pulled the shorter sword he kept in his belt. The archer gripped the blade that was buried in his flesh and stared at Ronin in horror. He tried to speak but blood spurted from his lips as he choked. Ronin slit the man's throat with his second blade, then tucked it back into its sheath. He withdrew his sword and stood up, turning around to see a group of raiders surrounding him. He did a quick count: twelve.

Ronin stood perfectly still, waiting for them to make a move. Their eyes darted between him and where Kyatta stood some distance away, lost in her bloodlust. Ronin waited patiently, placing his hands behind his back and locking eyes with the closest man, a challenge. The man snarled and ran at Ronin, swinging an ax. Ronin caught the blade against his and swiftly swept the man's feet out from under him and sent his sword through his head. He watched as the remaining raiders weighed their options. Him or Kyatta? Sword or blood moon? Weapon or legend?

Him.

Four raiders broke away from the group and charged him. Ronin ducked under the first blade and stepped out of another's path. He swung his sword up, blocking a blow meant for his neck. Ronin slit the raider's throat and moved to the next when he felt a sharp pain in his leg. He looked down to see an arrow, the head protruding just below his knee. Grunting, Ronin snapped the arrow, pulling it free just as a raider plowed into him. They fell to the snow, but Ronin kept his grip on the hilt of his sword as the man tried to shove his dagger into Ronin's heart. He pulled the raider closer and headbutted him, blood spraying from his nose. Throwing the raider aside, Ronin scrambled to his feet when he felt a blow to his back.

He stumbled forward and turned around to see a massive man with a club in his hands. He swung again, and Ronin dodged as the club crashed into the snow. Taking a careful breath, Ronin made a mental note of the damage. He had a broken rib, but he ignored the pain. On his feet, the raider stood a head taller than Ronin, but he was quicker. He dodged another blow from the club and swung his sword at the raider's side, but the man caught the blade in his hands. Ronin didn't hesitate to rip his sword free, slicing the raiders palm wide open. He cried out in pain, but rage burned behind his eyes. He advanced, forcing Ronin back further into the army. He skewered a raider behind him without looking, stepping lightly over his bleeding body. A club swung at his head, and Ronin ducked, sliding around him and slashing at his back.

Ronin's leg was throbbing from the arrow, and when he looked down, he saw a trail of blood following his every move. He kept his breathing as calm as he could manage, keeping his eyes trained on the club. The raider whirled around, swinging recklessly, and Ronin stepped up to him, leaning back to miss the club before slashing his blade across his chest then thrusting it through his heart. The raider fell to his knees, his blood blending into the redness of the snow, lit up by the moon overhead. He stole a quick glance at Kyatta and saw that she was being surrounded. The raiders were getting too close, and he could see her struggling to keep them all in her grasp. Ronin didn't hesitate.

He ran straight for them, yelling and drawing their attention away from Kyatta. He sliced through bodies, his sword slick with fresh blood as he drew them away. Ronin flew through the crowd, keeping one eye on Kyatta and the other on the swords swinging at him. He heard the screams of the raiders who were unfortunate enough to stay and fight her. A smile spread across his lips as the raiders ahead of him formed a wall. The pain in his leg was worsening and his breathing labored from the blow, but he pushed forward.

It was almost over.

The wall closed off around him as Ronin targeted the first body to step in his path. The man's legs folded beneath him as Ronin relieved him of his head. There were shields blocking his way but they lowered as a few archers drew back and sent their arrows flying. Ronin dodged a few but felt the impact as one arrow sliced his upper arm and another embedded itself in his shoulder. He snapped the back of the arrow and switched the sword to his other hand, challenging the raiders to advance. They happily obliged.

Ronin was a blur of dark robes as he sliced through one, two, three, half a dozen raiders in a matter of seconds. "Kill him!" someone bellowed from behind the wall. Ronin kept calm. He knew exactly what he was doing the moment he stepped out of the woodline. He thought of Ivy and her family, how their fates had been intertwined since before they met. Ronin believed the gods brought them together so that he could guide Ivy and teach her all he knew to sculpt himself into someone else. But she didn't take shape. Ivy was her own person with her own style of fighting and Ronin beamed with pride every time he watched her fight. Perhaps he should have told her more often how proud he was or showed his approval, but somewhere deep down, he trusted that Ivy knew. Ronin felt a calmness spread throughout his entire being; he knew Ivy would be all right and that she would do great things. The death of one legend only made room for another to emerge.

Ronin stumbled as another arrow sunk into his thigh. He grimaced at the pain and he was bleeding heavily now and started to feel lightheaded. Raiders stepped up to fight him, confident they would win now that he was injured, but Ronin wouldn't go down smoothly. He lifted his sword with his good arm, sending it crashing into the side of a raider's skull just as another sliced at his ribs. Ronin stepped back, not even taking a second to look down at the slice to his side. He could feel the blood leaking through his robes but ignored it. A group broke off from the wall, all attacking him at once. Ronin slid and twirled, blocking as many blades as he could and taking others to his leg, his back, and his sword hand. He dropped his sword in the snow and crashed into the first raider he saw.

They fell to the ground, and Ronin sent his bleeding fist into his nose, smiling at the sound of bone crunching. Another arrow struck his back as he fought the raider, who then threw Ronin from him, clutching his broken nose and swaying as he got to his feet. Ronin knelt down, pulling the copper bracelet from his pocket and slipping it over his wrist. He wiped the blood from the shiny metal, letting a smile spread across his lips. "I'll see you soon." His voice was barely a whisper.

Ronin stood up, grinning at the army of raiders around him. Some seemed unnerved by it, while others took it as a challenge. He picked up his sword and held it in both hands, widening his stance and waiting. The raiders rushed him, too many to slice his way out of, and Ronin smiled as they surrounded him, picturing Yacira's soft black hair, her copper eyes that shone brighter than the sun, and her warm smile, welcoming him into the Hall of the Gods.

THE MIRAGE

Ivy stared at the walls of Godstone, the snow-covered fields stretched far and wide, perfectly smooth and untouched. It looked like a calm, white sea, and Ivy hesitated to take a step into it, not wanting to disturb something so pure and untouched. Torches burned along the walls, and smoke drifted up into the night sky from the homes within the kingdom. Everything was peaceful, normal even, a kingdom untouched by the chaos of the world.

No.

Ivy blinked until the picture faded, and the real image took shape.

Just a mirage.

The fields were filled with screaming men, the snow sprayed with blood, or torn up from hooves. Everywhere she looked, Ivy saw death. It lingered in the air, thick and suffocating. She scanned the fields, tears forming in her eyes as she searched for her trainer. Ronin couldn't die. He was the best fighter she'd ever seen, a legend. Ivy spotted a shield wall forming a circle around one man. Her breath caught in her throat as she watched a dark figure, twirling and slicing his way through bodies. Ivy felt a brief moment of hope. Ronin knew what he was doing. Surely he wouldn't have walked off without having a plan, would he? Her eyes were wide and frantic as she tried to keep up with his movements, but he was like smoke, moving through raiders' paths as if he was never there. Her knees began to shake, her palms sweating as she watched, and then it happened. Ivy saw a large group break off from the circle and surround Ronin, and he went down.

Ivy's mind exploded into a million little pieces, the tears flowing like rivers down her cheeks. She grabbed Promise from her scabbard. Ivy couldn't stand by. She would rather die in her home than to never see it again. She took off in a sprint down the hill, the cold wind clawing at her face and pulling her tears back. A poor plan began to take shape in her mind when she felt a pair of arms wrap around her waist. They slid in the snow, tumbling down the hill to a stop. She whirled around to see Rayner, his hands still firmly wrapped around her. "Get off me!" she yelled and struggled to get away from him.

Rayner gripped her even harder, but his voice was soft. "It's not our time."

The words froze Ivy for a split second. She blinked at him, then shoved away and got to her feet. Rayner stood up and blocked her path. Over his shoulder, Ivy saw her family standing in the tree line, watching her. She tried to blink them away, but they remained where they stood. Ivy brought her hands up to her ears, trying to block out the screaming and thundering of hooves. She had tried to stop her dream from coming true, but the gods were adamant about it playing out. She looked past Rayner, searching for something she knew she wouldn't see.

Rayner stepped closer, his voice no more than a whisper. "You can't save everyone."

Tears stung her eyes as she stared at Rayner, but then a commotion turned her attention to the woodline. Grimm stumbled into the field and his eyes landed on Ivy. He looked mad, insane, as he searched for Kyatta, and Ivy saw it the moment he spotted her.

Grimm took off running toward Godstone, his eyes locked on Kyatta. Finn and Piotr ran after him and tackled him to the ground. "No!" he roared and tried to crawl away. Grimm shoved Piotr off him and got to his feet, but Rayner now stood in front of him. "Move," he growled.

"You can't go down there, Grimm."

Grimm's voice cracked with defeat, "I cannot lose her!" Rayner lowered his eyes, not wanting to see his friend in pain, but he knew Grimm would die if he went to help. Kyatta made her choice, even when they all tried to convince her not to go.

Ivy stepped up beside her brother and reached up, placing a hand on Grimm's shoulder. "Grimm..." she said through her tears. He shoved away from her and began to walk around them when Earl Rorik came up and wrapped his son up from behind. Grimm thrashed and started screaming, but his father held his grip. They sank down to the snow. Grimm was sobbing, but his tears quickly burned away with the anger nesting in his cheeks. Ivy looked back to see that a group of raiders had spotted them, likely drawn to Grimm's screams. They broke off from the army and ran straight toward them.

"We have to go!" Rayner yelled, grabbing Ivy by the arm and pulling her along. Rorik pulled Grimm to his feet and shoved him toward the woodline. Ivy took Finn's hand as they ran through the trees to get to their horses.

Aska and her family were already mounted up when they broke through the treeline. The raiders tried to cut them off, and Lord Cylas stepped in front of the horses, drawing his sword and calling back over his shoulder for them to go. Everyone mounted their horses and snapped the reins, taking off toward the camp. A few of Rayner's knights stood with Cylas, and Ivy turned back to see them standing in a line as archers began to shoot at them. She watched them until they were no more than specks in the distance.

Rayner jumped from his horse when they came galloping into the camp. "Get a perimeter around this campsite," he shouted to his men. Correlyn stood by her horse, looking pale and lost. Grimm slumped down from his saddle and sank to his knees, burying his shaking hands in the snow and softly sobbing to himself. Ivy started to go over to him, but Earl Rorik got there first. He bent down, placing a hand on Grimm's back. "I am sorry, son." Grimm pushed him away and got to his feet, storming off through the row of tents. Piotr went up to Correlyn and took her by the elbow, leading her back to her tent.

Ivy walked over to Finn, who stood by his horse with his eyes focused south. She stepped in front of him, but he wouldn't look at her. "Finn…what happened?" He didn't respond. Ivy lifted a finger under his chin until he finally looked at her. "Talk to me, Finn. Please."

Finn grabbed her hand and led Ivy back to their tent. He paced the room nervously while Ivy took a seat at the edge of their bed. The tent was dark save for a candelabra burning on the table in the center of the room. Finn walked over to the table and poured himself a cup of wine, downing the whole thing in a few gulps. He lowered himself on the bed next to Ivy, wringing his hands and keeping his eyes on his boots as he spoke. Finn told her everything, about Helvarr killing his family, the scar he left, about the man named Hal who led the raid. He hesitated when he got to Thorman but told Ivy what Helvarr claimed would have happened to his little brother if the raiders had taken him. Finn told her that some children were taken that day and that they might still be out there, but if Helvarr did know, he pretended not to.

By the time he was done, Finn's eyes were shiny with tears. Ivy didn't move the whole time, she could hardly breathe as Finn told his story. All that time, it had been Helvarr at the center of Finn's pain and guilt. A new flame of rage ignited inside her gut, but she doused it, for now.

"I'm so sorry, Finn…" No amount of sympathy would ever make up for what was done to him. Finn closed his eyes, and Ivy rested her hand on his thigh. He finally turned to look at her, then grabbed Ivy by the back of the head and kissed her. It was hard and desperate. Ivy leaned away and stared at him. His russet eyes were bloodshot, his hair hung limply across his forehead, and he looked undone.

She searched his eyes, and they looked hurt. "Finn...I don't think—"

"Please." His eyes stayed locked with hers. "I just need to forget. Even if it's only for now." Ivy understood wanting a distraction from your pain. Everyone had their own ways of dealing with it, but none of them were a cure. She reached out to brush his hair away from his face, wrapping her fingers around his head and pulling him in. Finn buried his face in the crook of her neck, wrapping his arms around her waist. Ivy felt him melting in her arms as she stroked the back of his head, his warm breath sending tingles up her neck. She brought her lips to his ear.

"Lie back," she told him. Finn broke away from her, kicking his boots off and flopping back down on the bed with a loud sigh.

Ivy got up to pour two cups of wine, handing one to Finn, who took a few sips before setting it aside. Ivy crawled onto the bed and sat behind him, lifting Finn's head to rest in her lap and stretching her legs out to either side of him. She began to gently rub his head, humming a soft tune as her fingers glided through his hair. Finn rested a hand on her lower leg and started rubbing small circles against her skin. After a moment, Finn closed his eyes and Ivy saw some of the tension easing out of his shoulders as he settled in deeper between her legs. She leaned down beside his ear and whispered, "We'll get them back, Finn."

He cracked his eyes open to look at Ivy. She slid her hands down to his cheeks, brushing her thumbs over his lips. "If you think your people are still out there," she went on, resting her hands on his chest. "Then we'll search for them and bring them home."

Finn eyes lit up some with the possibility, but it was only a moment before they went dark once more. "I don't even know where to look."

Ivy shrugged her shoulders. "Then we look everywhere." Finn smiled at her and lifted his hand to rest against her cheek, pulling her down until their lips met. His fingers tangled in her hair as he kissed her, and then he stopped and sat up, getting to his knees before her.

Finn gently hooked his hands behind her knees and pulled until she was lying down on the bed before he crawled on top of her. He kissed his way up her neck to her jawline before finding her lips again. Ivy buried her hands in his feathery hair as Finn started to unlace the top of her shirt. His kisses were warm and loving now, and Ivy parted her lips slightly, and his tongue slipped into her mouth, sending heat to her core. His other hand slowly worked its way up under her shirt, trailing along her hips and up her ribs, cupping her breast. A soft moan escaped her lips at the touch and Finn tensed at the sound, his back flexing as she ran her hands over them. Ivy needed to forget too.

Forget what Ronin did, how calm he was as he walked away to meet death, forget the last words he said to her. Was Godstone just a mirage? A place that sucked you in with the promise of peace and then trapped you there to die?

No. The mirage was thinking they could get it back without losing people. People would always die when there was something worth fighting for, or someone. *You will be a legend,* Ronin told her.

Ivy felt a tear roll away at the thought. Finn stopped kissing her and leaned back. He gave her a sad smile and brushed away her tears. "There's nothing you could have done to stop him," he whispered. Ivy knew that, but it didn't make the pain and guilt any easier to carry. She looked at Finn and wondered how he was feeling. He'd known Ronin since he was nine years old, and Ronin had saved Finn from starving after he fled his home. Perhaps what Helvarr had told Finn left no room for more grief in his head, but Ivy knew he would feel it eventually. She cupped his cheek, and he leaned in to her touch.

"Ronin was proud of you." Finn lowered his eyes and nodded

slightly. Ivy knew it was true, even if Ronin rarely praised them, but she knew pride when she saw it, and Ronin beamed with it every time he watched Finn fight. "He cared about you," Ivy went on. "Maybe he didn't show it as often as he should have, but I could see it."

Finn smiled at her and caressed both her cheeks, bringing his lips back to hers. He kissed her long and slow at first, and then his lips began to move faster. Ivy tugged his shirt off and threw it to the floor. Her blood started to race as Finn unlaced her shirt and slipped it over her head, immediately lowering his mouth to her bare neck. Ivy shucked out of her pants and Finn unbuttoned his before lowering himself between her legs. Her skin was on fire as Finn kissed her again, hungry and eager. He groaned as they came together, and Ivy hooked her ankles behind his back, which flexed with his movements.

Ivy needed the distraction as much as Finn did. There were too many things rolling around in her head for sleep to come anyway, and she wanted to feel something other than fear and pain, if only for now.

Grimm sat under a spruce tree at the edge of the campsite, refusing to take his eyes off the path that led south. He was afraid that if he even blinked, he might miss her. He dug his nails into the center of his palms, trying to control the trembling that worked its way from his core to his fingertips. Grimm's eyes darted all around the path—every shadow was Kyatta, every rustle of dead leaves that still clung to their branches. Everything that stirred set his heart pounding against his ribs, hoping it would be Kyatta.

Grimm couldn't believe she had used her powers on him again to keep him from getting in the way. Kyatta had been right though. Grimm never intended to let her go, but he thought that Rayner's offer to Helvarr might have changed things. If Helvarr had taken the deal and Lady Oharra had kept her mouth shut, they wouldn't have been forced to fight the raiders. Grimm didn't know what exactly happened with Correlyn and her mother, but he did know Correlyn had been pushed to the breaking point. Oharra knew how to get under people's skin, and he figured Correlyn had enough of it. Grimm was glad that she was dead. Oharra had ruined so much of their lives, and all of them wanted revenge, but Correlyn had more reasons than any of them to seek hers.

They all had tried to think of every way they could stop Ivy's dream from coming true, they took precautions, but it still wasn't enough. It was like being lost in a maze, and the gods were purposefully cutting off any path that might have led to a different outcome.

Grimm brought his knees up under his chin, thinking about the last words Kyatta said to him.

I love you.

Had he heard right? Or was it just his mind playing a cruel trick on him as her powers forced him to sleep? Grimm wanted to believe that his ears didn't betray him, but at the same time, he couldn't deny how strongly he felt about Kyatta. Even back on Kame Island, he knew he was falling for her, but still, he tried to keep his distance. He told himself that it was too much of a risk, that Kyatta would be his undoing like Fey had been. Now he knew that she was a risk worth taking, and all he wanted was to see her beautiful face again, feel her soft hair between his fingers, and see that smile that made his stomach flutter.

Grimm shot to his feet when he spotted a figure walking down the path. He pulled his ax from his belt, immediately knowing it wasn't Kyatta. He caught a glimpse of orange hair as he drew near and huffed out a sigh as Lord Cylas came walking up to him, clutching his ribs. Grimm looked past the lord, searching the path for someone who wasn't there. "What happened?" Grimm asked, keeping his eyes south.

Cylas shifted to face him, sucking in a sharp breath. "We killed them, but King Rayner's knights died."

Grimm glanced down at his ribs. "You are bleeding."

Cylas waved his words away like a pesky fly. "Arrow. It just grazed me."

Grimm turned his eyes back south. "Did you see her?"

Cylas looked back, too, as if he was expecting her to walk up the path. He shook his head. "There were too many bodies. I'm sorry." Cylas left Grimm to go bandage his wound, leaving a small trickle of blood in his path.

The blood moon was receding, and Grimm knew there wasn't much time left before Kyatta's powers would disappear. He couldn't stand there for the rest of the night and watch an empty path—he'd go mad. Making his way back to his tent, Grimm spotted Cylas and Elana in a warm embrace. Cylas leaned over her growing belly, pressing a kiss to her cheek and taking her by the hand. Further along, he saw his father talking with Zion; the old man hung his head, mourning his friend's death. Luna croaked just above Zion as if offering her condolences before taking flight and heading toward Rayner's tent.

Back in his own tent, Grimm snapped the flap closed behind him and went over to the small table that held a flagon of wine, some cheese that was half-frozen, and some bread. Grimm snatched the whole flagon of wine and sunk down at the foot of his bed, leaning his head back against the wood and running his fingers along the fur pelt. He took a swig, letting the alcohol burn his throat as he thought of the last time Kyatta had been in his tent.

It was the night before the blood moon, and Grimm couldn't sleep. He lay sprawled out on the floor, using the fur pelts as cushions and staring up at the canopy. He felt overwhelmed with worry about what would happen when they traded hostages back and what Helvarr would say to Rayner's offer. There were too many things that could go wrong, and even though they prepared, something still didn't feel right. He had sensed someone standing at his tent, and when he sat up, he heard footsteps slipping away. Grimm stumbled to his feet and poked his head outside to see Kyatta, walking away.

"You cannot sleep?" he called after her, careful to keep his voice low. She halted and spun around. Her eyes were big, as if she was surprised he'd heard her. Grimm stepped outside and walked to her, offering his hand. "Come, I cannot sleep either."

They entered his tent, and Grimm offered her a cup of wine, which she took. He lowered himself back into his spot on the furs, watching her over the brim of his cup. There was a nervous energy buzzing in the room between them. Grimm stood up, walking behind her and lifting the white cloak from her shoulders. "Stay awhile." His voice was soft against her cheek. Kyatta stepped away from him and sat down in the furs, cupping her wine in both hands. Grimm sat across from her, the silence eaten up by the crackling of fire from a small brazier to the left. It bathed the whole tent in an orange hue, giving Kyatta's hair the appearance of glowing.

"Why are you awake?" she asked, looking into her wine.

"Too much on my mind." She lifted her eyes to his, and a blush warmed her cheeks. "Why did you not just come in?" Grimm asked, motioning to the tent flap.

"I wasn't sure if…I didn't know—"

"Kyatta." He leaned forward, his voice soft. "You can always come to me for anything."

Kyatta stared at him, her lips slightly parted. Grimm's gaze wavered to them for a moment before settling back on her eyes. She nodded.

"You are worried about tomorrow?" Grimm asked cautiously. She nodded. Grimm was nervous for her, too, but he didn't want to add his own worries to hers. She had come to him for something, perhaps just a distraction?

He shifted closer. "What can I do?"

Kyatta hesitated at the question. She took a sip of her wine and turned her eyes to the fire. "Tell me a story." When she looked back to him, Grimm smiled and bowed his head. He scooched closer before spreading out on his back and twisting his lips, thinking. Kyatta nestled in further, getting comfortable and watching Grimm. He tucked his hands behind his head, staring up at the canopy. "I have a story you will enjoy."

Grimm told her a story that had been passed along for generations. It started with a man named Torsten, who was one of the strongest and largest men in the whole village, and many people looked up to him. Torsten decided one day that he was going to sail south, all the way to the Serpent's Pass, and slay the beast. Men thought he had gone mad, others praised him, women wept for him, thinking him a dead man. Torsten asked which of the men were brave enough to accompany him as he could not sail the small longboat alone. Men shied away from the offer, and Torsten scolded them for being cowards. Finally, one man stepped up and offered to go. His name was Hamyr, and he made Torsten look small in comparison. It was said that Hamyr could lift entire trees over his head, that he could row a boat by himself and that no horse nor caribou could support his weight. Torsten was delighted to have such a powerful man accompany him.

They set off immediately, sailing when the winds were fair and rowing when they had to. When they reached the Serpent's Pass, Hamyr asked how Torsten planned to slay the beast? Torsten pulled the head of a wild boar from a bag and said the giant serpent would not be able to resist. He would then snag the beast as he fed on the boar's head and spear him when they got close enough. Hamyr was doubtful and began to grow more worried the closer they got. When they reached the spot where the beast was most often seen, Torsten hooked the head of the boar on a line and threw it into the waves. Hamyr paced the length of the boat nervously while Torsten whistled a tune to himself. After a while, he felt a jerk on his line and yanked back, yelling, "I have caught the beast!" Hamyr went pale as he beheld the serpent, writhing and thrashing in the waves as Torsten tried to pull it on board.

Torsten used all of his strength, pulling the head of the serpent into the boat. He strained so hard that one of his feet shot through the bottom of the vessel, and seawater began to pour in. Hamyr panicked as he watched Torsten wrestle the beast, the head of the boar still visible behind its piercing teeth. Torsten yelled at Hamyr to help him, but he stayed planted in his spot on the other side of the boat. Torsten reached for his spear, the serpent still wriggling and trying to bite him, but he finally got it. Just as he lifted it above his head to pierce the beast, Hamyr cut the line and kicked the serpent's head back into the sea. Torsten was so furious that he killed Hamyr and tossed him overboard, then leapt into the sea himself and swam to shore as the boat sank.

Kyatta giggled all throughout the story at the different voices Grimm used for the characters. He beamed at the sound of her laughter and couldn't help but join in. Kyatta slid down in the furs, lying on her back beside Grimm. He reached out and brushed his fingers against hers. Kyatta turned to look at him, letting her eyes fall on his lips. "You're a good storyteller." She smiled.

"Only for a certain crowd." Kyatta rolled on her side to face him, tracing her finger along his jawline and over his lips.

"Will you tell me another one?" she asked softly.

Grimm smiled. "Of course, as many as you like."

Grimm told story after story, Kyatta laughing herself silly at his ridiculous voices and gestures. Grimm watched her the whole time, sometimes losing his place in the story as he stared in awe at the woman beside him. After a while, he could see she was beginning to get tired, which meant Grimm had done his job. Kyatta closed her eyes, still smiling as Grimm continued with another story. He reached out, brushing the stray hairs from her face, and Kyatta scooched closer, nuzzling her head on his chest. Grimm's heart fluttered as he wrapped her in his arms, wishing she'd stay there forever. Grimm lowered his voice, stroking her hair, and only stopped the story when he was sure Kyatta had fallen asleep. He kissed the top of her head. "Good night, Kyatta," he whispered against her hair before he too drifted off to sleep.

Now, Grimm recalled every detail of that night as he ran his fingertips over the soft fur. He wanted nothing more than to curl up with Kyatta again and listen to her laugh as he told her tall tales. He took another swig of wine, hoping to numb his mind. Grimm didn't want to feel like this, not again. He told himself to stay away from her, that it would only bring pain, but he couldn't fight it anymore. Grimm couldn't afford to get lost in himself again, not when they still had work to do.

He sat in his empty tent, drinking his worries away and listening to the camp around him. He doubted anyone would sleep tonight, not after what happened. Helvarr and his raiders could come upon them at any time and attack, so they had to be ready. His head began to spin from the wine but he gulped the rest and lay down in the furs. He spread his arms out to his sides and closed his eyes, feeling with his fingers for someone who wasn't there, but hoping the spot wouldn't stay empty forever.

THE FALLEN

Death never looks the same. Some like to accept it, while others break at the sight of it. But as Helvarr sat there looking at Oharra, he thought that she looked peaceful. As if she knew she was going to die, and in her final moments, she accepted death and let it take her away to the Hall of the Gods. Death never looks the same, but Oharra did.

Helvarr sat in the middle of the Hall, clutching Oharra's cold hand in his. Her midnight hair was swept to one side, cascading across her shoulder, and her pale skin seemed to shimmer in the dancing flames of the candle. Her lips looked as soft as ever. He reached out and ran his finger over them, feeling her lips one last time. The blood from the arrow wound was now a dull brown. Helvarr didn't know how long he'd been sitting there. Time stopped for him yet the world went on around him.

Outside, he could hear the faint sound of his men screaming, but he couldn't move. He couldn't go out there and face King Rayner's army. He'd already lost, and his whole world sat cold and stiff on the floor of the Hall. Oharra had been his first love, the mother of their daughter, and her fall left him broken and hollow. An empty shell forced to live on in the world he helped destroy.

Helvarr knew Oharra had changed; he could see it in her eyes the past few months. Every hateful glare toward Correlyn, every order she gave to have her beaten or starved. Oharra had taken things too far, and he let her. Helvarr would never forgive himself for standing by while his daughter was tortured. When they first captured her, Helvarr willingly pushed Correlyn. He needed to see what she was made of as if confirming that would make the fact that she was his daughter more real. Helvarr had struggled to tell her at first, and a part of him still couldn't believe that he'd finally gotten back to his family, but it wasn't how it was supposed to be.

After so many years away from his daughter, Helvarr wanted to see her, to truly see her. Raw and vulnerable. He needed it for himself before he could decide whether or not to tell her the truth about who he was. In a way, it was like a test. If he could see what Correlyn was made of while being held captive, then he would see what kind of person she was. Helvarr knew the moment she spat in his face, insulted him, and challenged him with the same glare he'd seen so often in Oharra's eyes, he knew then that Correlyn was a fierce woman not to be reckoned with and it didn't take much more convincing for him to grow to love her.

Correlyn was everything he dreamed she would be. She was smart, witty, funny, beautiful, stubborn, and deadly. He couldn't help but feel an overwhelming sense of pride at the woman she grew to be, but then a stab of pain dulled that feeling because he knew he had nothing to do with it. Oharra had raised their daughter alone and taught her from a young age to fight and take care of herself. He could see the pain in Oharra's eyes when she realized that Correlyn would never again accept her as her mother, and yet she continued to push Correlyn to the breaking point. Was this what she wanted? To force Correlyn into killing her, as if to prove a point? Helvarr couldn't believe it. Oharra wanted more, and they had worked so hard to get their family back together and claim Godstone. Why would she throw all that away?

Helvarr couldn't blame Correlyn for killing her, not really. Oharra was out of control, and he knew it, yet his love for her never died. She had been the one thing holding him together throughout his banishment, and he knew she risked everything to help him get back. He never expected Correlyn to forgive Oharra for what she'd done, not after she was forced to watch Magister Ivann be slaughtered. Helvarr didn't know at the time what Oharra planned to do but he liked to think he would've stopped it if he had. But would he? He stood by for so much of Correlyn's torment and held his tongue while Ser Oby broke her ankle, beat her, choked her, and threatened her. Yet even Ser Oby knew what a monster Oharra was and gave up his life to try to get Correlyn out. He wondered when Ser Oby had decided to betray them and help Correlyn escape. Helvarr had almost been relieved to find out she'd escaped but at the same time, he couldn't let her go.

He wasn't ready to give up hope that he could have some sliver of a relationship with his daughter. He had a lifetime of sins to make up for, but he would spend the rest of his life trying to prove himself to Correlyn if he had to. He wouldn't give up on his daughter until the day he was dead, and even then, Helvarr knew he'd fight the gods himself to be allowed to walk the earth as a ghost and keep watch over Correlyn. He had destroyed so much, taken so many lives, but there was still one thing he could do right.

Helvarr looked back to Oharra's closed eyes and felt his own start to water. He let go of her hand and reached out to brush a strand of hair behind her ear. Leaning down, he pressed his lips against her cheek. She was cold but soft. A tear slipped down his cheek as he closed his eyes and whispered, "I love you, my lady of ravens." Then he stood up and didn't look back as he walked out of the Hall.

The screams of his men drifted over the wall and disturbed that quiet place he'd been in. The blood moon was receding in the sky, and the sun would soon be up. Helvarr made his way to the western wall, picking up his pace and listening to the screams grow louder and louder. He peered out over the edge of the wall, expecting to see two armies slaughtering one another and King Rayner fighting with his family. Instead, one woman stood in the center of his men, surrounded by mounds of bodies. Her hair was whiter than snow, and her arms seemed to glow with strange marks. Helvarr had never seen anything like her before, but he recalled reading something once in a citadel in Volantar.

He shook his head, trying to make the woman disappear from his vision, but she was still there. Helvarr looked down at the raiders standing at the gate, shaking in their boots. He needed to get everyone back inside before his entire army was wiped out by one woman. "Open the gate!" he screamed. The raiders snapped their attention to Helvarr and hesitated before swinging the gates open. "Get inside!" he ordered. Other men began to yell, telling everyone to retreat back inside.

Helvarr scanned the field and the distant woodline, but he didn't see any sign of King Rayner's army or anyone. What happened? Why wasn't King Rayner fighting his men? He looked back to the woman who had her arms stretched out, fists clenched. A few of his raiders tried to run back with the rest of the army, but she held them in place, and Helvarr watched in horror as she snapped their necks without laying a finger on them. His stomach turned at the thought that one woman had killed a sizeable chunk of his army. Scanning the sea of bodies, his eyes settled on a group of raiders.

They were scattered in the snow, at least twenty of them. Helvarr could see some had missing limbs, and others' heads were severed entirely from their bodies. It couldn't have been the woman who did that. She wasn't even touching his men and yet she managed to kill so many. He squinted and leaned over the wall, scanning every face he could make out until he saw him. "No…"

Helvarr's heart thumped in his ears. He tried to blink away the face, but he remained. Sprawled out in the middle of the raiders was Ronin, his former trainer, and father. Helvarr felt sick;

he doubled over, his breathing coming too fast. Ronin couldn't be dead; the man was a legend, unkillable. He'd taught Helvarr everything he knew. He admitted to being his father and at the time, Helvarr didn't want to believe it, but it explained so much.

Ronin was always watching Helvarr, trying to lead him on the right path and teach him to control his anger. He had so many opportunities to tell Helvarr the truth, yet he chose a moment when it was too late. What had he expected Helvarr to do? Throw down his sword and embrace him? Tell his army to go back to King Caato? It was too late, and Ronin knew it. He often wondered if Ronin felt responsible for Magnus's death and for everything that Helvarr did. Helvarr used his anger and hate that day to thrust his dagger into Magnus's heart. He felt the stab as much as Magnus did, but he couldn't back down. He'd gone too far and done too much to lie down and die.

Helvarr struggled his whole life with his demons, and yet Ronin never thought about telling him the truth. Helvarr wondered if Ronin showed the same coldness toward Correlyn as he did with Helvarr. Ronin was her grandfather, and if he had told Helvarr the truth years ago, perhaps things could have been different. Ronin might have stayed in Godstone forever, he would have had a relationship with Helvarr and his granddaughter. But it was too late for all that now. Helvarr and Correlyn were the last ones left in their family, and he had to do everything he could to keep it that way.

He stood up and took a deep breath. Helvarr didn't want to be like Ronin and abandon his child. He wouldn't. Helvarr could still turn things around and be a better father than Ronin ever was. He looked down at the field again, but the woman was gone, and all his men were gathered inside the walls. Helvarr shouted to a few men standing near the gate and commanded them to go back out there and retrieve Ronin's body. They exchanged a look and poked their head out the gate to make sure the woman was gone before running over to where Helvarr pointed. Ronin's body was carried through the sea of the fallen and toward Godstone.

A THOUSAND LIFETIMES

Kyatta walked through the cold, silent trees of the Blackwoods. The moon had since been pushed out of the sky, and the sun was just about to come up. Using her powers all night left her feeling utterly drained and weak, but still, she couldn't rest. She didn't want to go back to the camp, not just yet. She needed time to clear her head.

Kyatta knew that Grimm must have been going insane the longer she stayed away. She wondered if he would look at her differently once he saw all the bodies, all the men she'd killed. She'd broken her bloodstone and given in to her powers fully. If she was honest, Kyatta was surprised she walked out of there alive. Kyatta knew full well what she was doing when she broke the stone and expected to be one of those bodies that now lay cold in the field.

The raiders retreated just in time because the sun was on its way, and Kyatta knew that she would be killed the moment her powers left her. She wondered why Helvarr had called them back. Perhaps he had been out there in the field with his men, and he too now lay dead. Kyatta couldn't remember the faces of the men she killed. Her powers blocked the part of her brain that allowed her to remember, and for that, she was grateful, but it also made her dangerous.

Kyatta recalled the night Grimm brought her out of her murderous state back on Starry Point. She'd been hurting Ivy, but she didn't know it at the time. She had no control over who she hurt; her brain just told her to kill anyone who got in her way. It made her sick to think about. Sighing, she sat down under a tree and drew her knees up under her chin. The world was turning gray in the first light of day, and Kyatta knew she had to go back. She didn't want to be questioned or swarmed the second she walked into camp. All she wanted was to curl up in Grimm's arms and sleep.

Kyatta recalled the night she went to him and how he told her story after story just to help her fall asleep. She had been nervous about using her powers, and she could sense that Grimm was worried for her, too, but he held her together anyway and pushed his fears aside. She felt guilty about using her powers on him last night, but she didn't have a choice. Grimm was extremely protective, and she knew that there was no way he was going to let her go.

She pushed off the ground and started back to camp. They would only come looking for her if she didn't come back. The tents rose up in the distance, and Kyatta moved around the outskirts to keep from being spotted. Smoke drifted up into the sky from several fires still burning around camp. She had hoped everyone would be sleeping, and she'd be able to walk through without being seen. What did everyone think of her? Did they all make it back safely before she crushed the bloodstone and went on a killing rampage? Kyatta felt a sick twisting in her gut at the thought of killing one of her people. The elderly women who had trained her felt the full wrath of her powers when they tried to interfere.

She moved silently around the backs of tents, keeping out of sight of Rayner's knights. She couldn't face them all—not yet. She hesitated before stepping into Grimm's tent just as a few knights came around the corner. Kyatta stood silently just inside the flap until they passed by.

The tent was dark, save for a dim light from the dying fire. She stepped closer and saw Grimm, curled up in the furs on the floor with one arm outstretched as if reaching for something. Behind him, an empty flagon lay tipped over on the furs. His breathing was deep and heavy with sleep. She stared at him for a moment, taking in his broad shoulders, his short blond-red beard, the swirls of black running down either side of his scalp. Kyatta slowly lowered herself down beside him, keeping her eyes on his face. She gently lifted his outstretched arm and placed it on her waist and scooched closer. His breath was warm against her forehead, and Kyatta felt a sense of calm wash over her.

She reached a finger up to brush over his lips. He was the most handsome man she'd ever seen. Tall, broad, and strong, but she knew how soft and kind he was on the inside, with those he loved. Grimm loved with everything he had; she'd seen it with Ivy and her family. The way Grimm lost himself the night that Ivy fell from the ship into the sea. Kyatta saw then just how hard he loved when he let himself get close to someone. She told herself for a long time that she didn't love him. She thought he would never feel the same, but she still couldn't deny how she felt. Grimm guarded his feelings, building a wall of armor around it until someone strong enough finally broke through. Kyatta never meant to fall in love with Grimm.

She edged closer, wanting to feel the heat of his body alongside hers. Their faces were mere inches apart. She lifted her hand again and cupped his cheek and saw his eyes start to move under their lids. He mumbled something, and she ran her thumb over his cheek. "Kyatta…" he whispered. Her heart fluttered as Grimm began to stir awake.

Grimm cracked his eyes open, blinking rapidly as if trying to discern whether he was still dreaming or not. "Kyatta," he repeated, locking eyes on her. She smiled and ran her thumb across his lips, feeling his warm breath on her fingertip. His eyes grew wider as he realized it wasn't a dream. He shot up to a sitting position and looked down at her, his head shaking as if his eyes were deceiving him. Kyatta sat up too and held her breath, waiting for what he'd say.

"You are here," he whispered, his voice raspy. "You are all right, you are—" Tears formed in his eyes, and Grimm pulled her in before he could finish his thought.

"I'm here," Kyatta whispered against his ear. Grimm's arms wrapped around her, and Kyatta allowed him to pull her onto his lap. He stroked her hair, squeezing her tighter with his other arm. Kyatta began to cry, and she could feel Grimm's body shaking beneath her. His powerful arms gently held her together as she quietly wept. Her arms wound tight around his neck, and she buried her face, letting her tears wet his beard.

"I'm sorry, Grimm—" she choked on the words. He hushed her and hugged her tighter, pressing her into his chest, like he never wanted to let her go. Kyatta cried even harder at that. Grimm had likely gone mad last night and drank himself to sleep, yet here he was, holding her together and letting her cry through her fears. He never put himself before anyone, never allowed his feelings to trump those of the people around him. Grimm brought his lips to her ear and whispered, "I love you."

Kyatta stopped breathing. He'd said the words to her back in the Moon Wood, but this felt different. Grimm drew back to look at her and gently cradled her face, wiping away her tears with his thumbs as they fell. "I thought I lost you." His voice sounded distant. Kyatta put her hands against his chest, feeling how quickly his heart was pounding. She wrapped her legs around his waist to face him fully, and he kept his hands resting against her cheeks. "I tried to come after you," he admitted, and Kyatta felt the knot in her stomach twist. "I went mad, I tried to think of every possible way that I could get to you, but they would not let me." Grimm's eyes were more intense than she'd ever seen them.

"I got back here and started thinking about all the things I wanted to say to you and never got the chance. That I might not ever get the chance again. I thought about all the time I wasted being afraid to get close to you just because I did not want to lose you. It was stupid and selfish."

Kyatta didn't breathe, didn't dare move or speak. Her heart hummed loudly in her ears.

"You have had me since the first time I saw you smile, *really* smile," Grimm said. "And you have locked me in with every smile since. Every giggle, every sharp look you gave me. The way your brow lifts slightly when you're thinking. So do not tell me you are sorry because I am the one who has everything to be sorry about.

"After I kissed you that night in the Moon Wood, I thought I would have you forever. But then last night you were just…gone. Alone with an army coming after you, and I thought of every single thing I never said to you and felt sick at the thought that you might die alone, thinking there was no one out there who loved you. If I could go back and do it again, I would have told you sooner. I would have told you how you drive me crazy. How you kicking my ass in the pit only made me love you more. How you have completely destroyed me in the best possible way. I have been powerless to you all along.

"I am sorry for the time we wasted, and I want to make up that time with you, Kyatta. A lifetime with you would not be enough. I will find you in the next life whenever that comes, I will find you again and will not waste a single second on being afraid to get close to you. I would trade anything for a thousand lifetimes with you. I am completely in love with you, Kyatta of the Moon Wood, and I will do anything to keep you by my side forever."

Kyatta couldn't breathe or even blink. Grimm looked at her in a way that made her feel completely exposed yet comfortable. He dropped his hands from her cheeks and let them rest on top of her thighs. Kyatta brought her hands up his chest, feeling his heart flutter as she snaked her fingers around his neck and locked them.

She had so many things she wanted to say, so much she wanted to tell him, but she only said, "I love you too, Grimm." She swore his body relaxed with utter relief. "I have for a long time," she whispered. Grimm watched her lips, and before she knew it, she was kissing him.

Grimm grabbed her face, caressing her cheeks. His kiss was so soft and gentle, it made her want to cry. She could feel the love with every brush of his lips against hers. She shifted in his lap, hooking her ankles behind his back, and Grimm's hands slid back to tangle in her hair. He parted his lips slightly, and Kyatta let her tongue slip between them. He groaned against her lips, and heat pooled between her legs at the sound. He slid his hands down to her waist, untucking her tunic and allowing his fingers to trail across the small of her back. Kyatta arched, and Grimm grabbed her around the back and lifted her from his lap before laying her down on the furs ever so gently. Grimm kissed his way down her neck and Kyatta turned her head, exposing more skin for his lips to taste. His fingers began unlacing her pants and she grabbed the back of his head as his teeth grazed her collarbone.

He pulled her pants down and she lifted her hips to help him, then she sat up and leaned away from him. Grimm's eyes were dialated as he stared at her. "We do not—"

He began to say, then stopped as Kyatta lifted her shirt and threw it off to the side. Grimm's mouth hung open slightly as his eyes traveled over her naked form. His eyes followed the tattoos at the top of her arm, where the pattern swirled at her collarbone and dipped down to the center of her chest. She felt vulnerable under Grimm's eyes as they traveled across every swirl of black ink.

His eyes found hers again. Grimm peeled his shirt off and Kyatta's breath caught in her throat. She'd seen him shirtless before, but this was different. She took her time running her eyes over his many tattoos, his pecs and his chiseled stomach. Desire buzzed in her stomach at the man before her. Grimm ran his hand up one of her legs and hooked it behind her bent knee, then gently laid her back down. Their lips crashed together again as Grimm worked with one hand to unbutton his pants. He struggled slightly and Kyatta smiled against his lips. He pulled back to look at her. "Are you laughing at me?" he asked, smirking.

Kyatta shrugged her shoulder. "Maybe."

Grimm lowered his lips to her ear, gently nibbling her lobe. She shivered as he whispered, "And here I was, ready to pleasure you."

"Don't stop," she said in a breathy voice not her own.

Grimm leaned back and smiled. "Would you mind repeating that?"

She snarled and he grinned. Kyatta grabbed the back of his head and brought his ear to her lips. "I said, don't stop." Her tongue traveled down the side of his neck and Grimm's whole body went rigid. "Pleasure me, Grimm."

He groaned as he began kissing her neck, then their lips crashed together again. His hand traveled up the curve of her hips to her chest as he tasted the skin at the base of her throat. Kyatta shifted beneath him and Grimm grabbed her hips and lifted them. Her entire body was on fire, every nerve in her burned for him and they finally came together. Grimm whispered her name once, twice as their hips moved together and Kyatta melted for him. He grabbed the back of her head and pressed his chest into hers. He kissed her again, slow and tender this time and she threw her arms around his neck. Grimm wrapped his arm around her back and sat up, pulling Kyatta into his lap. She moaned slightly at the shift in position and Grimm's breathing was fast and uneven as she moved against him. Her hair cascaded down her back and she tilted her head, exposing her neck. Grimm grabbed her neck and pressed gentle kisses to both collarbones then slowly made his way to her chest. Her cheeks flushed as she looked down at him. She slowed her movements then pressed her hand flat against his chest, pushing him to lay back in the furs. Grimm's eyes never wavered from hers. Kyatta leaned over him, bracing her hands on either side of his head as her hair slipped over her shoulder and hung like a curtain around them. Grimm grabbed her hips as she lowered herself on him, and his grip tightened. She smiled and kissed him again as they tangled in the furs until they were both exhausted and out of breath.

Afterward, Kyatta lay on her back, trying to catch her breath as Grimm did the same next to her. The camp was awake by then, and voices could be heard outside the tent, but Kyatta still didn't want to go out there. She wanted to stay in this moment, with Grimm forever. He rolled over and propped himself up on an elbow, looking down at her. She smiled and reached out to caress his cheek. Grimm closed his eyes and leaned in to her touch and kissed the palm of her hand. "A thousand lifetimes." His voice was soft and sweet. Kyatta lifted, bringing her lips just under his.

"Starting now," she replied and kissed him again. Grimm quickly scooped her up, forcing a surprised shriek to escape her. Kyatta laughed and hooked her ankles around his back as Grimm stood up. He kissed her all the way to the bed before setting her down. Kyatta laid back and Grimm crawled over her, kissing her stomach and the center of her chest where the ink stopped and letting his lips travel up to her collarbone, her neck, before finding her lips again. She craved him in a way she'd never felt before, and Grimm seemed happy to satisfy. He lowered down onto her, and Kyatta moaned against his lips at the pure pleasure that washed over her from head to every curling toe.

Grimm knew they stayed like that well into the morning before Kyatta finally curled up against his chest and drifted off to sleep. He pulled a fur over them and listened to her soft breathing and savored the feeling of her warm breath against his chest. Grimm allowed himself this time with Kyatta, knowing everyone else was likely worried about her. But he had time to make up for, and for once he let himself be selfish and give in to what he wanted. They were making up time lost, and still had a thousand lifetimes to go, starting now.

A FIGHTING CHANCE

Ivy slipped out from under Finn's arms and quietly got out of bed. Last night came back to her in flashes. The way Finn's hands roamed her body, how his breath in her ear sent fire to her belly. She looked at him now. His hair was tousled, and his back rose and fell with deep, sleepy breaths. Finn had been through so much, and it angered Ivy to think of it. She got dressed quickly and kissed Finn's cheek before slipping out of the tent.

Outside, the sun was just beginning to crest the horizon, and the world was still painted in shades of gray-blue. Ivy made her way to the horses and saddled the first one she saw before taking off. She rode south toward the battlefield. Ivy didn't know what she expected to find when she got there. Would Kyatta be walking back to camp? Would she have to see Ronin's body?

She had seen Ronin fall when a group of raiders swarmed him. She knew he was gone—she could feel it like a cold empty hole in her core. She felt it in her bones like that way she felt it when her father fell.

Ivy slowed her horse to a trot as she came up over the hill. Her stomach flipped. The battlefield was strewn with bodies—hundreds of them. They lay cold in the snow-covered field that was now bright with blood. The full destruction of Kyatta's wrath.

She scanned the bodies, looking for one with a head of white hair. But they were too far off to see, and Ivy didn't dare get any closer. Helvarr could be watching from the walls.

Kyatta was nowhere in sight, and that worried Ivy even more. How could she have let her friend walk off alone? To face an entire army by herself, with no one to back her up? Cold, hard guilt stabbed her at the thought. Ivy dared a few steps closer, looking for another body that wasn't there. There were so many men that Ronin could be any one of them. Ivy couldn't explain the connections she felt with people. Like how she was sure Correlyn was alive for all those months, or how she could still feel Rayner when he was thought to have been dead. She could feel it now, with Kyatta. But where was she?

Ivy turned back and headed toward the camp. She swung down from her horse when she spotted Aska and Arytin sitting by a fire. Aska lifted her eyes to Ivy as she came closer. She lifted her chin defiantly and stood up to leave before Ivy could say anything. Arytin shrugged his shoulders and motioned for Ivy to come sit by the fire. He offered her a mug of tea, which Ivy took but mostly used it to warm her hands. Ivy kept her eyes on the fire, but she could feel Arytin watching her.

"She's angry with me," Ivy said quietly.

Arytin shifted toward her. "She just wanted to help. We all did."

Ivy looked up at him, and his dark eyes were locked on her. "I'm sorry," she said. "I didn't mean to upset you, I was just...scared."

Arytin took her hand in his. "You could never upset me, Stormbringer." He winked and released her hand, taking a sip of his tea. "My cousin, on the other hand, is...sensitive."

Ivy raised a brow. "Aska? Sensitive?"

Arytin smiled at her. "She's more complicated than her quick tongue lets off." They both chuckled, Arytin watching her over the brim of his cup. Ivy grew quiet and stared into the flames, listening to the camp come to life around them. She needed to find

Kyatta, but where? And she needed to apologize for snapping at Aska. Arytin broke her from her thoughts.

He leaned in close. "I'm sorry."

"For what?" She turned to face him.

"For everything that's happened to you. Your friends, your family. I came to help you, so don't push us away. We all know what's at stake." He sat back, observing her. "You remind me of Nova." Ivy blushed. Nova had been Arytin's best friend back on Starry Point. She knew how much her death had hurt him. "Nova was so willing to put others before herself that she never thought to guard her back against a knife." Ivy lost her smile and looked down at her boots. Arytin grew quiet as well, studying his tea as if it were the most interesting thing.

Ivy hesitated before speaking. "You loved her."

Arytin seemed to flinch and snap out of his blank gaze. He kept his eyes down, nodding slowly. "I never got the chance to tell her." Ivy felt her heart snap for him. She could sense there was something more that Arytin left out whenever he talked about Nova.

"Does Aska know? Or Macon?"

Arytin only shook his head.

Ivy reached out and took his hand. "I'm sorry." He turned to her, his eyes deep, dark pools. "Nova was like so many other people," she went on. "Willing to lay down their lives for those they love. I think you'll find more of those people the more you look."

Arytin ran his thumb over the back of her hand. "I already have."

Ivy smiled. "I hope you find someone who makes you happy."

Arytin gave her a shy grin, then looked past her and gestured to someone. "Is he your happiness?"

Ivy turned to see Finn walked toward them. "Yes."

Arytin released her hand and nodded to Finn before leaving them. Finn beamed when he rested his eyes on Ivy. He leaned in and kissed her cheek before pulling her in for a hug. Ivy breathed in his scent. Finn leaned back, brushing her hair from her cheek. "Where did you go?"

Ivy held his gaze. "I had to see it for myself." She looked past him as if she could see the battlefield from there. The bodies piled up in the snow. Finn shoved his hands in his pockets and looked down.

"I'm sorry about last night," he said. His brown hair hung over his eyes. "I didn't mean to…use you like that."

Ivy furrowed her brow and lifted his chin, "Don't apologize. I needed it too." And she did. Ivy needed any distraction she could get. If it hadn't been Finn, it would have been a sword in her hand or a flagon of wine. Anything to cut or drown out the screaming chaos in her head.

Finn stepped up to her, his russet eyes soft but intense. "Did you sleep all right?" he looked genuinely concerned. Ivy smiled and wrapped her arms around his neck. "I always sleep better when you're beside me."

Finn smiled shyly and leaned in to kiss her. It was long and deep. "I love you," he said against her lips.

Ivy's heart fluttered. She didn't think she'd ever get sick of hearing those words. "I love you too, my Finn." He chuckled against her lips and wrapped his hands around her waist, kissing her in the middle of the camp while people strolled by, going about their business.

Rayner walked through the camp, his hands buried in his pockets and head down. The sun was working its way higher into the sky, and Rayner knew he couldn't waste any more time. Correlyn had been a steel trap last night and wouldn't talk to Rayner about what happened. He let her cry in his arms until she ran out of tears, and her eyes lids grew heavy.

Rayner hadn't expected Correlyn to kill Oharra, but he couldn't blame her. He still didn't know all the details of what happened during her captivity, but he imagined the worst. Oharra was a monster, and Rayner knew that. As much as he wanted her dead for what she'd done, it still came as a shock. He knew Correlyn had more reason for wanting Oharra dead, and it was her revenge to take, but Rayner didn't feel any better about what Oharra had done to him. He wondered if he would have felt better if he'd been the one to kill her.

Rayner imagined that Correlyn didn't shed those tears for her mother's death, but for what she came to be. How Oharra had pushed Correlyn to the breaking point, and in the end, Correlyn gave her exactly what she expected. He could also see that Correlyn felt sorry for Helvarr, whether she would admit it or not. Helvarr was so desperate to have a relationship with his daughter that he was willing to give up everything he'd taken. It pained Rayner to see his wife so torn between what to do. He knew she was confused by it all, not knowing what to feel or what to believe. Even Rayner had been confused by the desperation in Helvarr's eyes. He was sincere in his offer and truly believed that Correlyn might want to repair their relationship. What had happened between the two?

Rayner didn't ask. Correlyn would tell him everything in her own time. Right now, he needed to find Kyatta because no matter how many men she might have taken out, any amount heightened their chances of winning. He only hoped that Kyatta had survived.

He made his way toward Grimm's tent, nodding at his knights as he passed. Grimm would want to join him in searching for Kyatta. If she hadn't come back, she could be hurt somewhere. Rayner spotted Ivy and Finn, wrapped in each other's arms and kissing in the center of the camp. He paused for a moment, smiling at their happiness before turning away.

He tapped on the flap of Grimm's tent. "Grimm?" he called. No one answered, but he heard movement inside. Rayner stepped inside the tent, and it was dim and warm. Grimm walked over to him, shirtless and tying the laces on his pants. His hair was messy and his cheeks red. "I'm going to find Kyatta. I thought you'd like to go." Grimm gave him a shy smile before stepping aside. Rayner looked back to the bed and saw a head of white hair swept across the pillows and Kyatta's bare back poking up from under the furs. Rayner started to speak but snapped his mouth shut.

Grimm stepped back to block his view and crossed his arms against his bare chest. Rayner lowered his voice to a whisper. "When did she get back? What happened? Is she all right?" The rapid-fire questions made Grimm smile. He held up a hand to stop the king's chattering.

"She got back before sunrise, and she is fine. She needed to rest."

Rayner smirked, crossing his arms and gesturing to the bed. "Rest, huh?"

Grimm narrowed his eyes and Rayner grinned even bigger.

"Right. Well, both of you need to come to see me when you're done...*resting.*"

"Of course, Your Grace." Grimm gave Rayner a dramatic bow, and Rayner smacked his arm and laughed before stepping out of the tent.

Kyatta was alive and unharmed. He still didn't know how much of Helvarr's army she had gone through, but he could feel it in his bones. They would come up with a plan and move out soon. The longer they waited, the more time Helvarr had to plan. Now they would go and take their home back. Now they had a fighting chance.

THE FINAL NIGHT

After going over plans all day, straining his eyes on maps, and arguing with Grimm, Rayner finally let himself relax. Grimm and Kyatta had come to him earlier that day, and she told the king everything about what happened the night before. At least what she could piece together from the carnage that lay in the field. Grimm and Rayner had argued about Kyatta using her powers again when they stormed Godstone. Rayner had insisted that it wasn't up to them, that Kyatta needed to decide for herself. Grimm thought that was utter madness and angered at the thought of her being in danger like that again. After what seemed like endless hours, Kyatta finally stepped forward and claimed that she wouldn't use her powers again. Not when she would be in such close proximity to Rayner's men and could potentially hurt the wrong people. Grimm's whole body had shuddered with relief, and Rayner didn't argue further.

Tomorrow night they would finally get their home back. Tomorrow night would be the start of everything. But as Rayner sat back in his chair and looked around to all the smiling faces, he couldn't help but worry that this was the final night that he would see some of those faces. The final night that they would all be together like this, maybe forever.

Rayner sat alone, scanning the crowd, and sipping his wine. A feast had been put together to honor Ronin and to celebrate his life. A large tent had been set up in the center of the camp, and all four walls were left rolled up. Large bonfires dotted the land, and the beat of drums and other instruments drifted through the camp on a breeze.

He spotted his beautiful queen from across the tent. Rayner smiled as he looked at her; Correlyn wore a dark dress that trailed in the snow behind her and a fur-lined cloak that rose high on her neck. Her midnight hair was messily braided and thrown over one shoulder carelessly. She was seated beside Elana, who was beaming with happiness and rubbing small circles on her growing belly. Lord Cylas sat next to her, snaking a protective hand around her waist.

Rayner wondered what would become of his mother and Lord Cylas when the war was over. He noticed they had been spending a lot of time alone together as if they knew it was almost over and that they may be forced apart again. Lord Cylas would never abandon his city and offer to stay with her in Godstone. Rayner knew he loved Elana; he could see it in the way he looked at her when his mother's attention was elsewhere. But he had a city to run and people to protect.

Rayner averted his eyes, not wanting to think about his mother in pain again. He looked to the other side of the tent and saw Grimm and Kyatta sitting side by side. Their hands were clasped above the table, and their eyes locked. Rayner smirked. It was about time Grimm stopped fighting against what he wanted. He'd never seen Grimm like that before. His eyes lit up whenever he spotted Kyatta; his back went rigid, and he couldn't fight the smile that spread across his lips. Rayner was happy for his friend. Grimm turned and caught Rayner staring. He glared playfully at the king to which Rayner grinned and lifted his cup.

A loud cackle turned his attention. At a table just outside the tent, Macon and Arytin appeared to be arm wrestling while Aska judged from across the table. Macon slammed Arytin's arm down on the table, right into a meat pie that just so happened to grow legs and move across the table on its own. Aska threw her head back in laughter, almost falling backwards off the bench. Arytin grimaced and flicked the pie at his cousin before getting to his feet and jumping over the table. Aska dodged him and took off running, while Macon smiled triumphantly at his victory. Rayner shook his head but allowed himself to smile. The feuding cousins from Starry Point had become a welcomed part of their group. It lifted the spirits of so many, and Rayner knew they would be sorely missed once they returned home.

Luna came and perched on the back of Rayner's chair, ruffling her orange feathers. Rayner turned sideways, throwing his legs over the armrest and reaching up to stroke Luna. She cocked her head, carefully watching the surroundings of her new king. Rayner had managed to keep Luna away from the raiders last night, but he knew they would need her help tomorrow. Luna lowered her head as if she understood the king's struggle. "You'll be all right, won't you, Luna?" he said quietly. She lifted her head and blinked at him before stretching her massive wings and sweeping through the tent without a sound.

His eyes trailed after her and outside, he noticed it had begun to snow. The musicians took shelter under the tent and began to play a joyful tune. The strumming of strings and beating of drums filled the air with their rhythm. Luna swooped down low, her tail ablaze and creating small sparks of ash that drifted down with the snow. Everyone was smiling, laughing, and joking, and Rayner let himself feel all of it. Every smile, every giggle, every sound of pure happiness, not tainted by worry and loss. Because tomorrow, some of those faces would be gone.

He spotted his sister, swaying to the beat of the music. Finn's arms were gently wrapped around her waist, and his gaze locked on hers, as if she were the only person in the world. Ivy hugged Finn close, and then she motioned for someone over Finn's shoulder, her grin wicked. Rayner scanned the crowd and saw Piotr sneaking behind Finn, a large horn in his hand and a mischievous smile plastered on his face. Ivy pushed away from Finn suddenly, just as Piotr tipped the horn over Finn's head, soaking him with a dark ale.

Ivy and Piotr both doubled over in laughter. Finn whipped around, and Piotr cursed, then took off in a sprint. He turned back to Ivy with a smile on his face as he tried to grab her. Ivy slipped through his fingers and ran in the direction Piotr had gone. Finn chased after, pushing knights from his path and nearly slipping in the snow.

Ivy grabbed Arytin by the collar and yanked him to his feet as she passed. Finn collided with him, and they went tumbling to the ground. Aska spit up her ale and laughed until her face was beat red. Arytin scowled as he got to his feet, scooping up some snow as he did. He rolled it in his hands and threw it. The snowball exploded on Aska's cheek and she stopped laughing to wipe the snow from her face before launching to her feet and scooping up some snow in one swift motion. Rayner leaned forward in his chair to watch as a snow war broke out in the camp.

I vy ducked under a snowball and returned fire, hitting Finn in the shoulder. Piotr came out of nowhere and shoved a snowball down Finn's back. His eyes grew wide and he hissed through his teeth at the icy bite. Turning away, Ivy spotted Arytin and hit him in the back of the head. He turned, locked eyes with her, and charged. Ivy shrieked with laughter as she evaded her attacker. Aska and Macon took up posts on opposite ends of the large table and began to rapid-fire on each other. A stray snowball hit Grimm in the center of his back, and he shot to his feet, scanning the group when his eyes fell on Ivy. She stared back at him, a challenge in her eyes as she casually tossed a snowball up and down in her hand. Grimm cocked his head, daring her to throw it. Ivy obliged and aimed for his head, but he caught it and crushed the snowball, letting it slip through his splayed fingers.

"Shit," Ivy said, lowering her arm which was still raised from the throw.

Grimm grinned. "Yes," he said, slowly bending down and scooping up a massive amount of snow before crushing it into a ball. *"Shit."*

Ivy smiled as he stood up straight and began walking toward her.

"Run!" Kyatta yelled from behind him, giggling.

Grimm whirled on her, feigning hurt. "Whose side are you on?"

Kyatta only shrugged, smirking.

Grimm whirled around, throwing the snowball as he did. Ivy barely had time to dodge, throwing her head back as the snowball sailed over her face. She righted herself and glared at Grimm, who was now charging her.Everyone turned on Grimm and began to fire, but his eyes stayed locked on Ivy. He caught up to her and grabbed Ivy around the waist, lifting her like she was made of cotton and throwing her over his shoulder. Grimm spun Ivy around and she took two snowballs to the back that were meant for him. He chuckled as she pounded her fists into his solid back, but then he slipped. They went crashing down into the snow face-first.

Ivy rolled off him and tried to catch her breath as he did the same. They laid on their backs and Ivy turned to look at him. "I'm happy for you and Kyatta," she said between breaths.

Grimm turned to look at her, still smiling. "Your brother told you?"

"He didn't need to. I see the way you look at one another."

Grimm reached out, taking Ivy's hand in his. "Thank you."

Ivy propped herself on an elbow and leaned in. "You sure are a softy for such a large man."

Grimm shoved Ivy away playfully, his cheeks burning bright

red. Ivy leaned back in and gave him a quick peck on the cheek. "I love you, softy."

Grimm got up and offered his hand to Ivy. "I love you too, Iron Heart." He hauled Ivy to standing, then wrapped his arm around her shoulder as they made their way back to the tent.

Ivy spotted Aska sitting with her family. They still hadn't really talked since Ivy yelled at her the night of the blood moon. Grimm seemed to read her mind and slipped away to find Kyatta as Ivy made her way toward the Cosmians. Arytin spotted her and winked, then grabbed Macon's collar and pulled him to his feet, giving the two some privacy. She sat down next to Aska, whose eyes were focused on the dancers, twirling around in the snow. Aska handed Ivy a horn of ale without looking. They sat silently for a moment. Ivy took a sip of ale and turned to face her. "I'm sorry I snapped at you. I didn't mean it. We're all grateful for your help. We might not have gotten Correlyn back if it wasn't for Macon, and I would be dead in the Siren Sea if it wasn't for you."

Aska grinned into her cup and gave Ivy a nudge in the ribs. "It's all right, Stormbringer. No harm done."

Ivy let go a sigh of relief.

"I'm going to miss all of you," Aska said, turning her attention back to the camp. Ivy followed her gaze and felt a pang in her heart. Ivy had grown so close to everyone in such a short amount of time, and in a way, they were like family. Thoughts of Aska and her family leaving plagued her, but the battle was upon them. It was almost over.

"We'll miss you too." Ivy said, banishing her sorrow for another day. "But you're always welcome in the North."

"I know Ary will miss you." Aska mused, a smile pulling at the corner of her mouth. "He's grown very fond of you, Stormbringer. It seems you have that effect on people."

Ivy snickered. "And to think, he once threatened to hand me over to raiders."

Aska snorted and waved a dismissive hand. "Ary is so dramatic." They both chuckled.

Ivy set down her ale and turned to face her friend. "Will you promise me something?"

Aska wrinkled her nose. "That depends."

"When you get back home, will you talk to that girl? Valeria?"

Aska's cheeks immediately flushed with color. "Why do you—"

"I'm serious, Aska. You deserve to be happy, and you shouldn't be afraid of what others will think. Just promise me you'll at least talk to her."

Aska didn't answer and turned her eyes down to her ale.

Ivy sat up straight and crossed her arms. "The great Cosmian Aska, afraid of a black-haired beauty?" Ivy snorted and leaned in, locking eyes with her. "I thought you liked a challenge?"

Aska flashed her teeth but couldn't hide her smile. "Very well, Stormbringer. I accept your challenge." She held her hand between them and Ivy took it.

"Good."

Rayner sat alone, lost in thought as Earl Rorik came up to him, plopping down in Correlyn's chair with a sigh. "Are you enjoying yourself, Your Grace?"

"You don't have to call me that," Rayner insisted. "Just Rayner."

Earl Rorik grinned. "Are you enjoying yourself, *just Rayner*?"

Rayner rolled his eyes and chuckled, but his smile faded as he nodded in response. Rorik adjusted in his seat, turning to face him better. "Your father was very informal as well." Rayner lowered his eyes to the cup cradled in his hands. "A king with no crown," Rorik went on and Rayner heard the smile in his voice. "Magnus insisted he be treated like any of his other knights. Your father did not need titles or a ring of gold atop his head to earn respect. I think you will rule as your father did, and I know he would be proud." Earl Rorik reached out and gripped Rayner's shoulder, turning his attention. His smile was warm and Rayner couldn't help but return it.

"Thank you, Earl Rorik."

"Just Rorik," he replied with a wink. He patted Rayner's shoulder then got to his feet.

The earl bowed as he passed the queen as she made her way toward Rayner. He stood as Correlyn came closer. She tangled her fingers in his hair and pulled him in for a kiss. Rayner let his wine spill into the snow, then dropped his cup, slipping one hand around her waist while the other rested against her cold cheek. His heart played an uneven tune as she kissed him deeply, before leaning back to look in his eyes.

"Come," she whispered and grabbed his hand, leading him out of the tent. People moved from their path as Correlyn led him out into the snow. "Dance with me."

Rayner smiled as Correlyn wrapped her arms around his neck, and he placed his hands on her waist. They swayed slowly, and on cue, the musicians changed the music to better fit the king and queen's dance. "Do you remember the last time we danced?" she asked. Her eyes were dark pools of smoke.

Rayner remembered the night exactly. Their wedding had been the happiest day of his life. He smiled and brushed a stray hair behind her ear. "I remember stepping on your feet." Correlyn giggled, and it was far sweeter than the music that surrounded them.

Something shifted in her eyes, and Rayner furrowed his brow. He was sure many demons still haunted Correlyn, and he wished she would talk to him about it. Perhaps voicing her fears would just make it more real, and she'd rather forget. Rayner understood. He'd held onto his fear of the horned knight for too long, and it almost broke him. He lifted her chin, and she smiled, taking his hand in hers.

"When this is over," she started, her voice severe and

confident, "we will have to rebuild our home, our family. But it's also a chance to start something new." Rayner's heart fluttered with anticipation at what she was about to say. "I want to think about starting a family of our own."

Rayner stopped swaying and stood frozen in place. Rayner knew he wanted children with Correlyn, but he didn't expect her to want the same thing so soon. Especially after all that had happened to her. "Correlyn…you don't—*we* don't need to think about that right now. There's plenty of time, and I don't want you to feel rushed or—"

She pressed a finger to his lips. "It's all I thought about. You're all I thought about during my captivity. I want a family with you, Rayner. And you're right, there is no rush I just want us to start considering it. Do you want that?"

Rayner gently grabbed her face and brought his lips to hers. "Nothing would make me happier," he whispered.

Correlyn kissed him and then hugged him close, burying her face in the crook of his neck. "I love you, Rayner."

"I love you, my queen." They stayed wrapped in each other's arms and began to sway to the music.

All around them, people drank, and their laughter filled the air. Rayner let himself smile and soak up every feeling, every scent, and every sight. He could have never imagined the amount of pressure that would weigh on him when he became king. Especially one who wore no crown. Rayner tried to enjoy his final night with his family and friends, but there was a fear lurking amongst his people. It moved silently through the camp, wrapping its cold fingers around unsuspected victims and clouding their minds. Tomorrow was the beginning of the end– or was it just the end? Tomorrow night, everything would change, but right now, wrapped in Correlyn's arms, Rayner wasn't anxious to find out just what that change would bring.

UNBROKEN

Rayner checked his sword belt for the hundredth time that night. His armor was strapped, sword sheathed, and mind clear. They would win back Godstone tonight. They had to. His entire army was gathered just over the hill and out of sight. Atop his horse, Rayner trotted to the front line of his men, then dismounted, pacing in front of his people before turning to face them. He found comfort in the eyes of his wife, who smiled encouragingly.

Rayner brushed his hair back from his face and met every eye that stood in the front line. Ivy, Finn, and Piotr all watched him intently. Grimm and Kyatta stood side by side, backs straight, and faces stern. Lord Cylas stood beside Correlyn's horse with his hands clasped in front of him and a prideful smile on his face. Rayner took a breath and scanned the sea of men and women.

"Everything will change after tonight." He paused, and some leaned forward to hear their king. "I came to many of you on my knees, begging for your help." His eyes found Lord Cylas and Zion before he turned back to the army before him. "You could have turned me away. Told me that this was not your fight, and I wouldn't have had any right to argue. Those of you from the South could have turned their heads and let the North be taken, but you didn't. Some of you even offered your help without being asked." This he directed to Aska and her family.

"I can never repay you for your help, or your sacrifice in standing with us. But like my sister once said"—Ivy straightened under Rayner's gaze—"there is nothing to repay because we do not owe each other a debt. We are all fighting for the same thing, and Godstone is that first step toward a different future. Those of you who live south of the border have lived in fear for so long, have distanced yourselves, or stayed hidden. But no more. This change starts here by taking back the North and claiming what is ours. Helvarr is no king!" Rayner raised his voice and pointed in the direction of Godstone. "And there are no more kings in the southern mainland, and it will remain that way. Helvarr thinks he has a claim to my home, to *our* home. But we will show him that he's wrong! This—" Rayner drew his sword and plunged it into the earth. He bent down and scooped up a patch of frozen dirt, crumpling it in his hands.

"This is the North. This is our land!" He walked over to a knight and gestured for his hand, which the man produced. Rayner sprinkled some dirt into his palm and closed his fingers over it. "This is your land." He said to him before moving down the line. "This is the land of my ancestors." He sprinkled some dirt in Ivy's hand, and she smiled down at him. "This is the land of the first Daemonts!" Piotr's brow creased with sadness as he held out his hand. "The land of the first clansmen!" Rayner continued, offering soil to Grimm. "The land of those lost!" Finn lowered his eyes but held out his hand. "This has been our land." He stopped in front of Kyatta. "Since the moon first showed its face in the sky, and it will be our land until the moon is gone, and there is nothing more of this earth!"

Rayner reached up to his wife and wrapped her fingers around the last piece of frozen dirt. "Helvarr has challenged us, broken some of us, and killed more. But tonight, we return his wrath!" A few cheers rose up from within the crowd. "My father once said that sometimes the only weapon you have left is fear, so let's show them what that looks like. Some of you will fall tonight. Maybe it's the person next to you, perhaps it will be me, but not all of us will make it to see the sunrise again. But the sun will rise, and with it...the North." People began to cheer, thrusting their spears or swords into the air. Rayner felt his heart leap as more people began to roared in approval. His voice boomed out across the army. "So let's remind them of who we are. We are the North! Together!"

"Unbroken!" the army roared.

"Together!"

"Unbroken!" The army continued to cheer, and Rayner walked up to his wife's horse and took her hand, "Let's go get our home back."

ow, Rayner sat on his horse in front of half his army. Zion and Earl Rorik led the people from the Isle of Fire and the rest of the clansmen to wait just outside the northern gate. Once he gave the signal, they would attack from the north while Rayner's group hit the main gate. Rayner's heart was steadily thumping in his chest. He looked up to the sky and saw clusters of stars poking out through the slow-moving clouds. It would have to do. It was tonight or never.

He could hear raiders along the wall starting to yell orders as they spotted Rayner's army. He looked back over his shoulder. There must have been close to a thousand people formed up and hundreds more with Zion and Rorik. He told himself it was enough. That Kyatta had wiped out too many raiders, which now evened the odds. But Rayner still worried. He turned back and spotted braziers being lit along the wall and archers forming up. Piotr turned his horse to his men. "Get a wall of archers in front of the king. Now!"

"Yes, my lord," one his knights replied, and Piotr faltered at the title. He still wasn't used to being called lord, and Rayner wondered how he would react to the decision that he had yet to inform Piotr of. Piotr held his head high, and his men didn't seem to notice his discomfort.

Luna called out from above, and Rayner turned his head up to see her circling, her flames gone, waiting until she was signaled. He walked his horse a few paces ahead, Piotr's archers moving with him. "Helvarr!" he roared, letting the anger carry his voice. There was commotion behind the walls and raiders ran to their positions. Ivy came up alongside him and unsheathed Promise.

The gates opened slightly, and Helvarr came riding out on a black horse. Ivy's grip tightened as she recognized Eclipse, Ser Osmund's old horse. Finn had told them that he'd ridden Cassius when he was taken to Godstone and that her horse looked well. As Rayner looked at his sister, he could see the anger flickering in her purple eyes, though she seemed to be trying to hide it.

Helvarr stopped some distance away, eyeing the archers who nocked back arrows and took aim. Rayner held out a hand, and they lowered their bows and spread so that he could walk his horse closer. Helvarr looked unhinged, and it took Rayner by surprise. His black hair hung limp around his face, and his copper eyes that usually burned with rage seemed to have been doused. Rayner reminded himself that Helvarr had many masks, and that perhaps this was one. "King Rayner," Helvarr said slowly, caressing every syllable.

"It's over, Helvarr." He reeled back his anger. "This is your final chance."

Helvarr grinned. "Isn't it funny? We were here just months ago, though you were standing in my spot."

Rayner snarled.

"Did you give up then?" He tapped his chin. "No, you didn't. So why should I?"

"You're outnu—"

"You killed her!" Helvarr snapped and looked back to

Correlyn. Rayner blinked. He was falling apart at the seams. Helvarr smoothed his wild hair back. "She's gone, and now I have no one. This is what we fought for, she"—he pointed to Correlyn—"is what we fought for, and you want me to just lie down and die? No. If you want your home back so you can play king with my daughter"—his horse stepped closer—"then come and take it."

Rayner expected as much; he just needed Helvarr distracted for a few moments. His raiders had been slowly trickling out of the gates, the *wooden* gates. Rayner smirked, and Helvarr snarled at him. "Very well," Rayner drawled and lifted his fingers to his mouth and let out a shrill whistle. On command, Luna burst into flames and shot down from the sky like a dying star. Helvarr's eyes went wide as Luna flew straight at him before spreading her massive wings and gliding, heading right for the gates.

Raiders screamed and ran from her path. They tried to close the gates, but it was too late. Luna opened her beak and sent a comet of fire straight ahead. It hit with such an impact that one of the doors shattered and flew from the hinges. The other roared with fire and quickly began to split and crack. Rayner whistled again, and Luna took off north to aid Zion and Rorik as they broke in that gate. Helvarr was already riding back toward the entrance when Rayner looked up. Raiders along the wall began nocking back arrows while others poured out of the hole in the wall where the gate once sat. Rayner drew his sword and lifted it in the air, then swiped it down, and his army burst to life.

They screamed and charged ahead of the king. Piotr's archers stayed with him and began firing at the raiders along the wall. Rayner turned to Ivy and gave her a firm nod before they both took off. Rayner slashed his first raider as he charged through the body of men that writhed with battle. He saw a burst of fire in the distance and knew Zion and his people were fighting to get in. He tried to keep an eye on Ivy but realized she didn't need it.

Ivy jumped down from her horse and landed on a raider's back, sending Promise down the length of his spine. The man crumpled, and Ivy found her next victim. Finn ran alongside her, ducking and slashing their way closer to the wall. An arrow whizzed by her head, and Ivy turned to see the man nocking another back. She shoved Finn out of the way just in time, and the arrow hit one of Piotr's knights. Ivy bolted for him, shoving past men and drawing Rayner's dagger as she ran. The archer fumbled for another arrow, but Ivy was on him. She turned the blade and dragged it up the length of his neck and up through his jaw. His eyes were wild before his pupils dilated and he collapsed in Ivy's arms. She turned to see Finn skewering a man with his own spear and Piotr wrestling another to the ground. Ivy jumped over a body that fell in her path and tackled the man off Piotr.

He pulled a knife from his boot and waved for Ivy to attack. Adrenaline rushed through her veins, her body buzzing with energy. The raider widened his stance, gripping his dagger and waiting for Ivy. A challenging grin split her face as she slid Rayner's dagger back into her belt.

"Come on, then," she said, waving for the man to attack. He hesitated only a second before charging her. Ivy threw her head back, the blade missing her neck by mere inches. Extending two fingers, Ivy quickly jabbed the raider on the inside of his arm. He tried to swing again but found his arm now useless. He looked at Ivy in confusion then anger when she smiled at him. Switching the blade to his other hand, he attacked again, thrusting the blade at her heart. Ivy slipped from his path at the last minute, then hit the pressure point in his side and he fumbled. She grabbed his wrist and hit the point in his other arm, which went limp. Then she kicked the back of his knee and he fell to the snow, his eyes now round with panic. Only then did Ivy pull out her dagger and walk up to him. The raider tried to lift his arms, but to no avail. He snarled in anger as Ivy leveled her blade to his throat.

"You'll never—"

Ivy slit his throat and his words were replaced with hot blood that sputtered past his lips. "I'm sorry, were you going to say something?" She mused as the raider dropped to the ground, bleeding into the earth. "I didn't think so."

Arytin ran through the army of raiders with Macon at his side. He pulled his two long daggers and slit a raiders throat as he passed, then dropped and slid on his knees, cutting the back of anothers ankles. Aska was somewhere behind them, but Arytin kept his focus on the wall. They were supposed to make it inside and then harness their powers from there. The snow was quickly melting under the hot blood being spilled and becoming red slush. He ducked just as a raider swung his sword. He slid behind him on his knees, then pounced to his feet and thrust his dagger into the man's ribs and twisted. He cried out in pain, dropping his sword, and Aska came running up. She cracked her whip just over Arytin's head. Behind him, a raider dropped to his knees and covered his bleeding face. "Watch it," he snarled at Aska.

"You're welcome, Ary," she replied with a tight grin. Arytin twirled around and put the raider out of his misery before turning to look for Macon. He couldn't see him in the frenzied crowd of moving bodies. They were supposed to stay together until they got inside the kingdom.

A loud roar drew his attention to the wall. Luna clapped her wings together, creating a burst of fire that soared over the wall. Raiders tried to run from the flames while others hurled themselves over the wall rather than burn to death. Arytin grabbed Aska's hand and started to run, hoping that Macon was already inside. They made their way to the wall, and Arytin unwound the grappling hook and tossed it up. There were still too many raiders trying to block the gates, and Rayner and his group were slowly chipping away at them. Arytin hoisted Aska up, and she started to climb.

"Watch your back, Ary," she called down.

"Shall I watch yours as well?" Arytin turned around as a raider came barreling toward him. He pulled a knife from the belt across his chest and took aim.

"If it isn't too much trouble," Aska replied, and Arytin could hear the smile in her voice. He rolled his eyes and hurled the knife.

The blade stuck in the man's eye socket, his head whipping back from the force of the throw. "Hurry up!" he called to Aska, who replied with an annoyed scoff. Then he spotted Macon coming toward them, and he took off running, leaving Aska on the rope. A raider cut off his path, swinging his sword, but Arytin jumped, twirling his body over the blade and slitting the man's throat before his feet touched down again.

"Show off," Macon breathed. Arytin grabbed him by the arm and yanked him forward. They got back to the rope just as a raider landed with a crunch in front of them. They snapped their heads up to see Aska, waving for them to hurry. Macon rolled his eyes and started to climb while Arytin covered him, throwing more knives from his belt.

"Get on!" Macon called over the wall. Arytin grabbed hold of the rope, and they started to hoist him up. He continued throwing his knives as the raiders scrambled to snatch the end of the rope. Aska was already harnessing her powers when Arytin made it over the wall. She dropped raiders in their paths; some screamed in pain while others began to cry hysterically. He watched as Aska forced a group to stand on the edge of the wall and spread their arms out before leaning back and falling to their death. "She sure knows how to enjoy it, doesn't she," Macon grumbled.

Arytin looked down and noticed a pool of blood below his friend. "You're bleeding," he said. Bending down, he sliced the bottom of Macon's pants.

"It's fine." Macon waved Arytin away. "We need to finish the mission."

Arytin ignored him and looked at the bleeding gash that ran up the length of his lower leg. "This isn't fine, Macon. You need stitches." His anger rose as he stood up. Macon sheathed his sword and waved him off again. "Macon—"

"We don't have time for this!" he interrupted, and Aska turned her attention to them. "We need to finish the mission and move the raiders outside the walls. Take Aska and move to the southern wall, I'll go check on the others."

Arytin hesitated but nodded. They turned back to Aska, whose eyes were wide with worry as she looked at the pool of blood running over the stone. "Macon." She stepped forward, and then her whole body jerked forward as an arrow struck her.

Macon stepped forward and caught her as she fell. Fear coiled so tight around Arytin's lungs it made breathing almost impossible. When he looked behind her, there was an archer, reaching for another arrow. Tears burned in his eyes, and before he knew it, he was running. He glanced up at the sky and felt his powers coursing through his veins and mixing with the adrenaline. The archer stopped dead when he spotted Arytin's glowing eyes and face twisted with rage. Arytin jumped up onto the wall and flipped through the air, cutting off his path. The archer was trembling and tried to slowly back away. Arytin rushed him, pinning him up against the wall and grabbing him by the throat. He entered the man's mind, flipping through all his fears and worries until he found the one that would break him.

Arytin flashed his teeth and brought his fingers up to his mouth and whistled. Luna called back and swooped down, landing just beside the raider. "Afraid of fire?" Arytin growled. The archer looked like he was going to throw up and pass out. Arytin shoved him back, and the archer crumpled to the ground, begging and crying. Arytin gave another quick whistle and watched the fire build in Luna's mouth before she released it. The archer sprang to his feet as the flames consumed him, thrashing and twisting to try and put himself out. Arytin grabbed hold of the man's mind and forced him to stand entirely still while the flames burned him, and all the while, the archer was fully aware that he was on fire. Arytin could feel his pure terror, fighting and trying to escape, but he held firm on his mind until the flames charred his body.

Arytin released his powers and ran back down the wall, but Aska and Macon were gone. A large pool of blood covered the middle of the walkway.

"Aska!" he yelled. "Macon!"

Scanning the crowd of people below them, Arytin searched for his family, but he didn't see them. He spotted Rayner, no longer on his horse, but covered in blood as he fought his way closer to the open gate. He expected the path to be clear of raiders by the time he got there. Arytin's mind was racing; he turned back to see a massive crowd of raiders still inside the walls of Godstone. He couldn't do this alone. He couldn't force all of them out without his family. He needed them, but where were they? Arytin snapped his eyes shut. He couldn't afford to fall apart, not yet. He told himself that Aska was alive, and Macon was all right. He opened his glowing eyes and ran down the wall.

THE PLAN OF DECEPTION

Blood sprayed on Grimm's face as he cut down another raider in his path. Kyatta kept one eye on him as they moved together toward the gate. Rayner was just ahead, fighting hard to keep the gate open and clear. They needed to get inside Godstone if they had any hope of taking it back, but first, they needed to get the king inside. Kyatta knew the plan. They had gone over it again and again, all in agreeance as to what they needed to do.

Grimm turned and grabbed Kyatta by the arm, pulling her along. He kicked a raider in front of him before driving the tip of his sword through the man's eye. He let go of Kyatta to swing his sword up to block as another raider came barreling toward him. Their swords clashed, and Grimm kicked him in the gut then slit his throat. A mounted knight cut off their path, and Grimm barely had time to shove Kyatta aside before the knight's sword came crashing down.

Kyatta grabbed an arrow and nocked it, but she couldn't get a clear shot. Grimm raised his blade to catch the blow before reaching out and yanking the knight by his boot. He tumbled off the horse and landed on top of Grimm, who grunted in pain as he shoved the knight from him, getting to his feet. Kyatta's attention was pulled from them. Rushing footsteps at her back had her turning just in time to put her arrow through a raider's throat. As he fell, another jumped over his body, ax raised as he screamed in rage. She swung her bow, cracking him across the face before pulling her dagger and stabbing him. She turned back to see Grimm and the knight on their feet. The knight thrust his sword forward, and Grimm deflected it, but the knight was quick. He stepped into his jab and sliced Grimm across the arm, only turning in time for the blade to miss his heart. Kyatta reached for another arrow, but Grimm shouted at her to get on the horse and go. Her fingers stilled at the boom of his voice and the fear in it. Fear for her.

Grimm dodged another blow and swung his sword, forcing the knight to back up a few steps. He turned to Kyatta. "Get on! *Now!*" Kyatta ran and swung up onto the horse's back and started firing arrows, clearing a path. She looked over her shoulder, to where Grimm and the knight were struggling against one another, and Kyatta felt a wave of panic. "Go!" Grimm ordered, but she wouldn't leave him. She couldn't lose him. Grimm headbutted the knight through their crossed swords and locked eyes with Kyatta before slapping the horse on the rear.

The horse took off in a sprint. "Grimm!" Kyatta called back, but her voice was drowned in the screams of battle. She watched Grimm be swarmed by raiders, his sword slicing through necks like butter. She swallowed her tears and turned ahead. Kyatta couldn't think about losing Grimm; it would destroy her before they completed their plan.

She rose in the stirrups and placed one foot in the center of the saddle. Raiders blocked her path, but Kyatta brought them down with an arrow through their skulls. The horse trampled over the fallen bodies like they were nothing. She spotted Rayner up ahead and dropped a few raiders that surrounded him. Rayner snapped his attention up to Kyatta.

"Get on!" she ordered. Rayner swung up behind her, sinking his sword into a skull that grabbed for them, and the horse took off again. They galloped straight for the gate, but the raiders still blocked it and created a wall of shields across the hole. The horse raged on past raiders and men on fire. She felt Rayner grip her tighter when he realized that they weren't stopping.

"Kyatta," he yelled in her ear.

She snapped the reins, urging the horse to run faster.

"Kyatta!"

Kyatta looked back over her shoulder as she slung her bow. "Hold on!"

Rayner kept one hand on his sword and wrapped the other around Kyatta's waist. The shield wall held, and Kyatta drew in a tight breath as the horse launched itself into the air, soaring over the shields and through the burning gate. As soon as the hooves were on the ground again, Rayner jumped off the back of the horse. He turned around and slit a raider's throat, nearly taking off his head with the force of his swing. Kyatta stopped the horse in the middle of the main yard and stood up on its back. She unslung her bow and dropped a raider at Rayner's feet before turning to another.

Rayner's heart was racing with the rush of battle and the fact that he had made it in. He was inside Godstone, his home, his kingdom. He looked around and realized Aska and her family were nowhere in sight. They were supposed to have cleared the gates so Rayner and the rest of the army could get in. He couldn't see Zion or Earl Rorik either. They should've made it in by now through the northern gate. Where were they?

His thoughts were forced away as a raider's spear almost pierced his foot. He moved just in time and grabbed the shaft, ripping it from the raider's hand. He pulled a knife and charged Rayner, nearly slicing off his ear as he stepped aside. Rayner kicked the raider's leg, forcing him down to one knee and driving his sword through his neck, spraying a warm mist of blood. An arrow whizzed past his head, and Rayner whipped around to see a raider dropping face-first in the mud. He turned to Kyatta and offered a grateful smile.

Just to the right of him, a wall of fire rose from the ground. Raiders paused to look at the fire, and Rayner did the same. It reached two men high, and when it parted down the middle, Zion stepped through. He looked like a god or a demon, Rayner couldn't decide which. His robes swirled with the dancing flames as he held his arms out, commanding the fire. A shrill cry drew his attention to the sky, where Luna swooped down and headed straight for Zion. Her beak parted and she bellowed out a comet of fire. Zion held a hand out in front of him, his palm facing the sky and the fireball stopped just before him. He clenched his fist, and the fire compacted into a tighter ball. He put his hands together, then opened them, the heel of his palms still touching and the fire soared across the yard to a group of raiders. It exploded on impact, and raiders were thrown off their feet; others tried to run from the flames that clung to them like a shadow. Luna did the same with Zion's men, and the fireballs started soaring across the yard, their impact sending a wave of hot air that blew Rayner's hair back.

Rayner only peeled his eyes away when Piotr and Correlyn came running up behind him. Piotr's archers stood around him, and Rayner had an idea. He told Piotr to get them formed up in a line facing the yard. Rayner whistled for Luna and gestured toward the line of raiders. He didn't know how Luna understood what he wanted, but she did. It was as if they had some unknown connection between them, and he wondered if Magnus had felt it too. The archers held their arrows out in a straight line as Luna blew past them, the flames of her wings just brushing the tips of the arrows. One by one, they were alight. The archers nocked their arrows back and aimed. "Loose!" Piotr bellowed and the flock of fire arrows ripped through the sky.

The main yard was packed with bodies and crawling with fire. Some surrounding buildings caught, but Rayner couldn't worry about that now. He needed to find Helvarr and end this. Shouting from the gate turned his attention. Ivy and Finn assisted Grimm, who was limping badly. Kyatta bolted for him, slamming into Grimm's chest and nearly knocking him over.

"I am all right," he said through his teeth. Ivy ran up to Rayner, Finn following closely with his sword and ax drawn. The king's knights quickly surrounded them and held off the raiders who weren't occupied by Zion's flames. Rayner brought a hand up to Ivy's cheek and tried to give her a reassuring smile, but their work wasn't done yet.

Ivy looked around the yard, then asked, "Where's Aska?"

"I don't know," Rayner answered and then realized they were missing someone else. "Lord Cylas?" Ivy only shook her head and said that she lost sight of him.

Rayner had to think; he couldn't lose anyone else in this fight. He had no idea where Helvarr was or how many more raiders lurked deeper in the kingdom. He had to lure them all outside the walls before it was too late. Aska and her family were supposed to lead most of them out, but they were nowhere in sight. He had to go with plan B.

Rayner turned to Kyatta. "Get up on the walls with Piotr and his archers, and start firing down on the raiders who still remain outside the walls." He turned his gaze to his sister. "You and Finn go find Aska and the others. We'll start to lead the raiders toward the gate." Ivy looked at Correlyn and seemed to be asking her something that Rayner couldn't discern. Deciding to ignore the look, he turned and yelled for Zion over the screams of burning raiders. They locked eyes and Rayner gave him a firm nod: plan B.

Zion nodded in return.

Rayner looked around to everyone for a moment. He didn't want to split up, but he saw no other way. He had to trust that their plan would work, and they would be able to lead the raiders outside. Helvarr was nothing without his army, and if Rayner could get them away, that only left Helvarr to deal with. He locked eyes with Ivy, who gave him a smile that looked sad. "Together." He held out his hand.

Everyone reached a hand in, placing it on top of the king's.

"Unbroken," they answered and broke off to take up their posts.

Rayner grabbed Correlyn by the hand and took off, running deeper into the kingdom. He looked back once to see Zion pushing a firewall at the raiders and forcing them back out the gate, but there were still plenty ahead. His knights ran alongside him, their swords slick with blood. Rayner knew he had to get behind the raiders and somehow force them all toward the main yard where Zion would be waiting. He was in the middle of a half-baked thought when a stallion cut off their path. Rayner looked up to see Earl Rorik, covered in blood and his leather armor shredded, revealing a large gash to his side. Panic started to dance in Rayner's head as he looked at the wound that was still seeping with thick blood.

"Plan B," Rayner called up to him, and Rorik's face shifted. His attention turned to the streets that were crawling with raiders and Rayner's knights who were fighting to keep them away. Rorik looked past the king and nodded once, his expression unreadable.

Rayner spun around to see Lord Cylas running up. His red hair was caked with blood, and his brows were drawn together in what looked like sorrow. The lord's men ran up and joined the circle of Rayner's knights. "I'm sorry," Lord Cylas said and glanced back up to Earl Rorik.

Rayner shook his head, frustration and confusion fluttering in his belly. "What are you talking about? We need to—"

"All hail King Rayner the Unbroken!" Earl Rorik bellowed, turning the raiders' attention to him. He beat his chest and bared his teeth at them. Rayner stepped forward, but Cylas grabbed him by the arm. Rorik unslung a bone horn from his back and blew. The sound was guttural and deafening. Raiders from further down the street all snapped their heads up to the earl. Rayner felt a knot twisting in his stomach and sweat running down his back as he realized what was happening.

"All hail the king!" Earl Rorik roared and blew the horn again before leaning down and locking eyes with Rayner. "It's been a pleasure, just Rayner." He winked and snapped the reins of the stallion.

"Rorik, wait!" Rayner shouted and tried to run, but Cylas wrapped his arms around him. Earl Rorik charged the sea of raiders, shouting and blowing the horn until they followed him.

"What the fuck are you doing?" Rayner demanded.

"This was always the plan." Cylas let go of him. "For you to survive. Everyone agreed. You've done enough and got us in, now let us fight for you."

Rayner felt sick, and his whole body began to shake. "No!" he roared again and tried to push past Cylas. The knights tightened their rank around the three. He thrashed against Cylas and thought of Ivy. Where was she? Did she know about this plan to deceive him?

Rayner remembered the look his sister gave Correlyn. He turned his attention back to his wife, who gave him a sorrowful look. She knew too. Correlyn grabbed his face between her hands. Behind them, the sound of Rorik's horn was fading as he moved further from them. "This is all for nothing if you fall." Her voice was a calm breeze. "A kingdom with no king is nothing but stone and walls."

Rayner gaped at her. "Correlyn?" But he couldn't even finish his thought.

She stepped closer. "It will be all right," she assured him. "Everyone has their orders."

"Orders? From who?"

Cylas answered. "From the queen."

Rayner felt sick, like his chest was caving in, and he couldn't breathe. He couldn't let his family fight without him. They had come this far together.

This was his fight as much as it was all of theirs, if not more so. How could Ivy agree to save him above everyone else? Rayner couldn't comprehend it. He didn't think his life was worth more than any of those that he fought alongside. How could he just stand by while his family and friends fought for him?

He grabbed Cylas by the collar. "What are they doing?"

"Just what you said. Lead the raiders outside the walls." His eyes were intense and bright. "But it was always the plan to get you safe once we got inside."

Rayner stepped back. He tried to think of what he could do. There was still time. He could make it past the knights and get to his family. He would rather die than live as king with no one he loved left to fill his kingdom. He looked past the knights. He could hear screaming in the distance and see flashes of fire shooting through the air. Rayner blinked as he realized there were no raiders left around them. Earl Rorik had successfully led them all toward the main yard, but what happened to him? Did he continue riding outside the walls?

Correlyn grabbed his hand in hers as if she could sense that he was about to take off. "Everything will be all right," she repeated and turned Rayner's face to look at her. "The gods have already woven our fates, and there's nothing we can do to change that. *You* can't change that." Rayner felt tears forming and tried to blink them away. "You were meant to rule, Rayner. You will be the greatest king the land has ever seen, but you can't do it alone. Let us help you." He closed his eyes, and Correlyn rested a hand against his cheek. "You have carried the kingdom around on your shoulders for months, and I'm sorry that I couldn't be there."

"Correlyn—" He choked on the words, and she hushed him.

"You have given so much for your people already, and I won't watch you strain under the weight anymore. You are selfless and brave. I have no doubt that if I let you go now, that you would be all right–that you would kill any man in your path. But I'm not willing to gamble with your life, and you shouldn't either. This will be over soon, but that doesn't mean the work will stop. I told you we have a new life to build here, and I need you by my side to do that because I can't do this without you."

The battle and knights seemed to fade away as she spoke, calming the screaming panic in his mind. She gave him a faint smile and ran her thumb over his cheek, catching the tears he hadn't realized escaped.

Rayner was so close to getting his home back, not only for him but for the whole North. Perhaps Correlyn was right, and he needed to trust his family to wrap things up. Rayner had been carrying his worries and fears for months. He buried them deep inside because there was always someone else who needed help, and he couldn't justify putting his own first. He never thought he would become king so young, but the gods often threw new rings to jump through just when your feet touched the ground again.

Correlyn pulled him in, wrapping her arms around his neck as he buried his face in her hair. Cylas waved off the knights who ran toward the main yard to offer their assistance. Rayner pulled away and mustered up a smile before turning back to Lord Cylas. "What do you need me to do?"

Cylas grinned. "There's still the issue of locating a certain banished knight." Rayner nodded and took a deep breath before grabbing Correlyn by the hand and heading through the streets. Helvarr was hiding somewhere, and Rayner thought he knew where.

THE HARDER THEY FALL

Get the king inside, then keep him safe.

Ivy knew the plan, yet she felt a pang to her heart for deceiving her brother. Everyone had been in on it from the first meeting that was held about how they were going to attack Godstone. Rayner had been late, so everyone got started without him. It was Earl Rorik's idea to go along with whatever Rayner came up with but then go with their own plan if things went wrong. And they had.

Aska and her family were nowhere in sight, but Ivy had to keep herself calm, or at least try. Zion and his people were pushing the raiders outside the wall while Kyatta and Piotr's archers took care of them once outside. The whole main yard was ablaze, and everywhere Ivy looked, people were screaming and fighting. The constant clash of swords was like a mantra.

Ivy had watched Lord Cylas run off toward Rayner only a moment ago, and she could only hope that her brother didn't try to do anything rash. They needed Rayner alive, Godstone needed its king, but Ivy needed her brother.

I'm your brother before I'm your king.

Rayner's words ate a hole inside her, but Ivy knew that being king was a more important job, no matter how much it hurt to admit that. The whole North would be under his command, and they were so close to winning it back. Ivy wondered if Rayner had told Piotr the news yet. She looked up on the wall to see him shouting orders to his men, his feathery blond hair sprayed with blood and a determined look on his face. Piotr had been through so much in the last stretch of the journey, and nothing could take away his pain, but Rayner was going to try to bring something good out of something bad.

"Look out!"

Ivy whipped around just as Finn tackled her to the ground. A few raiders had broken away from Zion. They were armed with spears and targeting Ivy. One nearly took off Finn's head as he shielded her from the attack. Back on her feet, she whistled for Luna just as another raider threw a spear. Luna swooped down and shot out a stream of fire, burning the spear to ashes midflight. One of the raiders threw down his weapon and charged Finn.

Ivy stepped away to go after the other one while Finn fought off his attacker. The raider smiled at Ivy before thrusting his spear toward her sternum. She turned on the balls of her feet and felt the tip of the blade slide against her back armor. Before the raider could attack again, Ivy was at his back, her sword to his throat and Rayner's dagger to his side. "Where's Helvarr?" she hissed and pressed the blade in further. The raider only chuckled at her, and Ivy stabbed him in the side, careful to miss any major organs.

"Where is Helvarr?" She asked again, slowly, as if talking to a child. The raider screamed in pain and threw his head back, catching Ivy in the jaw and forcing her to stumble back. He grabbed for her knife, but Ivy pulled it away and sheathed it before swinging Promise. The raider ducked and rolled, snatching up his spear and holding it out in front of him. Ivy snickered at him and lunged. She slid Promise down the length of the spear and slashed at the raider's chest, but his leather armor protected him some. Ivy twirled around him and brought her sword down in an arc, chopping the head of the spear off. He had no weapons

left and his eyes went to Ivy's sword, then back to her. A challenge.

Ivy sheathed Promise and grinned, waving at him to attack. She stole a glance over to Finn to make sure he was all right. The raider took it as an opening and charged. Ivy slipped from his path and brought her elbow down into his spine. He grunted, more so in anger than pain she thought. He balled his fists and swung at Ivy's face, but she dodged swing after swing. Keeping her eyes on his feet, she waited for him to step into his punch again, then grabbed him by the collar, slid her foot behind his ankle and threw him to the ground.

Ivy stomped her foot down, aiming for his stomach, but he rolled away and kicked, catching her in the back of the knee. She stumbled, and the raider grabbed her leg, pulling her down as he reached for her knife. Ivy jabbed her fingers into his upper arm to try to hit the pressure point, but his armor blocked her attempt. She tried again for the one in his thigh. The raider flipped her over and pinned Ivy to the ground. His hands wrapped around her neck, and Ivy choked for air. She reached down for her dagger, but the raider caught her hand before she could grab it. The adrenaline was like a shock to her body. She grabbed him by the collar and pulled him down closer, thrusting her hips up and throwing him onto his back. She quickly reached for her dagger and stabbed him in the chest. It didn't go all the way through the armor, and the raider was now fighting with her to pull the blade out. Ivy punched him in the ribs and forced all her weight on the handle, her hands shaking with the strain. His hazel eyes went wide as Ivy gave one last push and felt her blade slip between his ribs. She rolled off him, trying to catch her breath and staring up at the night sky.

Her heart started to speed up again as she watched a tight cluster of stars burn out. Ivy shot up and started scanning the yard for Aska, but it was Arytin she saw instead. His white eyes burned with rage, and his fists were clenched so tight Ivy thought the bones might break through his skin. Raiders ran from him, but he broke into their minds and forced them to stand still while he tormented them. Tears streamed down his face. She turned in a circle, hoping to see Macon or Aska, but he was alone. Ivy ran to him, fear burning her throat as she tried to discern what that look meant. When she reached him, she turned him around and Arytin snarled at her. Ivy stepped back and watched as it took a moment for Arytin to realize who she was.

The glow in his eyes receded, and his dark brown eyes were bloodshot and shiny. "Arytin." Ivy stepped up to him. "Where are they?"

His bottom lip quivered. "I don't know. We were up on the wall, and there was an archer, he…he shot Aska." His voice broke at her name, and Ivy's stomach sank. "I ran after him, but when I came back, they were gone. Macon was already hurt." Ivy tried not to panic—they had to be hiding out somewhere. If Macon was hurt and Aska was…

No. She couldn't think like that. This battle wasn't over yet.

Finn came running up a moment later, fresh blood splattered across his face. He took one look at Arytin and knew immediately something was wrong. Ivy turned in the direction Rayner had gone, and just then, she spotted Earl Rorik riding toward them. His eyes were focused, and lips curled around a bone horn as he blew. A group of raiders charged after him, and before Ivy could yell or jump into his path, Finn shoved her back and the stallion raged through the yard and out the gate. Zion quickly herded the raiders like sheep and began pushing them toward the open gate, where Earl Rorik had gone.

She looked back and saw Grimm mounted on a horse, killing raiders as they tried to break away from Zion and Luna's fire. Grimm's back was turned, and Ivy knew he hadn't just seen his father ride out through the gates. Dread pooled into every inch of her body, but she had to find Aska and Macon before it was too late. They couldn't lose anyone else. "We'll help you find her." Ivy turned back to Arytin then nodded to Finn. "If Macon is hurt, they couldn't have gone far. Did you see a blood trail?"

Arytin nodded. "But it stopped further down the northern wall." Ivy tried to think. Arytin didn't know the kingdom like Macon did. Where would he have taken Aska? How far could he have made it? There were a few possible places.

Ivy started running toward the stone steps, calling at them to follow. They would have to find the blood trail again and go from there. Ivy was halfway up the steps when she heard shouting from up on the wall. She ran faster, taking them three at a time and pulling Promise from her scabbard. Raiders that had been pushed outside the wall were now climbing back over it. Ivy peered over the edge to see that they had ladders all along the wall. "Shit," she cursed to herself. They must have had them hidden around the outside, just in case. Ivy and her people weren't the only ones with a backup plan.

A ladder was pushed up right where Ivy's hand had been. Finn and Arytin ran up behind her and started killing the few raiders who managed to make it over. Ivy poked her head out and waited until the ladder was full of raiders. Just as they were about to reach the top, she looked out over the edge and smiled at the first one before grabbing the ladder and shoving it back.

Ivy turned to see Kyatta standing on the edge of the wall, firing arrows along with Piotr's archers. Finn was just behind her, throwing the body of a raider down a ladder and knocking the rest from the rungs. Arytin harnessed his powers and forced a group of raiders to climb up the ladder and over the edge, then walk straight to the other side and hurl themselves from the wall. Ivy cringed at the sound of their bones crunching just below. "Come on." She waved for them to follow.

She went up behind Kyatta, who turned for a split second and nodded, letting Ivy know she was all right. Kyatta was much like Ronin during a battle—her face was calm and poised, her bow an extension of her own arm. Further down the wall, Piotr was fighting a raider who swung an ax while more started to pour over the sides. Piotr didn't notice them, and Ivy took off running before she could think to yell and warn him.

Piotr's back was turned to Ivy as he dodged the ax. The raider swung it with such a force that it became stuck in the stone wall, and Piotr lunged for him. The raider ducked and plowed into Piotr, pushing until his back slammed up against the edge. Piotr sent the pommel of his sword down on the raider's back, but he didn't even flinch. Ivy willed her legs to run faster, swerving around the archers and dodging raiders in her path. Her heart rose to her throat as she watched Piotr shove the man back and raise his sword. He swung and sliced the raider's arm open, but he still wasn't stopping. He dodged another swing and stepped up, punching Piotr across the jaw. His head snapped back, and Ivy suddenly felt like she was running in place. The punch was enough to knock him out, and the raider didn't hesitate to grab him behind the knees and lift Piotr up on the edge, before shoving him over the wall.

"Piotr!" Ivy screamed with all the breath she had left. The raider snapped his attention to her just as Ivy ran up on him. She put all her strength into her arms and swung Promise, the blade whistling as it cut the air in half. The raider stumbled back as the blade sliced across his chest, but Ivy didn't give him a chance to lunge. She stepped into her jab and sunk her sword into his ribs then kicked his body off her blade. The raider fell to his knees, and Ivy quickly swung her sword across his neck and watched his head bounce and roll to the other side of the wall.

Finn and Arytin were right behind her and held off the other raiders still trying to climb up the wall. Ivy looked over the edge and saw Piotr in the yard below, his eyes closed and body still. "Piotr!" she screamed, and before Finn could grab her, she took off running again. Ivy jumped down the stairs of the wall and quickly slit a raider's throat who stood in her way. Piotr lay off to the left of the gate, just past Zion and his men. Ivy pushed through the raiders being led out. The wall of fire rose about five feet. Ivy knew she couldn't clear it, but she didn't care. She had to get to Piotr. The flames seared her face as she got closer. Her heart skipped as she pushed off the ground and soared through the wall of fire.

She slid on her knees to a stop, dropping Promise and looking down at Piotr's face. A thin streak of blood trickled from his nose, and his eyes were closed. Hot tears washed away the grit and blood on Ivy's cheeks, leaving a pale stream in its place. "Piotr..." She choked on his name. Ivy brought a finger to his neck, searching for a pulse but her own throbbed so frantically that she couldn't tell. She lowered her head to his chest; it wasn't moving. Ivy's hands were shaking as she fumbled to get the straps unlaced on his armor. Piotr couldn't be dead, he had to live, he was meant to be...

Ivy sobbed just as Finn dropped down beside her. He moved quicker than she had, pulling his straps loose and lifting the armor off. His brown eyes were wild and searching as he felt Piotr's neck. Arytin stood silently behind Finn as he worked. Finn lowered his face to Piotr's, trying to feel his breath. Ivy reached out and brushed his hair away. "Please, Piotr," she sobbed. "You're going to be all right. We're here." She knew the words were more for her sake than Piotr's, who likely couldn't hear her.

Arytin crouched down. "Is he..."

Finn lifted his face from Piotr's and looked at Ivy. "He's alive." Ivy choked back a sob, covering her mouth with her hand. "We need to get him inside," Finn urged. But where? The only healer was back at the camp with Ivy's mother, and they couldn't go back out there now, not with all the raiders being pushed from the kingdom. Ivy looked down at Piotr. She knew he might not make it even if they did try to make a run for it. There wasn't time.

Finn scooped up Piotr in his arms, and Ivy stood. "Magister Ivann's room," she said and started running toward it. Finn and Arytin followed, the latter guarding their backs as they moved through the yard and down the long building where the Magister used to stay. Ivy knew he was dead and had no idea what Helvarr might have done to his room, but she only hoped there was something left behind. Surely Helvarr would have kept medicine even if they didn't have a healer.

She kicked in the door and held it open for Finn then barred it once Arytin was through. A few raiders tried to stop them, but Arytin had forced them to walk east, and Ivy guessed they would go all the way until they hit the Shadow Sea and then keep going.

The room was bare save for a dust-covered bed in the corner where Finn had once spent days after suffering from a fever. Finn laid Piotr down while Ivy worked on lighting a lantern. Arytin covered the window with a blanket, and Ivy began to scan the shelves. Nothing but empty glass jars and bowls sat on the shelf. Ivy cursed and kicked the bottom cabinet in frustration. Finn grabbed her shoulder, and she crumpled to the ground. Her whole body started to shake. This couldn't happen, not now, not when they were so close. Finn kneeled down and took her face between his hands. "Ivy, I need you to stay with me." His voice was shaky, but his hands were stable and calm. She nodded and took a deep breath, forcing her tears back. As she grabbed Finn's hand to stand up, his eyes went down to the cabinet she had kicked.

"What's that?" He crouched back down and pulled the piece of wood that split from her kick. Inside the cabinet, a hidden compartment was revealed.

Ivy bent down and saw all the usual herbs and liquids that Magister Ivann used to keep on his shelves. Finn started taking everything out, but Ivy just stared at it. There were herbs, nightshade, different colored powders to be mixed with water. Magister Ivann must have started hoarding his own medicine when he was forced to treat Correlyn during her captivity. Perhaps the Magister knew he wouldn't last long and wanted to leave something behind should Correlyn ever escape and rummage through his room. Ivy felt a sickening twist as she thought of the other possibility. That Magister Ivann had hidden all of his medicine and claimed to have no more left. Was that why Lady Oharra had killed him? Because he was no longer useful? Ivy couldn't dwell on that, not now.

Finn moved over to Piotr, and Arytin held the lantern above, casting a dull orange circle across Piotr's chest. Finn cut away Piotr's shirt and saw a large bruise already creeping its way around his ribs from his back. He pushed lightly on his ribs but said none were broken. Piotr's armor must have protected his torso, but Ivy had noticed outside that something was wrong with his leg. Finn saw it too and cut a slit up his pants. Piotr's leg was bent at an odd angle, and his knee and ankle were swollen. Ivy breath caught at the sight of it.

"I have to set it," Finn said quietly. He turned to look around the room and pointed to a chair. "Break two of those legs off and find me some wrapping." Arytin worked on the chair while Ivy rummaged through the rest of the cabinets but found nothing. She pulled her dagger and began cutting strips of cloth from the blanket.

Finn ordered Arytin to hold down Piotr's arm and for Ivy to stay up by his head and try to calm him when he woke. "You think he'll wake up?" Arytin asked.

Finn didn't look up but nodded. "I saw my mother work on plenty of people when I was young. It pains me to have to do it. He'll thrash and beg for us to stop, but if I don't set the bone, Piotr will never walk again."

He sucked in a breath and gently grabbed Piotr's leg in his hands. "I'm sorry," he whispered and then gave it a quick jerk. Piotr's eyes shot open as Finn snapped the bone back into place. He screamed and writhed. Ivy clamped a hand down over his mouth and pressed a finger to hers. She couldn't be sure if raiders still lurked outside, but Piotr's screams would quickly draw attention. His eyes spilled over with tears, and Ivy gently wiped them away, taking her hand from his mouth. Piotr's eyes stayed locked with Ivy's, and she reached down and took his hand. He squeezed so hard Ivy thought her bones would snap, but she didn't pull away.

"I have to wrap it," Finn said.

Ivy stroked Piotr's hair as Finn lifted his leg to tuck the wrapping under it. Piotr's body went tense, his muscles contorting, and veins pulsing in his neck. Ivy scanned his bare chest for any more cuts, but there was nothing. She didn't know how he'd survived the fall—perhaps he was as stubborn as she was. Finn finished tying off the chair legs. It would have to do for now until he could make a better brace.

Arytin let go of Piotr's arms and stepped away, but his hand stayed wrapped around Ivy's, and his eyes fixed on her.

"You're going to be all right," Ivy whispered.

"I saw you." His voice was raspy and constricted.

"What do you mean?"

He took in a shaky breath and squeezed her hand. "I saw you running for me, and then I was just…falling."

Ivy snapped her eyes shut. She would never get the image out of her head of Piotr's body lying at the foot of the wall. Finn glanced at Ivy and then stood, telling Arytin to follow him into the back kitchen to look for food.

"I thought I was dead when I heard your voice calling to me, begging me."

Ivy's eyes burned. "You're not dead, Piotr. You're here, and I'm here."

Piotr winced as he shifted to sit up. His ribs might not have been broken, but he was still badly hurt. Ivy hooked his arm around her neck and eased him into a sitting position. He managed a tight grin. "I know I'm not dead, because if I were—" He blushed and stopped himself.

"If you were what?"

Piotr gave her an embarrassed smile. "If I were dead, my body wouldn't hurt, and you'd be kissing me." He shot her a sideways glance and grinned.

Ivy snorted. "Only in your dreams, High Lord."

Piotr's brows pulled together, his smile melting away. "What did you call me?"

Ivy pinched her eyes shut and cursed herself. Rayner was supposed to tell Piotr. She opened her eyes to find Piotr staring at her. "You're going to be made High Lord of the North, Piotr. Rayner has already decided."

Piotr sat back. His face twisted with pain and confusion. Ivy got up and grabbed one of the small vials from Magister Ivann's stash. She popped the cap and handed it to Piotr, who took it without question. Ivy reached out to brush his hair away, and he caught her wrist.

"High Lord?" he asked. As if he hadn't heard Ivy the first time.

"Yes, Piotr."

He let go of her and ran his hand through his hair. "What does that mean?"

Ivy sighed and placed her hands in her lap. "It means, should there be more lords to come north once it's safe again, you will be their high lord. Rayner was going to tell you himself, but you'll be his right hand and have all the authority of a king back at the Twisted Tower."

Piotr seemed to be soaking in the news and his eyes held too many emotions. Ivy saw the fear and uncertainty that came with ruling, the spark of sorrow for how he got this position, it all flashed across his features in a split second.

"Piotr?" Ivy's voice shook his worries away. "Are you all right? You look pale."

"I'm fine," he said. "I just need to…absorb."

Ivy smiled faintly. "I understand. I didn't mean to spring that on you like that."

Piotr smiled at her. "And here I thought you couldn't surprise me anymore."

Ivy smirked and leaned in, kissing him gently on the cheek. Piotr's whole face flushed. "Not so pale anymore," Ivy teased, and Piotr snorted a chuckle.

"You want a surprise?" Finn was standing in the doorway with a bowl of apples. Ivy turned to face him, and he gave her a warm smile before locking eyes with Piotr. "She jumped through a wall of fire to get to you," Finn said.

Piotr snapped his eyes back to Ivy and immediately started scanning her for burns. "You did what?" His voice rose with worry.

Finn walked in and set the bowl down, handing an apple to Ivy. "Jumped straight through it." He motioned with his hands. "We were right behind her, and before I could yell at her to stop, she jumped, and the wall rose up, cutting off our path. I don't think Zion saw us until Ivy was already through. We had to go around." Piotr kept his eyes on Ivy, who blushed under his gaze. She hadn't thought much about it at the moment; she just knew she had to get to Piotr.

"Anyone would have done it." She shrugged it off and took a bite of the apple.

Finn reached out and grabbed her hand. "No, my Ivy. There aren't many people stubborn enough to think they are immune to fire." He winked at her.

They sat in the room for a while longer, looking out the window to make sure the streets were clear. Arytin offered to go to the stables and find a wagon for Piotr. Ivy knew she had to find her brother and Helvarr before this battle was over. The night seemed to stretch into days, but Ivy didn't feel tired. Ivy had finally made it back into her home, and there was no way she was leaving. Helvarr had raised himself up to what he thought was a king, claiming power and taking from others. Ivy could only hope the fall would kill him.

TO THE DEATH

Rayner kicked in the door of the Great Hall, sending a shock wave up his leg and to his core. Correlyn and Lord Cylas stepped in behind him while the king's knights posted outside the door. The Hall was just as Rayner remembered it. Tables and benches lined the walls; his father's Blackwood throne sat in the center of the dais at the back of the room. But it wasn't his father who sat on the throne now.

Helvarr didn't even look up as Rayner stormed across the room, sword drawn and hands steady. His black hair swept over his brow, shadowing his eyes, which were cast down to his boots. Helvarr wore a sword at his side and light black armor that seemed to absorb the light of the dancing flames that came from lanterns above his head. Rayner stopped dead in his tracks, his heart stopping with his feet as he noticed two bodies off to the left, lying atop a table. Macon and Aska.

He ran to them, and Helvarr made no move to stop him. Aska's eyes were closed and her breathing labored, and beside her, Macon had a gag over his mouth, and his hands were bound in front of him. Rayner's hands began shaking as he brought them to rest on Macon's chest—he was alive. He noticed a trickle of blood coming from his head and snapped his eyes back up to

Helvarr. He was now staring right at Rayner, his copper eyes haunting and a tight grin forming at the corner of his mouth.

"What did you do to them?" Rayner demanded, taking a step closer. Correlyn stood frozen in place, mouth open, and eyes locked on her father. Helvarr sat back further in the throne, tapping his fingers on the armrest as if Rayner was wasting his time.

"I didn't shoot her if that's what you're implying," he said casually. Rayner looked back at Aska. She was lying in a pool of blood, but she wasn't bound or gagged like Macon. Rayner turned back to Helvarr.

"It's over, Helvarr. We've taken the kingdom, and your raiders are outside the walls." Rayner only hoped that was true and that the rest of his family was safe. He stepped closer, lowering his voice to a growl, "Now get out of my seat." Helvarr chuckled and snapped his fingers.

A group of raiders came marching through the back room, swords and axes hanging at their sides. Lord Cylas shifted closer to Rayner, and Correlyn moved over to the table where Aska and Macon lay. The raiders swarmed them, and Rayner grabbed Correlyn, pulling her away as they surrounded the table. "Give them to us!" Correlyn snatched her arm away and took a step toward Helvarr. "You don't need them." He looked at her curiously and narrowed his eyes. He was angry.

"You're right, I don't need them." He waved a hand through the air, dismissing them as nothing. "But, I'll keep them for assurances if I must." He looked over to Aska, whose face was pale. "She won't make it much longer."

"What do you want?" Correlyn spoke through her teeth.

He smiled. "You know what I want."

Rayner stepped up and gently grabbed Correlyn's arm, pulling her back. "That's not going to happen."

Helvarr shrugged. "Then I suppose I'll just kill her—"

"No!" Correlyn roared and stepped up to his raiders. They eyed her, and she lifted her chin defiantly. "Get out of my way before I make you." The raiders exchanged a look but let her pass. Rayner reached for her, but they shoved him back with Lord Cylas.

"Correlyn!" He could feel the panic starting to rise in his throat. He couldn't lose her, not again, not when they were so close.

Correlyn put a hand to the hilt of her sword as she stopped just below the dais. "Let them go," she demanded.

Helvarr eyed her for a moment and then nodded to the group of raiders surrounding the table. "I'll tell you what. I'll give you the girl now, and I'll release the other when we're far away from here."

"You're not taking her!" Rayner's voice was laced with rage. Helvarr ignored him and stared at Correlyn. His smile left, and his mask began to slip the longer he looked at his daughter. Correlyn knew he wouldn't just let Macon go, even if she did plan on giving herself up. She had to save them. Rayner had to sit on the throne and be king, even if that meant she couldn't be his queen.

She steadied her breathing and stepped up until she was directly in front of Helvarr, looking down at him. "I have a counteroffer."

Helvarr lifted his brows curiously and cocked his head, waiting for her to explain. She looked back at Rayner, his worried eyes locked on to hers. He seemed to be begging her not to do whatever she had planned. She ignored it and looked again at Aska and Macon before turning back to face Helvarr.

"I challenge you," she stated plainly, and Helvarr's wicked grin returned. "Fight me, one on one. If I win, you let them go and tell your raiders to get out before I slit their throats."

"And if I win?"

Correlyn clenched her jaw. "Then I'll come with you, alone. You don't need Macon, and no one will try and stop us."

"I'll stop you," Rayner stated. "You think I'm just going to let you take my wife again? My queen?"

Correlyn turned to face him. "No. You won't."

Rayner blinked at her. "Correlyn—"

"I am the queen," she interrupted. "And this is my choice. I can't let any more people die. Besides, it was always the plan to make sure you sat on the throne, not me." She turned back, snapping her eyes shut as she listened to Rayner protest. She could hear him trying to thrash against Lord Cylas's grip. It broke her heart and forced a tight knot to form in her stomach, but she hoped it would go away soon.

Correlyn took a deep breath and tried to block our Rayner's pleas. "So?"

Helvarr twisted his mouth, considering. He stood up, and Correlyn didn't back away. She knew Helvarr was a skilled fighter and that she might have just doomed herself and everyone in the room because if she lost, she knew Rayner would keep his word. There was no way he would allow Helvarr to take her away, no matter whose lives were at stake. She balled her fists to keep them from shaking. Helvarr's expression softened. "You would come with me?"

Correlyn knew from the flicker in his eye just then that he didn't believe her. She started sweating, and she took a step back, but he grabbed her arm.

"You're almost as good a liar as your mother was," he hissed in her ear. Correlyn shoved away from him and grabbed her sword, pulling it halfway from the scabbard, but he didn't move. His mask lifted back into place, and Correlyn doubted if she would see it slip again. "You killed Oharra." His voice had turned venomous. "I loved her as I thought I once loved you." Her heart pounded madly, and her eyes darted to his sword, but he placed his hands behind his back. "I suppose I was a fool for thinking I could ever win your trust."

"I suppose you were," she snapped back.

Helvarr growled and stepped toward her, and she backed away. "I have another offer, *daughter.*" He said the last word as if it burned his tongue. "I will fight you, but not to win your empty promise. You will fight me to the death."

Correlyn swore she heard Rayner's heart stop beating behind her, but he remained silent. She stared at Helvarr, and his eyes shone with anger, but his face remained as still as a porcelain doll. She knew he was serious. He was angry. Everything had been taken from him, and she had taken the last and most important one. Helvarr would kill her for what she did and live the rest of his days drowning in his own anger and regret. But first, he had to kill her, and she wasn't ready to die yet.

Correlyn pulled her sword from the scabbard and stood up straight, looking into those copper eyes that once looked soft, that shed tears for her and filled with longing, but now only burned with rage.

"I accept." She tried to keep her voice stern and indifferent.

Helvarr grinned and quickly drew his sword. "Good," he hissed and lunged at her.

His eyes betrayed nothing as he lunged at Correlyn, surprising her and forcing her back a step. She kept her eyes on him but heard Rayner struggling to get to her, the raiders holding him off. "Correlyn!" he yelled, but she blocked it out and focused on Helvarr. He stepped into his jab, and she twirled, nearly missing the blade that stabbed at her ribs. The arrow wound that her mother had given her screamed at her to stop, and her rib ached. She knew the bone wasn't healed yet, but she pushed through the pain. She would heal later, if she made it that far.

Helvarr swung his sword through the air, and Correlyn ducked behind the throne. His blade bit into the wood, sending black slivers flying like tiny daggers. She pressed her back up against the wood and took a moment to think, but Helvarr stepped around the throne and swung. She ducked, his blade striking wood as she slid away and brought up her sword to block another blow. Her arms shook with the force. She kicked Helvarr in the gut, but his armor took the blow, and he flashed her a smile. He swung again, and Correlyn backed up, blocking his blows until she was pushed back down the dais and into the middle of the room. In the corner of her eye, she saw Rayner being held back by Lord Cylas who kept his other hand on his sword, ready to fight his way out if Correlyn fell. A thick wave of nausea filled her stomach at the thought. What had she done? Could she really beat Helvarr? Kill him?

Helvarr's sword was fueled by anger. He fought with everything he had, and Correlyn knew that. Ronin had told them of Helvarr's fighting style. He'd watched him ever since Helvarr was a child. Ser Osmund had seen it too; Helvarr held nothing back, and the angrier he got, the harder he fought which meant he would get tired quicker. Correlyn knew what she would do.

When Lady Oharra had been their prisoner, Correlyn didn't speak with her the whole time, but Rayner had. He'd told Correlyn what Oharra said about Helvarr, about what she would do after everything was over. She dodged another blow and stepped back, narrowing her eyes on Helvarr.

"My mother didn't love you anymore," she spat. Helvarr blinked and hesitated for a moment, and Correlyn lunged, jabbing her sword and slicing his arm. He growled in pain and stepped back as Correlyn swung her sword again. "She told Rayner that she was going to leave you," she said between breaths, not giving Helvarr a chance to swing, only block. "She thought you had become soft." She flashed her teeth. "That you'd changed."

Helvarr smacked her blade away. Something in his eyes had changed. Correlyn continued. "She never planned to go with you to Kaspin's Keep, just like we never planned to give it to you. Just like I never planned to go with you." She could practically see the smoke coming from his ears. He was growing angrier with every word. He swung at Correlyn's head, and she leaned back as the blade whistled by. Stepping forward, he continued to swing, but she managed to block his blows. "You really think my mother wanted to settle down and play house with you?" she mocked, and Helvarr swung so hard her arm nearly gave out when she blocked the blow. "Did you think we would be a happy family?" Her voice shook with anger.

She blocked his blade and quickly slid hers up to his hands and ripped it away, cutting him. He flinched from the pain and stepped back, holding his bleeding hand. Correlyn held her sword in front of her, her breathing coming too fast. "You were wrong," she breathed. "This was always going to end badly, but you were stupid enough to think the gods would end it in your favor." Helvarr roared in anger and switched his blade to the other hand, letting the injured one fall to his side. Correlyn tensed, ready for his blow. He lunged, just missing her thigh, and she stuck her blade into his lower leg before stepping back. His blood seeped through his pants and began to trickle down his boot and onto the floor.

She straightened her back and glared at him. "I once told you that you were a rabid dog that needed to be put down, but I was wrong. That was my mother, you just failed to rein her in, so I put her down." Correlyn lowered her sword. Helvarr's eyes were wild and bloodshot, his mouth was frozen in a permanent sneer, and his breath pushed through his clenched teeth. She stepped closer, looking into his burning eyes and said, "She didn't love you anymore, and I killed her. You should be thanking me for sparing you a broken heart."

"She did love me!" he roared. He was coming undone, like a loose thread that you keep pulling until the whole shirt unravels. He just needed one more tug.

"No," Correlyn said calmly. "No one has ever loved you. Not Magnus." She stepped closer. "Not your father, nor the man you thought to be your father." Helvarr backed up slightly. "Not Ser Osmund, not my mother, and not me. How could anyone love such a monster?" She grinned at him, and he snapped.

Helvarr lunged at her, and Correlyn slashed at his ribs as she stepped from his path. He charged again, and Correlyn swung her sword, knocking his from his hand and watched as it skidded across the room. He didn't stop. He swung a fist, and Correlyn ducked before plowing into him. She let her own anger and hate for him fuel her, no longer feeling the pain to her ribs. They crashed to the floor, and Helvarr grabbed a handful of her hair and yanked her head back. She cried out at the pain and grabbed his hand, sinking her nails into the wound. He hissed and let go, and Correlyn sent a punch to his jaw before rolling off him. He grabbed her by the ankle and pulled her back. She kicked with her free leg, but her boot caught his armor. Correlyn reached for her sword that she'd dropped, but he pulled her away.

Correlyn turned and sent all her strength into a kick. Her foot made contact with his chest plate, but the force was enough to make him fall back. She scrambled to her feet and grabbed her sword before he could recover. Helvarr sat back up, but Correlyn's blade was pointed at his neck. He froze.

Correlyn's chest was heaving as she tried to catch her breath. Helvarr stayed on his knees, but the anger hadn't left his eyes yet. She pressed the point of her sword to his throat, and he let her. He made no move to grab the blade or try to fight, but she hesitated. Helvarr had ruined everything for her. He was the source of all her pain and the pain of those she loved. He stared at her, his eyes urging her to do it. Correlyn had won. She played the game better and came out on top, so why couldn't she finish it?

My little monster, her mother's words echoed in her head. Correlyn wouldn't be like her parents. For so long Correlyn had wanted to meet her father. She'd dreamt of what he might be like, how he would look. As a little girl, she'd painted a picture of a tall, handsome knight that would teach her to fight and let her ride with him on the back of his horse. He would have been loving and gentle yet strong and fierce. But that was just a dream.

Correlyn thought about those old dreams on the day of her wedding. She didn't have a father there to watch her get married or to dance with afterward, but the more she thought about it, the more she realized that she did. Magnus had been the father from her dreams. The man who was handsome and strong yet gentle and kind. He had taken Correlyn in and loved her like his own. Magnus had been there for her when she thought something happened to her mother. He had been there to protect her, to comfort her and to try and make her feel at home in Godstone. To Correlyn, Magnus was the father she never had, she only wished she'd realized it sooner and had more time with him.

Helvarr could never fill that role, not after everything he'd done. He deserved worse; he deserved to feel Ivy's wrath, or Finn's, or anyone's. So many people had a right to want him dead, Correlyn more so than any, but she didn't think he deserved it. Death was final, a way out. Life is difficult, and it will make you cry, it will make you laugh, it will make you bleed and drive you mad. Living is hard; dying is easy.

She locked eyes with Helvarr. His nose flared with hate, but his eyes were pleading. "Do it!" he yelled. Correlyn's arm shook under the weight of her decision. She couldn't do it. She lowered her sword.

"Correlyn?" Rayner's voice was frantic and confused. She didn't look at him but stared at Helvarr and watched his brows draw together in confusion. "Do it," he said again, more calmly.

"No," she said and sheathed her sword. "You don't deserve death. You deserve to live."

"Correlyn!" Rayner roared again. He sounded angry now.

"You deserve to live with all the choices you made." She spoke only to Helvarr, the rest of the room melting away as she blocked it out. "You will live a long life. I have no doubt. And every minute of it will be tainted with regret and shame. The choices you made created a rippling effect that changed the fate of all of us, starting with Magnus. Many people will want to see you hanging or tortured, but I know how you struggle with yourself inside your head. I know that it will eat away at you until there is nothing left, a hollow shell of a man. Then and only then, Helvarr," she hissed, "do you have my permission to truly die."

She leaned down. "I agreed to fight you to the death, and I have. You are cold and dead on the inside; anything I thought I might have seen in you was only another one of your masks. I may be your blood, but you were never my father, and you never will be." Correlyn straightened, and Helvarr's face crumpled. He didn't look angry anymore. The rage had died out in his eyes. He rounded his shoulders and lowered his head. Correlyn thought for a moment that he was crying as his body began to shake but then he snapped his eyes back up to her. He cackled wildly but Correlyn didn't falter.

"I still have raiders out there, Correlyn dear. Just because you don't have the guts to kill me doesn't mean they won't kill *you*." He looked back to the men who had once followed him. Correlyn followed his gaze and saw how unsure they looked. Many lowered their swords and just stared at Helvarr, confusion written on their faces.

Correlyn smirked. "I think they would rather leave with their lives." She spoke to Helvarr, but she eyed the remaining raiders. They looked to one another, exchanging glances until they stepped back. Lord Cylas released Rayner and held his sword out, waiting for the raiders to make the wrong move. Correlyn didn't let the surprise or her relief show as one by one, the raiders turned their backs on Helvarr and ran for the door.

Rayner's knights waited outside and would surely cut them down, but Correlyn let them try and run anyway. She couldn't help the wicked smile that passed her lips as they ran, abandoning Helvarr and leaving him to his punishment. How could they be expected to fight for a man who had nothing left? A man who had likely promised them things he could never give and a man who had just been stripped and broken down by the hands of his daughter?

Rayner ran to her side once the raiders had left. He searched her face; she gave him a tight smile. She knew he might not understand her decision, but he would support her. Rayner lifted a hand to her cheek as Lord Cylas came up and grabbed Helvarr, yanking him to his feet. Behind them, Macon began to stir awake, and they still needed to get Aska some help. So many things needed to happen, and their work wasn't yet done. Correlyn leaned in and kissed Rayner, long and deep. His lips returned her kiss before she broke away and glanced behind him.

"Your throne awaits you," she whispered. Rayner glanced over his shoulder to his father's throne. They had worked and bled and suffered for months to get here. He turned away and looked at his wife, the Queen of Godstone.

He took her face in his hands. "Later," he whispered. "I have a lifetime to sit on that throne, and you will be beside me, but right now, we need to finish this." She smiled at him and nodded. Rayner pulled her in for a hug, taking a full breath of relief and letting it go in one long sigh. The fight may be over and won, but their work wasn't done yet. They needed to find their family, get Aska help, and then figure out what to do with Helvarr...though Correlyn had some ideas already.

THE RISE OF A KINGDOM

"Where is she?"

Ivy stood in the doorway of Magister Ivann's old room. The whole building had been transformed into an infirmary for those who were injured during the battle. Macon laced on his boots and grabbed a walking stick, putting it under his arm and standing. He winced from the injury to his leg.

"Sit down, Macon. You'll tear your stitches. I'll find her." He smiled at Ivy and held up a hand in defeat.

Ivy turned around and bumped into Piotr. "Not you too?" She folded her arms in annoyance. Piotr's leg had been badly broken, and he walked with a crutch. Finn had made a better splint to keep the bone set in place while it healed, but after he put it on, he pulled Ivy to the side and voiced his worries. The break was bad but he'd told Ivy that Piotr would walk again, but not without the assistance of a crutch, possibly for the rest of his life. Ivy's heart broke at the thought, but when she'd told Piotr, he didn't have a reaction, which made her even more nervous.

Piotr grinned at Ivy, and she rolled her eyes. "Get back in bed, Piotr. You shouldn't be up and moving around. It's too soon."

It had only been a week since he fell from the wall. Only a

week since they won the battle and took back their home. "Is that an order?" he asked sarcastically.

Ivy snorted. "I don't imagine a high lord such as yourself would take orders from me. I'm just a knight."

"You're more than that. And I would happily allow you to boss me around." He winked, and Ivy punched him in the shoulder.

"Then get back in bed, High Lord." She stepped closer. "Before I beat you with your own crutch." Piotr chuckled and nodded, slipping past Ivy and back into the room.

Ivy walked down the streets of Godstone and toward the main gate. Repairs had already been made, and the gate had been replaced with a portcullis. Besides the fire from Zion and his people, not much damage had been done to the kingdom. Ivy had to admit, Helvarr had done a good job of restoring the buildings from the last time he attacked the kingdom. The knights' barracks by the front gate had been burned and the whole northern wall of the building had to be torn down. She walked past it, nodding to the men who worked on the building. Some were people from Tordenfall, Grimm included, and others were Rayner's men. She caught Grimm's eye, and he gave her a sad smile.

Earl Rorik's body had been found outside the walls the day after the battle. Ivy remembered watching him ride by on his horse, no fear in his eyes as he charged into the army of raiders outside the walls. Grimm took his death hard, and he still wasn't himself. He had insisted that his father's body be buried in Godstone, saying that he fought for this place and sacrificed himself, knowing he wouldn't be going back home. This is the place Earl Rorik's wife had died, and so Grimm buried his father next to his mother in a small area along the north wall. Ivy was surprised to see that Ronin was also buried back there and wondered if Helvarr did it himself. Rayner had sent a hawk to King Mashu and asked if he could spare a few Shadows to bring his father's body back north so that they could lay him to rest in Godstone.

As Ivy reached the top of the wall, she looked over to see men out in the west field, still burning the bodies of the raiders who fell. They had built massive pyres and stacked the bodies high before Luna set them ablaze. The raiders who managed to escape were spotted heading south, but Rayner didn't order them to be brought back. He hoped they would just go home since their leaders were dead. Lamira had lost its king, and Rayner knew he had to deal with that at some point, but the rebuilding of his kingdom was the priority. He asked Lord Cylas if he would be willing to speak with his council when he returned and nominate a lord to take control over Lamira. The city would likely start to riot and fall apart with no king or lord to rule over them and maintain order.

Ivy turned her attention away from the fields and spotted a figure up ahead. Her short-cropped, brown hair was snarled and messy from days in bed. She leaned over the wall, staring west at some unseen place. "Aska," Ivy called. She twirled around and winced at the pain but smiled all the same as Ivy approached. "What do you think you're doing?"

Aska smirked. "I thought I'd go for a walk."

"You know you should be resting. You're still hurt."

Aska rolled her eyes. "You try living in a cramped room with Macon for a week."

Ivy smiled. "You were shot, Aska. Besides, Finn needs to change your bandages."

"And when you were shot"—Aska crossed her arms—"did you lie abed for weeks on end?"

Ivy opened and closed her mouth a few times before speaking. "Well, no but—"

Aska held up a hand. "That's what I thought, Stormbringer." Ivy couldn't help but chuckle.

After the fighting ended and she saw Aska, lying in a pool of her own blood, she thought for sure she was dead. Aska had been shot in the back with an arrow and passed out on the wall. Macon said he carried her toward Magister Ivann's room, but that

Helvarr ambushed them and knocked him out. He'd been injured already, and Helvarr saw the opportunity, thinking he could use them to escape with Correlyn, but he was wrong.

"I suppose you'll need a nickname now," Ivy said.

"I'm open to suggestions."

Ivy tapped her finger on her chin and smiled. "How about... Aska the Unslain. Or Aska, the Stubborn. Aska, the Hard-Headed."

Aska snorted. "All very fitting, but I think I'll just stick with Aska."

Ivy shrugged. "Suit yourself. A nickname might draw the attention of a certain black-haired girl on Starry Point." Aska blushed and shoved Ivy, who chuckled and took her by the elbow. They made their way back to the infirmary, where she was hoping to find Finn.

Finn had been busy day and night for the past week. He slept in the infirmary, keeping an eye on those injured and taking care of wounds. Ivy tried to stay with him, but he insisted that she would get a better night's sleep in a real bed. But Ivy never slept well without Finn by her side. She worked all week on getting their room ready, replacing their two smaller beds for one large one. Rayner and Correlyn took the top chamber of the tower where their parents once slept. The rest of the rooms were reserved for their family. Elana and Lord Cylas had one, Grimm and Kyatta the other, and Arytin stayed alone.

Ivy got Aska settled back on her bed then went upstairs to the other rooms in search of Finn. Many cots had been brought in, and everywhere she looked, knights lay abed, some with cloth wrapped around their heads, some with arms in slings. Some of the clansmen had been injured as well, but the remaining Shadows from King Mashu seemed uninjured and had departed back to Kame Island yesterday as well as Zion and his men. The clansmen would return to their villages as soon as their injured were permitted to travel, and Lord Cylas planned to leave in a few days.

Ivy was startled by a pair of arms wrapping her in a hug from behind. The air filled with the smell of rainwater and pine trees and Ivy melted in it. "Did you find her?" Finn whispered against her ear. Ivy nodded. "Good, she's as stubborn as you are." He shook her slightly. Ivy smiled and turned around to face him. He had purple bags under his eyes, his brown hair was messy, and he hadn't shaved in days. Ivy smirked at him, and Finn raked his fingers through his hair, trying to straighten it some.

"You look tired," Ivy put a hand to his cheek.

"And you look beautiful."

"Finn…you need to rest. I don't need you looking like the dead in a few days."

Finn chuckled and pressed a kiss to her temple. "Everything will be perfect, I promise." He took her hand in his, looking down at the ring on her finger. "That is if you're still sure you want to marry me," he teased. Ivy answered by pulling him in by the collar and kissing him. A few knights in the room clapped and whistled, voicing their approval. Finn smiled against her lips before pulling away. "I'll find you later," he said and kissed the back of her hand.

Rayner stood with his arms crossed, staring at the throne as men moved around him, setting up the tables and sweeping the wooden floors. Correlyn came up beside him and followed his gaze. "What should we do with it?" she asked. Rayner let out a long sigh and walked up to the throne. He ran his fingers over the slashes from Helvarr's sword and crouched down behind it. Correlyn followed him and placed a hand on his shoulder. Rayner knew he couldn't get rid of the throne. It was his father's, and Rayner was always meant to sit in it one day; he just didn't think it wouldn't be so soon. He reached out to touch the names that were carved into the base of the throne.

Magnus.

Helvarr.

Rayner pulled out a small knife from his boot and began to carve.

"What are you doing?" Correlyn crouched down beside him.

"My father made this throne with his own hands. He sat in it for years, and though it was always meant for me. Helvarr sat in my place first." He paused to look at Correlyn. "I won't erase him from our history just because it tells of our defeat. Helvarr sat in this throne, and though he wasn't a king, he held a kingdom–my kingdom." He continued carving. "I will rise where he fell. This kingdom will rise again, and from now on, every person who sits on this throne will have their name carved into it. Helvarr is part of Blackbourne history, and I want our children to know what happened here. I will not hide him like my father did to us. What he did and what my father did affected us all, and it will serve as a lesson for generations to come."

He stood up and looked at his work. Correlyn turned his cheek and smiled at him, kissing him softly. "Our children will know our history," she said quietly.

Rayner caressed her cheeks. "The *world* will know our history," he corrected. They looked down at the carvings and smiled before linking hands and walking back through the Hall, leaving the throne where it was, with more carvings etched into its history.

Magnus the Mighty.

Helvarr the Banished.

Rayner the Unbroken.

The Hall was filled with people, their voices carried out into the street as Kyatta entered. She brushed the snow from her hood and made her way toward the dais. Rayner set up a large table just below for his family. He sat in the middle next to his queen and Ivy. Elana and Cylas sat opposite them, surrounded by Aska and her family and Piotr. Ivy smiled at her as Kyatta strolled up to the table and then looked over to Grimm. He was smiling and drinking, but Kyatta knew he was still hurting on the inside.

She lowered herself down in the seat beside him and took his hand. Grimm gave her a small smile and leaned in, gently brushing his lips against her cheek. "How are you feeling?" She couldn't keep the concern from her voice.

"Better now," he answered. Kyatta smiled and looked down the length of the table. Everyone was grinning and laughing, discussing normal things. It felt strange but comforting. No one talked about battle plans, or how many men they had, what weapons they carried or how many horses they would need. Instead, the table was filled with discussions of farming, riding to the nearby towns and trading goods, getting the central market set up again and, of course, Finn and Ivy's wedding. She glanced over at the couple and couldn't help but smile. Finn was leaning in, his eyes helplessly lost in Ivy.

She let her eyes fall on Piotr, who was talking with Arytin while Aska sat beside him, eyes rolling and sipping wine. She knew Aska and her family were going to travel back west with Piotr before they broke apart and went their separate ways. Grimm had offered to accompany them to help Piotr get settled in his home before he returned to Tordenfall, where he would be coronated as earl. Kyatta had been thinking for days now about what she was going to do. Everyone would be split apart again, back to their own homes, with their own family, but Kyatta didn't have any family back in the Moon Wood. Her family was in Godstone with Ivy, in the Twisted Tower with Piotr, on Starry Point with Aska...and in Tordenfall with Grimm. She couldn't imagine her whole family being scattered to the four corners of the world while she returned north, with her people but more alone than ever.

Kyatta turned back to Grimm, who had been staring at her. She blushed and squeezed his hand tighter. "I want to go with you."

Grimm furrowed his brow. "To bring Piotr home?"

"Yes, but not just that…" She hesitated, her heart beating madly. "I want to come with you, to your home, to Tordenfall."

Grimm's eyes grew in surprise as he stared at her. He shifted in his seat to face her better and took her other hand in his. "What about your people? The Moon Wood?"

"I've already talked with my council members, and they will elect a new leader. I have no family there. My family is here." She cast her arm out to the full table. "They're my family now, and so are you. I love you, Grimm, and I'm coming with you. A thousand lifetimes, remember?"

Grimm was beaming. He leaned in and kissed her, and Kyatta brought her hands up to his cheeks. "I love you, too," he spoke against her lips.

Kyatta broke their lips apart and looked down the table to see Rayner smirking at them. "You know," Grimm said. "I am earl now, and since Tordenfall is the closest settlement to Godstone, I imagine I will be traveling this way quite often to assist the king and queen in whatever they need. Is that something you think you can handle?"

Kyatta smiled even bigger. "Absolutely."

"Good." He grinned and wrapped an arm around her shoulder. "I am afraid I would get lost without you," he whispered against her temple. Kyatta nestled into his chest, and they sat in silence, sipping wine and watching their family.

After the Hall cleared out and the only people remaining were those seated at the king's table, Rayner stood up with his glass in his hand. The table hushed and looked up to Rayner. "There are so many things I could say," he started. "But I'll keep it short." He turned to Lord Cylas, who sat with his arm around Elana's waist. "I cannot thank you enough for everything you've done for us." He looked at his mother's smiling face. "Without you and your men, I'm not sure any of us would be here now." Lord Cylas bowed his head slightly, and Rayner turned to Grimm and Kyatta. "The same goes for the clansmen; without your numbers, Godstone would have fallen, but with your help, it is rising back up, and it will be a better kingdom than before." Grimm and Kyatta raised their glasses to the king.

He turned to Aska and her family. "I hope that your people don't feel the need to hide any longer and that peace will find its way to the South. We still have some work to do, but I'm glad to have you as allies. And Aska." She straightened as Rayner looked at her. "You saved my sister's life and almost lost yours for this kingdom. You and your family will always have a place under my roof." Rayner brought his eyes to Piotr and waved at him to stand. Piotr hesitated but stood, leaning with one hand on the table for support. "Piotr..." He swallowed and looked down at his leg. "You have lost so much in this war, people who can never be replaced. Your father was sworn to my father for years, and they were great friends, even if they didn't agree all the time." Piotr gave him a sad smile and lowered his head. "Though I haven't always liked you..." Rayner's tone turned playful, and Piotr smiled up at him. "I'm glad to call you a friend now. A brother. And I hope our father's friendship will carry on through us, and as High Lord of the North, I don't ask that you swear loyalty to me, I just ask that you vow to keep the North safe from harm."

Piotr stared at Rayner then looked down at Ivy, who smiled at him. "My father swore loyalty to Magnus when he could have easily sworn to King Cenric at Kaspin's Keep. But my father recognized a great king when he saw one, and I know that you will be even greater." Piotr picked up his cup and raised it to Rayner. "Though you don't require it, my House will forever be sworn to House Blackbourne. May this alliance carry over for generations to come. To the King of the North." The whole table raised their cups to Rayner and cheered.

Rayner stayed standing and turned to Ivy and Finn and kept his cup raised. "To my sister and her husband-to-be, Finn. I would be here all night if I thanked you for everything you've done, so I'll just say this." He looked at Ivy, and her eyes shone with tears. "Our father would have been so proud of you. He saw the fight in you from the time you were a small child, and though he held off on your training, I know he only did it out of love. You were always special to him, his sweetling." He winked, and a single tear rolled down Ivy's cheek. "I'm proud of you, and I hope you find the happiness and peace you deserve." Rayner looked to Finn. "You have done so much for my sister, and for that, I am eternally grateful. You have been a part of our family for a while now, and I wish you both happiness. To Finn and Ivy." He lifted his cup higher, and the group did the same.

Rayner went on to thank his mother and wife, cups lifting in their honor before the conversation started up again. He leaned back, holding Correlyn's hand and listening to Aska and Arytin bicker. The usual feuding settled his mind and warmed his heart. Piotr and Grimm were discussing their journey west and how long it would take to get there. Kyatta rolled her eyes and laughed as the two argued and playfully insulted one another from across the table. Luna slept in the branches of the throne as her king sat with his family, enjoying the night and savoring every moment. Soon most of them would be gone, back to their homes, some missing a few family members but with new ones gained.

Rayner knew everything would be different now and that their work wasn't over yet. Lord Cylas would help him put a new ruler in charge of Lamira, and Macon would continue his spying around the land, always looking for threats and keeping him informed. The South had lost their king, and Rayner doubted that all of the raiders would lay down their swords and go home. The South had been controlled and suppressed for so long, but Rayner hoped to change that. King Mashu would keep control of his island while Rayner's allies in the South worked to rebuild the cities which were once under the control of King Caato. It would take time and a lot of work, but Rayner knew he had a good team that could handle it and a family that would always stand by him.

23

THE PRISONER

The next day, Finn walked alone down the steps of the tower. It was early, and he'd slipped out of bed before Ivy woke. He couldn't help but pause to look at her before getting dressed. Her wavy auburn hair cascaded down her bare back that rose with even breaths. He had leaned in and kissed the top of her head before getting dressed, lacing his boots, and leaving his sword behind.

The kingdom was just waking up, and Finn could hear people outside moving about and preparing for the day. Some of Rayner's men would leave today to the town of Ashton in hopes of trading goods so that they could survive the winter. The Feast of Winter was tomorrow, and they would be celebrating it along with Finn and Ivy after they married. Ivy insisted on getting married on that day, and Finn didn't argue. He would give her anything she wanted without batting an eye. The Feast of Winter held a special place in Ivy's heart, and though Finn's people had a similar celebration, it was never on such a grand scale. The clansmen, Aska's family, and Piotr and his men were all staying for the celebration along with Lord Cylas and his knights. After that, they would all go their separate ways, and Finn knew it might be a while before he could see them again, especially since he was planning a trip with Ivy soon; he just needed some information first.

He crossed the main room of the tower to where a knight stood guard at the door. Finn glanced down at the table and noticed a tray with a flagon of water and an apple. "Is that for him?" he asked the knight.

"Yes, I was just about to take it down."

"I'll do it. I need to talk to him." The knight nodded and opened the door, letting Finn pass. He carried the tray down the spiral steps and stopped before two more knights who stood like statues outside the wooden door. They nodded to Finn and unlocked the door, telling him to knock when he was ready to leave.

Finn stepped into the cell, which was lit by one torch that hung in a metal hoop on the wall. He set the tray down on a small table, glancing at the corner where a mattress rested on the floor, and Helvarr sat eyeing him. Finn pulled out the only chair at the table and sat down, crossing his arms against his chest. Helvarr shifted to the edge of the mattress, his shackles jingling softly in the quiet room. Finn observed him for a moment—the black hair that hung limp around his face, the wild beard that grew around his jaw, and his copper eyes that seemed to have lost their shine. He had never seen Helvarr like this, but he had to admit, it gave him some comfort to see him defeated.

"Hungry?" Finn picked up the apple and rolled it across the floor. Helvarr grinned and stomped the apple beneath his boot before sitting back. "You could have just said no."

Helvarr smirked and cocked his head to one side. "It's a little early for visiting hours, isn't it?"

"Not when you're the only prisoner I have to visit."

"How lucky for me." Helvarr narrowed his gaze. "I'm afraid I'm busy. Perhaps you could come back another time."

Finn sat forward, leaning over his knees. "Cut the shit,

Helvarr. I came to ask some questions, and you're going to answer them."

"Am I?" he tsked. "And if I don't, you'll…what? Throw me in a cell? Kill me? The queen wouldn't like if you go against her orders."

"Correlyn showed you mercy; you should be glad you're allowed to breathe this filthy air."

Helvarr sat forward suddenly. "A blade across my throat would have been more merciful than this." He held up his hands and rattled the chains.

Finn sat back and grinned. "I think that was her intention all along. Some might call it mercy, but I know she wants you to suffer, and I'm glad you're not dead, because you're going to tell me something."

Helvarr chuckled. "And what's that?"

Finn got up from his chair and stopped a few feet in front of him before crouching down to look eye level. Helvarr lifted his chin defiantly, and Finn smirked at his effort to look like he wasn't falling apart. "You're going to tell me what happened to the children from my village."

Helvarr stared at him for a long moment and then threw his head back, cackling. Finn's eye twitched with anger, but he composed himself. "I already told you what happened to them, Finnick."

"Don't call me that," Finn snapped. Helvarr held up his chained hands in surrender.

"You told me what they were being captured for. You didn't tell me where they went."

Helvarr eyed him. "I told you already, I don't know where they went."

"And I don't believe you."

"Believe what you want. It won't make what I do know any less true."

"And what do you know?"

Helvarr grinned. "I know that no matter where they ended up, they're likely dead and gone by now."

Finn felt his heart sink at the thought. He had to believe they were still out there somewhere and that he wasn't the last of his people. "I don't believe you," he repeated. "You told me they would be sold as slaves or into pleasure houses. Why would they be dead?"

Helvarr shrugged as if he were bored. "Plenty of reasons. Disobeying their master. Trying to escape or injure the person they worked for. Some of the pleasure houses will throw you on the street if you don't bring in enough money, and for a child that has nothing left, that's as good as killing them." He paused and looked at Finn for a long moment. "Although it didn't kill you. You turned out fine, didn't you?"

"Ronin helped me."

"How poetic," Helvarr mocked. "He gave up one son and got a chance for another to make up for his mistake."

Finn went back to the chair and dragged it closer. He had never thought of Ronin as a father because Finn had known his father well and loved him; no one could ever take that position. Ronin was always a mentor to Finn and someone he could trust when he had no one left. He wondered if Helvarr truly was jealous and thought they had a closer relationship than they actually did. Finn knew that Ronin regretted his decision and lived with the guilt for the rest of his life, but Helvarr didn't seem to accept that.

"Ronin was not my father. You killed my father, remember?" Helvarr lost his smile, and Finn waited for him to mock him again, but he leaned his head back against the stone wall and sighed.

"I told you, I didn't mean to kill your father. Do you expect me to beg for forgiveness? A little light groveling?"

"No. I expect you to do the right thing now and help me find the children from my village that were taken."

"And what's in it for me?"

"You seem to forget that you're the prisoner here, and we can make your life a lot worse than what it is."

Helvarr gave Finn an approving smirk. "You are free to try." Finn sighed and pinched his brows together. He knew Helvarr would be difficult, but Finn had all day, and he would keep coming back until he got some answers.

"I tried to help you," Helvarr said. "I could have killed you."

"At least I would have been with my family."

"Ah, yes, but then you wouldn't have Ivy." Finn cringed at her name on his tongue.

After the fighting was over, and Correlyn told everyone what would become of Helvarr, Ivy lost it. She tried to run to the tower to kill him, but Rayner had caught her. She sobbed in his arms for a long time, saying she broke her promise to her father and that Helvarr needed to die. Correlyn didn't know what to say and so stayed silent while Rayner tried to comfort her. He told Ivy that their father never expected that of her, that she made the promise and thus could take it back. Rayner knew that Ivy wanted Helvarr to suffer for what he did to their father and Ser Osmund, for what he did to Correlyn and Finn, everyone, but he couldn't let Ivy kill him. He was Correlyn's father, and it was her decision to let him live. Rayner hadn't been happy about it at first either, but he agreed that it was satisfying, knowing Helvarr sat below the kingdom he helped destroy while they raised a new one over his head.

Ivy cried herself to sleep that night in Finn's arms, but by morning, her eyes were dry. Ivy said she had a dream that seemed to sway her opinion, but when Finn asked about it, she brushed him off. He didn't pry her again about it. Finn trusted Ivy and knew that her dreams were never the full picture. Perhaps she didn't want to reveal it until she knew more. She didn't seem upset by the dream, so Finn accepted her silence, and Ivy accepted Helvarr's fate.

"Ivy wanted you dead more than any of us." Finn raised his brow.

Helvarr cocked his head, smirking. "Wanted?"

"I'm sure she still wants to kill you," Finn said, shrugging his shoulders. "But she's accepted Correlyn's decision."

"How noble of her," Helvarr mocked.

"Watch your tone," Finn hissed.

"Are we done here?" Helvarr pretended to yawn.

"No, we aren't. And if I'm bothering you, then just answer my questions because I'll keep coming back until you do. We have all the time in the world."

"I want something in return. That's how this works, I give you something you want, and you give me something I want."

"Forget it, Correlyn won't—"

"I didn't ask for her, did I?" Helvarr scooted closer to the edge of his mattress. "I know she won't come to see me unless she wants to, so I could be waiting a long time for that. In the meantime, I want a window."

Finn furrowed his brows. "A window?"

Helvarr looked up to where the wall met the ceiling. "I know this cell isn't completely underground. There could be a small window right up there." He gestured to a spot high on the wall.

Finn shook his head and sat back. "That's not up to me."

"So convince someone who can do that. Like the queen." Finn thought for a moment. He knew it would be a risk, and the window would have to be barred, but he might be able to convince Rayner or Correlyn. That is if they planned on keeping Helvarr there. The knights' barracks were being rebuilt, and they already had cells with a barred window. It might be safer to keep Helvarr in the same building as all the knights. Perhaps he could convince Rayner to do so.

Finn leaned forward. "I have a counteroffer." Helvarr raised a brow, interested. Finn explained that the barracks would be ready soon and that he might be able to convince Rayner to move him. That way, Helvarr would have his window and not just to look at feet passing by but perhaps a view of the main yard. Helvarr scratched at his shaggy beard, considering.

"You think you can convince the king?"

Finn nodded.

"Very well. Once I'm snug in my new cell, I'll tell you what you want to know."

"No, I need to know now. I'm planning to go south after the wedding."

"Wedding?" Helvarr said quietly. He dipped his head into a bow. "Congratulations, I hope you'll give my best to the bride."

"Shut up," Finn said. "Tell me what I want to know now, or the deal is off, and you can rot down here in your dark cell." Helvarr snarled and pushed back to the wall.

Finn stood up abruptly from his chair, tipping it over. He got down in Helvarr's face and jerked him forward by the collar. His pulse was starting to race. He was so close to getting what he needed, and he didn't have time for Helvarr's games. Helvarr seemed delighted and snickered as Finn drew him in closer. "Tell me where they are," he growled.

Helvarr put his hands to Finn's chest and tried to push him away, but Finn slammed his back into the stone wall and leaned in closer. Helvarr hissed and glared at Finn, but he wasn't backing down. Helvarr finally held up his hands in submission, and Finn let go of his collar but stayed right in front of him. Raising his chained hands, he straightened his hair back and fixed his collar. He brought his eyes up to meet Finn's and held him there for a long moment before grinning slightly and bowing his head. "Very well, *Finn*. Get a quill and some paper."

Finn backed up to sit on his feet. "Why?"

Helvarr sighed impatiently. "Because you are going to give me a list of the children from your village with their physical descriptions. The more you remember, the better help I'll be."

"You can't expect me to believe you remember what they all look like."

Helvarr ran his eyes down to Finn's scar. "I remembered you, didn't I?"

Finn narrowed his eyes and stood up. "I'll be back with a list, and then you're going to tell me where they are, and if I think you're lying"—he grinned and looked to the door—"maybe I'll convince the guards to take a break and let Ivy in here to do whatever she wants."

Helvarr smiled at him, but something shifted in his eyes. "I'll tell you where they are," Helvarr answered. Finn nodded and knocked on the door of the cell.

24

THE HANDS THAT HOLD

A light flurry drifted down from the sky, which was turning crimson and fiery orange in the dying sun. A slight wind from the north combed its pine-scented fingers through Rayner's hair. He stood outside the southern gate, staring up at a face that seemed familiar and unfamiliar at the same time. Perhaps it was the way the shadows hid his stone eyes or the way the orange hue of the sky lit up his hair, making it appear auburn. Rayner turned his head from side to side, trying to figure it out when Correlyn came out of the gate.

The statue was immediately forgotten as Rayner spotted his wife. She wore a long gown the color of pine trees in the first morning light. Her sleeves were full, and the bodice was laced with small onyx stones that caught in the sun. She had swept her hair up in a loose knot and tied it with a red ribbon. Correlyn was beaming as she locked eyes with her husband. Rayner stepped up to her, snaking his arm around her waist and pulling her in for a kiss. Correlyn caressed his cheeks, letting her hands fall down to his collarbones. She pulled back and looked behind Rayner to the statue guarding the gate, the God of Judgment.

"It's finished," she said, stepping around him. Stopping at the base of the statue, Correlyn tilted her head, studying the face.

Rayner came up behind her, his chest pressing against her back, and let his hands rest on her shoulders. "What do you think?"

Correlyn was quiet for a long moment before she answered. "It looks like Magnus." Rayner looked back up to the statue with a new set of eyes.

Magnus had destroyed the statue of the god last winter when he thought Rayner had died. Rayner always assumed his father would one day restore it, but he died before he ever got the chance. After the battle with Helvarr and his raiders, Rayner had decided to have the statue rebuilt. There wasn't much damage done to the kingdom, and so he'd ordered his men to put a rush on it. He studied it again and realized Correlyn was right–the statue did resemble Magnus. His wavy hair, his strong shoulders, and the stern look of a king, yet his eyes remained warm. Rayner smiled and brought his lips down to Correlyn's ear. "Do you think Ivy will like it?"

"She'll love it." Correlyn turned around and wrapped her arms around his neck. "Speaking of Ivy, we're going to be late."

Rayner let out a small sigh. "I can't believe she's getting married."

Correlyn grinned up at him. "Getting cold feet, big brother? Perhaps you should lock her in the tower or send Finn away on a mission to win your approval."

Rayner narrowed his eyes. "That's not what I meant. It's just… so much has changed in the last year. Ivy and Finn will be leaving soon for their trip south. Grimm, Piotr, and Kyatta will be gone. My mother…will be gone." He lowered his head, and Correlyn pulled him in, nestling her face against his neck.

The night before, Elana had asked to speak with Rayner and Ivy alone. They went to her bedchamber, passing Lord Cylas in the hall. He had given them a small nod then averted his eyes. Rayner and Ivy stepped into Elana's room. She was seated in the corner in front of the hearth, humming and rubbing her belly. Elana would give birth around the time of the new year. She motioned for them to join her, Ivy sitting next to her mother and Rayner across from them. Elana fidgeted with her skirts before looking up. "I have something I want to tell you both." Ivy and Rayner exchanged a quick, confused glance but stayed silent. Elana cleared her throat nervously. "You know I love you both very much, and I'm beyond proud of all that you've accomplished. You have worked so hard to win back your home and claim your rightful seat as the king."

Ivy shifted to face her. "What do you mean 'your home?' This is your home too." Her heart was starting to pound faster as she searched her mother's face, but she was looking at Rayner. Elana reached out and took Rayner's hand, then turned to Ivy and took hers. "This has been my home for so long, and it always will be, but…I think it's time I find a new one. This is your kingdom, your time to rule, and I know you will both help one another and build a better kingdom."

"Mother…" Ivy choked. Elana quickly continued.

"I am still your mother, and I will always be. But you don't need me, not anymore."

Rayner sat forward. "Mother, that's not true." His eyes were streaked with worry.

"Yes, it is. You are both grown and have done much more than many your age, and I know that you'll be all right. I have decided that I will go back to Rahama, with Cylas." Rayner and Ivy both looked at each other, mouths open.

Ivy pulled her hand from Elana's. "But… what about the baby?"

"I assure you that Cylas has the best healers and that I'll be in good hands."

Rayner shook his head. "But...it will be the first Blackbourne not born in Godstone." Even saying it made him feel a knot in his stomach. He couldn't believe his mother wanted to leave, after everything they've done to get back home. Elana brought her hands to her stomach and lowered her eyes.

"The Blackbournes came from the South, and besides, it's time to start doing things differently, don't you think? This is the perfect time to start over."

Rayner studied his mother until she met his gaze. "You love him?"

Elana nodded.

They all sat in silence for a few long moments, listening to the crackling fire fill the silence of the room. Rayner looked at his sister and was even more saddened by the tears in her eyes. "Will you come back to visit?" she said in a small voice.

"Of course, darling." Elana took her daughter's hands in hers. "And I expect you and Finn to come visit when you're in the South."

"When do you plan to leave?" Rayner cut in.

"In two days, when everyone else will leave. I thought it would be easier to go then, so you don't need to say more goodbyes." Ivy started sniffing, and Rayner looked at his sister. He moved over and lowered himself down beside her, reaching across Ivy's back to grab Elana's hand.

"We understand, Mother." Rayner spoke for the both of them. "And we're glad that you found happiness, you deserve it." Ivy only managed to nod in agreement, leaning her head against Elana's shoulder. Rayner wrapped his arm around Ivy as she quietly sobbed.

After a while, Ivy calmed herself and seemed to find a silver lining. They sat for a while, discussing all there was to see and do in Rahama. They had all been there before, though for different reasons, and Ivy was excited to be able to see it again with her mother, who first told her all about the city when she was a young girl. A break in the conversation gave Rayner a chance to ask about the baby. "Do you know what you'll name it?"

"Him," Elana corrected with a smile.

Rayner furrowed his brow. "How can you tell?"

Elana smiled and looked down at her swollen belly. "I just know."

"Then what will you name him?" Ivy asked.

"I think I'll name him after the first Blackbourne king."

Rayner smiled, recalling the history he had heard of since the time he was a young boy. "Kitt." Rayner let the name fall like a whisper. Elana nodded and smiled.

"Kitt Blackbourne," Ivy said, trying out the name. "I like it."

Elana's smile lit her face up. "Me too."

Rayner and Correlyn walked back through the kingdom hand in hand. A large crowd was already formed around the maple tree just outside the tower. They spotted Grimm standing with Piotr and Kyatta. Piotr leaned heavily on a crutch, rolling his eyes at something Grimm said. Rayner kissed Correlyn's hand and made his way toward them. He nodded to Aska, who was dressed in one of Ivy's gowns with a cloak pulled tight around her face. Arytin and Macon stood with their arms crossed, deep in conversation.

Rayner looked up to the branches of the maple tree and smiled. Luna sat in a low branch with a colorful ribbon clutched in her talons. Red, green, and gold ribbons hung from the branches with silver bells tied at their ends. They jingled in the light breeze and caught the light from the lanterns. The sun would be setting soon, and his sister would be married. It all seemed like a dream to Rayner, but it was a good one. He stepped up beside Piotr. "Come with me."

"What for?"

Rayner leaned in closer. "The bride wishes to see you, High Lord. Would you deny her?" He flashed his teeth and waited for Piotr to answer.

"Of course not." Piotr followed slowly behind Rayner as they made their way to the tower. He spotted Finn, standing under the woven branches of the arch just at the base of the tree. He wore a black high collared tunic trimmed with gold lace and a light fur-lined cloak over his shoulders. His dark pants were tucked into knee-high black boots, and his brown hair was combed back. They locked eyes, and Finn gave him a warm smile before Rayner stepped into the tower.

Rayner knocked on Ivy's door before stepping in, and his breath caught in his throat when he laid eyes on his sister. Elana hovered over Ivy, finishing the intricate braid that ran down her spine and wove in and out of her wavy hair. Ivy stood up and turned around to face him.

Ivy's gown fit snug to her torso before flaring out slightly just below her hips. It was the color of gold, with black laces sweeping across the bodice. The sleeves were snug and long, with small black swirls stitched along the shoulders and running down the bodice. Ivy was beaming with happiness as she looked at Rayner. Elana kissed Ivy on the cheek and left the room. Rayner took a step toward her. "You look beautiful, Ivy."

Ivy put her hands on her hips and narrowed her eyes. "No snarky comment? I don't even know you," she teased.

Rayner gave her a playful glare and smiled. "I'm sure I could come up with something if you like. I wouldn't want to disappoint a woman on her wedding day." Ivy snorted and punched him in the shoulder, making him stumble back a step. Rayner hugged his sister, careful not to mess her hair or wrinkle the dress. "Are you nervous?" he whispered against her ear.

"Not at all," she answered.

"Good." Rayner stepped back and motioned for Piotr to come

in. He turned back to Ivy with a grin. "The High Lord of the Twisted Tower, my lady," Rayner dipped into a bow, and Ivy laughed and smacked the top of his head. He winked at Ivy and said he'd be waiting downstairs for her when she was ready.

Piotr stood frozen in place as Ivy motioned for him to come closer. She turned away and began searching a wooden chest at the end of her bed, picking up something wrapped in a blue cloth before moving over to her bed. "Come sit, Piotr." She patted the bed beside her.

Piotr willed his legs to move closer. He propped his crutch up against the bed and settled down next to her, careful to keep some space. Ivy rolled her eyes and scooched closer. She smelled of scented candles and apple, and Piotr drank in the scent while he could. "You look gorgeous," he said quietly.

Ivy blushed and pushed her hair behind her ear. "I have something for you."

"Shouldn't I be the one giving you a gift? It is your wedding day."

Ivy grinned. "By all means." Piotr chuckled and reached into his breast pocket, pulling out a small object wrapped in a purple cloth. He handed it to Ivy and held his breath as she unwrapped it.

Ivy held up the necklace and studied it. The heart pendant was about the size of her thumb, hanging from a delicate chain. Piotr sat, wringing his hands, and leaned in. "It's iron," he said. Ivy turned to him and smiled.

"Iron Heart," she breathed.

Piotr blushed. "I thought you should have something to resemble the nickname. It's very fitting."

Ivy's cheeks flushed. She ran her thumb over the small iron heart.

"May I?" Piotr held out a hand, and Ivy handed him the necklace. She turned around, and he slipped it around her neck, clasping the chain. Ivy touched the cold metal and turned back to face Piotr.

"Thank you, Piotr. I love it." She leaned in and brushed her lips against his cheek.

"You're welcome, Ivy Iron Heart." He winked. Ivy giggled and turned to grab the wrapped package.

"Now, I have something for you."

"Ivy, you shouldn't have got me anything—"

"Oh, hush and open it." She bumped his shoulder with hers. Piotr smiled and set the package in his lap and started unwrapping it. The cloth fell away, and Piotr felt tears beginning to form in his eyes. He held it up to the candlelight, running his fingers over the smooth, twisting wood. Ivy leaned in. "Do you like it?"

"I…it's…" Piotr didn't know what to say. The cane was a perfect representation of the Twisted Tower. The wood was expertly carved, twisting all the way to the top. Piotr knew it was from a Blackwood tree and ran his finger over the smooth wood. At the top, a large red stone was encircled by thin strips of metal that had been twisted together. Piotr turned back to Ivy to find her staring at him. "Ivy…"

"I know you can't use a cane just yet, but I thought perhaps you might want one with some style." She winked at him and stood up. "That's not all." She gestured to the cane. "Pull on the jewel." Piotr scrunched his brows in confusion and pulled. The twisted wood cane slid away to reveal a thin sword. The metal was black, with the pattern of flowing water running down the length of the blade. "I know it's not a proper sword, and you'll likely still carry your own, but this way you have a backup and the element of surprise."

Piotr balanced the blade in his hand, it was light, but he could see it was strong and had been folded many times. Piotr smiled and put the sword back in the cane and stood. He tried it out, leaning his weight into the cane. His leg was still badly broken, and he needed the crutch to walk.

When Piotr learned that he wouldn't walk normally again without the support of a cane, he felt a part of him die. He had tried to keep his face indifferent and not let his pain show, but it broke him on the inside. He knew he had to work hard if he were ever able to fight again or ride a horse properly. Ivy was too smart to think that Piotr wasn't hurting emotionally from his fall. They knew each other too well, and so Ivy immediately went to a smith and had the sword and cane made just days after Piotr's injury.

Piotr looked at Ivy, who was eagerly waiting for him to say something. He grabbed his crutch and set his cane down on the bed. "Well?" she said impatiently. Piotr stepped up to her and, with his free arm, reached out and pulled her into his chest. Ivy wrapped her arms around him, and he squeezed her tighter.

"I can't tell you how much this means to me," Piotr whispered. "I love it, Ivy. Thank you." Ivy pulled away and brushed his blond hair from his face.

"I expect to see you wielding that sword next time I come for a visit." Her smile was warm yet sorrow seeped into the edges of her features. Piotr took her hand in his and brought it to his lips.

"I will practice day and night if it means I'll see you sooner." Ivy smiled but there were tears building in her eyes, and Piotr's heart sank at the sight. She let a tear roll away; Piotr reached out to brush it with his thumb. "Come on now," he whispered. "I can't have everyone thinking I made you cry on your wedding day." Ivy sniffed as another tear rolled down her cheek to be swept away by Piotr's thumb. "Grimm would toss me in the sea if he knew I made you cry." Ivy giggled and nodded in agreement.

She gave Piotr another peck on the cheek and stepped back, smoothing her skirts and checking her hair and strapping Promise to her hip. "Are you ready?" he asked.

"I'm ready," she replied. Piotr smiled and reached for her hand, tucking it in his elbow.

They made their way down the steps of the tower and met up with Rayner, who took Ivy's hand and placed it in the crook of his arm. Piotr kissed Ivy on the cheek and nodded to Rayner before heading toward the maple tree. The rest of the kingdom had gathered, and the sun was already set. Orange glass lanterns hung from the maple tree, and others swayed on hooks down the length of the aisle. Ivy took in a deep breath before rounding the corner with Rayner and laying eyes on Finn.

Everyone else melted away in her peripherals as she stared at Finn. He shifted to look at her and their eyes locked. Ivy recalled the first time she had seen him, practicing in the pit with Prince Kal and the way his stare made her feel. From that moment on, Ivy was always aware of his eyes on her. He smiled from ear to ear as Rayner led Ivy down the path. She caught Grimm's eye, and he gave her a wink and a smile. Everyone's eyes turned as Ivy passed by, smiles, and happy whispers pushing her along until she stopped before Finn.

Rayner leaned in and kissed Ivy on the cheek before stepping around Finn to stand under the archway. Finn reached out to take Ivy's hand. His hands were rough and calloused but warm. She stood in front of Finn, not evening hearing Rayner's voice as he welcomed everyone. Finn's voice was the only one she heard as he leaned in slightly and whispered, "You are stunning."

Ivy smiled and ran her eyes down his chest, then back up. "You clean up pretty good yourself."

Finn chuckled quietly. "I look forward to a lifetime of your wit."

Ivy shrugged but couldn't drop her smile. "If you think you can handle it."

"I told you once, and I'll tell you again, I would follow you anywhere, and I will always be by your side, my Ivy. I promise."

Rayner cleared his throat, and Ivy realized everyone was silent and watching. "Trying to skip ahead, Finn?" Rayner teased.

Finn's cheeks blushed. "I'm just eager," he replied and turned back to face Ivy. "I've waited my whole life for you."

Rayner smiled and instructed them to exchange swords before he spoke the ceremonial words. He called for Luna, who swooped down with her wings alight. Rayner took the ribbon from her talons and began to weave Ivy and Finn's hands together while speaking the words. He glanced over to Correlyn while he was speaking, and her smile was warmer than the summer sun. Luna's flames created sparks that gently drifted down behind where Rayner stood as he finished the last of the vows. "Whether through good or bad, these hands will hold. And may this bond remain forever unbroken." Rayner stepped back and clasped his hands in front of him.

Finn stepped closer to Ivy and brought his free hand to caress her cheek, running his thumbs over her smooth skin. "Together," he whispered, his lips hovering just above hers.

"Unbroken," Ivy answered and brought their lips together. The kingdom cheered and hollered their approval, clapping hands, and whistling. Ivy smiled against his mouth and parted her lips slightly, deepening their kiss. Ivy absorbed everything she could, the way Finn's lips felt against hers, his hand on her skin, the scent that came from his skin. She drank up every sensation and tucked it away in her mind.

Finn reluctantly broke their lips apart and leaned his forehead against hers. Rayner clapped him on the shoulder, his smile broad and sincere. Finn looked around to the faces watching them, and time seemed to slow down. Elana had tears rolling down her cheeks in a steady stream while Grimm had the biggest smile Finn had ever seen. Piotr and Kyatta were clapping, Arytin and Macon whistling while Aska looked about to cry. Ivy hugged Rayner, and Finn caught him wiping away a few stray tears. He shot Finn a warning glare but then chuckled and hugged Ivy tighter.

Finn couldn't believe he was here right now. A year ago, he'd been alone on an island with no family to speak of. The day Ivy arrived had changed his whole world because she had become his world. Finn wondered what his life would have been if Helvarr had never come to his village, if the raiders hadn't come and killed his people. Anytime he started to wonder, all he could picture was Ivy's face and the future he would have with her. It was as if the gods wouldn't allow him to imagine any other possible outcome, because there never was one. Finn's and Ivy's futures were woven from the day Helvarr came crashing into his life. They were always destined to cross paths and fated to be together. Although Finn thought the gods took no part in him falling in love with Ivy. She had done that on her own with every smile, every time she snapped back at him, every shy giggle or uncontrollable laughter. It was all Ivy, and Finn had been powerless to her all along.

He looked at his wife, who broke away from Rayner and took Finn by the hand. Ivy would forever remain a Blackbourne as Finn didn't remember his family name. The people of his village had been simple farmers and fishermen. There were no lords or higher houses, only neighbors and friends, and so family names didn't matter. He had always been just Finn and when Rayner suggested taking their name, Finn declined. He already knew he was a part of their family, and no name would make that any more valid.

Finn declined because he needed to remember his people and their traditions. He would always be just Finn, but he would be Ivy's Finn, and that's all that mattered. Soon he and Ivy would head south and begin their search for the children that were stolen from his village. Helvarr had provided Finn with a list of places that he recalled the man called Hal talking about. Helvarr had parted ways with the raiders on the western coast, and so he couldn't be sure, but he had heard Hal discussing his plans on the boat back to Lamira. Finn thought he was telling the truth, and even if he wasn't, it didn't matter. Nothing would stop him from finding his people and bringing them back home.

Finn leaned in and kissed Ivy again, another round of applause shooting up into the night sky. He pressed his hand into her back and twirled her around, dipping her. Ivy laughed against his lips and ran her fingers through his hair. He broke his lips away but stayed close to her face. "I love you, my wife." He winked, and Ivy giggled, running her finger over the scar on his cheek.

"I love you, my husband." Ivy kissed him again and Rayner coughed loudly. She rolled her eyes, and Finn lifted her back up.

"Are you finished?" Rayner mocked with a tight grin. Ivy smirked and kissed Finn again in answer.

"Enough of that!" a voice yelled from the crowd. Ivy broke away to see Grimm, arms crossed, and a knowing smile painted on his face. "Some of us want to start the celebrations," he called out. Ivy glared at him, and Grimm returned it until he broke and began to laugh.

Kyatta shook her head and linked arms with Grimm, turning him around and heading toward the Hall. People began to shuffle off toward the Hall, where the games and dancing would begin along with a proper northern feast. Elana smiled over her shoulder as Cylas led her away. Rayner squeezed her hand then walked up to Correlyn and wrapped his arm around her shoulder. Ivy took a moment to look up at the bare branches of the maple tree that were adorned with ribbons and bells. She said a silent prayer for her father, who couldn't be there to see his little girl married. Ivy closed her eyes against the tears. She felt Finn's heat coming from him as he stepped up, wrapping his arms around her.

"You're not thinking of climbing in that dress, are you?" His tone was teasing, and it made Ivy smile. She opened her eyes to see his gaze drinking her in.

"No, I was just thinking of my father."

Finn reached his hand up to her chin. "I know he would be happy for you; he gave me permission to marry you long ago."

Ivy nodded and mustered a small smile.

"He loved you very much, and he'll always be here." Finn reached down to Ivy's sword, touching the golden scarf hung around the pommel. Ivy rubbed it between her fingers, remembering that day in the market with her father, the way he tried so hard to make her laugh and the look on his face when Ivy put the scarf up to her cheek. Magnus was always with Ivy. She knew that because Ivy had always had a special connection with her family. She could never explain it, like a string that attached all of them. Ivy could always feel them, and she could feel Magnus now.

Ivy looked up to the maple tree again and smiled at the memory of her father. One chapter of her life was coming to an end, but another would soon begin. Ivy had a new life to build with her family, with Finn and a kingdom to help raise with her brother. Finn placed a gentle kiss to her cheeks, and Ivy looked back to him.

"Are you all right?" His voice was deep and soothing.

Ivy smoothed his hair back. "I'm fine." Finn raised a brow and grinned at her usual response. Ivy chuckled and corrected. "I'm perfect. Come on, our family is waiting."

Finn grabbed her hand, and they headed toward the Hall. "Want to bet that Grimm will start the first fight?" Ivy gave him a sideways glance.

Finn laughed. "You're on, Iron Heart. Though I'm guessing it will be Arytin. Aska does know how to push him, and I think he's about to snap."

Ivy giggled, and they continued to discuss all the possibilities as they walked hand in hand toward their family. A flurry of snow started to drift down from the dark sky, swirling around the pathway with a certain bite to the air. Ivy shivered against it as the hairs on the back of her neck rose up, like a silent warning from the gods.

EPILOGUE

The weather was bleak, and a constant rain fell like a mist across the city of Lamira. It had been months since King Caato's soldiers returned home without their king. The city fell into a panic. They had relied so heavily on the king's presence and the constant abuse of the raiders that their absence only seemed to make things worse.

Since the fall of their king, the raiders had either gone back to their families, fled, or created bands of their own and were now terrorizing the city. They demanded taxes paid, land handed over, and rooms for free at the local inns. So far, no one had stood up to them because they never had before. The raiders still demanded the same amount of respect and control as if the king were alive, but he was dead and gone. Many of the locals still lived in constant fear of the raiders and the power they had over a kingdom with no king.

As he walked through the cold rain of the streets, Levi thought about what he would steal today. Being a young boy of only fourteen, Levi had grown up on the streets of Lamira, stealing and conning his way through life. His parents were poor and couldn't afford to take care of him and so gave him up at the young age of three. Levi made his way from orphanage to orphanage until he ran away some five years ago and started to take care of himself. He had hunted down his parents at first but soon found out that they died in a fire set by the raiders only two years after they gave him away. Levi made friends with other street kids, thieving and stealing to keep their stomachs at least half full. But Levi was different from the rest.

As he walked through the streets that led downtown, he spotted a tall man with black hair watching him from the shadows. Levi felt a shiver crawl down his spine and quickly turned away. He headed south, keeping to the alleys until he hit the market square.

Everywhere he looked, vendors had booths and tents set up, ready to sell their goods. He pulled up the hood of his cloak, his orange hair already wet from the rain. He scanned the booths, looking for his next subject. Many sold food such as fruit, vegetables, whole pigs laid across trestle tables, ready to be butchered. Others sold brightly colored fabric that seemed odd in such a dark city. Some sold spices from around the land, swords, and knives adorned with rare jewels, but Levi needed food. It had been two days since his last meal, and his stomach growled in agreeance as he stopped in front of a baker's booth.

The man was older with a head of gray hair and a beard that fell to his belly, wrapped in a leather cord. Levi scanned his surroundings, always looking for two ways out before he approached the booth. The older man was talking with a younger woman, perhaps a few years older than Levi. She had chestnut hair and rosebud lips that spread into a smile as she chatted with the old man. Levi shook his head, telling himself to focus. He locked his sight on a loaf of bread the size of his head. That could feed him alone for a few days, or perhaps he could split it with a few of his friends. His stomach growled, and he turned back to the elderly man, who was flirting with the young woman. Levi rolled his eyes and cleared his throat twice before the man peeled his eyes away from the young beauty. She blushed and dropped a few silver coins on the counter before disappearing into the sea of people.

"What do you want?" the man asked angrily, clearly upset that Levi had ruined his chances for something that would never happen.

"How much?" Levi asked, pointing to the large loaf of bread. The man followed his finger and scoffed. "Too much for you, street rat. Now get out of here, I have customers."

Levi felt his cheeks burn with rage but quickly doused the flames. "How about a trade then?"

The older man eyed him curiously. "And what could the likes of you have to offer me for such a meal?"

Levi hated that the man assumed a simple loaf a bread would be a meal to him, but he wasn't wrong. Levi locked his honey eyes on the older man and smiled. "Perhaps a riddle?"

The old man scoffed again, but curiosity danced in his blue eyes. He stroked his long beard as he considered. "Tell you what kid, if you can tell me a riddle I haven't heard before and can't solve, I'll give you the loaf."

Levi grinned, knowing the man would never have the chance to solve the riddle. He cleared his throat and began.

"I have no eyes, but see you well.
I follow you wherever you dwell.
The sun I love, but not the moon.
Shrouded in darkness will be my doom.
I'm free to touch, to grow, to feel,
But shackled to you at the heel.
When stars above flicker with light,
I fade away, dead for the night."

As Levi spoke the riddle, the man began to fall into a trancelike state. His eyes seemed locked on a distant object, and his arms hung slack at his sides. Levi smiled halfway through the riddle as he harnessed his powers and froze the man in place. Levi grabbed the loaf of bread, slipping a few delicious looking pastries inside his bag before he finished the riddle.

Before the man snapped out of it, Levi was down the street with a bag full of baked goods. He chuckled to himself as he grabbed an apple tart and stuffed it into his mouth. The sugary pastry danced on his tongue, and Levi paused in an alley, closing his eyes and savoring every bite. He would never get used to the feeling of his powers and how easily he could freeze people in time. It was as if they were lost in the moment, frozen to whatever else was happening around them. Levi could only control it for so long, so he used riddles to draw out the time it took to harness his powers and focus them. It was a simple thief trick to distract vendors with riddles while another grabbed the goods they needed, but Levi preferred to work alone.

He had never relied on anyone, and no one knew of his powers. Levi didn't know who he could trust. Even the honor of his thief friends wasn't to be trusted. He knew many of them would turn him in if they knew he had powers. A lot of people in the city were uncomfortable with people with such powers as it might give hope for a rebellion to start up. Anyone caught with certain abilities had been taken by the raiders and never heard from again, so Levi had been careful to keep his powers to himself.

He wished to leave the city one day but always seemed to find an excuse to prolong his journey. The raiders had brought back word of King Caato's death, but soon after, more raiders started to show up. They preached of a woman with white hair who wiped out half their army. Levi tended to hang around the local taverns, picking the pockets of the drunks, when one night he heard a raider describing something impossible. A woman who seemed to control bodies, twisting and turning them the way a smith forged metal. Levi had craned his neck, trying to hear what they were saying. Apparently, the woman fought for Godstone, a northern kingdom which they believed now held the only remaining king in the North and on the whole mainland.

Levi had since dreamed of going there to meet this white-haired woman and perhaps see if his powers were similar. If he could have a master to train him. Maybe then, Levi wouldn't need to be a thief anymore. He had heard many things about the king in the North, but he didn't believe any of them. Levi knew that King Caato was mad and was glad to hear of his death. The king in the North was thought to be a young and fierce king, taking his home by force after losing it during a great battle. Levi didn't know much about the war and got his information from loose-lipped raiders, but still, he didn't believe their drunken words because they stood with King Caato.

As Levi stood in the shadows of the alley, he let himself picture the North. Would he be able to handle the snow and cold weather? He shook his head. It didn't matter. He knew he had to go and perhaps this king would take him in, and he could find a new home.

He swallowed the last of the apple tart and pushed off the stone wall, making his way back to the sad shack he called home. It was no more than a hole in the wall, stuffed tight with plenty of other bodies and not enough food and water to go around. He was so lost in thought that he nearly ran into the man who blocked his path. Levi looked up and slowly backed away, feeling the hairs on his neck start to rise. The man was tall and lean with a handsome face. His hair was so black it seemed to absorb any light that made its way into the alley, and his eyes burned like fire, their orange hue searing a hole in Levi. It was the man who had been watching him earlier.

He felt a sudden wave of panic and backed away a few more steps, scanning his surroundings. Always two ways out. The man placed his hands behind his back and smiled, which only made Levi's stomach turn. He reached for the knife he kept tucked away under his cloak when the man spoke. His voice sounded high and deep all at once, guttural and alluring. Levi lowered his hand and shook his head in disbelief.

"What did you say?" he asked the stranger.

"The answer to your riddle." The man took a step closer, his smile never faltering. "It's a shadow, isn't it?" Levi felt knocked off balance, and something inside him seemed to tug in the direction of the man. No one had ever solved one of his riddles because he didn't stick around long enough for the person to realize they'd been frozen. Levi wondered how close the man had been when he harnessed his powers, and that sent another shiver of panic down his back. He tried to remain calm, standing up straight and lifting his chin.

"Yes," he answered. "It's a shadow."

The man smiled knowingly and stepped even closer, and his orange eyes seemed to burn even brighter at his victory.

"Tell me," he said in his strange voice. "How did you acquire a full bag of baked goods while that old man stood as still as a statue? He never even looked your way as you stuffed your bag full of food."

Levi felt sweat starting to form on his brow, his heart drummed quickly in his chest.

"I guess the old man must be losing his sight," Levi mused, trying to remain calm. The stranger smiled, and Levi felt that tug again somewhere inside his chest.

"Perhaps." He stepped even closer, and Levi tried to back away, but the man grabbed his wrist. "Or perhaps you're a lying, thieving street boy who abuses his powers to fill that empty hole below your lungs." Levi felt his heart drop into his boots. He quickly grabbed for his knife, but the stranger took hold of his other arm. He was entirely too powerful for such a lean looking man, and Levi's mind instantly went to panicking. He harnessed his powers, feeling it course through his veins like a warm embrace before he lashed out at the stranger.

The man threw his head back in laughter and squeezed Levi until the pain blinded him, and he dropped to his knees. His powers bounced back at him. He tried to think. Two ways out.

The stranger crouched down in front of Levi, taking his chin between his fingers and jerking it up until they were eye to eye. "Such a shame," he said. "The power of the gods wasted on no more than a common thief." He clicked his tongue and narrowed his eyes. "Disgusting. Allow me to relieve you of your burden."

Levi tried to scream, but when he opened his mouth, no sound came out. The stranger's eyes seemed to dance with fire as his hand rested over Levi's heart. He felt a strange sensation, like a tugging toward his ribs and his own being pulling back at the force. The stranger leaned in closer, his black hair enveloping every ounce of light that remained.

Levi tried to struggle and thrash against his grip, but he felt powerless. The man held his chin in place, making him look as he sucked Levi's powers from his body, along with his soul. The feeling was too much to describe, pulling and tugging, blows, clouded memory, flashbacks of everything he was, all that made him Levi. He felt a tear roll away as the stranger gave one last tug, and his soul drifted out from his chest in a bright red light and nestled snug inside the stranger's chest.

He let go, and Levi fell back on the wet, cold stone of the alley. His breathing was labored, and his vision began to waver. The stranger hovered above him, and Levi swore he was glowing with power. He couldn't begin to comprehend what had happened. The stranger kneeled down, grinning wickedly as Levi took in his last breaths. His entire body shook, and he felt a hole inside of him that he hadn't realized had been full up until a moment ago. He struggled to speak, and his voice came out shaky and timid. "Who are you?"

The stranger smiled and stood up, fixing his black hair that was slick with rain and glaring down at Levi as if he were nothing more than a piece of trash stuck to his boot. He smoothed out his tunic and pulled the hood of his cloak over his handsome face. The stranger bent down, jerking Levi's chin up to face him again.

"You mean you don't know?" he said in his strange voice of many emotions. "I'm the Supreme."

He let go of Levi and stood up, turning to make his way back through the alley and never looking back. Levi's mind was clouded, and his thoughts slipping as he tried to focus. The rain turned sharp and piercing, freezing Levi to the stone walkway. He only thanked the gods he wouldn't be around long enough the feel their icy stab.

The Supreme.

The first god who, if the stories were to be believed, had created the four gods that were now worshipped all throughout the land. He had taken Levi's soul and, along with it, his power, holding it as his own and wielding it however he saw fit. Levi sent a prayer to the four gods with his last breath, hoping they would send a warning to someone, anyone. As he closed his eyes, Levi was sure that the gods had heard him and that a warning had been sent to someone who might be able to stop a god. Someone powerful enough to change the fate of the world.

ACKNOWLEDGMENTS

One more book in the series to go! It feels like a lifetime ago that I sat down and wrote this series, spending endless hours in front of my laptop, weaving Ivy's story into words and pages. It's bittersweet, but I couldn't have done it without a lot of help from fellow writers, readers, and everyone who supported this journey. I'm going to keep this very short.

To my amazing editor, Sarah, for helping me form a cohesive sentence. Thank you for all your many hours invested in this story. Thank you, Sheridan, for creating the map for this series. I can't wait to work with you again on future novels. Coco- your work always amazes me, and any time I get an email with some line art attached, it's like a present on Christmas. You truly are talented, and your work speaks volumes. Thank you to Franzi for creating designs that embody the story and putting those final touches on my manuscript. Liz, you've been such a great help over the years with this self-publishing thing, and I couldn't have done it without you. Thank you for all the help you've been, not only to me, but to other authors; it means the world.

For anyone who's ever entertained a conversation with me about my writing, or given advice, feedback, praise, criticism, 1 star or 5 stars, thank you all. A book goes through many hands and dances on many tongues before it is formed, and without my fans, ARC readers, friends, and family, I wouldn't have written Ivy's story. There are too many people to name, but you know who you are. I am eternally grateful.

P.S. Yes. Helvarr is still alive.
We're not through with him yet.

ABOUT THE AUTHOR

BRITTANY CZARNECKI

Brittany is a self-published author of YA and NA Fantasy novels. After serving in the U.S. Army, she earned a BA in English at the Massachusetts College of Liberal Arts and is currently trying (very hard, I might add) to write her first Horror novel, so stay tuned. Brittany resides in Western Massachusetts with her pit bull, Zenitsu, who is nothing like his namesake.

www.brittanyczar.wixsite.com/brittany-czarnecki-b
www.etsy.com/shop/HouseBlackbourneShop

facebook.com/brittany.czarnecki
instagram.com/Brittany_czarbooks
tiktok.com/@brittanyczar_books